MW00769910

DEMON'S MARK

DEMON'S MARK I

NORA ASH

This is a work of fiction. Any and all likeness to trademarks, corporations or persons, dead or alive, is purely coincidental.

ABOUT THE AUTHOR

Nora Ash writes thrilling romance and sexy paranormal fantasy.

Visit her website to learn more about her upcoming books.

WWW.NORA-ASH.COM

ONE
SELMA

At twenty-seven, Selma'd long since learned that staring at monsters brought nothing but pain.

Which is why, when she saw three of them herd a woman toward a deserted alley behind the grocery store's parking lot, she ducked behind her car, shopping bag filled with last-minute ready meals clutched to her chest thanks to Mr. Jones' insistence that she work late yet again.

But the monsters didn't pay her any mind; their focus was solely on the girl between them. She was stumbling along the pavement as if drugged, headed toward the secluded spot seemingly without a shred of worry about the three males accompanying her.

Selma gave her a guilty glance as she fumbled with her keys to unlock the car door, her palms sweaty and shaking with the violent drumming of her heart.

She knew the monsters could bend a human's will and make them see things that weren't there—or not see things that were. They hid their grotesque appearance behind human skins, which was why no one else seemed to notice the scaled, horned creatures who walked among them.

No one except her.

Or maybe she was just crazy. Or *unbalanced*, as a multitude of doctors in white coats had told her concerned parents before she'd learned to pretend she didn't see the monsters anymore.

At least the woman wasn't putting up a fight. Whatever they'd done to make her follow them, she likely wouldn't remember what happened to her. She might not even realize it while it was happening.

Selma drew in a deep breath and focused on the key in her sweaty palm—but before she could look down, the girl turned her head, catching her gaze.

Large, panicked eyes locked on hers, and though the rest of her face remained slack and docile, those eyes spoke clearly that that woman was aware of what was about to happen to her.

A large, clawed hand came to rest on her shoulder and pulled her into the alley. Her eyes widened even further, the plea in them impossible to ignore. Then the darkness swallowed her, leaving the parking lot desolate once more.

Fuck. Selma stared at the gaping mouth of the alley, her heart thudding unevenly in her chest. Had she come out of the shop ten minutes later, she'd have been none the wiser, and guilt wouldn't have been gnawing at her to *do* something.

What was she supposed to do against three monsters?

"Shit," she muttered, easing the shopping bag and her purse to the ground as she fished out her phone.

"911, what's your emergency?"

"Hi, yeah, I saw three men drag a woman into an alley behind the shops on the corner of Smith and 31st, by the parking lot. Please, can you send the police?"

Selma spoke fast and low, not wanting to risk the monsters hearing. They were far enough away she couldn't hear them, but she knew all too well that some of them had enhanced senses.

"Can you see them, ma'am? Are they hurting her?" the voice on the other end asked.

Selma blinked at the question. "No, I can't, but it was obvious what they were going to do to her. She was fighting them." Or she would have been, had she been capable. "Do you need me to move closer so I have eyes on them?"

"No, don't put yourself in harm's way, ma'am. The police are on their way now. They'll be with you in twenty minutes. Can I ask your name, please?"

"Twenty?" Selma croaked. "You can't be serious—they'll have..." She trailed off as images flashed before her mind's eye of what it'd be like for that poor girl alone with those three for a full twenty minutes.

"Fuck!"

"They're coming as fast as they can, I promise," the voice soothed. *"Your name please, ma'am?"*

"As fast as they can" wasn't going to save that poor woman. Dread soured in her stomach, adrenaline and fear making her hands shake as she hung up and slid the phone back into her purse. Forcing herself not to think, she moved toward the alley. Maybe she could distract them long enough for the police to show up.

A metal pipe lay among bricks and rubble in the entry. Selma bent to pick it up, feeling just a tad better at the cold, heavy weight in her hands. She clutched it hard and pressed her back against the brick wall, peering around the corner and into the darkness.

She couldn't see anything but a couple of overflowing dumpsters, the faint light from the parking lot dying just a few feet into the alley. But from deep within, soft grunts echoed.

This time, Selma didn't have to force herself not to think. She slid into the shadows without hesitation, propelled forward by an equal mix of horror and fury. For a few moments, she didn't think about what the monsters could do to her, only what they *were* doing to that helpless woman.

A bit of light spilled in from the city's fluorescent skyline where the alley widened into a dead end, letting Selma's eyes catch up to her ears.

The three monsters were standing in a semi-circle facing the wall, the broad brute in the middle moving his hips rhythmically back and forth as his comrades chuckled every time the girl made a noise.

"Fuck, go faster, Cres. I'm busting out my fucking pants here," the monster on the left groaned, pawing at his crotch.

But Cres never got to answer, because Selma stepped forward and swung her impromptu bat with as much force as she could, cracking the metal pipe against his horned skull.

The strike sounded like a gong through the alleyway and vibrated up through Selma's arms and into her teeth.

"What the fuck?" The monster on the right whirled on her, mouth open as Cres let out an inhuman snarl. He pulled free from the girl, finally revealing her body as she sagged to the ground, and rounded on Selma.

His eyes were acid-green with slitted pupils, and his bared teeth were sharp as any predator's. Revulsion honed Selma's terror to a fine point. Suddenly, she was his full focus.

"You're one very dumb little girl," Cres hissed, reaching for her weapon.

Selma snatched it away just in time and delivered another whack, this time to his shoulder. "Get away from her!"

"Now, now... don't be like that, baby," one of the other monsters purred, his blue-scaled mouth twisted in a nasty smile. "We've got plenty of time to play with you as well."

"No thanks." She swung again, hitting Blue square in the face. "Get out of here *now!* The police are on their way!"

"Son of a bitch!" Blue staggered for a moment, bringing one clawed hand to his face. "Little cunt broke my fucking nose!"

"Feisty thing." The other beast, whose horns curled in

a strange pattern behind his head, grinned. “Calm down, pretty girl. Relax and it won’t hurt... that bad.”

A dark fog rose around Selma. It felt like thick, clammy soup clinging to her skin, setting every hair on her body on end as it tried to penetrate through her nostrils and mouth.

Magic.

This was what they used to make their victims docile and believe their lies. Some had tried it on her when she was a little girl screaming at their gruesome features. It hadn’t worked then, and it wasn’t working now, but she lowered her bat anyway, relaxing her pose.

“Now there’s a good girl,” Curly purred, stepping toward her with his hand outstretched. “Give me that nasty stick, why don’t you, and then you and me are going to have some fun.”

“Leave her alone!” Someone shouted from behind the monsters, followed by a metallic clang when a garbage can lid connected with Cres’ horned head. It seemed their victim had managed to shake their filthy magic while Selma distracted them.

Cres snarled and spun around, backhanding the woman to the ground, but that was all the time Selma needed. She raised her weapon again and aimed straight for Curly’s temple, putting all her strength behind her swing.

He let out a groan like a wounded animal and staggered back, stumbling over his feet and falling on his ass as he clutched his head.

"What the...?" Blue stared at her through narrowed eyes, for the first time taking up a cautionary stance as she rounded on him. "How did you break through his magic?"

Selma didn't answer, choosing instead to press her advantage. She leapt at him, but this time he was prepared. He easily side-stepped her swing, and when she tried again he twisted to block her, grabbing the metal pole in one huge, clawed hand.

She pulled, but he was so much stronger. With an easy yank, he ripped her weapon from her hand and tossed it into a dark corner of the alley, leaving her defenseless.

It was as if all the anger that'd propelled her into action seeped out through the soles of her feet as the blue-scaled monster rounded on her, lips curled in a snarl.

Out of sight, the woman she'd tried to save fought against Cres on the ground. This time, it seemed the monster hadn't deemed it necessary to drug her with his magic.

"Not so feisty now, huh?" Over Blue's shoulder, the curly-horned monster reappeared. Thin trails of blood trickled from his pointed ears, but that was the extent of the damage she'd managed to inflict.

She'd been a fool in thinking she could save anyone from these monsters. She'd never even been able to save herself.

"Hope you like it rough, bitch, 'cause we're gonna make your cunt pay for every blow you got in with that pipe," Blue growled, reaching for his belt buckle as Curly rushed forward and pinned Selma's shoulders to the wall before she could twist away.

Rough, cold brick bit into her back as they moved in, blocking the faint light from the city. She screamed and tried to force her body to keep fighting, but there was nothing she could do to prevent their clawed hands from ripping the clothes from her body or pushing up between her legs.

As a child, her fear of the monsters had been childish. She'd feared they'd eat her, that they'd hide in the dark underneath her bed or in her closet and devour her in her sleep.

Adulthood had brought a different understanding of their intent. She'd seen the hunger in their eyes as they chose their prey, and it was rarely to feed.

Her nightmares had long since morphed into this—into gruesome rape at the hands of the monsters who'd haunted her her entire life.

Selma screamed until darkness swallowed her.

TWO
SELMA

"Selma?"

Selma slowly turned her gaze from the tranquil gardens beyond the bay window-ledge where she'd been curled up for the better part of the morning. A nurse stood in the doorway, a kind smile on her face. Her name was Marie, if Selma remembered correctly. Her mind was still fuzzy from the drugs.

"The doctor is ready for you again. Would you please come with me?" probably-Marie asked.

The doctor. Selma didn't remember a doctor, but then she didn't remember much of anything from after the paramedics had injected her with whatever sedative they'd had on hand.

She unfolded from the window ledge with a sigh, slipping obediently to the floor. With an encouraging smile, the nurse led her from the small, high-ceilinged room she'd slept in and down a series of long corridors lined with the same large windows as the one she'd spent most of the day gazing out of. Although whoever had converted the old manor into a psychiatric ward had gone out of their way to make it look the part of a hospital, it still retained some of its grandeur from its glory days. It even smelled faintly of old wood through the acrid odor of cleaning agents filling the air.

There were very few indications of other patients or staff members on the premises. A soft humming from one of the rooms was the only noise apart from their footsteps echoing off the mahogany floors as they passed closed door after closed door. Only after climbing the staircase to the first floor did life seem to vibrate through to the hall: the low buzz of a radio flowing through an open door; the murmur of female voices; and the scent of coffee emitting from what must have been the staff break room.

The hallway grew quieter as they came to a broader stretch, where golden plaques engraved with doctors' names hung next to dark, carved door frames that matched the floorboards.

The nurse stopped to knock where the fancy sign indicated Dr. Martin Hershey had his office. Upon hearing an affirmative mumble through the aged wood, she offered Selma a reassuring smile before opening it.

"Dr. Hershey, your next patient is here to see you."

"Very good," a pleasantly deep voice said from within. "Show her in please, Marie."

Marie turned to Selma, the previously encouraging smile on her lips now spread wider. "Go on in."

Sighing inwardly, Selma moved past her and through the opening into the psychiatrist's office, feeling like she was stepping into the middle of an office romance. But romantic interest or no, patient confidentiality was patient confidentiality, and the door closed behind her, leaving Selma alone with yet another professional about to draw a blank on her condition.

"Come on over and have a seat, please."

Maybe he'd give up quickly—he would have had her medical records sent over from the other institutions and therapists she'd seen, and would probably come to the sad conclusion that his newest patient was a lost cause just like they had.

If she was lucky.

With another sigh, this time not so inward, she lifted her head to face the doctor... and froze mid-step at the sight of him.

He was certainly handsome, which was probably the reason for the nurse's sudden shift from reassuring professional to giddy schoolgirl. The first thing Selma noticed was his olive skin, strong, clean features, and thick, black hair. However, the neatly brushed, wavy strands did nothing to hide his pointed ears, nor the small horns protruding from just above his hairline. His almond shaped eyes watching her halted approach were a burning orange.

He was one of *them.*

No. How was she meant to get through this? She'd had to deal with them before, from her physics teacher to bank advisors, and even a supervisor at one point, but never had she been expected to open up about her illness to one. How could she trust him with her health—and her already fractured mind?

The slight tilt of one of his dark eyebrows brought her out of the maelstrom of her thoughts. If she were to have any hope of being released before the hospital notified her parents, she best get herself together!

Forcing her legs to complete the steps needed to reach Dr. Hershey's desk, she gritted her teeth and lifted her gaze to meet his. Apart from their disturbing color, his eyes held no dark threats.

"Please, sit." He indicated the chair next to him—a comfortable-looking one, perfect for therapy sessions and delving into childhood memories.

Selma obeyed, fervently wishing that he'd just hand her a prescription and be done. She had no interest in exploring her trauma with this... whatever he was, and even less desire for him to do so.

"Selma Lehmann, correct?" He lifted those dark eyebrows at her questioningly, waiting for her nod. "I am Doctor Martin Hershey, chief psychiatrist here at Ravenswood House. I suspect you don't recall me from last night, so it's a pleasure to meet you." He stretched his large hand toward her. Hesitantly she took it, bracing for the heat she knew he'd radiate. It wasn't unpleasant, but the warmth traveling from her fingers up through her arm felt mildly invasive, as if his touch attempted to cover as much of her skin as possible.

He smiled a little at her hesitation before letting go and leaning back, watching her in that therapist way she knew meant that every unconscious move of her body was being observed. It always made her fidget even more.

"I read your file this morning; this is the first time in ten years you have had a recorded incident. Did the hallucinations disappear in your late teens, or did you decide to deal with them on your own?"

Selma bit her lip. The way his fiery gaze locked on the gesture didn't ease the sense she was being scrutinized, but if she could make him believe that her latest "hallucination" had been a freak accident and not a relapse, this might be over quicker.

"I... haven't had an episode since I was seventeen. I think maybe it was just due to the stress of the situation, and I hadn't eaten all day..." Her voice died at his cocked eyebrow.

"You don't need to lie to me, Selma." His tone was mildly admonishing, but also gentle—the kind of tone someone would use to correct undesirable behavior in a skittish cat. "I am very good at recognizing deception. They never disappeared, did they?"

Splendid. So apart from having fire-eyes and horns, her new doctor was also a living lie detector. She shook her head.

"How did you manage them for so long on your own?"

There really was no way around it—they were going to talk about all the details of her miserable existence with this illness, and she was going to be permanently put back into a system that had no way of helping her, and every way of ruining what levels of contentment she'd managed to scrape together over the past ten years.

"I learned to ignore them," she said, voice low and defeated. "I found that if I didn't pay attention to them, the monsters wouldn't be able to tell me apart from everyone else. It's easier in the daylight."

Dr. Hershey cocked his head as he watched her, his burning eyes falling into shadow. He almost looked like a normal person, apart from the horns and ears. "Interesting. That must have been very hard."

Selma shrugged. "It was at first, but now it's easier than... than before." She gave him a pleading look. "I was doing alright. I really was. Last night was just..."

"What happened last night?"

She shot him a quizzical look. "Didn't they tell you?" She was pretty much used to having every detail of her life readily available in file format to anyone with a doctorate.

"They did indeed, but I would like to hear it from you, if you don't mind."

It was strange, really. She'd spent all her life keeping as much distance from *them* as she possibly could, and now she was sitting right in front of one who seemed genuinely interested in her well-being, almost... caring. It was intensely disturbing.

"I saw a girl being led away by three of..." She glanced quickly at his horns and stifled the words "your kind" from coming out of her mouth. "...uh, three of the *illusions*, and she looked very scared, so I couldn't not help."

"But they weren't illusions, were they? There were three men there, according to the police report. You did save a girl from her rapists," he said, leaning forward and supporting his chin in one big hand. The way he was watching her now, as if she were the most intriguing creature on the face of the Earth, was not much better than his previous scrutiny.

Selma shifted uncomfortably in her seat. "Well, yeah. But... to me, they didn't look like men, and... and when they tried to hurt me, I... panicked."

"You say 'tried to.' Did you fight back?"

She shuddered at the memory of the metal rod connecting with hard bone, sending shocks of vibrations down her arms. "Yes. It wasn't enough, though. It never is..."

When the police officers came, the tentative grasp she'd had on her broken mind snapped completely. A flash of the scaly monster who had ripped the pipe from her hands made her gasp. His claws tearing through her clothing had hurt, as had his fist locking around her throat.

Selma couldn't remember anything after that, apart from the sound of gunshots and the footsteps of the police officers sprinting to their rescue. She hadn't stopped screaming until the paramedics injected her with some kind of sedative.

"I... I'm sorry, I... don't recall the details so well." She wrapped her arms around herself in an attempt to quell the sinking feeling of despair. She would never escape the waking nightmare that was her illness.

Dr. Hershey patted her soothingly on the knee, transferring heat to her skin through the fabric. "That's quite alright, Selma. I know you must have been very frightened. Would you mind elaborating on what you mean by 'it never is'? Have you been hurt by people you see as monsters before?"

Of course he'd picked up on that. She bit her lower lip, nodding. "A few times, when I was a kid. Only one time really bad."

His orange gaze narrowed, something reminiscent of anger flickering behind it for a short moment before he managed to regain that soothing therapist-expression. "Sexually?"

"Oh, no. Mostly just..." She'd been about to say "normally," but thought better of it. Instead she rolled up the loose leg of the comfortable white pants she'd been given upon arrival, twisting her leg to reveal the long scar down her calf.

Dr. Hershey trailed his finger up it, leaving an electric trail in his wake, and the thought that she was happy she'd shaved her legs the morning before sparked in her mind. Blushing at that—*completely* irrelevant—contemplation, she resolutely stared at the horns sticking up from his wavy locks. Goosebump-inducing touch or no, horns did not belong on a man's head, and they certainly subtracted from the charms of his firm jaw and wide shoulders.

"This was vicious," he said, the softest touch of his

breath grazing her skin. "And certainly not a figment of your imagination. Did anyone catch the perpetrator?"

Selma pulled her leg back, shifting so the fabric slid down and covered her skin again. "No. Some passerby saw her, though. Said it was a young redheaded woman. She ran when he came to help me."

"And to you it was...?"

She grimaced. "A monster."

Dr. Hershey leaned back in his chair, staring straight into her eyes. "Are the monsters always evil, Selma? Is that what you see? A physical manifestation of inherently dangerous people?"

Before even realizing what she was doing, she shook her head.

"No?"

She flushed again and glanced at his pointed ears. "Uh... well, I don't know for certain. Many of them have left me alone, even when I... was staring at them. Or crying and pointing, when I was little. But I don't know if they are dangerous in other circumstances."

A small smile tugged at his full lips. "And do you see me as one of these monsters?"

THREE
SELMA

The excess blood—and then some—immediately drained from her face. *Oh god, how did he...?*

"No." It came out as a squeak.

Dr. Hershey raised an eyebrow in challenge. "Selma... I thought we had an understanding about telling the truth?"

Her brown eyes widened. Did he honestly expect her to explain that yes, she saw him as some form of nightmare creature—albeit a handsome one?

His defiant stare suggested that that was very much the case.

Shame hadn't rested this heavily on her since she'd been forced to apologize to Mr. Hubert, the physics teacher she'd confessed to suspecting was some form of demon. Gaze resting firmly on her knees, she nodded shortly.

"What do I look like? Please, describe what you see."

Defeated, she lifted a hand and made a vague gesture toward his head. "Horns, pointed ears..."

"Is that all?" He sounded idly amused, which really wasn't very polite.

Selma shot him an annoyed glare—she didn't enjoy feeling like the butt of a joke, having spent much of her life as one. However, his flaming eyes caught hers the second she looked up again, and the interest in them far overshadowed any indication of humor.

"Your eyes are like fire, but apart from that, you look... normal." She grimaced, feeling several shades of ridiculous. It was always uncomfortable to talk about her illness, but the fact that he was so... *intrigued* just made everything worse. Maybe it was his age—Dr. Hershey couldn't have been out of college for many years, and she was possibly his first non-standard patient.

He was, at least, looking at her as if she was some kind of rare and valuable find. "What color are my horns, then?"

Selma blinked, glancing up at said horns. "Er... black, with a bit of gray. Why?"

Something shifted in his eyes, as if he'd reached some conclusion in their depths. Then he smiled, turning his attention back to the computer that had gone into sleep mode, and moved the mouse to revive it.

"Simple curiosity. Now..." He tapped on the keyboard and looked at what she assumed was her file. "Have you ever heard of Sigmund Freud, Selma?"

"Yes." Who hadn't heard of that nut ball?

Her apprehensive tone drew another wry smile from his defined features. "I take from your expression that you aren't a fan. I hope you will keep an open mind, though, because there is a very good chance that we can help you by applying some newer theories that have their origins in his philosophy."

"Help me?" She had heard those airy words before, and each time had been a letdown. "Is there a new drug?"

Dr. Hershey shook his head, clicking his tongue disapprovingly. "Pharmaceuticals... It may be unorthodox, given my profession, but I rarely support attempts at altering brain chemistry with the use of drugs. The human mind is such a fascinating organism, and so much can be done just by finding a way to balance a patient's hormones."

Selma frowned—that was certainly unorthodox thinking for a psychiatrist.

"The paramedics took some blood samples from you last night. Do you remember?" he continued, ignoring her obvious doubt.

Hazily she remembered being pricked with a needle, but she'd not realized they'd done anything other than sedate her. She nodded anyway.

"There is an indication of a pretty rare hormonal imbalance in your results, one we haven't been able to test for until about four years ago. I suspect, and new research supports, that this could be the primary cause of your hallucinations."

That sounded really, really far-fetched, almost as

much as the horrible child psychologist who had suggested she needed some real life scares to overcome her fear of Bogeymen.

"But I've had them since I was a child," she pointed out.

The doctor turned his body fully toward her, leaned forward, and held out one large hand, palm facing up in an inviting gesture.

Tentatively, she placed her right hand in his, glancing at his face.

"Selma..." His fingers constricted slightly around hers, making them appear ghostly against his olive skin. "I understand that you've been through many failed treatments and how that must have affected your life. That you have chosen to deal with this disorder on your own for an entire decade makes it very clear that you have little trust left for any part of the medical profession, which I cannot fault you for. But this... this will change your life, I can almost guarantee it."

It wasn't that she believed he was right, exactly, but the conviction on his handsome face was hard to ignore... or remain unaffected by. And he wasn't going to use some experimental drugs on her, so what harm could there really be in giving it a try?

"Okay."

"Good girl." He closed his warm hand around hers again, firmer this time, before he let go and sat up straight. "The main goal is to even out your hormonal balance and encourage your brain to create new neurological pathways. That you see me as a monster will be helpful."

Selma cocked her head. "Why?" The only thing his monstrous appearance helped her with was to refrain from acting like that giggly nurse.

His brilliant smile returned. "We'll know if there is an improvement straight away." He opened one of his desk drawers and pulled out a notebook and pen. "But first I need to ask you some questions about your general health so we can establish a baseline for the treatment."

For a moment she'd feared he would be delving into electroshock therapy, but this sounded a lot more agreeable.

She returned his smile, lightness buoying her chest for the first time since that horrible incident the night before. Something about Dr. Hershey's conviction penetrated her otherwise jaded experiences with doctors trying to help her, and just the slightest sliver of hope was starting to shine through the dark. He was nothing like the other psychiatrists she'd dealt with, and if there was even a remote chance that her condition could be improved, she was more than happy to give it a shot.

Sometimes, like last night, she was certain she saw the truth and everyone else was blind. The clammy feel of dark magic still clung to her like a bad memory. But now, in the light of day? She knew the monsters couldn't have been anything but hallucinations. She was not a little girl anymore, and monsters and magic weren't real.

"Are you a virgin?"

Selma blinked, taken aback. "Uh..."

But the doctor was all business, which made her able to fight off a blush. She was twenty-seven, after all—there was no need to get embarrassed about sharing her history with her doctor.

"No."

"How many partners?"

"Three." One drunken one-night stand and two attempts at dating that had lasted fewer than three weeks combined, but he hopefully wouldn't need the specifics.

He moved the pen elegantly across the page of his notebook, creating beautifully curled script. Selma found herself mesmerized by the movement. He seemed to be adding a whole lot more detail than her one-word answers.

"Have you ever been, or tried to become, pregnant?"

"No." She had made her peace with never getting to bring a baby into the world long ago; no one deserved a mother who struggled with this kind of illness.

"Are you on birth control?"

One would have to have a sex life for that to be relevant. "No."

"How long since you were last sexually active?"

Selma blinked. Professional setting aside, admitting to a probably-rather-attractive-without-those-horns male that she had the sex life of a nun was still pretty humiliating.

"Two years."

Dr. Hershey looked up. "How often do you masturbate?"

There was no fighting the blood rushing to her face this time. "I... do you really need to know that?"

"I need to know everything that affects your hormonal production," he replied.

Well! Selma rubbed her suddenly clammy hands against her pants, wishing he'd look down at the paper again. "Maybe... uh, maybe... three times a... week?"

His forehead furrowed, and she managed to feel like a complete pervert before he said, "That won't do. Make sure you increase it—your body needs the surge in hormones. Do you have a healthy diet?"

Did he really just prescribe orgasms? She managed a weak nod to his question about eating right, as well as answering if she exercised.

"Excellent." Dr. Hershey snapped the notebook shut and got to his feet, gesturing toward a sofa half-hidden behind his book-laden shelves. "Please, come sit with me."

A bit apprehensive of why they might need to change their seating arrangements, Selma nevertheless got up and followed him to the sofa.

He sat down first and patted the cushion next to him, rewarding her with a smile when she obeyed.

"Now, Selma, I want to explain the procedure to you first. I know from previous patients that it can be... somewhat uncomfortable to submit to this sort of treatment, which is why we've adapted the methods a bit. I want you to know that you can ask for the standard procedure, but given what almost happened to you last night, I strongly urge you to let me make this as pleasant as I can for you, okay?"

Selma frowned, some of her hope dimming. "It's not... it's not electroshock, right? I've... it doesn't work on me."

Dr. Hershey grimaced and put a gentle hand on her arm. "My dear girl, no. I would never subject a patient to something so barbaric, and I'm so sorry that someone did. It's a sad truth that some doctors will resort to the most archaic and vile treatments when they're faced with a patient whose illness they can't cure, almost in some twisted act of revenge for putting their skills and reputation in question. I promise if you put your trust in my hands, you won't be harmed."

She shouldn't have trusted him—he was one of *them,* after all—but as she looked into his fiery eyes, she knew he meant every word. It went a long way to soothing both her fears and the painful memories of the experimental treatments she'd endured in the past.

Dr. Hershey must have picked up on her acceptance, because he continued, "For the first step, I will give you a pill. It's nothing but a concentrated dose of progesterone, and it will help your body accept the treatment. Now, have you heard of birth control implants?"

Selma nodded.

"Excellent. The device I'll be fitting you with works in a somewhat similar fashion. It's a small metal circle that fastens around your clitoris, where it will be able to constantly monitor your body's delicate hormonal balance and regulate it as necessary."

He said it as if there was nothing to be remotely alarmed about, but Selma jerked back from him with a start.

"You're—on my... Are you serious? No, I don't want that!"

Apart from the incredibly unsettling idea of having him touch her down there, his suggestion that her delusions could be cured by a piece of metal around her clit, of all places, sounded absurd. Where only a moment ago she'd felt overwhelming trust in him, her initial fear of what he looked like came rushing back on a flood of adrenaline.

"I know it's a lot to ask that you trust me on this, Selma," Dr. Hershey said, his face never betraying anything but patience. "And I know you've had little reason to believe in my kind before. But this procedure will change your life, and you need to be brave."

"Your kind?" she asked, eyes darting to his horns.

His smile widened a little. "Doctors. I'm just a man, Selma. One who wants to help you."

"And... and how would this procedure be done? Would *you...?*" She fidgeted on the chair, trying to not imagine him between her spread legs.

"Yes, it would be me. Attaching the ring requires some expertise—and a delicate touch. The way I strongly suggest you let me do this is in the privacy of my office. I'll help you get comfortable on the couch before we coax your body to allow me to place it. I promise it will be pleasant.

"Now, if you are uncomfortable with that, you do have the right to ask for a more formal procedure. That would be... less pleasant. There would be three doctors and a few nurses present, and I would have to put you in an examination chair in one of the procedure rooms. Instead of gentle stimuli, I would be using steel tools, and if I may be blunt—there's a strong chance you'd be tied down. Patients who've opted for this route in the past haven't been able to keep still, and with the tools, any wrong movement could injure the patient.

"I don't want that for you, Selma. I don't think it would help your healing process, especially not after your assault last night. I urge you to choose the gentle way."

Selma swallowed thickly, gaze darting to the door on instinct, then back to him. The image he painted had her heart thudding unevenly. She didn't want him to attach *anything* down there, not even a supposedly medicinal ring that would cure her hallucinations, but she especially didn't want to be tied down and gawked at by multiple people. She'd been in a straitjacket once, and the memory of being helpless while she was prodded at was nauseating.

"I... Can't I choose neither? Look, it was a one-time relapse; I've been doing fine for the past ten years. Please, I just want to go home."

Dr. Hershey put a large hand on her knee, and squeezed. "I know, sweetheart. But I can't let you go home while you're still seeing these *monsters*. If you were honest with yourself, you'd know you weren't doing fine this past decade. It was only a matter of time before your condition would flare up again. I don't want you to get hurt, so you have to stay with us until we've got a handle on this.

"Please, Selma. Please let me help you. I don't want to hand you back to the hacks who'll torture you with their electroshock treatments and drug you with pills that will leave you a walking vegetable."

She stared at him as the images he conjured sank into her mind's eye. Years of torture. Years of being too drugged to even think. She'd escaped that future when she convinced her previous doctors that she was cured, but now Dr. Hershey knew she'd been lying. There would be no escape from being permanently institutionalized—unless she submitted to this treatment.

If it didn't work, she could fake it. What was a few uncomfortable moments in the face of a much bleaker lifetime? He may have looked like a monster, but he was her only hope.

"Okay," she said softly. "Okay, I'll do it."

FOUR
SELMA

"Please take off your pants and undergarments and lay down on the couch." Dr. Hershey gave her an encouraging smile.

"I... didn't shave." It was silly to worry about her grooming habits before the most awkward medical procedure of her life, but the thought popped into her head before she could stop it.

He smiled a little wider, then shook his head. "You're a woman, not a little girl. Don't worry about it. Do get comfortable, please. I'll just need to fetch the ring—I won't be a moment."

It was a lot to ask of her—to get comfortable with her entire lower body exposed—but Selma obeyed nonetheless. She quickly got out of her pants and underwear, then lay on the couch waiting while Dr. Hershey rummaged around in his desk drawers on the other side of the bookshelf.

He was back by her side before she'd managed to calm her thudding heart, a small piece of gleaming metal trapped between his fingers.

"Can I see it?" she asked despite herself.

"Certainly." He held his hand out toward her, letting the little device rest in his palm.

It was a small hexagon that looked an awful lot like something a builder would use to secure screws with. A nut, she thought they were called. Some sort of letters were etched along the silvery sides, but they were too small for her to make out.

"What does it say?"

"It's just the make and serial number," he said, closing his hand around it and dropping into a crouch by her side. "Are you comfortable? Use the cushions to support your neck. That's it. Can you put one leg on the backrest for me?"

Selma obeyed, biting her lip as she lifted her leg up and out of the way, giving him access to her most private place. She stared straight up into the ceiling, avoiding his gaze—but he seemed to be focused on her sex rather than her eyes anyway.

"Good girl," he murmured, scooting closer as he knelt. His large hands encircled her hips underneath her linen shirt, warming her skin as he adjusted her position. Without asking her to move it, he grabbed her straightened leg behind the knee and lifted it off the couch, spreading her further.

"Very good."

His hot breath ghosted against the inside of her thigh, raising goosebumps in its wake. His hands followed, smoothing up along the inside of her thighs, spreading her wider still with a gentle, yet firm caress.

Her breath caught in her throat, every nerve in her skin suddenly alive with sensation. When Dr. Hershey brushed one hand up along her sex, she couldn't hold back a gasp.

"I'm going to stimulate you now," he said, letting the back of two fingers tease up and down her closed lips, tickling the hair there.

"S-stimulate?" Selma did her best to keep her voice calm, but she most definitely had never experienced an examination like this.

"We need your clitoris nice and plump for the ring to be fitted. In a more clinical setting, I would have to use tools to force it out—a rather painful procedure. But it's just you and me here now, and I can achieve the same results with some gentle stimulation instead."

"O-Okay." Neither option seemed ideal, but at least this way, she wouldn't get hurt. And regardless of what he was about to do to her, and how effective it may or may not be, once it was over she would have her freedom again.

When Dr. Hershey gently parted her slit with two fingers, she clenched her eyes shut and silently repeated that over and over.

"You are so tense," he murmured, breath grazing her

most intimate flesh this time. "Try to relax, sweetheart. It'll be over faster if you can."

"Yes, Doctor," she whispered, doing her best to obey.

"You don't have to call me 'Doctor' right now. I suspect it's not helping you relax. My name is Marathin," he said as he rubbed up and down her outer lips while keeping her slit spread open.

"Marathin?" The oddity broke her tense focus, her eyes fluttering open as she frowned. "The sign... said Dr. Martin Hershey?"

He cracked a half-smile, though his eyes didn't flicker up to meet hers. "Yes. I'm known as Martin here—when I was first hired, they misheard my name. By the time I realized the mistake, they'd already ordered the name plaque. But I'm mostly called Dr. Hershey by my colleagues and the support staff, so it never seemed worth the trouble to order a new one."

"But you ask your patients to call you by your given name?" she asked, grateful for the distraction of their conversation—even if it was hard to pretend like he wasn't massaging her sex in an increasingly intimate fashion.

Marathin chuckled. "Only a very few. Your condition is rare—but the intimate nature of the procedure doesn't lend itself well to formalities. I find most women prefer to pretend I'm not their doctor during this process." He moved his thumb from her outer lips to the soft flesh between them, testing with gentle presses.

It was uncomfortable, dry, and the sensation made her tense her thighs.

"Shh, it'll be better when you've lubricated," he murmured, moving one hand to press her thigh back up on the sofa's backrest. "You're starting to flush nicely. Just relax. We'll get you there."

Selma forced a deep breath as she stared at the white ceiling, trying and failing to ignore his insistent stroking of her sex. He wasn't touching her clit, but on every upstroke, he manipulated her inner lips just enough that her flesh tensed around the sensitive bud, stimulating it ever so slightly. It didn't take long before, despite herself, heat began to collect between her legs and a soft, pleasant throb stirred in her abdomen.

"Good girl," Marathin cooed when she inadvertently lifted her hips on another upstroke. "Very good." And then, before she could fully comprehend what he was doing, he'd popped his thumb in his mouth, wetting the pad before he pressed it directly at her still-hooded clit.

The zing of sensation was sharp and made her grunt, but it was far from unpleasant—which made it so much worse. She bit her lip hard and tried to shift her pelvis to lessen the stimulation, but he wasn't having it. He followed her movements with his thumb pressed hard against her little nub, rubbing in circles as he caught her hips with his other arm and grounded her to the couch.

"Easy now. Easy." His dark voice was huskier than before, which did little to calm the throb of her blood pulsing heavily in her tissue. "Give in to the pleasure, sweetheart. The more fully you surrender, the quicker it'll be over."

He had a point. The sooner he could get her body to respond enough that he could slip the ring on her, the sooner she would be free.

It took everything Selma had to relax her thighs and reopen her legs fully for him.

"That's it, well done," Dr. Hershey said, shifting so he could maneuver more easily. He brought the hand that'd been keeping her leg on the backrest down to her sex, wetting his thumb in dampness she hadn't know she was producing until he touched the hood of her clitoris.

"Let's see if we can't coax her out, hmm?" His low hum was followed by pressure on both sides of her clit. He rubbed up and down the tiny shaft, squeezing gently on the upstroke, just enough to set her nerves alight. Over and over he rode it, only changing it up by occasionally letting his free fingers brush along her spread lips, teasing her opening ever so lightly.

Soon she was squirming, not to escape, but to increase the pressure of his touch, her breath coming in soft pants.

"Starting to feel good?" he asked, and she could have sworn he was smirking.

Squeezing her eyes shut, Selma hoped it was a rhetorical question as a low groan made its past her clenched teeth.

Thankfully he didn't push for an answer, nor did he comment on her body's involuntary, but embarrassing, signs of pleasure. Instead, he doubled his efforts on her clit, pinching harder as he rubbed it up and down.

It was too much, too intense, but when she pulled

back he followed her, capturing her against the end of the sofa.

"Give in, sweetheart," he purred. "You want to feel better, don't you? I'll make you feel so good. Listen to your body—it knows."

Much as she wanted to, she couldn't deny the rising flood of heat in her pelvis, and despite her mewls of reluctance, soon her thighs spread wider of their own accord, inviting him in. It'd been so long since a man attended to her needs, and the doctor knew how to make her come alive as she'd never been before.

"Please," she panted, not knowing what she was asking for. "Please!"

"I see her," he rumbled, voice hoarse. "Starting to peek out from her protective hood. So pretty and pink, your little pearl. Begging for more, hmm?"

In a wild moment, she thought he might put his mouth on her, but her fevered thoughts were quashed as he twisted around, fingers still stroking firmly, and grabbed the metal ring in his free hand.

When he brought it back around, her eyes caught his —and something in her gut that had little to do with the pleasure he was forcing on her clenched.

There was a look in his fiery eyes then, something dark, and from deep inside a wave of fear bloomed despite her arousal.

Get away! Get away! Selma, get away!

The voice rang through her mind as clearly as if someone had shouted it into her ear. She gasped, choking on a groan when Marathin pinched her clit, forcing it fully out from the hood.

No, she had to get away! She had to escape. That voice—

Metal gleamed between her thighs and she kicked out, but it was too late. The doctor pinned her legs with his elbows, spread her labia wide—and in the next second, the cool ring slipped over her throbbing clit.

The moment the metal hoop touched her, darkness rose around them both. Yet despite a bolt of panic, Selma quickly lost the ability to care.

Marathin twisted the band, tightening it unbearably against her sensitive nub—and Selma screamed as black stars of agony exploded before her eyes.

"Take it off!" She managed to squeal despite the pain pulsing through her with every frantic beat of her heart. Reaching down, she tried to rid herself of the torture device. "Please, please—!"

Marathin caught her hands easily in one of his own, stilling her desperate squirming as he reached between her legs again. "Give in!" he growled, and then his hot fingertips pinched the still-free tip of her clit. "Come for me!"

It shouldn't have worked. The pain was so severe, and her panic so overwhelming that her nerves should not have been able to feel pleasure as well. But when he pinched her trapped little bud, warmth flooded her pelvis —and from nowhere, an orgasm rose hard and fast.

Her attempts to escape stilled, quashed on a tidal

wave of agonized bliss. Selma howled, arching up from the sofa as her doctor rubbed savagely at her clit. The darkness seemed to close in from all sides, but she was beyond caring.

"Come for me, Selma!" he commanded again, pressing his free hand against her forehead to push her down into the couch. Pain seared where he touched her, but it was brief and quickly swallowed by the torment he was inflicting on her sex.

Squeezing her eyes shut and closing out anything but the burning sensation of pain and ecstasy, she finally obeyed, screaming in agonized surrender as her body seized.

Marathin's thick fingers penetrated her weeping core, pushing her over the edge. He fucked her in rhythm with her cramping orgasm until her torment was forgotten and all she knew was ecstasy.

FIVE
SELMA

Selma's breathing was slow to calm. Echoes of too many sensations still sang in her blood, and her clit still trembled from the pained orgasm. The ring was no longer too tight, but its heavy presence was undeniable. It didn't hurt, but it was there, its grasp firm and inescapable.

She lay in silence while Marathin pulled his fingers from her wet sex, post-orgasmic peace washing away the memory of that voice screaming at her to flee. It seemed like nothing but a dream now. A nightmare.

"How long before I can take it off?" she rasped, voice still raw from shrieking.

"Does it hurt?"

"No. It's just..."

"I know." He stroked his warm hand soothingly up her thigh as he got to his feet. "I'm afraid it'll have to remain in place, if you want your delusions to stay gone."

Selma removed her gaze from the ceiling then, lips

halfway parted in protest, but when her eyes landed on Marathin, the words died on her tongue.

His black hair was horn-free and his eyes were deep amber. There were no flames, and no pointy ears. How was that even... possible?

She reached up, and he obligingly bent his head so she could stroke through the glossy strands. No bumps met her fingers, just soft, silken hair.

"You..." The implication slowly set in as he straightened back up, his now-human eyes evaluating her like any doctor would after a treatment.

"You cured me?" She couldn't quite make it into a statement, her voice rising questioningly toward the end. A lump she hadn't been aware of was building in her throat and made her swallow thickly, attempting to press back the tears building in her eyes. She was free. She was finally free.

"It is not a full cure, Selma." He grabbed her hand and gave it a comforting squeeze. "You need to take good care of yourself and maintain your hormonal balance—eat well, take the vitamins I'll give you, do some yoga for stress relief. It's all about management now, but yes; you should no longer see monsters."

There was nothing she could say, and nothing she could ever do to repay this man. Her tears spilled as she clutched at his hand, all resentment forgiven.

"Thank you, doctor. Thank you, thank you, thank you!"

THE EXHAUSTION FOLLOWING her treatment was bone-deep and lasted the rest of the day. If it wasn't for the nurses' kind, but strict insistence that she get up to eat and stretch her legs, she'd have happily stayed in bed.

Dr. Hershey—Marathin—had told her she was to remain at Ravenswood House for ten more days. She would see him every day to check on her continued progress and spend the rest of her time relaxing and getting into a routine of meditation, yoga, and regular meals.

Selma fought back a blush as she walked to the small en-suite attached to her room to get ready for bed. Considering how much she'd dreaded seeing the doctor that first time, she had a distinct lack of reluctance now.

He'd been more than kind after the treatment, helping her to her room and praising her for how well she'd responded. And since she no longer saw a monster when looking at him, it had been hard not to feel a little flutter in her stomach as he gave her hands a final squeeze, wished her a good night, and told her not to hesitate to call on him.

Not that there was any real chance of him dating his patients—not even the ones he'd gotten to know as intimately as he had her.

She smiled as she cranked the shower on and got out of her white pajamas while waiting for the water to heat. How many of his patients had developed a crush on him?

She was willing to bet the number was high, even if their treatment didn't consist of spine-shatteringly powerful orgasms, what with his handsome—and hornless—looks and kind mannerisms. Add to it that he saved minds for a living...

Selma sighed softly, stepping into the shower. She was well-aware that her sudden onset of interest had everything to do with the fact that he was the one to make her hallucinations go away and nothing to do with actual emotions.

However, as the hot spray from the shower worked on loosening her muscles, she found her thoughts wandering back to that room and how good it had felt as he prepared her for the ring. She gingerly rubbed her slick folds, careful not to press too hard on her still-tender clit, and leaned against the wet tiles while breathing deeply, letting her climax build.

Hazy thoughts of what it would've been like if he'd crossed the boundary from doctor to lover ran through her mind. Her hips jerked in response, and she had to keep them pressed against the wall to not over-agitate her ringed clit as her pussy clenched, bringing her over the edge with a whimper.

Panting, Selma rested her head against the tiles. She'd probably have to figure out a way to explain the ring to future lovers, but... she might actually be able to have a true relationship now, one where she wouldn't have to worry that her condition would drive them away. She might even be a mom one day.

A smile pulled on her lips, even as she reminded herself to talk to Dr. Hershey about the risk of the illness being hereditary. There was a chance that she could have a family of her own now, and she found years of suppressed dreams suddenly flurrying up inside of her as she imagined a white picket fence and serving lemonade to her blue-eyed kids.

She finished up in the shower, catching herself humming along to a tune she'd heard on the radio last week as she stepped out and dried herself. How much would her life change now that she didn't have to spend so much energy pretending everything was all right?

When she wiped the mirror free from steam, the wide grin on her reflection seemed so alien, yet so right. She couldn't remember when she'd last felt this happy—this hopeful.

Happily planning her future she brushed her teeth, humming around a mouthful of toothpaste with sheer joy. She continued the cheery tune while rinsing out her mouth with water from the tap.

It was when she straightened back up to grin widely at the mirror that she noticed it.

The faint shimmer on her forehead cut the melody short, her expression faltering as she leaned in closer. There in the middle of her forehead, where Marathin's hot hand had touched her just before her orgasm, was a round, silvery mark so faint that it almost blended in with her pale skin. If it hadn't been for its shimmer, she might not even have noticed.

But there it was, approximately the size of a walnut with odd symbols following the curved outer line branded into her forehead.

Was it another delusion? Had their nature simply changed?

Panic tightened in the pit of her stomach, and she staggered away from the mirror. No! This was too cruel, too unfair. Maybe it was just a normal side-effect that would disappear over time? Marathin would be able to tell her, to help her... and if there was any sliver of justice in the world, he might still be in his office doing some after-hours paperwork, because if he wasn't, she wasn't sure how she'd make it through the night.

Spinning around, Selma ran back into her room and fumbled into her clothes before trying the door. It was unlocked.

She thanked every deity she could think of for having been moved off the at-risk list as she ran down the empty hallways to the staircase leading to the doctor's office. It was a bit later than she'd realized; darkness stared back at her through the windows she hurriedly passed, and the upstairs offices seemed deserted for the night.

Selma didn't slow down until she came to the hallway housing Marathin's office, and she could have fainted from relief when she saw a small stripe of light shining out from underneath his door.

With about the same desperation as a thirsting man stumbling upon an oasis in the desert, she threw herself at the door, knocking quietly but with an urgent rhythm.

"Dr. Hershey!" she called, knocking again. "Marathin, please, I need your help!"

No reply came through the heavy wooden door, so she hesitantly turned the knob.

The door opened, and she had a moment of reconsidering practically breaking into his office like a desperate drug addict, but the alternative—a night of not knowing whether she was really cured—drove her to step in and close it behind her.

"Marathin?"

There was still no reply, and the man himself didn't seem to be in the room. But some paperwork was scattered over his otherwise neat desk, and the light coming from his computer screen indicated that he probably wasn't far away. She walked closer, glancing to see if he'd been away long enough that it had locked his user profile.

It hadn't, and she forced a deep breath through her lungs. He'd be back soon, and he would help her.

She sat in the same chair she had earlier that day, brushing her hands through her still-damp hair and letting her gaze wander. She hadn't noticed the many tribal-looking sculptures adorning his shelves among the thick books the first time she was here, and in the limited light, they were almost frightening.

She looked at the papers on his desk instead, wondering what her file now said about her and the treatment she'd been through.

Maybe the file was hers...? Feeling just a little guilty, she leaned closer, glancing over the pages of what appeared to be hand-written entries on top of a medical file. A file with her name on it.

No longer concerned about breaching any ethical standards, she moved to the other side, leaning against the desk as she let her fingers dance over the neat handwriting.

What she read made color fill her cheeks; the first page was a detailed description of her reaction to everything he'd done to her that morning and she quickly flipped the page, not entirely sure she wanted to know what else he had to say on that subject.

She let her eyes roam the next sheet for something less mortifying, but when she spotted a small diagram lower down on the opposite page, her heart skipped a beat and blood rushed in her ears.

It... it was...

She bent even further over the papers, staring at the small circle and the symbols within it. It was an exact copy of the image she'd seen on her forehead.

He'd... put it there?

The realization struck as a bolt of lightning, and numbness spread through her fingers where they pressed against the drawing. She didn't know how, but he'd marked her.

Selma shook her head, trying to clear her confusion. Why would he have done that? Even if she ignored the how, it made no sense. She brushed a hand over her forehead, eliciting an odd pulsing sensation against her fingertips when she touched the mark.

There had to be an answer on the pages.

Her pulse quickened as she refocused on the paper, finally reading the jarring words underneath the circle.

As suspected, Selma Lehman is a Breeder.
Application of the blinding mark removed her ability to see through my human disguise. Attachment of the breeding ring instantly enhanced her scent. She no longer fears me. No longer fears my presence; she will be ready for auction soon.

SHE DIDN'T READ any further, because when her eyes darted over the word "auction" for the second time, trying to find some meaning in it that didn't make her tremble, someone politely cleared their throat.

Selma jumped and tore her gaze from the paper, only to have it land on Dr. Hershey's tall form looming by the door.

He cocked his head, giving her the impression of a cat watching a mouse, as a wry smile spread across his handsome face. This time he made no attempt at hiding the devious quirk to it.

"Why, Selma... whatever are you doing in my office this late? Is there something you wish to discuss?"

She swallowed thickly, ignoring the teasing note to his

question. He knew without a shadow of a doubt what she'd seen.

"What did you do to me?" she whispered, trying her best to stop her hands from shaking. "What is that mark?"

He narrowed his amber eyes at her before twisting the doorknob so it locked with a menacing click. "That document was not for your eyes, sweetheart. But since you've seen it, I suppose you might as well learn what it means a little sooner than planned."

Taking his time because there was nowhere for her to run, he walked toward her, his shadow growing larger with every step.

SIX
SELMA

"What did you do?" Selma backed away from the desk. Through her fear of the man stalking toward her, a spike of anger rose, heating her chest and arms. "What did you *do?*"

He'd tricked her, had gained her trust with deceit and used her broken mind against her. For what gain she didn't know, but the page with the diagram made it painfully clear that it wasn't for anything pleasant.

"I took away your *delusions*. Isn't that what you wanted?" He tilted his head as he assessed her movements, obviously calculating how much closer he could come before she'd dart around the desk. "Does anything else really matter?"

His silky tone only made her heart thrum harder against her ribs. It was deceitfully kind, just like the man himself. She kept retreating, maintaining her distance. "You're dangerous!"

It was too late, of course. She should never have let her guard down around one of *them,* should have known that his caring words and manners were only meant to lure her in. Would anyone hear her if she screamed? The corridor had been deserted; they were likely the only souls in this part of the hospital.

"You will not be harmed." His soothing words aside, he matched her retreat, keeping his body between her and the exit at all times. When her back hit the far wall and her eyes widened in terror, he stopped, leaving a few feet of space between them.

"Have I been anything but good to you yet, sweetheart?" There was a taunt in his smooth voice, one dark eyebrow curving up as if to suggest that she was being ridiculous when her gaze instinctively darted around the room in search of some way out. She found none.

"You lied." Selma stared back up at the man who had her cornered. She set her jaw, hoping to convey something other than "weak female" to whatever instincts ruled him. "You took advantage of me."

Though she tried to keep her voice calm, it held a shrill note that spoke of her fear as much as the tremble of her hands, emphasized by the rustle of paper clenched in her fist.

"Hmm, whatever do you mean? You no longer see demons, correct? I promised you as much."

He took a step closer, causing her to flatten herself against the wall. So much for putting on a brave act.

"Y-You *branded* me!" She touched a hand to her forehead. "I saw it—in the mirror. *You* did this! Why?"

He glanced at her forehead with both eyebrows raised in what looked like genuine surprise before bracing an arm against the wall right next to her head. "You can see the mark? Oh, Selma... if only you knew how valuable you are."

Her breath hitched at his sudden proximity. He really was very tall, and his broad shoulders caged her in from above as oppressively as the rest of him.

"What did you do?" It came out as a scared whisper this time.

Marathin raised the hand not currently supporting his weight, and with the faintest of touches, he traced a circle around the outer edges of her mark.

"I blinded you," he murmured. "Really, Selma, you must have known deep down what we really are. Through every evaluation and every drug they gave you, you must have known."

She stared up into his eyes, trying to deny his words from taking root. He was right—of course he was right. Deep down, that nagging feeling nurtured by all the questions that couldn't be answered—the ones that had plagued her for years—had never been silenced... Like how a young woman without weapons could have left that scar on her calf, or why some of them would follow her when they saw her staring at their otherness.

She'd never dared to think the thought through,

because if she'd actually acknowledged the concept, she'd have lost her mind.

The shaking in her hands moved up her arms and down through her body until she was trembling like a leaf in the wind.

"Don't be scared." Marathin stroked an unnaturally hot hand down her arm. "Let it settle in. You're special, sweetheart. And so very valuable."

It wasn't that his touch soothed her, but it did jolt her out of her downward spiral. She flinched away from him, unwilling to give him any doubts about her feelings. "What do you want from me?"

His devilish smile returned as he boxed her in fully, placing the hand she'd shied away from against the wall next to her head. Selma swallowed nervously as a few flashes of how he'd touched her body during the "procedure" passed through her mind. This time there was no doctor's coat and no professional persona to hide behind—there was just the very large creature who'd tricked her into spreading her thighs for him, and her own raspy breathing.

"It is not a matter of what I want; it's what I need. You don't understand the value of what's between your legs, my sweet. You're a perfect Breeder, so incredibly rare. I thought you were just a regular Breeder—valuable, but nothing like what you truly are. Most we come across cannot tolerate a Lord's magic, but you... you see the blinding mark. Your innate resistance to our magic is strong enough that you can survive being mated by one of our most powerful."

"B-Breeder?" There was that uncomfortable word again, the one he'd scribbled underneath the diagram. "You want to... *breed* me? L-Like an animal? Are you out of you mind?!"

Monster or not—strike that; the fact that he was a monster definitely made it worse—that was not something you should want to do to people!

Marathin chuckled. "No, definitely not 'like an animal.' You will be bred by one of my kind, not another human. Your womb would be wasted on the rats already overpopulating this planet."

"I don't..."

She was about to tell him that she didn't understand, but stopped before she finished the sentence. There was nothing to understand—not now. She could mull over everything later when she was safe. Right now, the only thing that mattered was that she was alone with a man talking about *breeding* her.

"HELP!" She screamed at the same time as she drove the heel of her right hand into his ribs, swinging the other at one of the arms keeping her trapped against the wall. "SOMEONE HELP ME!"

Marathin grunted when she impacted with his chest, but that was about all her fighting did. Even when she kicked at his shins, he barely flinched, and when she tried to dive underneath his arm, he easily caught her. He pulled her in, twisting her around to constrict her movements by locking his arms around hers, pressing her back against his chest so she couldn't bite him.

"LET ME GO!" Selma tried to headbutt him by tossing her head backwards, but she only connected with his rock-hard chest, which seemed to hurt her more than it did him. She screamed again, struggling wildly against his grip, but he didn't budge.

"There seems to have been a minor miscommunication," he purred in her ear. "You appear to believe you are in danger; that is not the case. I took away your Second Sight so you could be more comfortable–nothing more. Calm down, sweetheart."

There was nothing more she could do–he was simply too strong. She went limp in his arms with a defeated whine, breathing heavily from exhaustion after her short, but wild struggle to get free.

"Good girl," he murmured, bending his head to rest it against hers. "You have nothing to fear."

Selma drew a shuddering gasp when he breathed in deeply, obviously taking in her scent. Something hard started growing against the small of her back, stirring terror in the pit of her stomach.

"Please don't rape me."

It was a ridiculous request, of course. He was some form of a... a monster, and his kind had no qualms about imposing their desires on others with or without consent, as she had seen from the three who'd attacked that girl. Not to mention the things the doctor had already done to her under the disguise of a concerned healthcare provider.

The monster chuckled against her ear. "Selma. What did I say? You won't be harmed, sweetness. You're much too valuable, and I am duty-bound to kill anyone who would do damage to your beautiful little pussy."

His erection suggested otherwise.

"Y-You say you won't force me..." She drew a deep breath to calm her nerves as the thing at her back reached full size. "Yet you want to... *breed* with me. And I don't... I don't understand!"

"Shh, calm down." Marathin cradled her closer against his chest—and by default, his straining cock—as if to soothe her with his body heat leaching through her clothing and into her skin. It didn't work.

"I will explain, little Breeder."

"Stop calling me that!"

His low chuckle, huskier now, brushed against her ear again. "It is a title of honor among our kind. You will learn in time, when you have grown accustomed to our ways."

"I have no desire to grow accustomed to the ways of monsters!" she snarled, anger taking a front seat to fear. "Why did you lie to me? If... If you really are a monster, why try to... why trick me?"

What she wanted to ask was why he hadn't just forced her instead of going through the scam of her "procedure," but despite her anger, she didn't think it wise to antagonize him too much. No one said he couldn't change his mind.

He hummed in an amused tone. "Demons, Selma. We are demons, not monsters. I ringed you to ensure your cooperation once your mate's won you at auction. I blinded you because it would have been easier to accept your fate if you didn't realize what we were for a little while longer.

"You must understand, the Breeders who find their way to this place are as scared and convinced that their minds are damaged as you were. They are slowly introduced to life with us so that the transition is minimally traumatizing. Of course, it's a little too late for you. I should have known you'd see the mark, but it's been so long since I have been around a Pure Breeder."

If he truly was trying to explain, he wasn't doing a particularly good job.

"But why me?" It was the question she'd asked herself so many times over the years, oftentimes while huddled in her bed crying, only to be answered with silence.

"Ah, I cannot answer that, I'm afraid. All we know is that women who can see through our human disguises are biologically compatible with us. Since our own females are... shall we say, less compliant, we look for mates among your kind. It's my job as a procurer to find these women and prepare them for their auction.

"And you, sweetheart... you're a perfect specimen. You may still be too scared to appreciate it, but your sweet little cunt will bring the strongest demons across the world to their knees. They will come from far and wide for a chance to win you."

The pride in his voice, as if she were a particularly precious pet, made her cringe. "Please... let go of me!"

"I will, if you promise to stay calm and not attempt anything stupid." The demon gave her body a squeeze, a gentle reminder of how superior his strength was to hers.

"I promise." As if she had any other option. No one had come when she'd screamed for help before, and she would not be able to make it to the door and out before he caught her.

Besides… as confusing and terrifying as this evening had turned out to be, a not-small part of her hungered for any answers he might possess. Answers she'd been too afraid to hope for all her life.

Marathin's strong arms loosened their grasp and she quickly stepped away, spinning around so she could keep a watchful eye on him.

The lazy smile spreading over his face as he leaned against the wall told her that her mistrust was not particularly well-hidden.

She didn't care.

"What are you going to do to me?" Selma stared into his coppery eyes and decadently handsome face, not bothering to keep the accusation out of her tone. "Are you just going to kidnap me from the hospital?"

He shook his head and folded his arms across his chest as he took in her stubborn, but frightened expression. "Missing girls lead to investigations, and it's crucial that we keep a presence in as many mental institutions as possible; Breeders are often sent here by ignorant humans. You will remain in my care for the next ten days, and then

I'll sign off on your paperwork before transferring you to the governor's house."

She gaped at him. "You expect me to keep quiet and just go willingly?" Demon or not, he must be insane. The second she laid her eyes on another human being, she would be screaming for help. He expected her to keep up pretenses of everything being all right for an entire week? Well, he had another think coming!

Something shifted in his eyes—something dark. Selma shrunk back from his suddenly threatening aura, any rebellious thoughts evaporating as he stared her down.

"That is exactly what I expect, Selma. Did you hope to rouse the humans to the fact that demons walk among them? Do not be foolish; they locked you in here for that very reason. Now, play along nicely and I will make your time in my care very pleasant. Fight me, and you will regret it."

SEVEN
SELMA

"You promised not to hurt me!"

It was a silly thing to cling to—the word of a demon—but it was all she had as his dark presence grew, forcing her to accept his control over her.

The shadows in his eyes and around his body faded as he took in her shaking form. With a soft sigh he raised a hand and brushed his thumb over her bottom lip. "My sweet, you will never need to fear for your personal safety; but I will not hesitate to silence any nosy humans, should you go running that pretty little mouth. Do you understand?"

Her eyes went round at the warning and she quickly nodded. Other people's pain always made her ache to help—it was the reason she'd run after that girl to save her, dumb as it was—and the threat of being the cause of someone's death...

No, she would have to find her own way out of this mess.

Which required knowledge.

"You keep saying I am meant for 'a Lord.' What are they? Demon royalty?" Her forehead furrowed at the thought of monsters having nobility.

Marathin's thumb moved from her lips to her cheek, stroking it adoringly. "Yes. They are the strongest among us; they are bigger and more powerful, and thus need a mate who can withstand their magic when they mount. Unfortunately, only the purest of Breeders are capable of that, and as you are so rare... our Lords are not producing enough progeny."

Selma paled and swallowed hard; that did not sound pleasant from the Breeder's perspective! Then again, she wasn't planning on letting anyone *mount* her, Lord or otherwise.

With an inward shudder, she released the rather intimidating mental images Marathin's words had conjured and focused on the problem at hand—getting all the information she could out of the demon who'd tricked her.

"So you're not a Lord?"

He shook his head, a regretful frown pulling on his dark eyebrows as his thumb swiped back over her lips. "I am not, so I will not be bidding for the pleasure of claiming you. A pity—I find myself enjoying your spark."

She wrinkled her nose. "Bidding—you're going to... sell me at auction? That's what the note said."

No matter his assurance that he didn't plan to have her bred like cattle, he sure didn't help the picture the more he revealed about their customs. She briefly wondered if there would be a line of scared, kidnapped women up for sale, being paraded around an arena for perverted demons' viewing pleasure.

"Yes, though monetary compensation is only a part of the price for claiming a Breeder. It is a complicated system—do not worry yourself with such matters, sweetness. Whoever your mate will be, he will ensure your well-being."

She couldn't hold back a disbelieving scoff at his dismissive attitude. "My well-being? I am expected to serve as broodmare for some oversized demon, but of course he won't rape me, I'll just magically lust for my *owner*, and now you tell me that he will care for my well-being! Who the fuck are you to think you can determine my life? Your kind has ruined me, and now..."

She gasped for air, a refreshing rush of rage blazing through her. "Now you act as if any of this is for *my* sake? Fuck you, and fuck your precious Lords!"

The demon took in her raging outburst with complete calm. The hand still cupping her cheek stroked over her chin, undeterred by her attempt at slapping it away, as his gaze dipped lower.

"Ah, I suppose I did neglect to tell you exactly how that pretty little ring I gave you works. You see..." He moved his hand to her shoulder, fingers trailing down her side until they got to her waistband. "You will lust for him, or whoever touches it. One small twist, and you will spread your legs and beg to get fucked by anyone and anything with a cock. It is only a safety measure, of course, to ensure that new Breeders allow frequent matings while they're getting used to their new lives."

"I will never want anything from monsters!" Selma spat, jerking away from his touch but getting stopped when her back hit the wall. "And I will never willingly let you touch me again. You're a fraud and a rapist and... *Nnh!*"

His eyes held a mildly curiosity as he slipped a hand inside her pants and twisted the ring on her clit before she could dodge him.

The sharp shock that rocked through her whole body took her breath away, but several seconds passed before the full wave of sensation hit her. Pain was the first to register, and her face contorted in agony that was soon dulled by dark desire unlike anything she'd experienced before.

She *felt* the magic enter her body from that cursed circle of metal, shuddered as it seeped into her flesh and penetrated all the way to her bones. It traveled up her spine in tight pulses that left her fumbling blindly for support, until it finally clouded her brain in a hormonal fog.

Every cell in her body was on fire, every breath making her linen clothes rub painfully against her skin.

When she finally regained her vision, she realized she'd fisted both hands in Marathin's shirt. He was watching her with an amused quirk of his full lips, one mocking eyebrow raised in question.

She growled, the sound of a furious mountain lion, not because of what he'd done to her—but because of what he wasn't doing.

Gone was her fear—gone was her care that he'd deceived her, trapped her. All she wanted, all she *needed...*

She hurled herself at him with a strangled cry, using his shirt for leverage to pull herself up against him, stretching for his mouth. Unfortunately, he was much taller than her, and instead of bending his neck and kissing her like every instinct in her suddenly throbbing body was screaming for him to do, he just... looked at her. As if that was helping anything!

Angrily, she let go of his shirt and reached up, grabbing the smooth, black strands of his hair and forcefully pulling him down where she could reach.

His surprised laugh cut short when their lips finally crashed together. Selma moaned in relief and opened her mouth to better taste that sweet heat emitting from him, all the while clenching her fingers in his clothes and hair to keep him from moving away. She needed him as close as he could possibly get.

Thankfully he responded to her need, parting his lips just enough for her tongue to dart in between. She moaned again, white sparks firing off behind her closed eyelids at the taste and feel of his tongue, and though it soothed part of her wild craving, it also sparked another—deeper—desire.

With desperate haste, she started pulling at his shirt with the hand she didn't have locked around the back of his neck to keep his mouth where it belonged, and succeeded in untucking half of it from his pants before he could react.

Marathin grinned against her lips and grabbed both her hands in his, encompassing them with ease before he pulled a few inches away from her face. "Now, now, Miss Lehmann—" Her impatient whine interrupted him, and he cocked a teasing eyebrow at her. "I specifically recall you stating that you would never want anything from 'monsters' not two minutes ago, and I feel a little uncomfortable with a patient of mine trying to undress me in my own office."

He dared mock her! Selma snarled at him; it was his job to make her feel good, not to taunt her for something he had caused.

"Touch me, you fucking prick!"

The demon's grin widened at her language. "I'd love to, but I wouldn't want you to feel *violated,* my sweet. If you want me to take you, you don't get to deny me again later. Is that clear?"

The thought of violation was laughable at that point—somewhere, she understood he'd caused the wild haze of lust to take over her now-burning body, but it mattered little to her. What he was and what he had done was irrelevant, because he was everything she needed right then—

the only one who could give her the release she so desperately craved. If she'd had the strength, she'd have happily forced *him* without remorse.

"Yes!" she snapped while futilely wrestling with his grip.

His warm breath wafted over her upturned face and made liquid want soak her panties as he took in her desperation with a calculating expression. Yet she saw that his own desire was beginning to crack his calm mask and felt bone-deep relief, and even triumph, as she kept struggling for his mouth's attention. It was only a matter of minutes before he would give her what she needed.

"You consent, Selma?" His voice, now huskier, pulled another whimper from her with the vibration it sent down through her spine, but she managed to nod through the fire in her veins.

"You're gonna give me that sweet little pussy willingly in exchange for relief?" He bent his head just a little more, his breath teasingly tickling over her lips now, and she thought she might pass out from the sheer strength of her need for his kiss.

"Yes, anything! Just...!" She stretched as far as she could, almost reaching his warm lips, willing him to give in.

He did.

The sweet rush of ecstasy when his wonderful flavor returned to her lips pacified her for a few seconds as she adjusted to the head rush it caused. Then the fire in her abdomen exploded.

"Easy now!" There was still laughter in Marathin's voice when she ripped his shirt apart, sending buttons flying—but that didn't conceal the dark thrum of desire, nor the growl she pulled from him by scratching at his skin to yank it completely off his body.

"Little wildcat," he growled, grabbing her by the hair and pulling her head back when she tried to bite him for delaying their coupling. "You want it rough?"

Selma shuddered wantonly at the promise in his eyes, relishing in the unabashed lust she saw there. All signs of his cool, professional façade had been wiped away, leaving nothing but a strong, lean male primed and ready to fuck. God, how she needed him!

Instead of answering, she let her hands smooth over his rock-hard stomach muscles, up to the chiseled chest where she dug in her nails, drawing blood and a snarl from the demon. His hold on her hair tightened painfully, but it only sent the slick heat pooling between her thighs and dripping down her legs as she dug her nails in deeper, pressuring him to take control.

She wanted, *needed*, him to claim her, to prove he was strong enough to take her as he pleased, and he was going to do just that, even if she had to rip him to shreds first!

Thankfully, he complied.

He yanked her head all the way back with a rough tug, exposing her vulnerable throat to him. His lips followed, burning up the column of her neck until he dug in his teeth in an unspoken claim of dominance.

Selma moaned, momentarily going limp against him

as he wound his free arm around her waist. Yes, this was it —this was what she needed him to do! The heat from his mouth and the sting from his bite only fueled her desire.

The second he released her throat, she was pulling at his pants, not quite able to work the buttons in her lust-filled haze. Finally something snapped, and she managed to rip them open before he pressed her against the wall with both her hands locked over her head in his large hand.

"Are you wet for me, sweetheart?" he asked huskily, trailing the fingers not around her wrists down her stomach and—ever so lightly—over the front of her pants.

"Oh fuck, please, please, more!" She strained against his grip, pressing her hips out in a desperate attempt at getting more friction against her painfully sensitive groin, but he easily kept her in place, drawing teasing patterns on the white fabric with just enough pressure to drive her crazy with need.

"I'll give you more, sweetheart." His amber eyes bored into hers, forcing her attention to them rather than his naked torso and the ache between her legs.

"Just fuck me!" she gasped and arched desperately, doing her best to reach his warm body with the part of her that needed him the most. "Please, for the love of God, fuck me!"

A feral sneer crossed his features, almost resembling the demonic features the brand had suppressed from her vision. Marathin stepped closer to her, pressing against her pleading hips roughly enough to flatten her against the door. "There is no god here, Selma. There is only me and the pleasure. Do not call out for one again, or I will make you regret it."

The threat might have registered if he hadn't been close enough for his breath to waft over her face as he stared her down. When he released her hands to grasp at her shirt, she lost all focus for anything but his powerful body.

He ignored her frantic hands as they clawed his torso and ripped at his pants, easily removing her top and pushing her bottoms off before he pulled his length out of his own ruined pants.

She didn't get a chance to drink in the sight of him as the next moment he lifted her against the wall, bracing with one of her legs on each side of his strong hips. Her muscles tensed in preparation of what they instinctively knew was coming, even as the entrance to her pussy softened further, weeping with need.

"Yes, yes, yes!" she chanted as he pressed his hard cock against her nether lips, but when she angled down to take him inside of her, her opening protested the stretch.

Marathin didn't give her time to prepare. With a harsh grunt, he pulled down on her hips, breaching her.

Selma tossed her head back with a wail, pawing weakly at his chest. She was slick with need, but he was rough and she'd not been with a man for years. The demon didn't care, pushing into her farther—and that's when she realized that something was wrong—terribly wrong.

The head of his cock—large and bulbous, and otherwise just what she needed—was fully inside of her, but along the rim, something hard and uneven dug into her slick channel, overshadowing even the rough stretch of unaccustomed tissue.

"It won't harm you if you relax." He grunted, his own instincts clearly fighting to take over and ram into her to the hilt. "I will explain after... Don't fight it; it'll feel good in a minute."

It wasn't like she had much choice; her body, though alarmed at the unfamiliar sensation, was too deep in the ring's spell to put up a fight, and when he pressed in further and those bumps ground against her G-spot, all traces of worry disappeared.

"God!" Selma tossed her head back against the wall again as jolts of uninhibited pleasure rushed through her form. *"Hnng!"* Her cries abruptly cut off as the demon pushed her down and simultaneously drove his hips up with a single rough jerk, ploughing his cock all the way into her.

She clung to his shoulders, gasping through the shock. Though her pussy was more than ready, her unused muscles protested at the violent entry. He was enormous and diamond-hard, her squeezing core not finding any give in the ridgid mass as she struggled to adjust.

"One more mention of a god of any kind and you won't be able to walk for a week, do you hear?" Marathin hissed at her through gritted teeth, but he might as well have spoken Greek for all the sense it made to her; her focus was solely on the need for him to begin the thrusting rhythm she instinctively knew she had to receive to quell her wild lust.

Whimpering at the unyielding pressure, she flexed her hips, trying to gain enough momentum from the wall and his strong hands holding her up to ride him, but he was so deep within her that she could barely move.

But her efforts forced the demon's attention to the same urge, and he growled with pleasure at her movements, drawing back far enough for the uneven bumps to once more massage her G-spot before he drove in again. And again.

Oh, this was it! This was exactly what she craved, what she was built for, what her entire universe was centered around!

Selma let out a sob of relief even as he pounded her viciously, her abused pussy numb to the ache and her mind swathed in endorphins. She dug her nails into his shoulders to ensure that he didn't pull away before she surrendered completely to his control. Even if she had wanted to, she could do nothing to alter his deep, rapid thrusts, and her efforts to ease the coupling by moving against him went ignored as he lost himself in his instincts.

It took a few minutes before the bliss of being filled and rutted morphed into something more, turning her throaty moans of contentment into sharp cries as the ridges on his cock over-stimulated the deepest parts of her, pulling her towards climax.

It swelled and grew low in her belly with the dull, deep sensation of mounting pleasure, so different from her normal clitoral orgasms. Yet the desperate need for its completion had exactly the same power over her as when he had rubbed her clit until her world shattered.

Frantically she writhed for Marathin, unnecessary pleas for more spilling from her lips even as he ravaged her with the full force of his inhuman strength until...

Yes, finally!

Selma clung to her lover, screaming as her pussy clamped down around him, squeezing his hard length for all it was worth. Black dots danced in front of her eyes as she peaked.

When her orgasm finally released her, she slouched against his shoulder, breathing hard while slowly regaining her bearings.

He had courteously stopped pounding her into the wall while she came, and now his strong arms and the heavy thickness she was still straddling held her aloft, her torso resting intimately against his. His warmth was comforting, even as the heady pheromones from his sweat forced her tired pussy to contract weakly in an attempt at responding to the demand for every last drop of her lust.

She groaned at the persistent fullness, the ache slowly setting back in as the endorphin rush ebbed. Every time he breathed, small spikes of pleasure would ripple through her from where the bumps on his cock dug into her cunt.

God, what were those things? Now that her craze was

dwindling, they weren't entirely pleasant as they pressed into the deepest, most sensitive spots inside of her, even though they had felt amazing during... whatever it was they'd just done.

Fucked.

She glanced up at the waiting man and shivered at the heat blazing from his eyes. Though he was allowing for her body to recuperate, nothing about the way he looked at her made her think she'd receive any additional mercy.

Goodness, what had she done? The twist of her ring had turned her into some wanton whore, had changed her completely until she was nothing more than an aching vessel for Marathin's semen—and now she was trapped, melded to a demon who had no intention of letting her get out of the role as his broodmare.

She had begged for this... How could she have given up control so completely?

His all-pervading heat was suddenly anything but comforting; it wrapped around her oppressively, demanding her continued submission.

"I want you on your knees, Breeder." His voice was husky and deep as he slowly moved his hips against hers again, pulling a groan from her weakly protesting body. It was as if he could sense that she was no longer under the ring's thrall and needed a physical reminder of the pleasure he could cause.

"Enough foreplay; you need to get on your hands and knees and take my cock so I can show you what a good little Breeder you'll be."

Foreplay? She'd never been fucked so thoroughly in all her life! This had to stop; they had to stop for a moment so she could regain her bearings—regain her sense of self.

"Marathin, wait. Maybe we could—*oh!*"

Her pleas choked off when he hammered his cock in to the hilt, keeping her pressed against the wall at the hips.

"Don't even try. You asked to get fucked—and that is exactly what's going to happen." He smiled darkly at her as she writhed for him. "But if you prefer, we can certainly make it a little easier for you again."

"No!" Her eyes flew open as he slipped his fingers in between their bodies. She pushed at his chest, but it was futile. If he twisted her ring again, she would be lost, swept away in the firestorm of desire, and she wasn't sure she could go through that again without breaking completely and permanently. How many times could she succumb to that bottomless need before there would be no way back?

"Yes." His warm breath ghosted over her forehead as he wrapped his other hand around her wrists and pinned them to the wall. The dark lust that had taken over his professional persona burned in his gaze, leaving no shadow of reason; he was as lost in her as she had been in him.

Selma panted as he moved slowly and deliberately inside her until her attempts at freeing herself stilled, her traitorous body beginning to wake and respond again, though somewhat more mutedly than it had during the short, wild heat caused by the ring. Marathin stretched her perfectly, and she was wet enough for the bumps to feel good when he thrust, rubbing them slowly over every sensitive spot inside of her.

"What are they?" she gasped, clenching her fists as he pulled out far enough for her swollen G-spot to receive their firm attention.

"Cartilage ridges along the edge of the head." He grunted when she squeezed experimentally around them. "Our own females are stronger than humans and often need to be kept in line during mating. Biology has given us a way to do that. Of course, for human women, it's just another way to make you beg, isn't it, sweetheart?"

Selma mewled in response as he pointedly thrust back in with a bit more force, her hands grasping at air in his grip. His anatomy certainly did quell any desires to attempt resistance!

"I said: Isn't it?" His lip curled up in a snarl, and before she could gasp a reply, he pounded into her with enough force to make the wall protest. Immediately he let his hips pick up pace to a merciless rhythm that had her thrashing and screaming.

"Yes, yes!" she cried, not quite sure if she obeyed to end his assault on her body, or to ensure that he didn't stop. "God, please, I—!"

Her high-pitched whine when he reached down and yanked savagely on the ring interrupted her plea and she stiffened, her back arching as hot tendrils shot through her brain and body in pulses, forcing her pussy to contract around him.

The demon toyed with the metal for a bit before he pulled out of her sopping channel and let her slide to the floor.

There was only blazing heat and the sensation of having the most sensitive part of her being stimulated continuously and unrelentingly. It was more than orgasmic, more than sexual—it was the essence of everything the universe had to offer, and she felt it crack her grasp on reality and her sense of self slowly dissolve.

When he stopped, it was like being ripped away from the source of life itself.

Furiously she launched herself at Marathin with every intent of ripping him apart to get to that blissful source she knew he possessed. Within him was the key to her salvation, to the sweet release of the dark power boiling in her blood.

He growled at her, forcing her to the ground and flipping her over, despite her struggles to tear out strips of his skin.

"On. Your. Knees!" It was a hiss against her ear, followed by his hands pulling at her hips violently enough to make her stop swiping at him. Her arms barely managed to support her own weight in time to keep her head from banging painfully against the floor.

It was a curious thing, really; the moment she was on all fours with her back to him and his fingers bruising her hips, she no longer wanted to rip him apart. Howling with need, she arched her back for him, her dripping opening clenching on air as her body recognized the true nature of her desperate situation.

Mercifully he mounted her, clearly understanding that he'd driven the Breeder past what she could bear. He plowed into her clamping pussy and growled alongside her sob of relief as he bottomed out, the rut descending fully upon him.

EIGHT
SELMA

It took three pained orgasms before sense returned to Selma. Her bucking stilled as she gasped through the aftermath of her last climax. Every muscle in her body ached, their consistency resembling that of jelly, and her breathing was ragged and wheezing.

With a whine, she gave up her attempt at staying on her hands and knees, sliding down on her stomach and leaving the man still hard and buried in her to follow.

He did, pressing his weight down over her, and though she was no longer under the mark's spell, her exhausted mind understood his display of dominance. It felt... good, but something half-muted tried to claw its way through the thick fog to remind her that she was in enemy hands.

Those same hands moved from her hips, smoothed down her arms as he readjusted his weight over her, and finally braided with her fingers as he lifted halfway up again. The next moment she grunted with him as he thrust into her.

It didn't hurt exactly, as she was still sopping wet and open, but with the craze lifted, she was acutely aware that her pussy was battered and swollen, and every push of his ridged cock tormented her over-stimulated flesh with pleasure she could barely withstand.

There was no reprieve yet, though—not before her forceful lover had found his release—so Selma purposely pushed the protesting part of her mind aside and lifted her hips so he could fill her more easily.

The smacking of his flesh against hers made it easier to drown out the objections from both her body and brain. She moaned, giving in to Marathin's dominance and cock yet again, drunk on his pheromones and the lazily mounting pleasure in her loins.

"Mmm, my sweet. Like that." His voice in her ear was hoarse with tension from an impending climax and the long, hard build-up for it. Growling, he bit the back of her neck, and when she whimpered her surrender, he released her right hand and let his own find its way underneath her to her sweet spot.

She jolted, straining up while clutching at the floor, but before she could adjust, he drove his cock deep. A few hard, full thrusts and she gave up fighting his touch, her keening taking on the shrill note of yet another orgasm as he once again proved his total control over her body.

She took his cock to the hilt over and over, gritting her teeth against the power he was driving into her with while her pussy struggled to bring her the release he was demanding.

It only took minutes before the pressure in her abdomen overcame her fatigued muscles and she came with a hoarse cry, milking the demon with the last bit of energy she could produce.

Thankfully, it was enough. A deep, inhuman roar ripped from the beast on top of her as he slammed in one last time before stiffening. Hot liquid pulsed against her cervix, filling the few crevasses of her pussy not fully stretched to their limits as he finally seeded her.

When Marathin collapsed on top of her with a satisfied sigh, the only thing she had energy left for was gasping air into her burning lungs and listening to her own thundering heartbeat.

She closed her eyes, tiredly hoping that there would be no permanent damage done to her system from the intense over-stimulation.

They rested together in silence for a long while, the warmth of his body shielding her from the world and enveloping her mind in his masculine musk, soothing her while she calmed down. Only when his heavy cock began deflating, letting warm semen ooze down her thighs, did her brain jolt back to life.

He'd *bred* her.

"Am I pregnant?" she whispered into the sinewy arm he'd curled around her head as tendrils of fear snaked their way through the pleasant afterglow. She had lost herself so completely to his demonic magic that she hadn't protested his desire to seed her, had even welcomed it when she felt his semen coat her womb.

"No, sweetheart." Marathin pushed himself up and she groaned when he pulled out of her, the ridges on his softened cock still prominent enough to tease her tender pussy. "It can only happen during your ovulation, and even then the chances are slim."

Relief washed through her; while her slowly returning sense of self-preservation might have questioned the truth in anything he said, his longing tone made it obvious he would have delighted in having even a small chance at impregnating her. So at least she wouldn't have to face a demon spawn growing inside of her while she tried to understand what had happened to her in the past few hours. Or in the last twenty-seven years.

"Shh." He placed a kiss on her shoulder blade before gathering her up and cradling her in his arms like a child. "Be calm, my sweet. There's no need for worrisome thoughts."

With a gentle peck to the top of her head, he twisted around to lie back down on the floor, this time using his body as cushioning for hers. Before she could put distance between them, he propped a knee in between her thighs to make her more comfortable, and probably not-so-coincidentally stopping her from rolling off him.

Selma hauled in a slow breath, tempted to give in to his warmth and heady scent trying to lull her back into that relaxed post-orgasmic state. But despite her exhaustion, her mind was slowly returning now that the hormonal fog was lifting.

"Good girl. Just relax. I'll take care of you, my sweet. You'll be safe with me." Marathin's voice was oddly muted, as if his thoughts were miles away while he absent-mindedly breathed in her scent.

He might have meant his words to be soothing, but they caused a jolt of fear to spike through her chest even as she stayed perfectly still in his arms.

He'd made her promise she'd never reject him again, and the way he was talking now...

"Don't be afraid," he mumbled before rubbing his cheek against the top of her head. "I'll take such good care of you."

Like she was a pet.

"I'm not scared," she whispered.

"I told you not to lie to me." There was annoyance in his voice this time. "Your scent changes with your emotions—fear, distress... It spikes through even the intoxicating smell of pleasured Breeder. I know when you lie. I won't tolerate deceit and disobedience."

She swallowed thickly, his ominous words doing nothing to ease her fear. Her pussy ached from the rough sex, and though there was no denying how much she'd enjoyed his attentions, it'd been forced on her.

And now, the way he was acting as if she was something that belonged to him? It stirred the same unpleasant sense of foreboding his words before he'd taken her had. Thankfully, it also awakened her survival instincts.

He was stronger than her, had trapped her and used her broken mind to clamp a magic mind-control ring on her most sensitive parts—and he could tell when she lied. If she wanted to escape, she'd have to play along until she found out how to get away.

And if his behavior now was an indicator, perhaps she could use whatever possessive asshole urges had arisen in him during the mating to help herself. Scary as the doctor was, she was relatively certain she'd stand a better chance at escaping him before he sold her.

"I can't help it," she said softly. "I'm going to get sold off to some… some *stranger*. And you… what we did… It's just a lot right now."

He was quiet for a bit, stroking her hair while he mulled over her words. Then he rolled to his side, careful to place his arm under her head. There was still no fire in his eyes, but possessiveness flamed in them nonetheless.

"What if you weren't to be sold? Would you like that?"

She arched an eyebrow. "Yeah, that sounds pretty good, not gonna lie."

He chuckled at her lip, his free hand coming down to pinch her naked backside. "If you agree to be mine, you won't have to go through an auction."

Selma frowned, biting her lip as she looked at him. "But you said—"

"I know what I said. And if I were found out, there would be a price to pay. But this is the length I'm willing to go—for you, my sweet. I'll keep you safe from the Lords and their brutality."

"Why?" she persisted. "How many other women have you—"

"None!" he interrupted her, lip pulling up in a silent snarl as he pushed her off his shoulder and rose to his feet. His eyes blazed at her with so much anger she shrank back against the cold floor.

Marathin pulled a hand through his hair, his look of anger fading into frustration. "You think I'd risk my standing for a regular little tart? You *call* to me, Selma. Your scent... it's so intense. Spellbinding. The Lords may think they deserve you, but I'm older than most of them. I am powerful enough to keep you. Strong enough to breed you. If you wish it, I will make you mine. You cower from me now, but in time, you will be grateful for my sacrifice."

And there it was: the true reason for his possessive urges. He wanted to own her because of her supposed "purity." Because he saw her as a rare and valuable trinket. There was no tender emotion in his amber eyes, no empathy for her plight.

In that moment, she realized he had no intention of giving her up. His hints that she had a choice in the matter were empty. The humiliating proof of how skilled a manipulator he was lay between her thighs where she'd let him ring her, and he was attempting the same now—trying to make her believe that she chose her own fate as he expertly guided her where he wanted her.

She might have been scared and broken when she came to him, even naive. But Selma wasn't stupid.

"I'm... still scared of you, I won't deny it," she said softly. "You're a demon, after all. But... you've shown me kindness. Pleasure. I will stay with you—if you'll have me."

Through her lowered lashes she saw his warm smile, the last vestiges of anger draining from his posture. He bent for her, lifting her to her feet before he pulled her close and pushed her hair out of her face.

"Then you shall be mine, sweetheart. For the rest of eternity, you will belong to me."

Selma let him pull her all the way in so his traitorous heat surrounded her from all sides, and she didn't flinch when he sniffed at her hair in greedy gulps. She'd play the submissive female for him until he lowered his guard. And then she'd be gone, and he could spend eternity alone for all she cared.

"I'll take you to your room," Marathin murmured against her scalp. "You need to rest, and I need time to draw up your contract. Once you've given your soul to me, I plan on teaching you exactly what a good little Breeder you'll make."

NINE
SELMA

Despite the worry rolling in her stomach, Selma had slept soundly, her exhausted body overriding her anxiety. Apparently getting fucked into a stupor did wonders for your REM cycle.

She stared at the ceiling as last night's endeavor replayed in her mind. The moment dreamless sleep fully released her from its grip, dread clawed its way back into her consciousness.

She'd never thought much about the concept of a soul, but it was pretty impossible to pretend Marathin had been speaking in metaphors when he'd mentioned giving hers to him. And signing a contract... Odds were he was being very literal—seeing how he was a demon and all.

But what other choice did she have? Tell him she'd changed her mind and get auctioned off to some other demon? Sure, she could take her chances at escaping then, but there was no guarantee she'd ever get an opportunity. Here, now, she knew she could create one.

It'd be ten days before Marathin could take her to his own domain, which meant it'd be ten days where he wouldn't be able to fully control her movements. Sure, Ravenswood House wasn't a place where you came and went as you pleased, but she'd be willing to wager that her chances of escape were a lot better here than they ever would be in another demon's grasp.

Which meant... She swallowed and closed her eyes, trying to push back the rush of panic. She would have to sign her soul over to the demon who'd captured her. Somehow, somewhere, there had to be a way of breaking the contract. She'd find it once she was safe.

Groaning from the pain shooting through every stiff muscle, Selma struggled to sit up—her next "checkup" with Marathin was booked for shortly after breakfast, and she needed to shower and somehow calm down before the nurse came with her meal.

She shoved the duvet aside, and with a wince swung her legs over the side of the bed. White streaks of dried semen had crusted on her inner thighs, and she had no doubt that the rest of her appearance would cause an even remotely caring member of staff to ask questions.

Selma shuddered at the thought, the demon's words ringing clear in her memory. He would silence anyone who so much as thought to intervene, and she couldn't bear the idea of some innocent person dying for her.

Carefully she shifted her weight to her feet and pushed off the bed. Her muscles protested violently, and she groaned at the effort she had to make to keep standing.

But the place that should have hurt the most—her violated core—seemed... perfectly fine. The muscles were tired, but there was no pain.

Gingerly she squeezed her pelvic muscles to test the waters further, but they reacted as they should, albeit slower than normal.

Huh.

Staggering, she made her way to the bathroom and managed to get out of the shirt and panties she'd slept in before stepping under the blessedly warm spray of the shower.

The relief was instant, and she moaned with pleasure as the hot water worked on her stiffened limbs and back, washing off the dried evidence of Marathin's indiscretions in the process.

She stood there until a firm knock rapped against the bathroom door, and Nurse Marie entered with no further warning.

The friendly woman rounded on her, a minor frown on her face as she ensured that her patient was not in the process of self-harming in any way.

"How long have you been in there, child? Your skin is starting to prune up."

Child. Selma estimated that they were about the same age, but being a patient at a mental institution tended to strip you of any authority. She turned off the spray and attempted a smile.

"Oh, too long, I'm sure. I always liked my hot showers. I'll be out in a minute."

The other woman stayed put, staring at her naked body. "How did you get those?"

Selma looked down, following the nurse's gaze, and blanched. On each hip, nearly black, finger-shaped bruises from where Marathin had held her when he took her from behind marred her pale skin.

"Er..." She grabbed the towel from the hook next to the shower and wrapped it around herself. "I think I got them from... from the attack."

Marie's kind eyes narrowed. "No, you didn't; you did not have them when you arrived here—they would have been noted in your chart. Where did you get them from, Selma? Has someone hurt you?"

"No!" It came out too quickly, and she could see the blooming concern spreading on the nurse's face. *Damn it.* She needed her to stop the questions now, to make absolutely certain that she did not risk being silenced by the overzealous demon.

"Look, I..." She stepped out of the shower, keeping a firm grip on the towel. "I did it to myself. Before Dr. Hershey helped me. It's been a way of coping. I know, it's not smart, but I really think I'll be able to deal with it better now."

She knew she was babbling in her attempt at throwing

the other woman off the scent, and it wasn't that she was massively keen on adding "self-harm" to her extensive file, but anything was better than Marathin taking lethal steps to ensure his continued free rein as a procurer.

"Honey..." Marie bit her lip. "Those do not look like self-inflicted bruises. If someone hurt you, you need to tell me."

"No one's hurt me." Selma attempted a bright smile. "Everyone's been so kind here. I promise; it was my own stupidity, nothing else. I'll ask Dr. Hershey if he thinks I need help with it, but I honestly doubt it. I think he... cured me. Isn't that amazing?"

The long, doubtful look she received for her efforts made her cheeks tighten, spreading the smile painfully across her face.

Please, Marie. Please believe me.

The urge to dry up before her skin cooled from the amazing shower and her muscles seized again only increased her need for the nurse to drop the issue.

"Is breakfast ready? I'm starving." Nothing like a healthy appetite to convey the image of an equally healthy patient. Not that she was lying about that particular part —last night's adventures had depleted her resources, and after the shower had loosened up her aching muscles, her body was now free to focus on the gnawing hunger in the pit of her stomach.

"Yes." Marie sent her another lingering look. "We are very understaffed this morning; most of the nurses, wardens, and doctors are at a meeting until after lunch, so I will leave you to eat while I finish up with the other patients. I'll be back to bring you to your appointment with Dr. Hershey in half an hour. After that, we will talk about those bruises some more."

"Really, there's no need ..." Selma paused at the pained expression crossing the nurse's face.

"Look, I... I shouldn't be saying this, but... Honey, you've obviously been hurt, and only members of staff have had access to you. In the past, we've had some... issues with some of the wardens. I know you're probably very scared, but I promise that I will go directly to the police. You won't have to see whoever did this again, and this time management won't get the chance to sweep it under the rug."

Selma frowned. They'd "had issues in the past"? She wondered if they'd really had wardens behave unacceptably toward other patients, or if Marathin had simply covered his tracks after performing his special brand of examinations on unsuspecting women. Patients as trapped and frightened as she had been and still was.

And now this kind woman was planning to stand up to the injustice she thought came from the hospital management, not realizing that she wouldn't just be risking her job in the process—she would be risking her life.

"No." Selma tried her best to look strong and convincing as she stood wrapped in her towel on the cold, white tiles. "Don't do that. There is no need, I promise."

Marie's lips pinched, the determination in her blue eyes unwavering. "Dry yourself off, Selma, and have your breakfast. I will be back shortly."

SELMA PICKED AT HER BREAKFAST, her growling stomach demanding nourishment even though she was sick with fear—fear of Marathin, fear for Marie, and fear for her own future. She really, *really* didn't need the added concern of a nosy nurse asking questions that could get her killed.

When Marie came to get her, she had finished off the plate, but her anxiety hadn't eased in the slightest.

"Are you ready, honey?" Marie asked with an encouraging smile, and Selma managed to nod in return and get up.

This was it; her entire future depended on whether or not she could fool the demon into believing she wanted him.

Her thoughts kept looping around what he'd make her do to prove her loyalty once she'd signed his contract, along with the fact that if he killed Marie for asking questions, Selma would be responsible. Cold fear knotted in her stomach.

"You don't look so well, Selma. Is something wrong?" The nurse's smile dropped. "Is it the bruises? Do you want to talk about what happened?"

"Nothing happened," she said, doing her best to wipe

the worry from her features. "I'm just a little tired. Is Dr. Hershey ready to see me now?"

Marie replied with another suspicious look, but ended up nodding and leading her out the door. "We will talk more after your appointment. I'm not letting another girl..." She stopped herself, and with a strained smile, closed the door behind them.

They walked through the empty corridors in silence, the sound of their footsteps echoing through the old building. Selma tried to calm herself, to remind herself that it hadn't been all pain and suffering last night, but when Marie rapped her knuckles on the door to Marathin's office, her heart leapt into her throat.

The door opened, revealing Marathin's tall and darkly handsome figure. He smiled at the sight of them, stepping aside. "Selma, Marie. Do come in, both of you."

Now what? Selma swallowed nervously. He couldn't possibly know that the nurse was suspicious of the bruising he'd left—could he? Oh god, what was he going to do to the poor woman?

She tried shooting him a pleading look, but he didn't notice as he led them both further into his office before turning to look at them again.

"I know you're very busy today, Marie, so I won't keep you long. I just want to hear if my patient has been eating properly and taking care of herself?"

His charming smile seemed to have the same effect on the young nurse as it had the other day; her cheeks went a bit rosy and she seemed like she was trying not to giggle.

Clearing her throat, probably to regain her professional voice, she looked to Selma.

"Well, she is eating well enough, but I noticed some bruises on her today that she insists she did to herself."

Selma paled. *No.* How was she meant to keep the nurse safe if Marathin knew what she'd seen?

Amber eyes caught her frightened gaze. "What's this, Selma?"

"It was before you helped me, Dr. Hershey," she whispered. "I've self-harmed in the past, but only because of... the monsters. I don't think it will ever happen again, now that I'm... cured."

"I'm not sure she's telling the truth," Marie stated bluntly, placing a calming hand on her patient's shoulder. "They don't look self-inflicted, and you know... what's happened in the past."

His gaze moved to the nurse and he nodded seriously. "I will look at them and talk to Selma, Marie. If it is not self-inflicted, we will take action, and if they are, we will incorporate that into her treatment."

Then the demon smiled. "We will get to the bottom of this. Thank you for being so diligent in your duties, even when the department is running understaffed today."

The blush returned full-force to Marie's cheeks. "I'm just doing my job, doctor."

"You do it extraordinarily well." His smile seemed extra-brilliant, and Selma had a feeling that he was working his demonic charms on the poor woman. "I won't keep you from your other duties any longer. Thank you again."

Marie nodded and moved towards the door, and a tiny blossom of hope bloomed in Selma. Maybe the issue could be solved without further involvement from her. Maybe Marie would be satisfied with Marathin proclaiming the bruises self-inflicted.

That hope lingered until he absentmindedly stroked a hand over Selma's hip to soothe the marks hidden under her clothes. His back was to the door, and he must have assumed the nurse had already left, or perhaps he'd just reacted on instinct to calm her. But Selma was still facing the door, and she saw Marie freeze with her fingers on the knob, her gaze locked on the doctor's hand.

Her eyes quickly darted to Selma's, comprehension making them widen in shock.

Oh, god! She was going to get herself killed!

Selma shook her head ever so slightly, willing the other woman to leave and leave *now* before she turned her attention to the demon, trying to keep his focus on her so he didn't turn around.

Hopefully if she said the right thing, the nurse would understand how important it was that she kept silent and left before Marathin realized what she'd seen.

"I'm sorry; I was showering and she walked in, but I didn't say anything. Please don't hurt her." Her voice was squeaky with fear, but she made sure it resonated loudly enough for Marie to hear.

Selma dared a glance at her and saw her eyes widen

even farther before she closed the door almost all the way, hiding her body from detection, but leaving enough of a gap to hear his response.

"I won't hurt her if I don't have to." Marathin cupped her cheek with his large hand, eyes carefully examining hers. "Because you ask it of me, my sweet. But if she goes any further with this, I will have to silence her. Do you understand? Play your part, and she may live."

Too terrified to do anything but nod, she prayed that Marie was smart enough to keep her nose out of it after hearing the consequences if she didn't.

Seemingly she was, because when Marathin released Selma's cheek and turned to lock the door, the nurse was gone.

Selma exhaled a breath of relief. Whatever happened next, at least she wouldn't be responsible for an innocent's death.

"So." Marathin's deep voice shook her from her moment's respite. The large man turned back around, eyes trailing the length of her body. "Let me see how bad the bruising is."

Silently she lifted her top and pushed the waistband of her pants down a little, displaying the dark marks.

He moved closer, letting a finger slide gently over her bruised flesh, humming low in his throat as he took in the damage. "Mating marks," he murmured. "They are inevitable, I'm afraid. Do they hurt?"

Selma shook her head and let her shirt fall to cover up her skin when he withdrew his hand.

"Did I hurt you anywhere else? I notice you move a little stiffly." He stroked a hand up her side, over her shoulder, and down her arm in a caress that made her shiver. Standing this close made her almost painfully aware of his unnatural heat, and fear bloomed from the pit of her stomach.

"I... My muscles are just sore." Her throat had gone dry, leaving her hoarse.

"Mmm. And between your legs?" His hand came to rest just above her pubic bone. "Did my semen soothe you as it should?"

Blushing was perhaps a bit silly, given how intimately he'd gotten acquainted with that part of her already, but heat touched her cheeks nonetheless. "Yeah. I don't hurt there. Is it... Does your...?"

"Demon seed has healing properties. It's not uncommon that an unwilling female sustains injuries during a mating—nature found a way to ease the problem."

Marathin pulled back a little, placing an admonishing finger on her lips when she parted them for more questions. "Ah ah, sweetheart. You shall have all the answers your heart desires—after you've signed the contract. It wouldn't be proper for me to share all my kind's secrets before you've committed to being mine, hmm?"

Selma swallowed thickly and forced a weak smile. "I... suppose not."

His amber eyes raked over her, the greed in them unmistakable. Then he stepped back and walked around his desk, pulling out a rolled-up piece of parchment. "Your contract."

She breathed in deeply and reached for it, the paper scratching delicately under her fingertips as she unrolled it. A single sentence was scrawled across the page with impressive penmanship. Somehow she'd expected a document that took her soul away to be more intricate—maybe with some scrollwork, or at least a bit of a fine print. But no—it was short and to the point.

I HEREBY DECLARE *that upon this day and forevermore, my soul belongs to the demon Marathin.*

MARATHIN HANDED her an old-fashioned quill with a sharpened point. When she frowned at him, waiting for the ink, he said, "You sign in blood."

Oh.

Selma took another deep breath and pressed the tip to the pad of her index finger. She hissed as it punctured her skin. The pen hungrily drank her blood.

"Sign."

Repressing a shudder, she brought the quill to the parchment. This had to be done.

The second she pressed the tip against the thick paper, something flared inside of her—a wave of desperation, some primal instinct screaming at her to stop.

Don't!

The thought didn't seem like it was her own. It burned in her mind, echoing as if shouted from far away.

But it didn't matter. Her sixth sense didn't need to tell her that this was a terrible idea. Her other five were perfectly capable of deducing that on their own.

Clenching hard around the quill, Selma signed her name in her own blood, selling her soul to the demon.

TEN
SELMA

The second she put down the quill, a sinister smile spread across Marathin's face. He grabbed the contract and closed his eyes, letting dark magic spill from his palm.

"You're mine," he said, voice rough. "*Mine*."

Selma swallowed, taking an automatic step back. But he was right; she was his. For now. And she had to play the part if she wanted her chance at escape.

"I am," she whispered. "Yours."

He opened his eyes again, his amber irises glowing from within. "Come," he said, holding out his free hand toward her.

She took it, breathing deeply to calm her beating heart when he wrapped her in his warm embrace.

"So timid, my little Breeder," he murmured, bending his head to rub his nose along her hair. "Don't be. Once I've taught you true submission, you'll know you'll have nothing to fear from me so long as you obey."

"You said... once I was yours, you would answer my questions," she said, trying to buy just a little more time. She had a good idea of what kind of "submission" he had in mind, and everything inside of her clenched with terror at the mere thought.

Yes, he'd given her pleasure last night, but also pain and unwilling surrender. He'd made her want it, and when it was over...

Selma would never forget the absolute helplessness he'd forced upon her.

"Hmm," he hummed, putting her contract on the table so he could swipe a thumb over her lips without releasing his hold on her. "I suppose... If it'll give you time to calm, I can indulge you. For a little while. What do you wish to know?"

"How many before me have you...?"

"How many Breeders have I personally procured? Ten, over the last decade or so. None who were Pure like you, my sweet." He smiled at her, as if that was somehow a compliment.

"Did you... sleep with them, too?"

His smile widened, turning indulgent. "You have no need for jealousy, precious one. You're the only one who has made me forsake my vows to claim a Breeder of my own. What worthless females I've sampled in the past can't hold a candle to you."

Jealousy. It was as far from what she was feeling as anything could be, but she lowered her gaze bashfully, playing along. It was better he think she had some fucked up sense of belonging to him than to let him suss out the horror she felt at having Marie's words confirmed. Yeah, some of the previous patients at Ravenswood had clearly been abused too—but it hadn't been by the wardens.

"What would have happened to me, if you hadn't found me? Those demons that attacked me and the other girl—they tried to hurt me. That young woman who gave me the scar... Would someone like them eventually have... killed me?"

Marathin stilled, his lip curling up in primitive anger. "Males would never kill you." His voice held carefully controlled disgust. "Once they realized what you were, they would either have handed you over to the local Lord, or... kept you as an illegitimate mate."

"Illegitimate?"

"The lower-ranking demons rarely get the chance to bid on a Breeder—they're not worthy of the honor. However, in the past there have been a few... incidents. The pull from your scent is strong, and small enclaves have captured and shared Breeders, keeping them hidden while attempting to form mating bonds. Of course, these groups always fall apart from within eventually; no demon can share a mate."

He seemed to notice the shiver in her at the explanation and placed a calming kiss upon her hair. "Don't worry; that scum will never touch you."

The irony of his assurance against being exploited by

other demons was not lost on Selma, but she found it wisest not to comment.

"Is that why that group attacked the other girl?" she asked, thinking back to the miserable event that had led to her current predicament. "They wanted to breed her?"

"No, she was just a regular human." He glanced down at her, clearly not happy about discussing matters that could be upsetting, but humoring her curiosity nonetheless. "Given the lack of Breeders, we occasionally find release with human women; we can sway their minds so they don't resist too much and forget any discomfort after."

There was no hiding the horror that rushed through her at his explanation. "Why can't you just be with your own females?" Surely they would be built to withstand the males' ridged anatomy more easily than human women.

His handsome face turned grim. "We are at war. Any female demon we impregnate will always choose to carry a daughter to increase their numbers. That's why we need human Breeders—you will only give us sons.

"The scar on your calf," he continued. "The female responsible must have realized what you would become and decided to ensure we'd get one less chance at reproducing, once you matured."

Selma frowned. "If she knew, didn't the other demons I stared at know too? Why didn't you... take me in before?" She barely managed to avoid the word "kidnap."

"No civilized demon would touch a child. It's in our best interest that our future mates have as natural an upbringing as possible. You make for much better mothers if we leave you with your parents to learn about family," he said, smiling softly at her when she blinked at the odd concept of honor they seemed to uphold. "Of course, not all abide by this rule, which is why you've had unpleasant experiences when you were younger."

"They always went away after a while," she said, thinking back to the terrifying times a monster had stalked her during her childhood. "Why?"

"The Lord of your area was informed and the perpetrators executed. Young potential Breeders are not to be harassed in any way."

The grim satisfaction of knowing that the worst of her childhood nightmares had been sentenced to death startled her. She'd never been a violent person, and wishing ill on anybody was far from her nature. But then these creatures had not exactly been kindhearted.

"I tracked down your old file—you were in the archives as a strong potential until you reportedly stopped seeing us at age 17." He stroked her cheek, pinching it lightly. "Little trickster. We would have taken you in on your twenty-first birthday if you hadn't convinced everyone that you simply grew out of a mental instability. You would have been mated, and likely a mother by now."

A mother. A stab of longing sliced through her and she ruthlessly pushed it down. She would have been a mother of demons—nothing but repulsion should fill her at that thought.

"So… can I hear why you are at war with the female demons now?" she inquired, tilting her head so she could look into his eyes in a way she hoped portrayed vulnerability and submissiveness.

Marathin sighed, letting his wandering hand slide down to her hip. It was obvious his patience was wearing thin, but nevertheless, he obliged her.

"We have been at war for centuries; few remember the time before. We used to be a patriarchal society, the males dominating in large thanks to our Lords. We are generally physically stronger than the females, but they are quick and not without strengths of their own. However, the Lords are far, far superior in every way, leaving the females with little choice but to accept their dominion. Until the Queen betrayed us.

"She made a pact with a goddess of fertility who sympathized with their cause, and as a result, all female demons would be able to decide on the gender of their offspring as it grew in their bellies. It did not take long before we realized just how devastating that was for our society. Even with the Lords, the females soon overran us in great enough numbers that they would be able to overthrow the male dominion and force us into subservience.

"Matings were banned. For years we were at a standstill, and on both sides, concern grew that our dwindling population would leave us weakened—that the gods would take advantage and shift the balance in their favor when we were too few to fight them.

"Negotiations started, though no one wished for them. It's not in our nature to share power with our females, and they had tasted freedom and did not wish to give up even an ounce of it. But before any agreements could be reached, something unprecedented happened."

He smiled and stroked a hand over her belly. "We have always enjoyed human company, and especially that of the few gifted with the ability to see through our illusions. Your scent has always driven us mad with lust.

"Just as we were about to concede to the females' demands, the King's human lover fell pregnant. No one had ever heard of such a thing being possible, but nine months later, she gave birth to what was clearly his child.

"And it happened again—human women taken for their ability to give pleasure while we were barred from mounting our own females grew round with our seed. We soon learned that it was only the ones with the Sight who could bear our offspring.

"The female demons were furious that they had lost their bargaining power, especially when it became clear that the new Breeders only gave birth to males. And so the war unfolded. They refuse to bend to us as their natural masters, and they fight vehemently to rid the world of Breeders so they can once again attempt to force us to negotiate—something we will not stand for.

"And so there is the explanation you asked for, my sweet; the reason for the attack you had to endure is the result of centuries of hatred and envy for the life you are able to give."

Selma gaped at him. They had fought for centuries for the right to treat their own females as breeding slaves? What hope did she have of ever being seen as anything more than a sweetly scented uterus, if that was all they wished for from their own species? Even when she escaped Marathin, she would spend the rest of her life hiding the mark he'd given her, either to prevent herself from being killed or to escape being dragged back to perform her duty as a broodmare.

"Shh, don't fear, my sweet." He hugged her when her scent undoubtedly took on a fresh note of terror. "I will keep you safe and happy. You and our offspring."

Selma stared down at Marathin's hand as it once again caressed her belly, and another horrible thought made it to the forefront of her mind. If she didn't escape before she fell pregnant, she'd truly be bound to him. Trapped for an eternity. She wouldn't be able to flee with a baby, and as much as her gut clenched with terror at birthing his demon spawn, she knew deep down she'd never be able to abandon her child. Even if it had horns.

"I think it's time I give you your second lesson," Marathin whispered in her ear as he slid his hands down to grab the hem of her shirt. "I'll show you I can take care of you. Protect you from all who'd do you harm. Who'd take you away from me."

Selma stood still as he undressed her, raising goosebumps along her arms with every stroke of his warm fingers against her skin. There was nothing she could do to escape this—nothing more she could say to delay the inevitable.

When she was finally naked in front of him, he drew a finger through her slit, toying with the metal ring he'd placed the day before.

"Your smell drives me wild," he murmured, the heat in his voice sending shivers down her back. "For centuries, no cunt has called to me like yours does. I know you don't want this—not yet. That's fine. You don't have to want it. But I'll teach you to take it."

Selma closed her eyes tight, drawing in a breath to steel herself for the pinch when he'd twist the ring and bring on the dark magic meant to take over her mind.

But just as his fingers tightened on the metal, the sound of a lock sliding open echoed through the office like a gunshot.

They both looked at the door as it banged open, revealing a uniformed police officer holding a pistol, as well as a smaller form half-hiding behind him—Marie.

Terror tightened Selma's throat as the officer's eyes widened, then narrowed. He lifted the gun, aiming it at Marathin.

"That's his patient," Marie said, her voice thrill.

Oh god, no!

"I heard him threaten her," she continued hastily. "He told her he'd kill me and anyone else who might get in the way if she didn't... *play along.*"

The demon growled low in his throat, eyes locked on

the officer who didn't seem to realize just how much danger he was in.

"Step away from the girl," the officer said. "No one needs to be harmed here, but you have five seconds to step away from her with your hands above your head, do you understand?"

Marathin's growl only rose in volume, his lip curling high as the shadows thickened around him.

It was like watching a slow-moving horror film play out in front of her eyes.

Selma covered herself with both arms, trying to put herself between the demon and the two humans. "Please, you need to leave." She pressed against Marathin as he shoved her to the side, desperately hoping to stop him from lashing out. "Right now! Marathin, don't, please..."

"It's gonna be all right, sweetheart. Stay calm," the officer said, not realizing the irony in his chosen endearment and not taking his eyes off the demon. "Three seconds, doctor."

Selma felt rather than saw Marathin's back muscles flex, his growl rising as something dark swept through the room, dimming the lights.

"Two."

Someone screamed. Selma wasn't sure if it was her or Marie. Maybe it was both of them. She stared at the place the officer had stood less than a second ago, her eyes refusing to focus on what was there now.

But then a horrific clarity set in. Marathin, drenched in blood, stood in front of the small nurse, his hand outstretched and clenched around something round and red. She could see his profile, see that his eyes were locked on Marie, who stood trembling in front of him, a small noise leaving her petrified lips with each of her rapid breaths.

The officer... Selma's eyes shifted to the ground between the demon and the nurse, and her blood froze in her veins. The policeman's chest cavity had been ripped open, blood oozing from the hole where his heart had been.

His heart.

The thing Marathin was clutching in his hand—the same hand that had been intimately caressing her not a moment ago—was a man's heart.

Her mind went blank a second before she doubled over to throw up.

"No, no, no. Please, no!" The sound of Marie's desperate voice rose over Selma's retching. "Please, don't kill me, please! Oh god, what are you? No! N—gh!"

"Don't." Selma gasped between heaves, supporting her trembling arms against the desk. "Don't hurt her, please."

When she looked up to plead with him, he'd already locked his bloodied fist around Marie's slim neck, the heart tossed carelessly to the floor.

"Marathin!" Panic finally made its way through her disbelief and she stumbled around the desk to throw herself at the demon. "Please, no!"

He pushed her away with his free hand, ignoring her

desperate attempts at wrestling his grip loose from the struggling woman. "Worthless human cunt."

Then he clenched his fist, snapping the neck of the young woman who'd tried to save her.

"What did you do?" Bile filled Selma's throat again as she slid to the floor where he tossed the nurse's still-warm body next to the officer's corpse.

"Oh god, no, no, no!" Her lungs felt too big for her body, pressing against her ribs and threatening to break them apart. How could he... How could they... They were dead. He'd killed them.

"Be calm."

She looked up through her tears and saw his face smoothing into its normal lines, as if the savage snarl spread across his features mere moments ago had never existed. As if he hadn't just slaughtered someone in front of her.

Calm?

"You killed them," she croaked. A shiver was making its way through her body until she was shaking on the floor in front of him.

"Of course I did." He frowned down at her. "I will not tolerate human interference with our plans, and certainly not from some human thinking he can tell me to step away from my mate." Without waiting for her response, he grabbed her underneath her armpits and lifted her up. "Come. You need to go back to your room and clean up while I get rid of their bodies."

She didn't move. Blood dripped from her thighs and

legs to the floor where he'd placed her. She'd sat in the officer's blood without realizing it, and now she stared at the deep red streaked across her pale skin.

"Selma!" the demon snapped. She flinched when he pressed his large hand against her cheek to bring her into his chest. It was splattered with blood that smeared over her face when he crushed her against him.

"Humans," he muttered against the top of her head before pulling back so he could lift her.

He carried her to his office chair where he sat her down, turning it away from the bodies. "Wait here. I will rinse my hands and get you something to help you relax."

She sat silently, staring at his many books while he left the room. Moments later he was back, once again lifting her by the armpits as if she didn't weigh more than a small child.

He got her dressed and pressed a blue pill into the palm of her hand.

"Look at me."

She did, wondering how even a demon could be capable of such cruelty.

"You're in shock, sweetheart." His voice had once again lowered to the soft, kind tone he'd used to coax her to relax before. "I apologize; I didn't consider how a young Breeder would experience it. I should have taken you back to your room first so you didn't have to see it. I will make it up to you later. For now, I need you to go back to the room and take a shower. Then take this pill. It will help you sleep, and when you wake up, all this will be taken care of."

Was she in shock? There was an odd numbness in the pit of her stomach that had spread through her entire body, leaving an unpleasant sensation of an echo in her mind, but she heard everything he said. And she understood everything that had happened.

"Selma." He stroked her hair. "Can you do this for me, my sweet?"

She nodded and he pressed a kiss to her forehead.

"Good girl. I will come for you in the morning."

Selma moved across the floor, careful not to look down before she'd closed the door to his office firmly behind her. Then she walked down the labyrinth of empty corridors and stairwells until she got to the small room she'd been kept in for the past few days. There she walked into the shower to wash blood and tears off her stiff body before climbing into bed. The blue pill she left on the nightstand.

He wanted her to sleep until morning so he could take her away. Even though she felt weak and hollow as she stared up at the ceiling, waiting for night to come, Selma knew this was likely the best chance she'd ever get to run. The only chance.

Two innocent people's lives had bought her the opportunity she needed.

WHEN DARKNESS FELL OVER RAVENSWOOD, she got out of bed and walked on bare feet to the cupboard where her personal belongings had been stored upon her arrival.

Five minutes later, she snuck out of the unlocked room and across the hall where a large, bar-less window let her escape into the night.

ELEVEN
KAIN

At first, Kain had no idea why the woman with the dirty walnut hair drew his attention the moment she stepped foot in the dingy bar.

He'd been lost in his thoughts, planning the scouting mission he'd be taking a handful of his best warriors on in a few hours, when he spotted her. She was practically creeping along the wall to the most secluded booth she could find.

Kain's gaze slipped from the crude map of the industrial center he was drawing on a napkin, where his scouts had spotted female demons a few times. He tracked the human girl as she pressed into the booth as if trying to meld into the shadows.

She was a scared-looking little thing, seemingly in her twenties and dressed in a baggy sweatshirt and jeans, with long dark hair and bangs that nearly covered her eyes—completely unremarkable in every way.

Yet there was something about her that nagged at the edges of his consciousness, poking and prodding, like forgotten lyrics to a melody playing on loop in his mind.

Irritated, he narrowed his eyes as he watched her order her food from a bored-looking waitress. She fidgeted and didn't look the other woman in the eyes, slender fingers playing nervously with the edges of the menu, and when she was alone again she curled in on herself as if she hoped she'd become one with the wallpaper.

What was it about her? He'd never seen her before—of that he was certain—she didn't set off any alarms of being dangerous, and he was more than used to seeing shady humans trying to dodge detection.

It was unsettling, really; the pull from somewhere in his gut resembled the instincts that kept him alert of potential dangers, but this little thing was no threat.

With a force of will, Kain pulled his attention back to his napkin. Whatever it was about her that had him on edge, it wasn't as important as his upcoming mission. If a band of females had truly set up a nest in his territory, he needed to get to them before they could fulfill whatever nasty purpose they had.

And—of equal importance—he'd need to extract any and all intel he could. As the Lord of the territory spanning most of Minnesota, he was located closer to the Queen's region than most of his kind. Any plans she had of coming down from the north, his territory was first line of defense.

Yet despite the urgency of this evening's mission, Kain

couldn't stop glancing at the human girl as she ate her greasy meal, her eyes closing while she chewed as if she hadn't had proper food in a while. She looked exhausted.

It wasn't until she brushed a hand across her face in a gesture emphasizing the tired draw of her mouth, displacing her bangs in the process, that he finally understood.

Kain stiffened at the silvery shimmer emanating from her forehead, all thoughts of the Queen and her scheming minions dissipating.

The woman shook her head, making the bangs fall into her eyes again, but he'd already seen it—*the mark.*

He inhaled deeply in her direction, testing the air, and found what a thick layer of deodorant and the contamination of the other patrons had kept hidden until then: the scent of an awakened Breeder.

Kain hissed softly and leaned back, eyes doing another sweep of the bar, but she was definitely there alone —unescorted.

A runaway.

His cock strained painfully against his tight jeans, alert after scenting the ripe female, and he silently cursed his body's reaction. Damned little thing didn't have to do anything but sit there for his hormones to attempt mutiny of his normally perfect self-control.

The fact that she was obviously scared didn't help—the undercurrent of decaying fear in her scent had his body in a state of arousal even before he realized what she was: a Breeder in need of a protector.

What the fuck was she doing in his territory? None of the surrounding areas had reported any new Breeders escaping. In fact, no one had claimed a Breeder in his or the surrounding areas for a few years now, and no woman who'd spent enough time with them would be stupid enough to try to run.

Fuck's sake.

The smart thing to do would be to cancel the evening's scouting mission, grab her when she left the bar, and bring her back to whoever had claimed her. It was his duty, and the little fool wouldn't be safe on her own—especially not here, now, given the recent sightings of female demons.

The Breeder stirred, perhaps aware of his intense scrutiny, and suddenly her chocolate brown eyes flicked up, locking on him.

She stared at him, eyes widening as if she could sense his demonic nature despite the mark blinding her.

Kain held her gaze. It was too late to pretend he hadn't been looking at her, and he was curious what she would do.

Her chest heaved with every shallow breath she drew, eyes darting from him to the exit.

When she grabbed her bag, tossed money on the table, and nearly ran for the door, he didn't follow.

Every instinct in his body raged for him to take up chase—to take her, protect her—keep her safe, warm, fed. *Fucked.* But the way the poor thing had been acting, it was painfully obvious she didn't want anything to do with his kind, and if he followed her, he'd have to capture her. Bring her back to whoever she'd escaped from.

Fighting back the overwhelming urge to give chase, Kain grunted with agitation and gripped the edge of the table until her lingering scent was too faint to reach his nostrils. He had no desire to force a girl into a lifetime of rapes, and as far as he was concerned, the fact that she'd fled meant that whoever had kept her had missed his chance at convincing her to stay as his mate.

Bringing her back against her will… He huffed in disgust before taking a deep swig of his whiskey, clearing his palate of the remaining taste of her. No, he had better things to spend his night on.

Like capturing the vile demon bitches who thought they could prowl his territory for easy pickings.

KAIN'S AGITATION grew exponentially as he paced along the boardwalk, waiting for his underlings to arrive for the mission. They weren't late—the arranged meeting time was not for another half-hour—but he'd been unable to focus inside the bar, his thoughts continually circling back to the little Breeder he'd scared off.

He'd thought some fresh air and patrolling might have cleared his mind, but as he stalked the pavement, the faint impression of her scent lingering in the air from where she must have passed more than an hour ago kept invading his nostrils. No demon would have noticed, not even a Lord like him, if not for his previous exposure, and he had to inhale deeply to taste her at the back of his tongue.

Irritated with himself, he stopped the full breaths he'd greedily been sucking in through his nose. *Damned pheromones.*

His body was tight with defensive reflexes ready to kick in at the slightest sound, and he knew it was because of the unmistakable touch of fear she'd left behind, as well as the terrified way she'd stared at him before fleeing the bar. That he was responsible for that fear didn't seem to affect his idiotic instincts roaring for him to protect her, and he groaned when something deep in his gut tugged insistently in an attempt to make him follow her trail.

Maybe he should, just to make sure she at least got out of his area safely. After that, she'd be someone else's problem.

Of course, that someone would probably bring her back to her mate, or keep her and fuck the living daylights out of her. But at least in the case of the former, she would be safe and off the streets.

His body had started moving down the boardwalk before he even realized it, gait smooth and fast as he tracked her delicate scent.

Yes, he would find her and bring her safely to the border of his territory, ensuring that no other male got his claws in her soft body...

The excited burn in his blood made him grit his teeth as he fought against the other instincts suddenly flooding up from the primal parts of his brain. He was hunting a

Breeder, stalking her scent while she fled from him—he'd need to keep his head in the game or the girl would be out of luck, despite his best intentions.

He hadn't walked far when traces of blood on the pavement caught his attention, his entire form stiffening at the odor that wafted up against him.

Her blood.

Mixed with...

Fury tinged his vision red as his instincts kicked into highest gear, overriding his self-control.

Female demons.

TWELVE
SELMA

He was one of *them*.

Selma hadn't needed her *second sight* to know—he was simply too big, and something about his looming form seemed off, as if too much mass had been pressed into the shape of a man. And his eyes...

She shuddered, forcing her legs to move quicker as she made her way across the walkway, cursing her decision not to park right by the bar. The sooner she got away from this place, the better, and having to run half a mile to get to her car wasn't helpful.

The theory had been that if the demons who hunted her managed to track the license plate on the hunk of junk she'd bought from a shady car dealer, and they found it while she was sorting out her pit stop, they wouldn't be able to find her just from which shop she'd parked in front of. Of course, in practice, the plan had a rather obvious flaw.

Gently she touched a hand to the silver mark marring her forehead, shuddering at the memory of the monster who'd blinded her. She'd always thought her ability to see demons for what they were was her curse. But now...

Now that she was blind to their true forms, she wished she could see them again. Running from monsters you couldn't see? Not easy. Only her constant vigilance, the continued moving from town to town, had kept her safe.

Until now.

At least this demon was so obvious even a regular person would be wary around him. His handsome face wasn't enough to hide the overly bulging muscles, nor the nearly palpable dark energy flickering off him like a looming thunderstorm.

Selma cast a quick glance over her shoulder to see if he'd followed, and drew a sigh of relief at the nearly empty stretch behind her. For whatever reason, Hulking Brute hadn't taken up chase.

But her deep breath of relief was cut short when something caught her ankle and she tripped, landing face-first on the pavement with a shriek and scraping her hands and knees in the process.

Pain shot from her cheek, knees, and palms, and she tasted blood from where she'd bit her tongue when she fell. *Just great.* Falling over her own feet while trying to escape a demon was not exactly a winning moment.

"Are you okay, sugar?"

Startled, she looked up from the pavement at two

young women, one of whom was bent over her splayed-out form. She hadn't noticed them before she fell.

"Y-Yeah, thanks." She scrambled to get up, only for the women to hoist her by her elbows.

"You don't look so good," the woman still holding onto her stated. "Why don't you come with us and we'll get you sorted out, hmm?"

Something in her eyes was off. The coldness there sent shivers of recognition down Selma's spine, and she pulled back in an attempt at getting free. "No, thanks, really—I'm fine."

The woman's grip didn't loosen, and when an unseen third person placed a hand on her shoulder, panic started bubbling in her veins, making her chest heavy with icy realization. In her desperate escape, she'd nearly forgotten that not everyone she needed to fear was male.

"Let me go!"

"Or you'll do what? Scream?" The redheaded woman who had yet to touch her pulled a blade from her sleeve, pressing it against Selma's stomach through her sweatshirt. *"Breeders.* Come now, or die on the street. Your choice."

"Please." Selma gasped as the woman pressed the knife closer, but she let her assailants drag her down a narrow passageway as all her thoughts turned immediately and sharply to the one singular goal: survival.

"Please, I don't want to be a... a *Breeder.*" She nearly spat the word. "You don't have to do this—I ran away from them. Please, just let me go—*oh!"*

Her pleas were cut short when she was shoved roughly through an open door and into what looked like a half-empty warehouse with sawdust on the concrete floor. She stumbled and nearly fell, but managed to catch herself on a wooden box.

Heart hammering in her throat, she turned around, swallowing thickly as the door closed. She was now alone in the half-lit room with what had to be three female demons. The still-drawn blade in the red-haired one's hand shimmered ominously.

She'd been warned. The demon who had captured and branded her had told her about the females of his kind—about the war between them and the males, and how the males had turned to human *Breeders* to procreate. He'd told her this with reverence, as if Selma would be proud she was one of the few humans who could carry a demon's spawn. As if needing his protection against the females dead-set on killing any Breeder they came across was a boon.

"God, please don't kill me, please! I'll do anything you want," Selma begged. She hadn't come this far, hadn't escaped one monster only to be gutted like a pig in a warehouse in Nowhere, Minnesota.

"Yes. Yes, you will." The one with the cold eyes stalked in a semi-circle around her, forcing her to twist in an attempt at keeping an eye on all three. "But first, little human... First, we want information. Who's your master?"

"I don't have a m-master." Under any other circumstances she probably would have been offended at the notion, but at that moment, her terror was too strong to allow for luxuries such as indignance.

"That pretty little mark on your forehead says otherwise." The blonde one—the one who'd come up behind her when she fell—took a few steps closer, and Selma drew up against the box again, pressing her back into it. It felt oddly good and solid—normal—in a world of nightmares made flesh.

"I ran away before anyone claimed me."

"Oh, really now? And how'd you manage that?"

Cold Eyes fell in from the side, trapping Selma against the box. Panicked tears blurred her sight, and she blinked rapidly to clear her vision. If she wanted any chance at getting out of this alive, she'd have to keep her wits about her. Whatever they wanted, she'd give them. She had zero allegiance to any male demons.

"I... I tricked him. Dr. Hershey—Marathin Hershey. The demon who captured me. I made him think I..."

Saying it out loud was harder than she'd expected, and humiliation burned her cheeks. What she'd been made to do in her captivity... it would haunt her for the rest of her life. Which might not be all that long, judging from the hard looks on these females.

Selma steeled herself, pushing through. "I made him think I wanted him. He said he'd spare me from... from the Lords if I..."

"The Lords?" Blondie cut her off, eyes widening, then narrowing to slits.

Selma nodded. "Y-Yes."

"She's *Blessed,*" Red spat. "Let's just gut her and move on. Too much trouble."

"Are you out of your mind?" Cold Eyes snarled. "She's a fucking Pure Breeder! Do you know what a Lord will do to get his hands on one of these? We play our cards right, the one ruling this territory might even give up Minnesota without a fight."

"*Might* being the operative word," Red said, edging closer. "It's too risky."

"I'll help you!" Selma gasped, pressing up harder against the box. "Please, I promise!"

"You think we'll be *rewarded* for handing a Lord an incubator?" Blondie asked, eyebrows raised as she looked at Cold Eyes.

"I think taking this territory is our first priority. It'll be years before any offspring he sires with this pathetic human is strong enough to fight—and at that point, it's going to be too late anyway."

Cold Eyes returned her focus to Selma, a nasty smile pulling up the corner of her lips. "But first... first we need to ensure she's in *suitable condition.* What do you say, little Breeder? Think a few cuts on that smooth skin of yours will make the Lord more amenable to our negotiations?"

THIRTEEN
SELMA

Selma screamed. Each time that wicked knife sliced through her flesh, claws raked her skin, and fists pummeled her gut, she howled in agony, pleas for mercy bubbling past her lips. She tried to curl in on herself, to protect her vitals, but the two demonesses not wielding the knife held her firmly between them, leaving her body open and vulnerable to the abuse.

They offered no mercy, each second only bringing her more pain. She lost track of time, lost track of everything but the searing agony and cackles of her captors, their amusement at her wails ringing through the warehouse—though to her, they sounded like they were filtered through water. The only clear sound was her own frantic heartbeat.

Until an explosion shook the building.

The three demons froze, turning toward the entrance

as one. Selma too lifted her head, following their startled gazes.

He was here—the demon from the bar. His dark eyes were wide and terrifying, his human features pulling into a mask of fury as he took in the scene, breathing heavily.

Selma snorted with weak amusement. She'd found him terrifying before—yet now even a normal human would have called him demonic. She'd never seen anyone look so angry.

"Lord." Cold Eyes seemed to regain her ability to speak, but there was a quake in her once-so-self-assured voice. "We have a trade to off—"

He *roared*, a bellow that vibrated through the warehouse and shook Selma to her core. He was a mountain of fury, molten rage spilling into the air in clouds of inky black.

Magic.

Both Blondie and Red released their grip on her, diving for cover. Blondie, however, was too slow. Black, sparking magic closed around her ankle before she could escape behind the box.

Her foot twisted with a sharp *crack*, suddenly pointing at an unnatural angle. The demoness screamed—a sound that turned shrill as the black fog gnashed up her leg like a hungry maw, rending her flesh and splintering her bones in a spray of blood.

Cold Eyes lunged for Selma and she squealed, twisting away from her drawn blade—but the demon didn't go for her throat. She grabbed Selma by the waist, twisting them both out of the way when the Lord leapt into the room, slamming down on top of the remains of the blonde female.

Snarling, he tore her head clean off with a wet popping sound, tossing it to the side. Then he spun around in a crouch, eyes fixed on Selma and her attacker.

Without preamble, the demoness shoved a hand down the front of Selma's pants.

Too late, Selma realized what she was doing. Before she could shove the demoness' hand away, her fingertips connected with the small piece of metal encircling Selma's clit.

Her humiliation. The ring that'd sealed her fate.

"No!"

Her cry came too late. Harsh fingers twisted the metal, squeezing it down painfully on her nub of nerves.

Fire burned through her pelvis, into her spine, and down her thighs. She fell to the floor with a gasp, shaking as the nefarious magic flooded her blood. Heat bloomed from the metal's vicious bite, overriding the pain.

And then... then came the *need*.

"No," she sobbed, clutching her hands uselessly against the concrete floor as she felt herself soften, sharp pangs of desire rising through her pelvis like an uncurling serpent.

She looked up then as if drawn by invisible powers, and her eyes locked on *his*—the powerful demon still crouched by the blonde female's mangled corpse.

His human irises were pitch-black, the pupils filling

them, his gaze fixed on her and her alone. His nostrils flared wide, taking in her scent.

She shuddered in terror of being this primal creature's sole focus—and with longing. Deep, intense, bone-melting *yearning*.

He was a demon, of that she was sure—but he was also big and strong, dominance radiating from his every pore. He was more than capable of saving her from the agonizing need growing steadily between her legs.

She let out a pained moan—a wordless plea as her mind fogged.

He moved then, shifting closer, but before he could rise and come to her, movement flashed behind him.

Selma cried out what should have been a warning, but it came too late. The redheaded demoness leapt at him from behind. Somehow he managed to twist at the last second, and the dagger that was aimed at his throat tore into his shoulder instead.

The Lord roared again, shaking the warehouse, and spun around to face his attacker, knocking the blade out of his shoulder in the process. The dagger clattered and skidded on the concrete as he snatched Red by the throat and immediately pounded her into the ground hard enough that her skull cracked like an egg. His fist followed, smashing into her face, breaking the front of her cranium and smattering her brain.

He spun and leapt to his feet, searching the warehouse for the third female. Judging by his frustrated growl,

Cold Eyes had taken the opportunity to run while he took out her second companion.

Go. Follow her, Selma silently prayed, even if her body wished he wouldn't.

The big brute took a few steps toward the warehouse's door, seemingly intent on taking up pursuit. But before he reached it, his steps faltered as he looked back over his shoulder. At her.

Shit.

Selma scrambled forward on her hands and knees until her fingers closed around the dagger that'd previously been buried in his shoulder.

"Leave!" she hissed, somehow finding the strength to push back up into a kneeling position. She aimed the blade at him with a shaking hand, using the other to wipe away the blood from her split eyebrow.

He paused, gaze flicking from her forehead to her knife. A deep exhale left his chest.

"Fuck." It was an exasperated growl, filled with frustration—and below that, husky need. The sound of it, of the rich, male rumble, made her core clench tight and a breathy gasp escape her throat.

No. *No, no, no.*

"L-Leave me alone," she whispered, incapable of putting conviction behind her words despite her brain's panicked screeching.

He didn't respond, but instead of exiting the warehouse, he turned around. And then he was walking toward her, heavy steps thumping in the emptiness until he was close enough to crouch in front of her.

She lunged at him, but he simply batted the weapon out of her hand before he wrapped his huge arms around her and lifted her as if she weighed nothing more than a kitten.

He smelled like sulphur and *male.*

"P-Put me... down." It was so hard to remember why she was supposed to run from him. His infernal heat penetrated her flesh through his black leather coat, soothing her aching muscles and pulling her into a cocoon of safety.

"No." He shifted her in his arms, eyes roaming her damaged body. "Did they cut you deep?"

"I don't... I don't think so," she croaked, though it was hard to feel the extent of her injuries through the involuntary lust pulsing in her veins.

He didn't say anything further. He simply carried her out into the night.

As soon as they were clear of the building, he adjusted her position again so he could free one hand to grab his phone. There was a sequence of digital tones as he dialed a number, and then his gruff voice resonated in his chest and in the air above her.

"Thomren, I need you to get Pete and his crew to come to the Spearhead Quarter down by the warehouses. I need a clean-up. They'll be able to find it by the scent. But before they get here, I need you to sort out a car. I'll meet you by 127th and Pearson. Got it?"

The person on the other end must have answered in the affirmative, because the demon hung up without another word, quickly stuffing the phone back into his pocket before he wrapped his arm securely around her again.

"Where are you taking me?" she croaked.

"To my home, Breeder," he said, not sparing her a look as he strode through the empty back streets, eyes scouting for more enemies in the shadows.

His home.

He had saved her from death, but in the end, her fate would be exactly what she had sacrificed everything to escape.

Dread and sorrow warred with the excited twinge in her abdomen at the thought of surrendering to this powerful male. It was too much. Everything she'd been through, the constant running, the torture, the humiliation —it swelled up in her throat and came out in loud, ugly sobs.

The demon jerked, his face whipping toward her.

"Shh, little one." His voice pitched in startled concern and he pulled her closer to his heated body. A moment later one of his hands, the palm of it the size of her face, curved around her cheek in a surprisingly soft caress. "Don't be scared. Shh, it's all right. Come, look at me."

Gently he tipped her head up—and up—until she finally saw his face. His eyes were still black, but somewhere behind her grief she realized his irises were naturally that color.

He looked at her as he walked, supporting her body mostly with the arm not cradling her cheek. Concern colored his now perfectly human features, the absence of anger removing the visual cues of what he was.

"You're safe," he soothed, clumsily stroking her cheek. "No one will hurt you again, I swear it."

Slowly his soothing words and warm touch calmed her shaking form so that she could gasp in a few deep breaths, quelling her anguished cries. Without thought to who and what he was—simply needing the comfort his large hands and deep eyes promised—she leaned in and rested her forehead against his broad chest, willing her body and mind to release its pent-up tension to his heat.

"Good girl," he muttered above her, strong hands caressing her face and tangled hair again and again in an obvious effort at keeping her calm. "Just breathe. I'll take care of the rest."

When he came to a stop a little while later, she had gotten enough of a hold of herself that she dared another look up at him again. His scent and his warmth made her pussy pulse hotly, the ever-growing ache making it hard to remember that she couldn't stay in his arms—and that, come the morning, she would regret her easy surrender.

"Please. Let me... Let me go. You didn't take me before, in the bar..."

A rumble of displeasure thundered in her ear and his arms constricted tighter around her.

"I can't," he gritted. "If I'd taken you in the bar, none of this would have happened."

"Please, I don't want—"

"I know what you don't want," he snapped, his tense features softening when she flinched in response. "Even if I let you leave now, your scent will draw every demon within a fifty-mile radius. I am the Lord of this territory, and your well-being is my duty. I will care for you tonight. But after..."

"After?" she whispered, the reluctance playing across his features allowing a seed of hope to sprout somewhere past her fog of need.

He stared down at her, mouth set in a grim line. "I have no desire to force an unwilling Breeder into an eternity of service."

She knew he could be lying—that he probably was. Lying was like breathing to his kind. She knew his words, as beguiling as they were, didn't promise her freedom. But right now, they were enough. She didn't have the strength to fight anymore, not tonight.

Closing her eyes against the fear and pain radiating in her body, she pressed her cheek against his leather-clad chest and surrendered to the fog promising blissful oblivion.

The demon stroked a thumb over her exposed cheekbone and she felt him bend his body around her, encapsulating her in his hard muscle to shield her from their harsh surroundings. His mouth and nose nuzzled at the top of her head, causing her pussy to throb, and a rumble rolled through his chest in response.

Selma mewled and pressed in closer, rubbing her face

against him. Now that she was no longer fighting it, her magic-induced need burned hotter than ever, making her yearn for release. She pressed her thighs together, rubbing them to alleviate the throbbing, but it only worsened.

"Please..."

He cursed and pulled his face away from her hair. "What's your name, little one?"

He was trying to fight the pull of her scent, she realized. She knew what it was doing to him, had learned the hard way what a male demon would do to get at her once the magic from her cursed ring had been activated. And still he was fighting it, trying to distract himself with conversation.

Marathin would have fucked her in that warehouse, not caring that she was injured and scared out of her mind.

"Selma." Perhaps she should have lied—Marathin might have put whatever the demon version of a missing person's report was out on her—but in that moment, high on hormones and magic and the knowledge that this man was fighting his base instincts for her, she didn't have the mind to. "I'm Selma."

"Selma," he repeated softly, as if testing the feel of it on his tongue. "I am Kain, Lord Protector of this city."

Lord Protector.

There were many kinds of demons, she'd learned, and the rulers among them—the biggest, the most dangerous—were the Lords.

And yet in Lord Kain's arms, she felt safer than she had her whole life.

FOURTEEN
KAIN

Thomren's nostrils flared wide the second he stepped out of the car, even before he spotted them in the shadows.

Kain let out a low, warning growl as he stepped into the light from the lonely street lamp on the deserted corner. Selma's scent had only grown stronger while they'd waited for Thomren, her breathing turning to small mewls and pants as her body surrendered to the magic of her ring.

He would have trusted few of his underlings in the presence of a wet and willing Breeder, even when she was under his protection, but Thomren had a mate at home. He'd still react to her, but he'd be less tempted by the beguiling scent drifting from her sweet little pussy so tauntingly close Kain could practically taste it.

"Blackened stars, man!" Thomren took in the sight of the woman's whimpering form before he stared wide-eyed at his Lord. "How have you not...?"

Fucked her to death was the obvious end to that sentence, but the man wisely held his tongue. The smell of a Breeder in heat was not the only scent perfuming the air; Kain could feel the testosterone boiling in his blood, and the tight leash he'd been keeping on his raging libido was threatening to ignite his fighting instincts instead. It took all his willpower not to explode out of his human disguise, shred the other male to pieces, and fuck the Breeder on the dirty ground until she broke.

Truly, the wisest choice would be to hand her over to Thomren and tell him to arrange for a trusted underling to take care of her so Kain could release his hormonal insanity by punching on the nearest gang of thugs he could find.

The problem was that, along with the most painful erection he'd ever experienced, the smell of the little Breeder—of Selma—also brought a violent urge to protect and claim. Her blood had his protective instincts firing on all cylinders, and after seeing her abused in that damned warehouse...

He would rather kill every last one of his subordinates than send her off with one of them.

Shooting Thomren one last glare, he slid into the backseat of the car, where he arranged the girl across his lap so that she would be comfortable. Or as comfortable as she could be, injured and needy as she was.

Selma whimpered when Thomren started the car, pressed her face against the hollow of Kain's neck, and breathed deeply in an obvious attempt to soothe herself.

Yet all it did was cause warm, wet slick to soak her jeans so thoroughly he felt it trickle onto his own thighs.

She moaned in frustration and rubbed herself against him, her wet little tongue licking at the column of his throat when, apparently, the magic swallowed the last vestige of her rational mind.

He was going to die. Probably from spontaneous combustion.

"Selma," he rasped, nuzzling into her messy hair once more when his self-control wavered. "You need to stop that. Now."

"You taste so good," she mumbled, her sweltering breath raising goosebumps on his skin. "Need you."

Kain's breath hitched when she resumed her teasing attentions, biting not entirely gently at his pulse point before her sweet, wet licks continued upwards. Blood was rushing in his ears, his head was light, and his groin heavy and pained.

Stars above! She smelled so good, *felt* so good... He needed her, needed to spread her open and conquer that sweet pussy calling to him—

Her small yelp pulled him back, and he found his fingers had inadvertently dug into the swell of her hips, undoubtedly aggravating one of her many bruises.

"Sorry," he ground out, releasing his grip on her injured body.

Selma hummed, her eyelids fluttering as she ground down against his straining cock, all thoughts of her injuries apparently forgotten.

Damned little thing.

Growling with the effort, he pushed her away and onto the seat beside him. She wailed at the separation and clawed at his clothes to get closer, and he lacked the strength to resist.

"Thomren, how much fucking longer?" It was meant as a snarl, but came out more like a desperate plea.

His underling had the good manners not to laugh, even as his eyes flicked to the rearview mirror in time to see Selma climb on top of Kain and start biting at his shoulders through the jacket.

"Two more minutes, my Lord."

It was the longest two minutes in the entire history of the universe.

When the car finally pulled up in front of the tower block that hosted his casino, hotel, and private apartment, Kain was shaking from head to toe. His hands were clenched hard around two chunks of the now-demolished back seat.

"We're here, my Lord," Thomren said, slipping into a more formal tone. The shift was undoubtedly linked with the man's personal experience of what it was like for an unmated demon to be around a Breeder in heat—and his understanding of what would happen if he accidentally pushed his Lord's temper right now. "Do you need... anything? For her?"

Kain knew what Thomren was asking, and thanks to the small reserve of reason he had left, he could appreciate the man's diplomacy and attempt at ensuring the girl's survival. Whether it was to preserve one of the rare mates or to attempt to save his master from the guilt of killing a Breeder, Kain wasn't sure, but in either case, he was thankful.

"I won't harm her," he grunted, taking a few quick breaths when the girl sucked wetly at his Adam's apple and pressed against his thigh to alleviate a little of her need. "I swear it. Do not tell anybody about her. I will call you in the morning."

"If you picked her up where you sent the crew to clean up, they'll be able to smell her all over it."

Damn. He was clearly not thinking straight.

"Fine. Muzzle them. If one word gets out about her, tell them I'll have their heads, you hear? I'll decide... tomorrow... oh, fuck!"

He arched against the ruined back seat when Selma's aimlessly roaming hands finally found the bulge in his pants that was nearly tearing his zipper in its attempt at getting free.

"I will take care of it. You get inside and take care of *her*... They get real vicious if you let them get too wound up." There was laughter, and sympathy, in his underling's voice.

Kain growled, more at the Breeder currently attempting to free his cock than at the other demon, and finally let go of the chunks of car seat so he could wrap his arms around her and push out of the car. His focus was solely on the private back entrance to his domain flanked by two armed guards—men Thomren would also need to keep quiet.

The two men went rigid when Selma's intoxicating scent hit their nostrils.

Kain let out a deep snarl in their direction, clutching the girl tighter. She clung to him like a baby koala, causing him to feel every one of her curves as he carried her, but he was too far gone for it to make much of a difference.

"She is *mine!*" he hissed when one of the guards, Brethor, took a step toward them. "One more fucking step and I swear it'll be your last!"

The underling blinked, one foot frozen mid-air, and shook his head from side to side as if to rid himself of the lustful haze spurred by the Breeder's proximity.

"Hold your breath," his older and wiser comrade choked out next to him.

Kain watched with narrowed eyes as Brethor did as instructed. Clearly struggling with his raging instincts, he stepped back into position before staring into the distance with a tormented expression.

Kain rushed past them and into the building, pushing back the urge to fight the male who'd thought he'd get to mount a female belonging to his Lord Protector. Nothing but wasted time and—eventually—regret would come from slaughtering the man, and all he needed right now was to get the girl up to his chambers.

He went straight for the private elevator, easily holding Selma with one arm as he pushed the top floor's button with more force than necessary. Leaning his head on top of hers, he breathed in her scent. The gentle nature of it calmed his violent instincts, and he nuzzled deeper into her messy hair with a relieved sigh.

"I will take good care of you. I promise," Kain mumbled in response to the wordless noises the Breeder was muttering into his shoulder and chest. He was fairly sure that her discontent was centered on the lack of sexual stimulation he was providing.

He caught sight of them in the elevator's mirror and grunted in annoyance. They were both splattered with blood, and she was dirty, tear-stricken, and not at all in the sort of condition a prized female should be kept in. It tore at his primitive desires to protect, and he knew he'd need to patch her up and soothe her before he could mount and claim her.

Kain paused in his musings, biting off an angry growl at his easy slip into the role of a male claiming his mate. He was not mounting, nor claiming the frail-looking girl, and unless he got himself moderately in check, he'd kill her with the dark magic emanating from his core in slow pulses.

Even more frustrated with the situation than before, he didn't wait for the elevator to open when the small bell announced their arrival at the top floor. Shifting Selma to one hip, he kicked the doors ajar and stomped through the debris toward the only apartment on this floor of the high-rise. It took him seconds to unlock the front door and type in the code, and then he was finally within the safety of his own walls.

He didn't pause as he strode straight to his bedroom and deposited her on the sturdy California King-Sized bed flanked by four carved, wooden posts.

Selma whined at being separated from the comfort of his body, but then seemed to realize where she was. Her slim fingers clenched in his black sheets as her gaze quickly darted around the room, lingering on the bed beneath her. Then she turned those lovely chocolate-colored eyes on him once more.

Kain groaned with want at the complete surrender in them and had to grasp at the nearest bedpost to stop himself from ripping the clothes from her body so he could ravage her.

"Take me." Her voice rasped in an odd mix of a plea and a command. "I need you. Take me now, please!"

As if he had to be reminded of how much she needed to have his cock fill her greedy little cunt—the air was laden with the smell of her heat, mingling with the musk of his own hormones.

"I can't. I need to heal you first, and then I will help you." His hand clenched around the wooden pole marking one of the bed's corners while he desperately tried to regain a bit more control.

She might have been too far gone on the magic to feel her injuries, but he'd never forgive himself if he hurt her further while he sated her.

But Selma had other plans. She narrowed her eyes, shifting the expression on her pale face from pleading to feral.

Faster than he would have thought a human of her stature could move, she launched to her feet, staggering on the plush mattress, and then threw herself at him. He managed to catch her just as she pressed her lips urgently against his, her tongue demanding access with soft, but persistent strokes.

Kain moaned when her nails scratched at his nape, inadvertently allowing her to deepen the kiss until all he could sense was the soft warmth of her mouth, the taste of her tongue, and the sensation of her slight body pressing against his. His hands found the swell of her backside—and shortly after, her jeans' waistband, which he shredded without effort.

He tore the maimed pants and underwear off her legs, never breaking away from her desperate kiss, then grabbed her sweatshirt and bra in two handfuls and ripped, wanting nothing but to feel her—*all* of her—naked against his searching palms.

Only when his fingers brushed over one of the many cuts on her skin did he manage to pull free of her once more, pushing her down on the mattress with a growl.

"*Stay!*" he snarled, putting his full authority behind the command when she made a move to launch herself at him again.

Selma growled in response, baring her blunt human teeth and looking so much like a feral kitten he couldn't contain a rumble of amusement.

"Stay," he repeated, softer but no less firmly this time.

She obeyed, remaining propped on her hands on the

bed, eyes glued to his every move.

In turn, he did his best not to look at her as he shrugged out of his leather coat and carefully sat down at the foot of the bed, knowing he wouldn't have the strength to withstand seeing her sprawled out naked for him.

Selma crawled into his lap the moment he sat down, rubbing up against him like a cat in heat.

"Please," she rasped.

"I know," he mumbled, letting his hands find her soft skin. His cock spasmed achingly, trying hard to break through its confines.

Kain held his breath and reached inside for the part of his magic he so rarely used. It welled much more easily from his inner core than he'd expected, flooding through his hands and into the girl, searching for the damages she'd sustained.

There were many, and not all of them as superficial as he'd thought upon first inspecting her. His anger welled, dampening his desire, and he used it to focus his magic.

Healing was not something that came naturally to demons, but as a Lord he had more than enough power to mend the Breeder's flesh and soothe her deep bruises.

Only when not a single scrape remained on her pale skin did Kain finally draw in a deep breath, his eyes fluttering open as her rich scent filled his nostrils. Her eyes were wide and unfocused, her forced lust so strong now there was barely anything left of her true nature. Postponing the inevitable any longer would be cruel.

It was time.

FIFTEEN
KAIN

The Breeder was soft and smooth under his hands as he eased her off his lap and down on her back against his sheets.

It seemed either the healing had gentled her, or she understood that he was finally about to give her what she'd been begging for, because she lay down obediently despite her panting breaths and the still all-consuming scent of her heat.

Kain brushed his palms up her stomach, frowning at how thin she was. His instincts, already on a knife's edge, snarled at a precious Breeder having been left malnourished, but the impulse to feed and bathe the dirty little thing was quickly overridden when she whimpered at his touch and spread her thighs for him.

The smell of her heat hit him full-force as she displayed her sopping cunt, the dark hair covering her vulva matted with the liquid proof of her desire.

Black dots danced at the edges of his vision as he fell to his knees on the floor, grabbing her around the hips and yanking her to the edge of the bed in one move.

Kain brushed over her mons, shuddered with longing at the gentle scratch of her pubic hair against his palm, and finally parted her soft flesh to inspect her offering.

Selma whimpered and tensed in response, arching her hips in a plea for relief.

Silver shimmered between her parted lips, encircling her engorged clitoris in a band of inscribed metal. Her Breeder's Ring—the tool used by Procurers to force Breeders into acceptance of their new status. One pinch on the magic-infused little trinket and the girl would plead with her captors for release, willingly parting her thighs for the demons she feared.

He growled at the look of it wound much too tight around her most tender spot and knew she'd be in pain from how carelessly the demoness had twisted it. Unthinking, he leaned in and brushed a soft kiss to her throbbing clitoris, yearning to soothe her the only way he knew how.

The second his lips connected with her swollen flesh, the Breeder turned wild underneath him.

She screamed, her hands snaking down and snatching on to his hair as she convulsed. Spurred on, he flicked his tongue over her clit, teasing the tip where metal met flesh.

Selma howled and wound herself around him, clasping his head between her thighs while she ground against his tongue, desperate for the promised release.

Kain let her ride his face, pulled her in closer by her ass, and finally gave her what she needed. He sucked her swollen bud in hard, sharp pulls, swirling his tongue around it mercilessly until she froze, every muscle in her body seizing.

She cried out as she came, an agonized sound that spoke of the torment inflicted on her poor clitoris until she collapsed onto her back again, panting heavily.

He slid his hands from her hips to her thighs, enjoying the silkiness of her skin against his callused palms before he opened up her lips again, inspecting the ring.

"Please," Selma gasped as he brushed a careful finger to the clamped metal. "Please, make it stop."

The magic still held fast, trapping her poor nub much too tightly. That was the curse of it—she needed penetration, or she would be driven to insanity.

Kain pushed off the floor, his head swimming with desire of his own and his willpower waning as she writhed below him. He dragged her up farther on the mattress, not even taking the time to enjoy her near-naked body before he fell on top of her, immediately finding her pussy between her eagerly spread legs.

He drove two fingers into her wet embrace, shuddering in delight at the fluttering sensation of her slick muscles clamping on his digits. Her pulse beat rapidly from within, and he fought the urge to take over and ram her deeply so he could feel that sweet rhythm against his thick cock. Instead he breathed in a mouthful of her beautiful pheromones before relenting to her cries for more and sliding a third finger into her thrashing body.

Selma yowled, but not from pain as he had half-expected. The human women he occasionally brought to his bed when the dark need inside of him became too much to bear usually struggled to take a third finger, but Selma only bucked, desperate for more.

The black dots dancing before his eyes turned red as his self-control slipped, drowning in the pounding rhythm of his pulse.

She was a Breeder. *His* Breeder.

Kain raised up above her, bracing himself on his free hand. Three of his fingers remained buried deep in her quivering pussy, hooking into the spongy zone on her frontal wall.

"Yes! More!" she mewled, clawing at his arm.

He let out a deep growl filled with his claim.

Selma's eyes popped open at the sound and she stared up at him, mouth half-open, chest heaving in time with her moans and her eyes shining with pure, dark lust. Her tangled bangs had been swept away, exposing her silvery mark, and the rest of her dark hair was fanned above her head like a matted halo against his black bedding.

She was the most beautiful thing he had ever seen. She was the only thing he would ever need.

"Fuck. Me!"

If he hadn't been lost in a rush of hormones, he would have laughed at the small woman's angry demand. No one dared order him about like that, not since he'd left his father's domain, but this little thing... she looked about ready to maul him if he didn't comply.

She reached up to rip at his clothes, already snarling with impatience, and it set his dominance aflame. His blood seemed to boil underneath his skin, erasing everything but his need to mark, claim, *take*.

Growling again, Kain grabbed her wrists in one hand and shifted his weight so he could undo his pants with the other. His cock burst free, immediately drawn to her sopping entrance so willingly thrust up against him. Her dripping lips kissed his ridged head, and the shockwaves of pleasure that shuddered through him had him unthinkingly pushing against them, seeking entry.

"God!"

The hated word was the only thing that tore his conscience back into his body, the impact of it making his eyes flutter open, gaze zeroing in on the woman underneath him.

Her mouth was open in a silent "O," her forehead furrowed and her hands curled into claws while her body bent in a frozen arc as her pussy stretched to take him.

The shudders of raw pleasure her wet embrace inflicted upon the crown of his cock were nearly enough that he gave in to every screaming instinct in his mind and body demanding that he fill and fuck her. Yet as he saw her lying there, so completely defenseless underneath his massive form, some part of him remembered that she was under his protection—and that if he gave in, he would kill her.

Roaring in frustration he pulled back, releasing her wrists as he knelt on the bed with his fists pressed into the mattress. He only narrowly resisted the urge to swing them at the nearest solid object.

"No! What are you doing? Please, you can't stop now!" Selma jolted upright, scrambling to reach him. Her shaking hands slid over his shoulder, nails digging into the fabric. "Don't stop! Please, *please,* I need you, I need—!"

Kain gritted his teeth and tried focusing on his breathing, the alluring scent of her slickness battering at his self-control. "I *can't*. I'm a Lord—my magic will kill you."

"It won't! I can withstand it, please!" Her eyes were glazed with frantic need as she did her best to convince him, hands rubbing at his shoulders, arms, and chest.

But she couldn't. He'd killed enough women before he'd gained the self-control to resist. He knew how his magic ate up any human woman he penetrated from the inside out, leaving nothing but a pile of blood and entrails behind. Even a Breeder would succumb. Only the rarest few, the most precious among them, could withstand, and Selma wasn't one of them. The second a Pure Breeder was found, every Lord across the globe would have been notified.

Reaching into a reserve of strength he didn't know he possessed, Kain got off the bed. He shook with the effort of moving away from her tantalizing scent, but managed to scramble to the drawer where he kept the articles he now used for entertaining the human women he brought home.

He grabbed a thick dildo and turned back around to where Selma had collapsed on her back, sobbing quietly in anguish.

"It'll be okay soon," he mumbled, more to himself than the delirious Breeder. His own need for release might be left unattended for now, but the main thing his entire being struggled against his restraint for was to conquer and pleasure *her*. As long as he could pummel her dripping pussy into submission with *something*, he would be able to deal with the onslaught on his senses.

Kain knelt back on the bed and stroked a hand up her creamy thigh. She whimpered and spread her legs wider at his touch, letting him slide to her weeping pussy. It was so infinitely soft, beckoning to him to explore and taste, but he knew if he buried his mouth there again he would mount her no matter the consequences.

Spreading her lips with two fingers to fully expose her eager sheath, he pressed the dildo's rounded head against her opening and sighed with her when it sank in to the hilt.

She was certainly a Breeder. It was not a small toy, and previous women had had to be coaxed and gentled before taking it. Selma simply moaned and lifted her hips, urging him to go deeper while pleading for more.

He obeyed, pressed deeper, and enjoyed the shudder of her pleasure that transferred through his arm and down his spine. He hadn't intentionally tapped into the dark core of magic within him, but the Breeder's sexual energy drew it from him with effortless ease, pulling him deeper into her spell.

"Damned little witch!" Through the fog of lust, anger swelled within him, a small vestige of sanity clawing its way through the hormonal chaos. He didn't *want* this burning desire to fuck, possess, and protect a Breeder! He'd done everything in his power since maturing into adulthood to avoid the responsibility they demanded, but here he was—one whiff of her cursed scent and he had been after her like a dog on a chain.

The fact that even he—so stoic in his resolve against the mating practices of his kind—had no choice but to act like a lovesick Neanderthal in her presence enraged him.

Clenching the dildo, he let the anger mix with his need for her surrender and drove it into her core far more savagely than most women would have enjoyed. But even though Selma squealed and screamed like a woman possessed, her hips still rose to meet every thrust.

Kain closed his eyes and imagined that the wet noises being pushed from her body came from driving his own mass into her, that the echo of pleasure itching underneath his skin was more than just his unleashed magic. He wanted her pussy to surrender, to force her to accept him as her master as much as he wanted to punish her for stirring those primitive urges in him.

Her pheromone-laced scent and the exquisite sensation of ramming her quivering channel into submission swallowed him whole in their dark torment, and he gave himself to the madness.

Only after several minutes did he realize that her screams and cries were not entirely from pleasure.

The shock—those two seconds he thought he had harmed her—broke the haze like a bucket of ice water, allowing him to hear her shrill pleas through the thrashing and shrieking.

"Please! More! I can't...! Please!"

Reining in his wits, he noticed her desperately lifted hips and flailing arms weren't just thrusting back against the intrusion and clutching at the bedding—she was squirming and angling her pelvis, attempting to get a rougher stimulation, and her hands pressed desperately against her clit to help her climax along. Only it wasn't helping, and the tears streaking her distorted face felt like a punch to the gut.

In the back of his mind, the memory of the lessons his father had bestowed on him concerning Breeders—given back when he had still hoped his son would one day take a mate—made him growl before pulling the near-useless dildo from her quivering flesh. She needed the harsh shape of a demon's anatomy once her ring had been activated—and he couldn't give it to her.

"Please!"

The pained sob made him look around the room in panic for something, anything that could help her.

His eyes fell on one of the carved bedposts. It didn't have the ridges, but its shape flared into smooth edges and bulbs...

Kain reached out, wrapped his hand around the post

midway up, and broke it in half with a flexing of muscles already tense with raging testosterone before he turned back to the girl.

She had stopped flailing since he pulled the dildo out of her and now lay limp in front of him, thighs spread so her glistening slit was fully visible. Tears rolled silently down her flushed cheeks, and a soft but persistent whimper made his stomach clench with need to soothe and comfort.

Humming a vibration he'd never produced before, he slid his fingers up her cleft, spreading her open once more.

Selma moaned in response, but when he pressed the rounded end of the bedpost to her opening, her eyelids fluttered open as she gasped in surprise—and then again in strained pleasure as the violently shaped staff forced her to open around its blunt end, sinking into her wet depths inch after torturous inch.

Seeing her stretched for the thick tool, its carved surface grinding into her walls almost as forcefully as a demon's cock would have, was nearly as stimulating as her sudden keening.

Kain groaned as the first ridge on the bedpost hit something good inside of her, and she spasmed so hard around it he could see her abdominal muscles twitch. His panic evaporated, once again replaced by the all-consuming need for pleasure.

He thrust the bed knob in until she couldn't take anymore before reversing the movement. Her slick, pink sheath desperately clasped on to the bedpost, following the thrust. Brutally he shoved it in again before finding her throbbing clit with his free hand.

She was too busy clutching at the bedding and panting to pay him any notice, but her body reacted with a violent clenching, nearly halting his ministrations. He put more force behind the thrusts, spearing her spasming pussy faster and faster.

Her rhythmic moans and cries thrilled down his spine and made his erection throb and ache. The humming in his throat turned to a possessive growl as he fucked her faster and faster, abandoning all concerns that she might get hurt. She was a Breeder; she was born to take it, born to fuck.

Too soon her cries of pleasure turned to hoarse screams, her body tensing until finally she stiffened completely in an arc, head tossed back into the mattress while her pussy milked the bedpost for all it was worth.

"Oh, fucking god! *Yes!*"

Her release filled the room, the air, his nostrils, and mind. She was beautiful in her climax, pale skin flushed pink, hair spread out like a dark halo, and that perfect pussy opened wide around the carved wood. He would never get enough of her.

Ignoring her startled yelp, he pulled out the now-dripping staff, grabbed her by the hips, and flipped her over so he had her on her belly. He needed to see her come again, this time like a female should be mounted. He needed the sweet scent of her release to soak into every pore of his skin so he would never, ever lose the smell of her.

Selma was still panting from pleasured exhaustion, resting with her head against her arms when he reached for the broken bedpost once more to press it against her swollen entrance.

"No." The Breeder's protest was weak and not supported by her body, which opened willingly around the tip of the staff, but it was enough to make him pause the onslaught.

"I can't..." He hissed a shallow breath, trying to rein in his need to see her pussy pounded into submission. "I need more!"

Groaning, she pressed her backside up so her beautiful slit was presented in invitation. "Please. Gently."

Clearly she was familiar with the fruitlessness of denying a demon in full rut. His heart gave a painful lurch somewhere past the burning need to fuck her into a stupor.

Tossing the carved pole aside he fell on top of her, careful not to crush her. It was physically impossible for him to leave her at this point, but he could ensure she wouldn't be violated by having to endure an unwanted penetration, however much he might make her enjoy it.

She angled her hips to allow him to push in, but he slid his aching cock past her entrance and through the cleft of her nether lips, pressing up against the soft flesh which so eagerly coated him in her warm juices.

When his head—and ridges—stroked firmly over her clit, she mewled in surprise and jerked underneath him. Before she got a chance to move away from the pressure, he clamped his legs around hers and pressed them together so her soft thighs squeezed his cock, creating a slick tunnel for him to burrow through. It was how he pleasured himself with human women these days, usually after swaying their minds with magic and stuffing their pussies with a dildo until they thought he was truly fucking them.

Selma might know the truth, but she'd still enjoy the stimulation.

And so would he.

Kain groaned long and deep as her warm, pliable flesh slid along his throbbing shaft. Sharp spikes of pure pleasure shot up his spine at the friction. The hot, wet gush of moisture coating him from her opening allowed him to imagine that he truly was pushing up inside of her, filling her tight cunt to the brim.

She whined softly when his ridges caught her clit again, but her struggle against the pressure and his hold eased as her body realized his intentions.

"You feel... so good," he whispered when the rush of her surrender made the edges of his vision blur. The feel of her, her small body underneath him, her skin and the way she moved against his chest, rubbing herself against his cock for more... No demoness, nor any human, had ever felt this good—had ever *sounded* this good.

Embracing her fully and ensuring every inch of her skin was touching his, he allowed himself to forget about everything else. There was only him and her, only their shared need and her intoxicating presence.

It didn't take him long to reach the point of no return after she started bucking more insistently and tensing, signaling her impending climax. Kain would have preferred to stay in the blissful haze for hours, but his body had been tormented for too long and the sensation of another of her orgasms was too much.

Roaring, he raised off her while pinning her pelvis to the mattress with his own and hammered his cock against her twitching clit as she screamed out her orgasm.

The flood of moisture her pussy released over his cock was the final trigger he needed. The sharp pleasure intensified to an all-consuming torrent, until finally his balls emptied and he was released from the raging inferno.

Kain collapsed, barely remembering to catch himself so he didn't crush the girl underneath him. His breathing was ragged and his heart pounded far harder than the physical exertion should have caused, but he was too pleasantly numb to give it much thought. His entire body sang with relief and endorphin-induced pleasure, and it was all because of *her*.

Selma turned her head from the tangle of his sheets to gasp more oxygen into her lungs, and he raised up on his elbows a little so he could nuzzle her wild hair and stroke his cheek against hers. "You okay?"

She nodded silently, not bothering to open her eyes, but from the smile curving her full lips, he knew she was in a similar state to himself—gone on hormones and exhaustion too bone-deep to be purely physical.

Pulling his softening member from between her

thighs, he let his hand find the semen he'd soaked the sheets and her stomach with, gathered a good amount on his fingers, and rubbed them against her nether lips and clit before dipping two into her still-fluttering channel. He may not have fucked her properly, but that bedpost was unyielding. The potent magic in his semen would go a long way toward easing the ache of the rough penetration.

She hardly did more than sigh when he smeared his seed deep into her well-used pussy, nor did she protest when he climbed back up and rested halfway on top her, possessively shielding her from the chill of the room with his own flesh.

He was well aware that his instincts had cast him in the role as her mate and protector, for the moment ignoring the fact that she could never truly be his.

As he settled against her soft body, he couldn't bring himself to care.

SIXTEEN
SELMA

When Selma woke up, she was toasty warm and buried in a very comfortable bed. Her brain was still dazed from the first proper sleep she'd had in over a month, only allowing her to sense that she was warm and safe.

She shifted with a pleased sigh, then realized the heavy weight which rested halfway on top of her firmly enough that she couldn't move, yet lightly enough to not crush her, was the reason she felt so warm.

Startled, she forced her eyelids open.

Bulky muscles covered in olive skin caged her from all sides. When she yelped, it constricted around her already pinned torso, gathering her closer to a massive male chest.

At the same time as his oddly familiar musk registered in her mind, memories from the night before flooded back —Memories of the female demons who had tortured and humiliated her, of the gut-wrenching *need* they'd forced on her, and of *him*: Lord Protector Kain, the demon who'd saved her.

He had taken her to his home, and... Truth be told, she wasn't entirely sure what he'd done, because while he'd sated her desperate need and taken his own pleasure from her, his approach had been far different than Marathin's. In fact, he had seemed pretty unwilling to bed her...

Selma frowned into the mattress when she recalled what he'd said—that his magic would kill her.

The demon who'd captured her had told her about the demon Lords and their magic—of how it killed any but a few humans who were inexplicably immune to taking their dark energies inside. The so-called Pure Breeders.

Of which she was one.

But Kain... Kain didn't know. And so long as she kept it that way, he might not try to lay claim to her like Marathin had.

She breathed deeply in an attempt at letting his soothing scent placate her waking brain. She was nowhere near as terrified as she should have been, waking up naked in the clutches of an enemy, most likely because his heady scent had been playing tricks with her mind while she slept.

She bit her lip, trying to shake her thoughts free of the drugged feelings of safety and complacency. He might seem kind and caring, but he was still one of *them,* and she would never again forget what they truly were: monsters only capable of kindness as an act of deceit.

She would have to bide her time and attempt to play him like she had the demon who had captured her. She'd escaped once before—she could do it again.

As if her whirling thoughts had pulled him from his sleep, Kain groaned into her hair a few moments later. Then one of his oversized hands slid up her bare stomach to round over a breast.

Selma flinched despite the lazy simmer of lust low in her belly, her thigh bumping into something hard that scraped tantalizingly against her skin.

His spiked dick.

Oh, God.

She may have already been up close and personal with the large male fondling her in his sleep, but she'd been lost in the ring's curse. Feeling him shift against her, touching her so intimately, reminded her that he was truly a stranger... and that she was at his mercy.

His groan turned to a rumble that vibrated through his chest. He kissed the top of her head as if he sensed her panic even in his sleep and tried to soothe her, but after a few seconds, he stopped. He was awake.

Withdrawing his hands from her body, he rolled off her. "Are you okay?" His voice was gruff, and not entirely from sleep.

Selma dared a look up, truly taking the Lord in for the first time. His features were all angles and sharp masculinity, too strong to be called beautiful, though they were softened by his full lips. She could still sense the *otherness* vibrating from him like she had in the bar, his power almost too much for her brand to blind her to his true form.

He was an attractive man, even if she knew what he was. Rough and big, with stubble on his chin, hair the color of rich mahogany, and eyes so dark they looked pitch-black even in the dim morning light. Three deep scratches marred his right cheek, and dried blood crusted on the shirt he'd kept on while they slept.

"I am." It came out as little more than a whisper. "Thank you for... saving me."

Heat rushed to her cheeks as he briefly let his eyes slide over her naked body. Now that she was no longer wrapped up in his warm embrace, she felt cold and exposed lying uncovered next to this stranger, and she couldn't stop her arms from moving to hide her breasts and sex.

Kain heaved a deep sigh before he rolled over with his back to her and sat up. "Go take a shower, little one. The bathroom is past the door by the mirror. When you're done, we'll talk."

Talk. Selma watched him rise and walk out the door opposite the end of the bed—the end, where one of the intricately carved bedposts had been broken off—and frowned. No doubt he would either force her to the auction she'd run from, or...

Or he would realize what she was and would try to claim her for himself.

Either way, as much as he had saved her last night, she

knew the only things she could expect from him now were chains and an eternity of servitude.

Selma bit back the onset of hopelessness and pushed out of the bed. She had survived so far—she had to remember that. She'd been captured, blinded, raped, and tortured, and yet she'd survived.

Whatever she had to do to escape this time, she would. Which meant that she'd need her wits and strength about her, or she might as well give up and accept a future as a broodmare for these monsters.

The bedroom was framed by a black carpet and white walls, one of them completely covered by floor-to-ceiling windows sporting an unsurpassed view of the city. The large bed and a dresser in matching wood were the only pieces of furniture in the room, but when she craned her neck she could see that the third door, opposite the one by the mirror Kain had pointed out as the bathroom door, opened up into a luxuriously large closet.

He was clearly wealthy, despite his sparse—and rather male—sense of interior design, but then again, she supposed a demon Lord was bound to be.

Selma walked naked to the bathroom, enjoying the sensation of the soft carpet underneath her feet. She hadn't exactly been able to afford much comfort while on the run; many nights she'd opted to sleep in her car instead of spending any of the savings she'd withdrawn on a motel room.

The luxurious shower was a welcome gift, despite the

circumstances that had brought her here. She used his expensive shampoo and fancy soap to wash away the dirt and semen that still covered her after the attack and Kain's tending to her. The hot water soothed her tired muscles and heavy heart, and afterwards she wrapped herself in clean, soft towels.

The shower didn't manage to clear away her sense of dread and anxiety over being captured by an enemy, but it did allow her a slightly clearer head and calmer outlook, and for that she was grateful.

She would make it through this somehow, even if she didn't quite know how yet.

Still wrapped in the black, fluffy towel, she padded back into the bedroom and found a man's shirt spread out for her on the bed. It didn't offer the modesty she'd hoped for, but it was long enough to cover well past her mid-thighs. It was clean and crisp, smelled like detergent, and faintly of *him*.

Flushing with embarrassment, Selma stopped sniffing the collar, scolding her excited ovaries for the sudden dampness between her thighs. She bit the inside of her cheek hard until her mind stopped looping over the things he'd done to her the night before.

So long as he didn't touch the cursed ring between her legs, she'd be able to keep her head clear. And now that she was clean, the first port of call was to find out what he planned to do with her so she could start working on her escape.

Selma walked to the bedroom door and peered into the dim hallway. Not too many steps to her right was the locked and bolted front door to the apartment. Just for a moment she considered running for it, but she had no idea where she was in relation to her abandoned car, and she'd dropped her purse with her car keys and most of her money when the female demons dragged her into the warehouse

No, even if she could get past all the locks, her only option was to find the demon Lord and see what game he intended to play.

SHE FOUND him in the kitchen, hunched on a bar stool in front of a marble-countered island hosting an obscenely large display of food. He was slouched with his chin resting on his knuckles and a facial expression that could only be described as *brooding*.

Selma hesitated at the threshold, uncertain how to proceed. Despite the safety and comfort of waking up in his embrace, his looming form made her draw in a shaky breath. Now that she was conscious and aware of what he was, she felt more than a little nervous in his presence.

"Come. Eat. You need food—a Breeder should never be so malnourished."

She blinked at the command and pressed a hand against her stomach. Sure, she'd lost some weight while on the road, and she hadn't made the healthiest food choices when she did scarf something down, but in no way would she be considered malnourished—not by human standards. Apparently demons preferred their sex toys somewhat plump.

Biting back a retort for his presumption that her weight was any of his business, she slid closer in silence. She *was* pretty hungry, and the spread on the counter made her mouth water. Just at a glance she noticed smoked salmon, bagels, strawberries, eggs, and a variety of cheeses.

"Did you prepare this for me?" she asked as she scooted onto the too-tall bar stool next to him. It seemed like the polite thing to do—and she wanted to stay on his good side for as long as possible.

"Room service," he grunted.

It seemed this Lord wasn't a morning demon.

Selma decided to leave him alone until he wanted to begin that talk he'd mentioned earlier and dug in.

"I sensed no mate claim on you."

Selma coughed. He'd chosen the exact moment she'd taken an enormous bite of bagel layered with cream cheese and salmon to finally break the silence. She shot him a sideways look and realized he was staring down at her from his higher vantage point, taking in every movement of her face and body as if she was an opponent whose next move he was trying to decipher.

"I don't have a mate," she confirmed after finally swallowing.

"You have been marked." He narrowed his eyes, probably trying to detect any hint of deceit. "Ringed. Which means you ran from your Procurer. How?"

Selma bit her lip and looked down at her hands next to the well-stocked plate. They shook a little, as they always did when she remembered Marathin and what she'd had to do.

"There was... an incident. I got away while he was busy trying to cover it up."

A surprisingly gentle touch to her chin made her look up, his dark eyes easily capturing her gaze.

"What did he do to you, Selma?"

She swallowed thickly, something in her heart fluttering at his gentleness. It seemed... real. Even though she knew what they were like, knew how easily they lied and deceived, something in his soft touch and dark eyes made her *want* to trust him.

"There has never been a recorded incident of a Breeder escaping her Procurer in the entirety of our history. They are taught to be gentle—and, above all else, cautious. If you fled... he did something he shouldn't have."

There was a fire in his dark gaze, a smoldering anger on her behalf. Perhaps it was the night they'd spent together—how he'd reined in his own desires to ensure he didn't harm her. Perhaps her mind was still swathed in his calming scent and influence. Or maybe it was that she hadn't had anyone to confide in before.

Kain might have been a demon, but he was also the only one who'd ever protected her from others of his kind.

"He..." She swallowed again, unsure how to find the words.

"From the beginning, little one," Kain said, releasing her chin in favor of wrapping his hand around her knee. It sent a trickle of sensation up her thigh, but he didn't move it higher and the warmth was comforting. "I need to know everything, from your first meeting with him until you escaped."

"I was brought into a... a mental health facility." Her eyes darted to his in search of any judgement, but he only nodded. She supposed it wasn't entirely unheard of that their Breeders ended up in mental hospitals. Not a lot of doctors took continued talk about demons as a sign of good health.

"He was the head psychiatrist there," Selma continued, forcing down a shudder at the memory of her time at Ravenswood House. "He... tricked me. Said the ring was a treatment, that my... *visions*... were a hormone imbalance. I... I should have known that the 'treatment,' that how he put it on me, wasn't a legitimate medical procedure, but I... wasn't in a good state.

"And after—I thought it'd worked. That I was cured. I didn't notice the mark before I looked in a mirror later that night." She brushed a hand over the silver circle marring her forehead, biting her lip at the memory of the horror that came after.

"You can see the mark?" Kain said, a frown drawing down his brows.

A spike of anxiety made her eyes flick to his. *Stupid!*

Marathin had discovered what she was after she'd seen the mark he'd placed on her forehead. A normal

Breeder wouldn't have been able to detect it; the magic in the sigil was supposedly invisible to them, unless they possessed the qualities of a so-called Pure Breeder—the women who could resist most of their magic.

The women a demon Lord could mate.

Kain might have fought his instincts to take and dominate last night, but she wasn't keen on her chances if he found out she could withstand his rutting.

"I thought I did," she lied. "So I freaked out. I thought I wasn't *cured*. It was just a smudge, but I didn't realize until it was too late. I ran to him and I found his notes about... about what I was. About the auction he was planning on sending me to.

"He saw me. Knew that I knew. He demonstrated what the ring does to keep me in line. And then he raped me. He made me *beg* for it. But after... after, he was... different. Possessive. He said if I wanted to escape the auction, I could. I could stay with him."

Kain's gaze blazed with anger, his free hand curling into a tight fist on the counter, but when he spoke his voice was soft.

"For a Procurer to betray his responsibilities, he would have wanted to claim you as his mate. Why is his mark not on you?"

Selma looked down at his hand anchored on her knee. "He was going to... but we were interrupted. There was a nurse. She tried to save me, but he... killed her. I escaped while he was busy covering up the traces of her murder."

"What's his name?" Kain brushed his hand from her

knee to her chin once more, and though the contact was light as a feather, it kept her frozen as surely as if he'd grabbed her.

"Please don't take me back to him." She swallowed again, trying to read the expression in the bottomless eyes staring down at her. She hadn't meant to plead with him; she'd planned on finding out what his intentions were before trying to sway him one way or the other. But her fear of being brought back to Dr. Hershey after the way she had tricked him made cold sweat trickle down the back of her neck. If he got his hands on her, she had no doubt she would live to regret running away.

Kain's gaze narrowed before he finally moved his hand from her chin. "His name, Selma. And the state of this mental hospital."

"Promise me," she whispered. "Promise you won't send me back."

"I promise." She wasn't sure demons could ever be trusted, but the conviction she saw in Kain's eyes then made a sliver of the tension in her chest ease.

"His name is Marathin Hershey. Ravenswood House is in Massachusetts."

He drew in a sharp breath, finally releasing her knee to refocus on the breakfast buffet. "I know of him. He is old. Crafty. You did well running from him."

"So... what now?" Selma asked, looking dubiously at him.

"What now?" he repeated, still keeping his gaze on the food.

"Are you... bringing me to an auction?" she asked, hating that she couldn't stop herself. Her life had been uncertainty for so long, she needed to know his plans, even if keeping quiet would have been the smart thing to do.

He was silent for a moment before he answered, "It is my duty."

Anger flared in her gut, along with a sense of betrayal she had no right in feeling. He was one of *them*. That he'd cared for her meant nothing—his loyalty would always be lie his kind.

But since she'd been in his care, she'd felt... safe. For the first time in as long as she could remember. And yet he was going to force her into a lifetime of service?

"This may come as a shock to you, but I don't want that," she bit out. "I'm not a fucking broodmare!"

Her outburst was met with silence.

Fuck. She'd managed to keep her temper in check with Dr. Hershey, gauging what reaction he wanted from her. But not this time. Perhaps it was the stress of it all, the fear of being back in their clutches after a month of running.

She braved a look at him. He was staring at her, his gaze as distant as before, though a small frown around his full lips made the hairs on her nape stand on end. Something about him really set her on edge—perhaps the hovering threat of his power looming just underneath the human facade, or the way he seemed to be hyperaware of every little movement she made, his dark eyes following her fidgeting like a hawk.

"You have seen the alternative." His voice was soft despite his unsettling gaze. "The world is not safe for you, little one. If you accept a mate, you will be protected from those who wish to do you harm. Cherished."

"You mean trapped," she muttered, finally finding the strength to break eye-contact. "I will essentially be some monster's sex slave to do with as he pleases, and if I object... Well, we both know what happens when someone touches my ring. Don't pretend like this is all for my own good."

"So you would rather spend your life on the run, risking death and rape every single day, than build a family with a man who would worship the ground you walk on? Have sons who would love you?"

"At least it would be my choice." Selma prodded irritably at the food with her fork. She didn't understand his motivations as she had Marathin's, so the only option she saw was to just be straightforward with him and hope he could sense her honesty. Maybe then he would be less vigilant when the right moment to escape revealed itself.

"Your kind says that you treat Breeders oh-so well," she continued, "but what you truly want is a slave. What if I'd had a human husband? Human children? Would that have mattered when you ripped me away from my life to serve whoever has enough money to buy me? I know it certainly wouldn't have mattered to Marathin."

Once again she was met with silence. A long silence.

She'd begun to fear her honesty had snapped his temper when he finally spoke.

"There might be a third option."

Her eyes hesitantly shifted back up to his. He had stopped staring at her and was now frowning at the enormous amounts of food on the kitchen counter.

"You mean... I could stay with you?" she prodded, cautious to keep her tone neutral. If he thought his magic would kill her if he were to be intimate with her, it was a bit of an odd suggestion, but perhaps her scent had affected him enough that he wasn't thinking rationally. Marathin had apparently been lost enough in it to go against their rules in order to claim ownership over her.

But instead of being pleased with her suggestion, Kain's face contorted in a grimace of disgust and anger. "*Never!*"

SEVENTEEN
KAIN

The Breeder jumped at his sharp retort, eyes widening in fear.

He was used to people scurrying away in response to his foul moods, but seeing the woman his instincts clamored to soothe and protect recoil made something in his gut clench.

With a deep breath he forced the despair-filled anger down, locking it deep in the part of his heart where it belonged, rotting away in the darkness. With effort, he carefully smoothed out his facial expression.

"I'm sorry, I... didn't mean to frighten you." Of its own accord, his hand moved to her shoulder in an attempt at offering comfort. She instantly went rigid, and he caught himself missing the pliable softness her body had responded with the previous night.

He pulled his arm back, letting it fall awkwardly to his

side. “I do not desire to take a mate. Ever. And even if I did, my magic would kill you when we coupled.”

Selma’s wrinkled her forehead in confusion. “Then how…? Can you remove my mark? The ring?”

Kain didn’t miss the desperate eagerness flashing across her face. “No. Your mark is permanent, and if I were to remove your ring, you would die. But there are… rumors.”

He grimaced, looking the woman over again. What he was about to suggest—if anyone ever found out, he’d be executed as a traitor. But if he didn’t…

Kain clenched his fist to alleviate the flash of rage conjured by the thought of her beautiful brown eyes dulled like his mother's had been. Broken.

“There are rumors of a place where Breeders can seek sanctuary. Somewhere my kind can’t follow.”

Selma stared at him, suspicion blatant in her pretty eyes. He couldn't blame her, really—she had very little reason to trust his kind.

“And why would you take me there?” She straightened her back in an effort to look confident and strong, but confusion and fear swirled in her otherwise so delicious scent.

He knew she was clinging to her composure by her fingernails, her scent betraying her stoic facade. She was a brave little thing, trying to hide how terrified she truly was, and the heated image of claiming her as his flashed before his mind’s eye. She’d make a good mate—courageous and strong despite her small stature.

But even if he'd wanted a mate, even if his innate magic weren't a guaranteed death sentence, how long would it be before he'd snuff the light within her, leaving what'd once been a spirited woman a hollow shell?

"Because if I don't, you will die." He managed to keep his voice calm this time. "You have run away once—you will do so again, until you find yourself in trouble without anyone around to save you. I cannot promise that this place is more than a rumor, but I will give you the option of finding out."

Her eyes lit up, hope blossoming behind the wall of mistrust, though she looked far from convinced. "And how is it that you know this secret, Kain?"

His name on her lips made a shiver run down his spine and materialize in his ever-straining cock. He hadn't been able to fully get rid of the raging erection he'd woken up with; ever since she sat down next to him, it had been standing at more than half-attention.

He had been around a few Breeders before, none of whom had invoked such a strong response from his instincts. Perhaps it was that she was unmated and in need of a protector, or that their first contact had been while she was in full heat, but in either case it was annoying as all fuck. Not having a clear head at all times was a new sensation for him, and he didn't appreciate the experience.

"My mother kept a diary." He rose, suddenly overwhelmed by the urge to escape the room she'd unwittingly poisoned with her irresistible pheromones. "Finish your food. I will make some preparations and then we will leave."

He could feel her haunting eyes follow his retreat.

"I APPRECIATE YOU COMING, Thomren. And you, Meredith." Kain nodded at his second-in-command and his mate, making sure his gaze didn't linger on the pregnant woman. It'd taken a direct command to get the otherwise unfalteringly loyal demon to bring his Breeder along in her current state, and Kain wasn't about to disrespect him. "I trust you are well, my dear?"

"Oh yes, thank you. Though this one has been extraordinarily overprotective since I became pregnant. This is the first time he's let me go farther than the front porch in three months." Meredith laughed.

"Thomren is very kind to honor my request that you accompany him today. I will remember this." Kain nodded at the other man.

"You're not supposed to run around in your condition," Thomren muttered, the growl in his voice only barely contained as he glared at his Lord Protector.

"Oh, will you stop it?" Meredith sighed, swatting his arm. "I'm fine. And if Lord Kain needs my help, we aren't going to argue—*are we?*"

Thomren pinched his lips at the intonation in his mate's voice, but some of the anger in his gaze died. "How's the girl?"

Kain sighed, extending an arm toward the kitchen instead of answering the question—because frankly, the thought of voicing out loud that the Breeder under his protection wasn't settled and happy was too much of an affront to his ego, even if there was no reason for her to be anything but scared out of her mind. "I'll introduce you."

Selma sat stiffly on the barstool where he'd left her, her tense pose making it obvious she was nervous about the newcomers.

"Selma, there's someone I'd like you to meet," he said, not missing how her wide eyes did a double-take of Meredith's rounded belly. "This is Thomren, my second-in-command, and his mate, Meredith. She's agreed to look after you while he and I work out a few details.

"Details?" Her voice was filled with suspicion.

It pulled at something in his gut—that innate urge to protect and soothe that her presence forced upon him—and he'd crossed the floor and placed a calming hand on her shoulder before he'd even realized what he'd done.

She shivered under his touch, fear mixing with uncertainty, and Kain cussed internally as his cock stirred.

Fucking pheromones.

"Yes. Details. If I am to follow through on my promise to you, there are preparations to be made, and we will need to leave before your presence in my territory becomes common knowledge. My men are loyal, but if you linger in my residence, rumors will spread. The sooner you are out of here, the better."

Except the longer he stared down at her, the harder it

became to bear the thought of handing her over to whichever divine being hosted the sanctuary his mother had noted in her journal.

Again with the fucking pheromones. He'd never been this riled up by a Breeder—she had every instinct in his body on edge, desperate to claim and possess.

But even if he didn't keep his promise to her, he'd still have to give her up—and to lowly demons who'd fight over the right to rut her like common beasts.

"We leave in half-an-hour. Be ready."

Brusquely, Kain released his grip on her shoulder and motioned at Thomren to follow as he strode through the door, doing his level-best to keep his raging instincts at bay. Entertaining the urges flooding his mind and body would bring nothing but frustration.

Thomren followed him, clearly unhappy about releasing his grip on his mate, but the fact that there was only another Breeder left behind with her seemed to dull his second's protective urges enough that he managed to obey his Lord Protector.

Kain led him to his study, leaving the door cracked so they could hear the women. It was for his own sake as much as it was Thomren's.

"All right," Thomren sighed, folding his arms across his chest. "I'm gonna guess you didn't ask me to bring my pregnant mate around if I'm just here to take the girl back to her master."

"She's scared of us," Kain said, fingering his shirt

sleeve in an effort to keep the anger at Selma's ordeal down. He needed a calm, rational mind to plan his next move. "She wasn't given to a mate. Her Procurer tried to keep her for himself—abused her in the process."

Thomren frowned, horror plain on his face. "So you are going to bring charges against him? And the girl? Will you arrange for her auction yourself?"

"No." Kain looked at him, ensuring he had his full attention. "I'm going to help her disappear."

The demon blinked twice, his mouth parting in shock. "*What?* Kain—have you lost your mind? If you do this—"

"I will be a traitor to our kind. I know." Kain didn't blink, keeping their gazes locked. "You once swore a blood oath to me, my friend, to follow my command through eternity, but that is not why I'm asking you to help me do this. I am asking you because I trust no one like I do you. I will not command you in this, Thomren—but I will ask. Will you help me?"

Thomren looked at him for a long time. Finally, he breathed out, the frown on his forehead smoothing. "This is about your mother."

Kain broke their gaze, forcing down the swell of anger and despair any thought of *her* always brought. Very few people knew that story—and of those, exactly one he would let live for mentioning the Breeder who'd borne him.

That one person was Thomren, the man who'd brought his pregnant mate to his Lord Protector's home because he'd needed Selma to see that some demons could be trusted to keep a Breeder safe. Content.

"It's about not dooming a woman and the children she'll bear to an eternity of misery," he said, voice low. "Her introduction to our world has been too violent. She'll never accept a forced mate bond. And the thought of her enduring rape and torment because I followed the fucking rules, and sent her to an auction?"

Thomren clasped his hand on Kain's shoulder. When their gazes met again, there was understanding in his second's eyes. And pity.

"When I first saw Meredith, the thought that someone else might win her made me sick with rage and sorrow. And I know had I not won her bid, you would have done anything in your power to ensure she'd still become mine. So I will do this for you, my friend. If making her disappear is what you can do to protect your Breeder, I will help make it so."

"WHAT ABOUT MY THINGS?"

"They are in the trunk. Thomren got them out before dumping your car in the river," Kain said, keeping his focus on the road ahead.

A small, indignant gasp sounded from the passenger seat. "You dumped my car? I spent a quarter of my savings on that!"

He refrained from mentioning that, according to his underling, that moving pile of junk was better suited for the bottom of the river than transporting anyone around. "It was too easy to track. If your Procurer is following you, he'll have a harder time tracking you this way."

"Will this... this sanctuary truly stop him?" She looked at him through fanned lashes, the intensity of her gaze making him glance at her out the corner of his eye. She looked so *vulnerable* his instincts reared up hard, desperate to soothe, to prove to her that she'd made the right decision when she put her faith in him to keep her safe.

"The contract he made me sign... he... thinks he *owns* me." She shuddered.

Kain's looping thoughts came to a screeching halt, his eyes widening as he whipped around to stare at her. "You signed a fucking *contract? Fuck!*" He slapped both hands against the steering wheel so hard the car swerved before he caught it again.

"Is... is that very bad?" she squeaked.

Only the spike of fear in her scent made him take a deep breath before answering. "You signed a contract with a *demon!* Yes, it's *bad.* Dark skies above! What exactly did this contract say, Selma?"

"T-That I... That my soul is his," she whispered. "You don't understand... I had to sign. It was my only chance at escaping him. I—"

"I understand," Kain ground out. It suddenly made a

lot more sense why a demon as old and crafty as Marathin had let a Breeder he wanted to claim out of his sight long enough that she could escape. A contract on her soul meant he'd be able to track her—and that he most likely was.

"What happens now?" she asked, the tremble in her voice more than evident that his reaction had alerted her to how completely fucked they were. "Can... Can you not help me after all?"

Kain rubbed the bridge of his nose. No. He couldn't. Nothing and no one could break a contract, and there was no escape. Even if this sanctuary turned out to be more than just his mother's desperate pipe dream, the magic in any contract made with a demon was binding and final. Somehow, some way, she would end up in the hands of her captor.

He could break the law and help her disappear—but even a demon Lord couldn't break contract magic.

But if he abandoned her now...

He glanced at her again, and clutched the steering wheel at the ache blooming in his chest at the desperation in her brown eyes.

He knew what demons did when a human tried to break a contract. He'd carried out such punishments himself more than once.

But what was he supposed to do? Kill an ancient demon and start a war in a doomed attempt to right a wrong that could never be undone anyway? Saving this little thing would not bring back his mother.

But as he looked at her out of the corner of his eye, saw her scared face and smelled her fear at the memory of the man she'd run from, he knew he would try, consequences be damned.

Fucking pheremones.

"I won't let him hurt you," he said softly. "I'll find a way."

They sat in silence for a little while, the miles eaten up by the steady thrum of the car's engine, until she spoke again.

"Why?"

"Why what?" It came out snippier than he'd wanted.

"Why are you helping me?"

Kain scoffed. He hardly knew the answer himself. The swirling inferno of emotions and instincts that had been warring inside of him made clear thinking excruciatingly hard.

"You have no idea the impact your scent has on us, do you?" He was aware that he sounded bitter.

"But Marathin... All my scent did to him was make him want me, not want to help me. Why is it different for you? Are you tricking me?"

His lips twisted in dark amusement. "If I were, you think asking me would make me tell you?"

She sighed. "No. I just... If you are, please just tell me, okay? It's not like I can get away from you, and I can't bear getting my hopes up if... if you're planning on selling me or something."

The defeat in her voice made his heart twist.

"I'm not out to trick you, little one. It's a little different for Lords. Most regular demons don't realize it, but our reaction to Breeders is... stronger." Kain sighed. "It's not just about sex; it's about providing you with protection and safety. When you are frightened or upset, your scent messes with my brain chemistry until I act to make it better. And yours is... potent."

She was silent again for a little while, until finally she said something that nearly made him crash the car.

"I'm sorry."

"You're what?" He was almost certain he'd heard her wrong.

"I'm sorry. I know what it's like to have your mind play tricks on you and force you, and I hate that I'm doing the same to you."

Her small hand found his arm, a little awkwardly, but the feeling of it burned through his coat and shirt all the way into his bloodstream.

How could someone that small, that soft, shake him to his very core? And how could someone who'd been put through the kind of abuse she had, have any empathy for anyone of his kind?

The chuckle at the absurdity of her apology erupting from his throat made her pull her hand away. "What?"

He offered her a gentle smile. "Breeders are known to care about others more so than most humans, but you apologizing for how your scent affects me? That's... a first. And I appreciate the sentiment. Quite a bit."

Her responding blush made his blood heat again, this time more predictably from arousal.

He forced his focus back on the road instead of on the odd little Breeder who made breathing difficult.

EIGHTEEN
SELMA

They drove all day and well into the night before the demon finally pulled over at a seedy motel off the highway, where he left her in the locked car while he sorted out room arrangements. Which turned out to be one small room with twin beds.

"I'm sorry for the cheap room. We are more likely not to draw attention if we stay off-grid." He actually looked mildly ashamed as he watched her take in the floral bedding, the stained carpet, and the dingy furniture.

Selma bit the inside of her cheek as she glanced at him. It wasn't the standard of the room she was concerned about—it was sharing it with a ginormous demon. Kain might have been helping her, but she knew from last night's debauched events and the near-constant bulge in his jeans that he was fighting his desires tooth and nail.

He'd admitted as much himself—that he had the same urges to take her as Marathin had. The fact that they were apparently mixed with an insurmountable urge to ensure her comfort and protection was likely the only reason he had yet to give in.

"I spent most of a month sleeping in my car. This is practically luxury in comparison," she said, offering him a small smile to hide her anxious thoughts—though judging from his frown, he could scent her fear just fine.

"Last night..." he began, hesitating for a moment as if he'd rather not continue that sentence. "I did what I did because I had to."

"I know." She *did* know. The metal ring hidden between her lower lips had been demonstrated enough during her time with Marathin that she understood Kain had had no other option.

She avoided his gaze and walked to the bed furthest from the door, dropping onto its floral surface to a squeak of springs. Horny demon or not, she'd much rather he was here with her than not—there was no arguing he made a mighty fine meat shield. Plus...

Selma looked up at him again through her eyelashes as he moved about, checking the small bathroom and windows. She couldn't deny that she felt infinitely safer with him around than she ever had on her own. He was big, strong, and demonstrably powerful—and the care with which he treated her made her heart soften despite her innate fear of demons. He was risking everything for her when in reality, he owed her nothing.

She kicked off her shoes, but kept on the dress Meredith had brought her as she climbed underneath the covers. Exhaustion pulled on her eyelids and relaxed her muscles, and when Kain turned to his own bed, sleep wasn't far away.

"Selma?"

"Hmm?" When she'd been alone, it had been hard to relax enough to fall asleep. Apparently her own instincts were only too happy to trust in her male companion to keep her safe during the night, no matter how much her rational side muttered about him being a stranger.

"Tomorrow we will arrive at the city where my contact is located. It is a place with many demons, and they may notice me—and you, by extension. If we are approached, you will have to act as my mate."

The thought of clinging to Kain's arm and fawning over him like a lovesick schoolgirl made her giggle, halfway gone on sleep as she was. "Mmhmm."

"If we are not approached... There are laws for Lords passing through another's territory, such as first presenting oneself to the local ruler before going about one's business in his Area. We do not have that option because any Lord will know that you are not my mate, as they have never attended your auction. If we are not approached, there is every chance we are instead being observed, which may result in an attack. I want you to understand how dangerous this is before you agree to it."

Selma knew she probably should ask him questions, but she was so tired, and deep in her core she knew the man whose subtle scent had her head spinning would protect her from anything and everyone. There was no true danger while he was present.

A low thump followed by a muttered cursing made her startle back from the brink of sleep—and when she saw the reason for it, she couldn't help but crack a half-smile. He'd evidently stubbed his toe against the bed frame while sliding his jeans off, and there was something endearingly human about such a clumsy act.

"You okay?"

"I'm fine," he growled, tossing his jeans over one of the chairs and letting his T-shirt follow.

Selma drew in a small breath and hurriedly bit her lip to quell the sound so she didn't alert him to her attention. He was *built*. Sure, she had some hazy memories from last night about his ridiculously muscled torso, but she'd written off her intense attraction to his physical appearance as a result of the ring.

Now though, as he moved around the room in only his boxers to turn off the few lamps, letting the lights from the parking lot illuminate him through the flimsy curtains... Yeah, there was no denying he was very handsome in his human disguise. His thighs were thick as tree trunks, his biceps almost as wide, and his chest and back spanned more than a yard across, narrowing to a tight, but thickly muscled waist. He was the epitome of male strength.

Only when he climbed into his own bed and turned his back to her did she dare to exhale, shame heating her cheeks. What was the matter with her? She knew what he was underneath his disguise: exactly what she'd given up everything to escape. Yet here she was, not even under her ring's cursed influence, imagining the heat of his strong body sliding underneath the sheets with her...

A pang between her thighs served as the first warning that her thoughts were going to get her into trouble. She could mostly ignore the ring, despite its tight fit over her most sensitive nerves, but as blood rushed to her nether regions the trapped nub swelled against the cold circle of metal, sending shocks of sensation through her pelvis.

Shit.

She glanced at Kain's broad back, praying silently he was a fast sleeper, but from the way he moved on the uncomfortable bed, she was pretty sure she wasn't that lucky.

He's going to smell me.

A jolt of unwelcome excitement mixed with her anxiety, blurred images of his furious lust when he'd broken off the bed post the previous night flashing before her mind's eye.

Against her will, her sex softened at the memory and she bit down on a groan. She needed to stop. This was only going to end one way—a way she certainly didn't want.

Even if the thought of Kain pinning her to the bed didn't fill her with dread like it should have.

But he wasn't like the others. She felt... *safe* with him and had since the second time she'd set eyes on him. When he'd carried her from the warehouse and healed her wounds... sated her desperate desire, broken demon laws to save her… he'd proven he was nothing like the beasts who'd haunted her her entire life.

She looked at him again and noticed the hard outline of his tensed back muscles in the low light from the window. He'd smelled her, all right.

Selma swallowed thickly, her breath slow but shallow. If he got up from that bed… if he came for her… would she resist?

Her clit pulsed hard against the vicious metal encircling it as she lay in the darkness, waiting for him to follow the temptation of her scent.

But he never moved so much as a muscle—and when she finally fell asleep some long hours later, she still wasn't sure if she'd wanted him to.

NINETEEN
KAIN

The woman next to him seemed surprisingly relaxed, considering how close the demon she'd shared a room with had come to losing control.

Kain knew she'd realized what her scent was doing to him, her small breaths and the sound of the scratchy motel sheets as she looked at him betraying her anxiety that he might react like his instincts had been screaming for him to.

It had taken all his considerable willpower not to pin her down, rip the fabric clean off her body, and fuck her into oblivion once that sweet, heady smell of her arousal hit his nostrils and made every cell in his body *ache*.

He shot her an ungrateful glare out the corner of his eye. The little Breeder was contentedly humming in the passenger seat as he maneuvered the car through the busy city, watching the world go by as if she had not a care in the world. How was she so fucking calm? Kain himself felt every nerve stand at attention, his senses hyper alert as he watched for other demons. Yet Selma... Selma had been calm ever since he woke her up, all traces of fear and anxiety gone for reasons unbeknownst to him.

Perhaps it was just the result of a good night's sleep, because while he had sat awake, staring at her passed out form and struggling with the onslaught of mixed emotions and raw desire her presence brought up in him, she had slept peacefully.

And through it all, his instincts were practically purring with contentment that the Breeder in his care finally trusted him to protect her. It was maddening.

"Are we close?" She looked out of the passenger side window as if searching for the demons she could no longer see while he pulled into a parking lot. "And is it demon-free?"

"Yes and yes, as far as I can tell." Kain turned off the engine and looked over at her. "Listen, if things go wrong, I want you to stay calm and close, okay? I will talk us out of any trouble if I can, and if not, I will fight. Most likely, things will run smoothly. Just be prepared."

She nodded obediently, and slid out of the car.

HER NEWFOUND CALM remained as he guided them through the crowd, one arm securely wrapped around her shoulders as he scouted for potential trouble.

"No demons around then?" she asked again, offering

him a smile that would have distracted him from his vigilance if he'd let it.

"Over there," he murmured, indicating a couple of demons who were watching them from a distance. "They don't look like trouble, though. Just keeping an eye on me."

As much as he'd dampened his natural power, there was a limit to what he could do. Demons didn't get fooled by human disguises, after all, and anyone who saw him would have no doubt he was a Lord—a Lord who didn't belong in this territory.

He shot the two a hard look, silently reminding them that he could end them if he wanted to, before shifting his focus back to the crowd. With any luck, they'd not want to get involved in a potential dispute between him and the Lord residing over this territory, and would keep their mouths shut, at least until he had Selma safely out of there.

"You know, this is the first time I've been able to walk among this many people and not worry," she hummed.

Kain shot her an incredulous look. He'd been *very* clear how dangerous this step of the plan was.

"When I was on the run, I'd never know if I was being stalked by a demon disguised as a human. And before that, I never knew if I'd see one. And if I'd stare too long—get his attention," she explained, leaning her head against his arm as if it was the most natural thing in the world.

Hot, heavy need coiled low in his belly at the little Breeder's obvious display of trust, his mind fogging with urges to show her how else he could please her. He knew her own instincts were likely being lulled by his presence, that she was predisposed to his pheromones. They'd been in each other's company for long enough now that his magic would be messing with the mark she'd been branded with. But that knowledge did little to help him concentrate while she was snuggled up to him.

"Stop that," he hissed through gritted teeth. "I need my head clear."

She looked up at him, startled by his tone, but understanding broke behind her pretty eyes at the look of hunger in his.

"Oh." A hefty blush spread across her cheeks and she pulled her head back with a jerk. "Sorry!"

Kain breathed deeply next to her, trying to get his body back under control. This was too important for him to let himself get distracted—one moment's inattentiveness and he risked being snuck up on.

"Fucking Breeders," he muttered under his breath.

"Well, 'fucking demons' right back," she snapped. "It's not like I choose for my body to get all screwy around you!"

He barked a hoarse laugh and constricted his arm tighter around her for the briefest moment. He liked this version of her—unafraid and confident in his presence, a feat not even many fully grown demons managed.

"All right, little smart-mouth, we're almost there." Kain gave her a tight smile, nodding for her to turn her attention up the street.

He'd been here once before, and the memory of that time made his mood sour instantly. It was a small and dingy shop, currently empty of customers as he pulled Selma through the door, the little bell jingling merrily upon their entry.

Kain headed straight for the counter, where a slender man with bad skin was too busy fiddling with a magazine to look up at them.

"Fred."

The man gave an odd sort of jolt at Kain's near-growled greeting, his head bobbing up with a snap.

"Oh god, you!" He flinched and backed up as if searching for an exit, but only managed to hit the back wall, knocking off a couple of bags of candy in the process.

"Indeed." Kain stopped in front of the counter, placing both of his massive hands on it so he could lean in. "I'm pleased you remember me. That should save us the trouble of you pretending like you can't answer my questions, shouldn't it?"

The man, now sickly pale behind his adult acne, nodded. "W-What do you want?"

"Precise directions to the place I asked you about last time."

Fred swallowed. "Man, you know I can't." Kain growled again, making the slender man shake harder. "It's a spell! I can't!"

Kain scoffed. "Oh, really? I suppose we'll just have to see if a little of *my* magic will help, then."

"No! Please, no!" Fred huddled in on himself as darkness suddenly filled the room, solidifying in tendrils that snaked toward the quivering man.

The Demon Lord hadn't gone this far the last time he visited—but the stakes hadn't been as high as they were now. Using his magic in another's territory? That was bound to draw attention from the residing Lord Protector. But if he was quick enough, he and Selma would be gone by the time anyone came to investigate.

"Kain!" Out of nowhere, a small hand slapped hard against his back, breaking his single-minded focus. "Stop that! Right now!"

Kain blinked, his dark magic receding as he snapped his head around to stare down at Selma. "What?"

"What do you mean, 'what'?" she stuttered, some of the unease she'd displayed their first morning together flickering in her gaze despite the stubborn jut of her chin. "Stop attacking the poor guy! You can't just... bully someone like that!"

He cocked an eyebrow at her. "I gave him ample opportunity to speak of his own accord. He chose not to."

Selma blinked. "He said it was a spell. I'm not entirely sure how magic works for y'all, but that doesn't sound like he could just choose to *tell* you. How about you *ask* the man?"

"What, ask him nicely and see if he'll comply? Look, I know you're a Breeder and therefore predisposed to being overly kind, but that's just not how the world works, sweetheart."

The fear on Selma's pretty face was swiftly replaced

by anger at his patronizing tone, but before she could lay into him, the clerk interrupted.

"If the girl is a Breeder, I can tell *her,*" he croaked, slowly straightening behind the counter.

Kain flicked his black gaze back to Fred, pinning him in place. *"Explain."*

He gulped. "Well... the spell ensures we only tell Breeders of the location. If she's a Breeder, I will be able to tell her. Though... you should leave the room while we..."

Kain's raised eyebrows made Fred falter.

"Uh, but I suppose we can ignore that." He fidgeted nervously. "She'll have to ask me directly."

Selma glanced up at Kain, likely to ensure that he was once again safe to be around before she walked closer to the counter so the man could look at her without also getting an eyeful of the threatening demon.

"Where is the place that demons can't go?"

Fred exhaled, undoubtedly from relief. "Colorado, in the mountains. Here, let me show you on a map."

While he bent to fish the map out from under the counter, Selma side-eyed her companion. "Yes, I see how much easier threatening people is. Why does anyone waste their time *talking*?"

Kain narrowed his eyes at her, but couldn't quite suppress a flicker of amusement at her lip. "You should watch that smart mouth of yours."

She didn't retaliate, choosing instead to focus on Fred

as his head reappeared and he slapped a map of Colorado in front of them.

"Here it is, just west of Routt National Forest off Route 40." He pointed at the map. "But if you bring him, he won't be able to take you closer than three miles."

"What's there?" She eyed the area that looked to be just a stretch of mountainous terrain. "Why can't demons enter?"

Fred's fingers twitched around the edge of the map. "I... I'm not sure." He quickly glanced at Kain. "B-But it's a sanctuary. They take in Breeders who find their way there. The ones who can't accept their lot in life."

Kain sighed. "Fred, don't make me do unpleasant things to you in front of the lady. She doesn't want to see that."

The clerk swallowed nervously, his Adam's apple bobbing in the process. "Right, it's just... I really, *really* shouldn't, and... this will not make you any less pissed off, and I can't afford to have you trash my store, okay?"

Selma frowned. "So it isn't a sanctuary?"

"Yeah, yeah, it is." Sweat shone on his temples, the glances he kept casting at Kain resembling a nervous twitch more and more.

"He won't harm you or your shop," Selma said, casting a stern look at Kain. "I promise."

Kain arched an eyebrow at her. How she thought it safe to presume he'd honor her promises, he didn't know.

"It's protected by a goddess," Fred whispered.

Kain's snarl came unbidden from the depths of his

chest. He fucking *knew* it! Some nosy bitch of a goddess was hiding away their precious Breeders, and here he was, prepared to voluntarily hand one over to an enemy!

Without turning her attention from Fred, Selma reached back to place a calming hand on Kain's chest, anchoring his aggression with the light touch as easily as if she'd cast a spell. "A... A goddess? But why?"

"I don't know, honestly. I swear. I just know that she is the only one who will protect you from the demons, and I'm one of her Secret Keepers. My only job is to tell Breeders about this place if they find me. And keep it safe from *them*." He made a vague gesture toward Kain.

"So you're a supernatural being, too?"

"Nah, man, I just owed her a debt. Fell in with the wrong crowd, was about to lose my goddamn soul, and she got me out of the pinch after I swore an oath to do this gig for her."

"Lose... your soul?"

"Made a deal with a demon." Fred shook his head. "I was young and stupid and wanted a new car."

Kain put his hand on her shoulder, interrupting what was undoubtedly going to be more questions. "That's fascinating. Selma, we need to get moving before Lord Harisham shows up."

Selma jolted at the reminder. "Yes, right. Thank you, Fred."

The clerk nodded and gave her a half-wave, only offering Kain a grimace. "Good luck."

The moment they exited the shop, a wholly familiar

sense dug in between Kain's shoulder-blades and he growled, jerking his head in the direction of the threat.

"What is it?" Selma pressed in against his side, an automatic reaction to his tension.

Kain wrapped his arm tighter around her shoulders and hurried her along the pavement in the direction of their parked car. "We're being watched."

TWENTY
SELMA

Selma blinked and looked over her shoulder as Kain whisked her down the street. In the shadows by a fruit stand, two men in honest-to-god trench coats and hats stood looking at them.

"Demons?"

"Yeah, and they're not acknowledging me. Come, little one. We need to get you out of here—*now*."

"You think they're his employees? Lord Haris... something?"

"I'm not sure." He didn't elaborate, but they made it to the car without incident, where Kain opened the passenger side door and practically shoved her in.

"What do you mean, you're not sure?" she asked.

The second he'd slammed his own door, he started the engine and reversed so fast the tires squealed. He didn't answer until they were out of the parking lot.

"I mean that they looked more professional than the

average lackeys. They could be Lord Harisham's, or... they could be agents sent by your Procurer."

An uncomfortable flutter made her stomach clench. "But it could just be the Lord's men?"

"Yes, but that's not much better. Not until we are well out of the city, at least."

THE DRIVE WAS AGONIZING. Every time they had to slow down or stop for traffic, Selma's pulse picked up speed, and every sound or movement outside the car made her jump.

Finally, Kain placed his hand on her knee and kept it there, only letting go to change gears. It allowed a little of her previous calm to return, her instincts whispering to her to trust that he could get her to safety.

When she'd woken up that morning, something had shifted between them. Or perhaps more accurately, something had shifted within her. He hadn't touched her, despite her carelessness. He'd only guarded her while she slept, and now she knew one thing with absolute certainty: she trusted Kain. Completely.

As the high-rises disappeared in the rearview mirror, Selma sank back in the passenger seat, breathing a sigh of relief as she smiled at her companion. Once again, he'd gotten her to safety.

"So... the whole 'selling your soul to a demon' is a thing, then?" she asked.

"Yes. You should know—you signed a contract handing over yours," Kain answered dryly.

Selma ignored the jab. "Have you ever... taken someone's soul?"

"I'm not that kind of demon."

Something eased inside of her. "Oh. So what do you do? Just fight the female demons?"

He snorted, returning her gaze for a short moment—long enough that she caught the sarcastic glimmer in his black eyes. "You mean am I the good kind of demon?"

A hot blush crept over her face. That's exactly what she'd meant.

"There's no such thing, little one, and anyone who tries to tell you differently is attempting to deceive you. I rule the underworld in my territory—I destroy lives on a regular basis."

Oh. Right. She bit her lip and looked away again. He certainly looked the part of a devilish bad boy, though she wasn't keen on knowing the exact details of what he meant by 'destroying lives.'

"Then why are you helping me? I know you said my scent makes you a bit crazy, but..." But he'd gone above and beyond. There was more to it than pheromones and instinct, that much was becoming obvious.

Kain didn't answer and she turned back to face him. His decadent lips were pinched as he stared at the road.

"You said you knew of Fred because of your mother's journal. Did she go to this place?" she prodded.

"My mother is dead," he finally said. "She killed

herself because she couldn't escape my father. Or me and my brother. When I was seventeen, I went to that shop because I wanted to see if she truly could have lived in safety—happiness—had she gotten away."

Though his voice was detached, distant, the words hit her like a punch to the gut. Before she realized she'd moved, she had pressed her hand to his arm in an attempt at alleviating whatever pain festered inside of him.

"I'm... I'm so sorry. That's horrible. Why was she so unhappy? I thought... I thought most Breeders came to terms with it."

"She had a family before she was captured. A human husband and daughter. She never stopped loving them—or resenting us for taking her away from them. Most Breeders do not have a violent entry into our society, but she did. As did you."

That explained why a Lord Protector would try to save a stranger—he was trying to right the horrors of his past.

Tears stung her eyes and she closed them. "Kain..." There was nothing else to say. She didn't know him well enough to cross the barriers of indifference he had put up around himself, however much the part of her that couldn't bear to see someone suffer screamed for her to do just that.

Silently she placed her lips against the leather of his jacket just above where her hand rested, offering her sympathy and gratitude where words would not be welcome.

The big male grunted at the gesture, but didn't move away. She left her hand in place when she lifted her head again, squeezing gently. Maybe he wasn't a good person in the usual sense, but someone who could experience that sort of grief and come out with the resolve to not let history repeat itself could not be purely evil, either.

"Fuck!"

The sudden outburst made Selma jolt back in her seat just as Kain slammed on the brakes. The car screeched to a halt.

"What...?" The question died on her lips the second she looked out the windshield. Three black cars were parked across the road and seven men in dark trench coats were standing in front of them, arms folded. One of them she recognized.

"No... Kain—it's *him!*"

Marathin. Her tormentor had found her.

"Stay calm." Kain gritted his teeth and released the steering wheel. "There are too many for me to fight and ensure your safety at the same time, but the fact he's not here alone means I can negotiate. He won't want what he's done to become public knowledge."

Selma stared from the nightmare waiting for her on the road to the man by her side. "Please, Kain. Don't let him take me. He'll hurt me, he'll punish me for leaving—"

"It'll be okay." Kain's voice was unusually soft. "Come. I don't want to leave you unguarded in the car."

Giving her one last, lingering look he opened the door and slid out.

Selma took several deep breaths before she managed to shakily unclasp her seatbelt and stumble after him.

Kain waited for her by the hood of the car. He closed his large hand around hers when she reached his side, keeping her steady as he led her toward the man who'd tricked her.

It'd been more than a month since she'd last seen Marathin Hershey, the demon who'd abused her when she was at her most vulnerable. His eyes lit up at the sight of her, that cruel smile she recognized all too well pulling at the corners of his mouth.

Flashes of her time with him passed through her mind's eye—of the humiliation when he snapped the ring around her clit; the fear rising in her throat when she read his intentions for her; the anguish when he forced her legs apart and seated himself inside of her; the horror as he tore apart the people trying to save her from his abuse.

She trembled and clutched harder at Kain's hand. She wasn't alone anymore. She wasn't his victim.

"That's her," Marathin said to his six companions. "Selma, you're safe! You made me very worried, young lady."

Selma shuddered at the eagerness in his eyes as he raked them over her body, before focusing on Kain.

"My Lord," Marathin continued, "I thank you for bringing me my charge. She's been a very naughty girl, running from her procurement in Massachusetts."

Kain made no motion to release his grip on her hand, his focus on one of the other demons. "I am uncertain what makes you think to stop a Lord Protector, Agent, but I suggest you state your business *quickly*."

The demon—apparently the leader of the group—hesitated for a moment. "Sir, we're here to bring the Breeder back to her Procurer."

"The man who let her escape in the first place?" Kain arched an eyebrow. "And who failed to alert the proper channels? Since when does the Agency handle runaway Breeders?"

The leader narrowed his cold eyes ever so slightly. "The Agency's business is confidential, my Lord."

"Confidential or not, you are proposing a Procurer who has failed to keep a new Breeder safe—and who failed to follow protocol once she escaped—simply be handed over responsibility for her care once more. No. The girl is under my protection. I will bring her to her auction—and if she requires further preparations beforehand, I will oversee them." The massive demon by her side seemed to grow even taller as he asserted his dominance.

"You are outside your jurisdiction, young Lord," Marathin said, his voice barely managing to skirt insolence. "The Breeder is mine. She should be of no interest or consequence to a Lord—and I am sure you have a territory to run."

"I'm not going with you!" Selma hissed, pressing closer to Kain as she clutched his hand. "You're a rapist and a murderer, and I'd rather slit my throat than have you touch me ever again."

"I'm sure you misspoke—a Breeder can never *belong* to her Procurer," Kain said, spearing the doctor with a dark stare. "And this one is frightened of you. I think we can all agree it would be much better to let her be handled by someone she's comfortable with."

"I have been a Procurer far longer than you've been alive, young one," Marathin said, the barest snarl penetrating his voice now. "It's no use coddling a runaway—she needs to learn her place, and *I* will teach her. These Agents are here to ensure I'll get what's rightfully mine, and Lord or not... I suggest you don't stand in my way."

"Please, my Lord," the leader of the Agents said, holding out his hand as if he expected him to hand her over like a dog on a leash. "She is not a Pure Breeder—this girl is of no concern to you. I know your father—you're of a strong bloodline, and I would rather not lose any men today. But I will if I must."

They weren't going to let her go.

Selma stared from Marathin's barely contained snarl to the six Agents standing ready to spring into action at any moment. She knew that if she didn't do something now, she would be back in her tormentor's clutches before the day was over. For good this time.

"I am." The words were out of her throat before she could pull them back. "I'm a Pure Breeder."

She would have continued—would have begged them to let Kain take her, told them that Marathin had lied to them to keep her to himself in the hopes that their loyalty was with their kind over the doctor—but she never got the chance.

As if they were one and the same, five of the Agents lifted their right arms and pointed them at Kain. Dark energy swirled around their palms.

"Step away from the girl. Now!" The leader no longer sounded calm. His voice was hoarse with stress, though he didn't take his eyes off the bigger demon.

Kain's hand had frozen around hers, and when the Agent not aiming at him with magic moved closer to pull her away from him, he didn't move to stop it. He simply stood as if carved from marble.

"Kain!" Selma fought against the man who had a firm grip on her, but his strength far surpassed hers. "Help me!"

"Shh, it'll be okay," the Agent murmured, obviously trying—and failing—to soothe her. "No one is going to hurt you, precious one."

"Is it true?" the leader rasped, still not looking away from the Lord. "Is the Breeder Pure?"

"Certainly not," Marathin hissed, taking a step toward her—but the Agent who held her took a step back, lifting his hand in warning. Her Procurer stopped, anger blazing in his eyes. "This is nonsense! You saw the contract—she belongs to me!"

"Gerriol," the leader said, "confirm."

The demon holding her gripped her body tighter, dark magic rising around them both like a nightmarish fog.

Selma gritted her teeth at the slimy touch of it against

her skin, but it only lasted a few seconds before the man gasped and the energy disappeared once more.

"It… It's true," he whispered. "She has no reaction to my magic."

"Please, just let me stay with Kain," Selma begged, writhing against the Agent to free herself. It was no use—he gripped her too tight, even if he was very careful not to hurt her. "I won't run away again, but please—let me stay with him! H-He's a Lord. You don't need to take me to an auction. I'll stay!"

"Have you forced a mating bond with her?" This time the leader snapped his question at Kain, completely ignoring her pleas.

Kain responded with a low, threatening growl. "I have not. She lied to me—I had no idea she was more than a normal Breeder. And neither did you, it would seem. Perhaps you might care to wonder why her Procurer didn't mention this when he sent you after her like a pack of obedient dogs."

"Careful."

"Sir, he's right," one of the other Agents whispered from behind her. "Contract or not, we can't give him a Pure Breeder."

"I'm aware." The leader gave Marathin a long look before he returned his attention to Kain. "We will bring her to the Governor instead, on the condition that you do not try to stop us from leaving with her. If you wish to see her again, you will be invited to her auction as tradition dictates."

Kain's black eyes burned into hers, the anger in them knocking the breath from her lungs. "I have no such desires. Take her."

"No! Kain, I'm sorry! Don't leave me! *Kain!*"

Selma struggled against the demon holding her, desperation flaring in her gut as the only protector she'd had turned his back on her and strode toward his car, leaving her to the very fate she'd signed her life away to escape.

TWENTY-ONE
SELMA

The Governor's mansion was a lavish, old plantation-style building somewhere on the southeastern coast. The Agents wouldn't tell her which state they'd brought her to, but the Spanish moss drooping from the sycamore trees lining the long, winding drive to the mansion tattled on the general geography of their location.

"It would be wise not to mention anything about contracts to the Governor," the leader said as they parked in front of the whitewashed mansion. He'd spent the drive by her side in the backseat of the Jeep, never so much as closing an eye despite them not even stopping for the night and a golden chain keeping her tied to him by the wrist at all times. "Nor whichever Lord claims you as his mate."

"You mean so your friend doesn't get into trouble for trying to poach one of your so-called Pure Breeders?" she bit.

He smiled a half-smile, tugging gently on her chain to make her follow him out of the car. "It would certainly look problematic for him, but Marathin is very old. Demons his age always find loopholes—that's why they get to live as long as they do. There is every chance you'd find yourself as his breeding slave in the end. And trust me when I tell you I've known him long enough to say that you would not enjoy returning to him after he'd taken whatever punishment would befall him for his misdeeds."

"And if I stay silent, he will just give up and let me go?" She snorted as they climbed the stairs, a silent guard opening the door for them. "Somehow I doubt that."

"He will." He gave her a hard look. "As I said, he's very old. He's not dumb enough to throw his life away pursuing a piece of pussy so long as giving you up saves his own skin. Even one as sweetly scented as yours."

"How comforting," she muttered, coming to a sharp stop when he jerked the chain again.

The Agent otherwise ignored her, focusing instead on the demon crossing the grand entry hall, an expectant smile on his ageless face as he looked her over.

"Agent Azir, welcome. And is this the Pure Breeder we were notified of? The Governor's house has been all aflutter with the news of your arrival, precious one."

"Indeed it is, Nemar. I have orders to bring her straight to the Governor. Please let him know we've arrived." The Agent gave the other demon a stern look, breaking the other's trance-like stare at her.

"Oh. Of course. Please, bring her to the second reception room—it's been secured in anticipation of your arrival." The demon gave Selma another look before he turned on his heel and disappeared farther into the mansion.

THE GOVERNOR WAS a demon the size of Kain, his power more than evident despite his human disguise. He was a Lord, Selma was sure. He was only the second of his kind she'd ever seen, and the reminder of the man who'd given her up sent a stab through her chest.

She knew she'd deceived him by not disclosing what she was, but his betrayal had still stunned her. He'd told her he didn't want a mate, yet knowing she was a Pure Breeder had made him turn his back on her in the blink of an eye, sealing her fate.

"Miss Selma Lehmann," the Governor said, a wide smile pulling at his lips as he spread his arms in a welcoming gesture. "My dear, we are so very pleased to have you join us. Come, child. You must be weary from your travels."

Selma raised both eyebrows at him. Did he really think she'd come of her own free will? She raised the hand tethered to Azir's, rattling the chain.

"Yeah. Hi. I'd shake your hand, but—I'm a bit tied up."

The demon Lord turned his disturbing gaze to the Agent, who tensed under his attention. "Agent Azir, one day you must tell me how a group of the Agency's best happened across the first Pure Breeder we've seen in over thirty years—but for now, I hope you'll excuse my lack of hospitality. I am locking down the property until the auction and no unauthorized personnel can be present."

"Of course, Your Excellency." The Agent gave a half-bow and unhooked the chain around Selma's wrist. "I will take my leave."

It wasn't that Selma was sad to see the back of the man who'd forced her to the auction, but when she was alone with the Governor, a new level of unease crawled up along her spine.

She stared up at the huge male, digging her nails into her palms to force herself not to cower in his presence. Whatever it'd been about Kain that had made her relax around him, this demon Lord didn't possess it.

"You have nothing to fear from me, my dear," he said, fixing her with another unsettling smile. "Your scent betrays your anxiety. Has it been a tough few days?"

Was he really asking her about her state of mind?

"Yeah. I guess getting kidnapped can be kind of stressful." She set her jaw. "I know it doesn't matter to any of you, but I want you to know that I don't want this—any of this. You can all act as if it's some great honor you're bestowing upon me, but we both know that all you've got planned for me is rape."

His eyes sparked and he let out an amused chuckle. "Oh, my dear girl! Such lip. My own Valarina is from a time when human women were gentler, but I'll wager whichever Lord wins your companionship will have fun taming you."

He reached out a hand, offering it to her palm-up. "Come, precious one. Let me bring you to your room."

Selma debated not taking his hand, but despite the Governor's friendly facade, she felt the dark steel behind it as clearly as she did the heat emanating from his skin. And something about that outstretched hand very much seemed like a test—one she wouldn't enjoy failing.

His smile turned a little sharper when she gingerly placed her palm against his.

"Very good," he murmured, brushing his lips against the back of her hand. "You'll find the process much easier this way."

He led her up the grand staircase and down a series of wide hallways decorated with lush runners and beautiful paintings. At the end of one such corridor, he fished out an iron key from his pocket and stopped by a heavy door. It had been painted white like the others they'd passed, but was obviously much sturdier.

The Governor laid his hand against the wood and murmured some words in a language she didn't understand. Black light flickered around his fingers before he stuck the key in the keyhole, twisted it, and opened the door.

The suite on the other side had been done up in a style that spoke of centuries past. A large bed dominated the room, but there was also a pretty white sofa set over by a dead fireplace. Two doors led from the main bedroom—and steel bars covered the windows.

"Your bathroom and dressing room," the Governor said, nodding at the two doors.

Selma hesitated, her eyes sliding from the bars to the bed. "What... What happens now?"

The demon chuckled, releasing her hand to rest his on top of her shoulder. She felt so small and vulnerable as she stared at the bed, trying her best to prepare for what came next.

"I smell your fear, precious one," he rumbled, petting her hair as if she were a treasured cat. "But I only have desires for my mate. You will not be penetrated before your auction. I will set it for three weeks from now to allow the Lords interested in claiming a mate to get their affairs in order. Until then, you will spend your time in this room, resting as you prepare to be claimed by the Lord who places the winning bid. Worry not—you will be well-cared for."

Finding strength at his assurance he wasn't going to force himself on her, she turned to look at him. "Will I have any say in who claims me?"

He smiled as if amused by the notion that she wanted any agency over her own fate. "Your mate will be the Lord willing to sacrifice the most and fight the hardest for you. Were you hoping for love, little Breeder?"

She flushed and looked down, angry at the flicker of Kain that danced before her inner eye at that word. It hadn't been love—but being with him was the first time she'd ever felt safe, and she knew whoever claimed her in three weeks...

Well, she was unlikely to feel anything but terror for them for a very long time to come.

"Most mates find contentment in their lot," the Governor said, nudging her chin up with a finger. "Eventually."

"And if I don't?" she asked through gritted teeth.

"Best not to worry your pretty head with such dark thoughts, dearest girl." He removed his hand from her chin, but her relief was short-lived. "Now if you would please undress for me."

She started, her heart slamming into overdrive as she automatically drew a step back. "W-What? You said—"

"I said you won't be penetrated. You will, however, need to be prepared for your claiming. Now don't make a fuss, hmm? It's in your best interest as well."

"How is it in my best interest?" she hissed, withdrawing several more steps until the large bed was between them. "You want to make me more pliant—to make it seem like I'm willingly submitting. I won't. I will *never* submit to any of your kind."

The large demon didn't move, but the air around him seemed to darken and she dug her nails into her palms at the crackle of his power. When he spoke, his voice was soft, but deadly.

"It is in your best interest, Breeder, because there is going to be more than a hundred and fifty demon Lords fighting for the right to seed you. Women have died during their claiming, ripped apart from within as they screamed underneath their new mates. The more pliant you are, the better chance you'll survive.

"I am not about to let you face your auction with anything but the best preparation, so either you strip for me of your own volition, or I will do it for you. But Selma —before I leave this room, one way or another, you *will* yield."

TWENTY-TWO
KAIN

Deceitful, traitorous, *cunning* little bitch!

Kain roared and punched yet another hole in his living room wall before tossing the letter to the floor. Governor Maell had sent out the invitation to *her* auction, and the arrival of it had sent his already spiraling mood into another fit of rage.

Ever since the Agents had taken Selma from his side, he'd been alternating between anger at her for lying to him and a nearly insurmountable desire to kick in the Governor's door and rescue the cursed little Breeder so she would be safe.

He knew what had to happen to prepare a Breeder for auction, and the mere thought of it made bile rise in his throat.

Panting, Kain leaned against the ruined wall. He knew how scared Selma would be during the few lucid moments they'd allow her to have. She'd risked everything to avoid this exact fate—the fate Kain had promised he would protect her from.

He still remembered her cries for him as they took her away. *Why* did she have to be a fucking Pure Breeder?

A snarl made its way up his throat as he recalled those cursed words leaving her lips. She'd pleaded to stay by his side, promised she'd no longer run. He knew they'd been lies spurred by her desperation to avoid an auction, much like she'd lied to him in her failure to mention what she truly was.

Kain understood why she'd lied—he'd been a tool she could use to ensure her freedom, but she would've been dumb to entrust him with that particular secret. He was a demon Lord, after all. She wasn't going to risk him going back on his word, tying her to his side with a mate claim despite his promise to set her free.

No, the anger churning in his gut wasn't because she'd lied. But acknowledging the true cause...

He grimaced and fisted his hands tightly as a wave of intense *longing* rolled through him powerful enough to make his body shake. Every cell in his body had craved her with an intensity like hellfire from the first moment he laid eyes on her, had craved to fuck her, protect her... *claim* her. And it'd been bearable while he'd believed he never could, that forcing his cock inside of her would cause his innate magic to turn her to ash and bloody pulp in his grip.

But *now*...

He glared at the letter beckoning him to come bid on

the pretty girl he'd promised to keep safe, the yearning deep in his gut making it impossible to ignore how much he wanted to win her. Possess her.

He was furious with her for *being* a Pure Breeder, not for lying about it. When she'd just been a regular Breeder on the run, he could pretend like the longing for her from the very core of his being stemmed purely from hormones and that there was nothing he could do about it.

Now he was forced to acknowledge that she could be his. He *could* win her. Claim her. *Possess* her. And by all the stars in the sky, he fucking *wanted* to.

Which was the problem.

He'd sworn to never, ever claim a mate—just the thought of tying a Breeder to his side made him ill. It was all primitive urges, something he'd made sure would never dictate his life until Selma waltzed into his territory.

Selma. Just her fucking *name* made him shiver with need.

It was more than just the instinct to claim and protect. Her gentle spirit, the way she'd obviously ached for his loss when he told her about his mother... Something in those chocolate brown eyes spoke to him more than he would ever willingly admit. Even the way she'd back-talked him like no one else ever dared had increased his fondness for the girl.

Just the thought of having her by his side loosened the tight coil in his chest that'd been there as far back as he could remember.

But she didn't want to be mated to a demon. She was

desperate to be free, exactly like his mother had been, and he would rather die than go through a loss like that again.

He couldn't claim her, even if he got the fuck over himself.

A soft knock on the door pulled his thoughts back to the present.

"*What?*" he snarled at the wood bearing his claw marks. Not one of his underlings had dared to disturb him since he returned, his dark mood hanging over his entire territory like a black cloud.

"Let me in, Kain."

Thomren. No one else would dare to address him so informally, let alone make demands of him.

"No locks are stopping you from entering," he growled, the challenge dripping off every word.

Thomren heaved a sigh, but instead of responding, he pushed the door handle down and slowly peeked in at the destruction in Kain's office. "Oh, my."

Kain glared at him. "What do you want?"

His second nodded at the crumpled letter on the floor. "To talk to you about that. I know the auction invitations went out."

"Out of respect for the pregnant Breeder you have at home, I will say this *once:* Get. Out." Kain flexed his hands, tempering the dark surge of anger simmering to be let out.

Thomren sighed again, his lips flattening to a thin line. "If you must take your anger out on me—if that's what it'll take to hear me—then so be it. I serve you, but you are also my friend. You need to go to this auction."

"You know I can't," he growled. "You of all people know."

Thomren nodded. "I know why you swore you wouldn't claim a Breeder, but this girl... Kain, you haven't been right since you came home without her. Everyone can see it, and we need you here. The females are on the warpath and your head isn't in the game. Without you, the northern border is vulnerable."

Kain snarled, slamming his palm against the door-frame right by Thomren's head. The rush of rage at a challenge to his leadership was a soothing balm that momentarily distracted him from his misery.

"You presume to tell me I'm failing my obligations to my territory? To my *face?!*"

"Aren't you?" Thomren visibly steeled himself as Kain's lip drew up in warning, but he still continued. "When did you last patrol anything but the area near the warehouse where we found her? The females aren't dumb enough to go back there. We need you north—*umph!*"

His voice died on a grunt as Kain grabbed him by the collar, pulled him into the room, and slammed him against the nearest wall.

"Don't you *dare* tell me how to run my territory! I am your Lord, and *I* govern these lands!" Darkness welled within him, flooding through the hand twisted in Thomren's shirt and into the other man. Blood trickled from the lesser demon's nostrils, ears, and the corners of his mouth.

"Kain," Thomren grunted, placing a hand on his Lord's chest. But instead of fighting to break the connection that was harming him, his touch was gentle. "I know your longing. I know what it's doing to you. When I saw Meredith, I *knew* she was mine, and I bid more than I had to claim her.

"*You* gave me the remaining balance; *you* saved me from losing her when it came time to pay up. And that's why I'm here. You need to claim that girl. For your territory, for your own sanity—but also for her.

"She's the first Pure Breeder to be auctioned since your mother. Every unmated Lord is going to be at that auction—I've even heard rumors that Prince Naharan may bid this time. And if you don't claim her... one of them will."

"It won't matter to her who claims her," Kain hissed. "She hates us all the same."

"Even if that's true... it'll matter to you, friend." Thomren's voice was strained, blood seeping faster from his orifices now. He wouldn't remain conscious much longer.

With an effort of will, Kain stepped back, breaking the physical connection to his underling. "Go."

Thomren staggered, clearly fighting to remain on his feet. He rubbed his throat with a shaky hand. "Kain—"

"*Go!* Before I change my mind."

With a regretful look in his direction, Thomren finally stumbled out of the office, leaving him alone with his thoughts once more.

Kain pushed off the wall and began pacing the room, hoping to calm his throbbing head just a little. Somewhere past his fury, he recognized Thomren's bravery—and his loyalty—for doing what he did, and that was the only reason he'd let him live despite his insubordinance.

Kain growled at the empty room as his friend's words echoed in his mind. The Breeder would be auctioned no matter what he did now. In less than a week, Selma would be on her hands and knees underneath whichever Lord won her, and that Lord's claim would be seared into her for eternity.

His knuckles itched with the urge to punch something —or someone. Sure, he could go to the Governor's manor and bid on the girl, but she would be just as miserable with him as she would with someone else. She'd proven that when she'd lied to him about what she was. She hadn't trusted him—she'd manipulated him to escape.

And just the thought of being the cause of her pretty eyes dimming the way his mother's had made his lungs constrict.

The letter lay innocently on the floor, tormenting him with its neatly curved writing. One week. One week, and she would belong to someone else.

TWENTY-THREE
SELMA

"It's time."

Time. It was a concept that'd long since stopped making sense.

Selma didn't have the strength to look up at the sound of Valarina's gentle voice, so she remained facedown on the bed, breathing shallowly through the pain.

At first there had been pleasure after Maell's manipulation of her ring, like there always was. Sick, throbbing, overwhelming pleasure as the dark magic locked within the sleek metal assaulted her trapped clit, driving her to insanity with need.

Yet there'd been no release no matter how much she'd begged, and she'd been aware enough those first few days to comprehend the humiliation all too keenly.

They'd kept her locked in this room since her arrival, Valarina bringing her food and water and urging her to eat to preserve her strength. And Governor Maell visited her once a day to tighten the vicious ring on her throbbing, oversensitive nub of nerves as she screamed.

There was only pain now. Pain and despair.

"Selma," the other woman murmured, the cool touch of a wet cloth pressing between her legs taking the edge off her torment for the briefest of moments. "It's almost over, child."

Selma managed to twist her neck to look at the blonde Breeder. There was so much empathy in her eyes, but no matter how often Selma had pleaded with her, she had never left the door unlocked.

It had been a while since she'd had the strength to plead.

"Over?" she rasped. When a glass of water pressed against her dry lips, she drank on instinct alone.

"Your auction is today. You just need to get through the next few hours and then... then it will be better."

Her auction.

"Better?" Selma bit, finding enough strength in her anger to push up into a half-seated position as she stared at the other woman. "They're... They're going to rape me. Hurt me. *Sell* me. You, of all people..."

She drew in a deep breath, gritting her teeth through the throbbing pain between her thighs as she moved. "How can you say it's *better?*"

Valarina grimaced, but stroked her forehead with a blessedly cool hand. "He hasn't broken you, has he? When I was in your place, I was willing to do anything to make the pain stop. I begged for it when he finally mounted me in that arena. But you're still fighting. I'm sorry. It would have been so much easier for you, but it doesn't change what lies ahead."

She was right. If there was one thing Governor Maell's torture had accomplished, it was to drive home the inescapable fact that there was nothing more she could do to escape the fate that had awaited her since birth. She didn't have the strength left to fight anymore, and no one was coming to save her.

The painful memory of Kain's stern face and black eyes made her heart spasm. Ruthlessly, she pushed it away. The time for fanciful dreaming had passed. Only stark reality lay ahead.

"I don't want this," she whispered as Valarina helped her to her feet.

"None of us do," the other Breeder offered gently. "But we all find a way to live with it, and so will you."

SHE WAS naked during her escort through the old mansion, save for a few chains decorated with precious stones wrapped around her body. Valarina guided her down creaking staircases and into a subterranean level deep in the bowels of the earth. The concrete underneath her bare feet spoke of the basement being from a more modern time than the rest of the house, as did the depth.

Valarina stopped in front of a pair of massive metal

doors at the end of the wide hallway. Here she turned to grasp Selma's shoulder with surprising strength.

"You can get through this. Just submit. It will make it easier."

Submit. The echo of Marathin's demand shivered up Selma's spine and she clenched her hands against the ensuing nausea. These beasts—these monsters—all wanted the same thing. But the price...

Despite the all-consuming pain rendering her weak and hopeless, she understood what the price of submission was. Marathin had taught her that.

"I can't," she whispered. "I... I'd rather die."

Valarina smiled, but only sadness radiated from her eyes. "They won't let you die. You're too valuable. Submit to them, little sister. There are other ways to fight. But first, you must make it through today with your sanity—"

The striking of a gong resonated through the hallway from beyond the metal doors, silencing her.

"It's time," she whispered. She gave Selma's shoulders a squeeze and stepped back as the doors swung open. "Go."

Selma drew in another shuddering breath and turned toward the bright lights shining from within. She was too weak to run, but she thought of refusing to enter of her own will. Let them force her in—let them know she didn't want any part of this sick show.

"It's better if you go," Valarina said softly.

She was right. Selma closed her eyes for a moment, mustering the strength she needed. She was about to experience every indignity a woman could. At least she could spare herself the humiliation of getting dragged in kicking and screaming.

Her thighs rubbed against the tight ring, making her bite her lip as she stepped past the threshold. Sawdust prickled underfoot. She sensed she was in a large arena, that outside the cone of light there was a vast space, but it was too bright for her to see anything but the floor.

"Ah, there she is. Selma, come here, precious one."

A murmur rose from somewhere farther away like the rumbling of distant thunder.

She gritted her teeth and wrapped her arms around her body, shielding it when the sensation of too many eyes became too much to bear.

"There, there, girl. You are perfectly safe. Come to me." A large man appeared in front of her, framed by the blinding light. She couldn't see his features clearly, even as he paused a few feet from her, but she recognized Maell's voice.

He held out a hand to her and she grabbed it on pure instinct, her body recognizing his potential to sate her despite her loathing at the sight of him.

"That's it," the Governor cooed, seemingly content with her body's response to his nearness. "Come to the middle of the arena with me so they can get a proper look at how beautiful you are."

Selma stumbled after the demon as he led her across the sawdust. There was nothing she could do at this point but obey.

Fight them later, Valarina had said. She wondered if Maell knew his cowed mate was capable of such rebellious thoughts.

He stopped next to a cage only a few feet taller than her and nodded at the open door. "Step in, little Breeder."

She hesitated for a moment, but the thought of being locked behind bars seemed unusually appealing—according to Maell, more than one hundred and fifty demon Lords were currently staring at her like she was a piece of meat. Despite everything, she still had enough presence of mind to realize she would be a lot better off securely locked away than out in the open, naked and oozing pheromones.

The door shut with a clank that echoed through the room once she was inside, and Selma felt rather than saw dark energy slither along the bars and over the lock—demonic magic ensuring her safekeeping.

And just like that, the light dimmed.

Selma blinked, her pupils dilating to adjust to the change. Slowly dark shapes came into focus, and she couldn't hold back a small gasp. In a cone shape straight ahead of her sat a multitude of men on raised benches, all their gazes firmly fixed on her.

It was a curious experience. While her first instinct was to cover her exposed breasts and sex with her hands, her body had a more positive reaction to the attention. A hot spasm from her core made her gasp again, then groan low in her throat when a rush of the liquid marking her readiness gushed down her legs.

Murmurs rose from the crowd, and several of the nameless faces moved restlessly. A dark force, faintly visible above the raised seats, started gathering like a thunderhead.

"Yes, as you can see, she's very, very eager to be claimed." Maell grinned, gesturing toward her with a flourish of one hand. "As your invitation stated, she is twenty-seven years old, extremely fertile according to her Procurer, and responds well to rough courting."

Selma closed her eyes and gripped at the bars while she tried to control her abdomen's shuddering at the many males in her presence.

"Those of you who wish to have a closer look at the young lady can approach now before we begin the bidding."

The instant racket of feet moving down wooden steps made Selma jolt backwards, eyes wide. They approached in a mob, the many faces nearing her cage too much to take in all at once. Despite the increasingly persistent throbbing between her thighs, she could hardly breathe from anxiety when they all surrounded her cage, blocking her view with bulky muscle and absurdly wide shoulders. Each and every one of them was as huge and overpowering as Kain.

"Shh, look up, honey."

"Little princess."

"Such a pretty girl."

"Lovely Breeder."

"Supreme."

"So beautiful."

Words cooed at her from all directions, undoubtedly meant to soothe and flatter. Selma whimpered and sunk into a ball on the floor in the middle of the cage as an impenetrable onslaught of pheromones assaulted her mind.

She wanted—*needed*—them. It didn't matter that they'd tear her apart; she needed the strength of their bodies and intoxicating scents, needed to be consumed by everything they were and everything they could offer. *Now.*

Selma staggered to her feet again and fell against the nearest bars, desperate for their heated touch on her bare skin, but when the demons tried to press their hands into the cage to oblige, black sparks flashed between the bars. Snarls erupted from the Lords close enough to get hit, but they didn't withdraw.

"Please," she gasped, pressing her own hands against the cool metal. No sparks flew at her touch, but she couldn't penetrate the magic either. "I need..."

Desperately her eyes darted over the bars and the demons outside in an attempt to find some way she could get to them, only to freeze to the spot when a black gaze locked on hers.

"Kain?"

She was vaguely aware of her mouth hanging open through the shock and continued throbbing in her nipples, clit, and throat. The crowd moved, continuing to block her full view of the owner of those black eyes, and even as she was afraid to believe, hope sprouted somewhere deep within.

Hope. She didn't have the mental capacity to try to reason the cause of this emotion, but she recognized it as she scurried along the bars in an attempt to catch an unobstructed glimpse of the demon's face.

"Kain!"

More words were being slung at her, but she drowned them out. They didn't seem to care that she wasn't responding to them; they were only preoccupied with how her scent and body affected them as they attempted to sway her in their direction.

"Everyone, return to your seats. It's time to begin the auction."

At Maell's command the crowd withdrew like an ebbing tide.

Selma bit down on her already bloody lip, trying her best to stay focused when her body started trembling with need for the males to return with their addictive scent, but it was useless. With a quiet sob she slid to the floor, her desperation to see if Kain was truly there suppressed by muted despair.

"My brothers," Maell boomed somewhere past the hot pulse coursing through her body. "You have seen the Pure Breeder and smelled her readiness, and have been able to judge if she is a suitable match to carry your offspring. If you desire to partake in the bidding to claim her, you may remain.

"Remember the responsibility that lays on the shoulders of a Pure Breeder's mate—her survival and comfort will be your main priority, even to the extent of abandoning your territory, should the need arise. Nothing will be more important than procreating to aid in our battle against the traitorous females and the gods by strengthening our ranks.

"Any who do not wish to make such a sacrifice for this Breeder may leave now."

Silence carried the echo of his words across the arena. Not one demon moved.

"Very well. Remember—killing is strictly forbidden, and if you place the winning bid, you must reactivate the Breeder's ring before claiming her." Once more he gestured toward Selma with a sweeping arc of his left arm. "Brothers... the auction has begun!"

Killing? Why on Earth would killing be part of an auction? Selma frowned, worry mixing with the hazed lust.

"Ten million dollars!"

The shout from the benches came from a blond demon five rows up who got to his feet with a slow, deliberate flexing of his bare chest.

Selma was nearly shocked out of her hormonal daze. Ten *million* dollars? She stared open-mouthed at the male as he walked down the stairs with a saunter that subtly highlighted his perfect body control. When he made it to the sawdust he turned to face the benches, resting his massive hands on his hips covered in tight leather pants. It was the position of someone issuing a challenge.

"Fifteen!" Someone yelled from the benches.

The Lord who'd greeted her when she stumbled through the door—the auctioneer—nodded at the first bidder. "Do you wish to concede, raise your bid, or fight the challenger?"

The blond turned his head and smiled wickedly, his flaming green eyes catching hers for the briefest moment. "I believe the little Breeder would appreciate a fight, Maell."

Another male stood up from one of the closer benches. He looked severe and determined as he made his way to the arena.

The moment his foot touched the sawdust, dark energy gathered in a swirling mass around the demon who'd first bid on her. With a flick of his arm it shot toward the newcomer.

The second bidder snarled and braced for the assault, raising his own dark magic to repel the attack.

The two men squared off, seemingly grabbing dark energy out of the air and hurling it at one another, leaving deep gashes bleeding onto the floor wherever it struck.

It finally ended when the blond launched himself at his opponent, and roaring like a wild beast, he pushed all the dark energy swirling around him at the other at the exact moment his fist connected with his jaw.

The newcomer didn't block the attack swiftly enough, and when he toppled backwards, his shoulders hit the ground with a muted thump. Maell jumped in to place a strong hand on the blond demon's shoulder just as he was about to press both hands against the fallen man's throat.

"Eirath wins! The bid stands at ten million dollars."

Both demons were growling, their eyes locked on each other as if they expected the other to jump at them while they slowly got to their feet. Blood dripped from both of them, and there was no hint of Eirath's casual arrogance when he finally took his gaze from his defeated opponent to look at her again.

His eyes were filled with something feral and terrifying, and though her clit spasmed longingly at the sight, cold terror made its way to her brain. This was what she would be fucked by and bound to for the rest of her life—the monster underneath their disguise that clamored to possess and consume every ounce of her.

Not even her rampant lust could hide the truth of what lay hidden behind their strong muscles and addictive scent—not after seeing what was truly behind the mask.

"Twenty-five million dollars."

The new challenger strode down from the benches. He, too, was clad in leather pants, and his hair was long and wild. He didn't even glance at her as he made his way to the arena, choosing instead to keep his gaze locked on Eirath.

Eirath charged at him the moment he entered the arena, dark magic bursting from both men as the fight began without delay.

This time it took what felt like twenty minutes before the scale tipped in anyone's favor.

Both demons were snarling, their naked chests heaving from their exertion. Several cuts littered both men's bodies from a mix of the dark magic as well blows from fists, elbows, knees, and feet that would have been deadly if they were human men.

It was during one short moment, when Eliath blinked to brush away the trail of blood from his split eyebrow, that the winner was decided. The long-haired demon leapt forward, and with a spinning kick powered by dark energy, knocked the blond to the floor with his heel.

"Loman wins!" Once more the Governor placed a restrictive hand on the winner's shoulder, undoubtedly to ensure he obeyed the "no killing" rule.

Eirath picked himself off the floor. His face was a mask of anger behind the bruises and blood, but he exited the arena with his back straight without looking at the prize he'd lost.

The bidding continued, more often than not followed by a brutal fight, and the gruesome display tore at her soul in a way even the ring couldn't hinder. Though watching them tear each other apart made her sick to her stomach, it also helped her hold on to her sense of self through the onslaught of her baser needs. She abhorred violence in any other capacity than self-defense, and nothing would ever change that.

After three hours the bids had reached a staggering ninety million dollars, and the fights had grown increasingly longer, and—if possible—more vicious. Maell had even had to use his own magic to physically separate contestants more than once.

"One hundred million!" a deep voice boomed through the arena.

Hushed murmurs followed when the owner of it strode down the stairs, his gaze firmly fixed on the current winner.

"Prince Naharan," the Governor greeted him, bowing lightly. "You honor us and the Breeder with your presence. Menor, do you wish to fight His Highness, raise your bid, or concede?"

The demon who'd won the last five fights spat in the sawdust and cracked his neck. "Fight!"

Naharan raised an eyebrow. "That is a foolish choice, brother, but it is yours to make." Dark magic crackled in the air around the Prince when he stepped into the ring.

Menor charged at him with a roar, raising his own magic.

The two collided with a shrill screech like metal being wrought out of shape.

Selma pressed her hands against her ears to block out the sound, and hid her eyes from the dark sparks igniting in the air around the two fighting males. When she looked up again moments later, Menor was slumped on the ground and a chunk of his shoulder was missing. She stared at the bloody mess for five horrific seconds before she realized that Naharan had ripped a piece of his flesh out—with his teeth.

The Prince's lips and bared teeth were bloodied, but it didn't seem to concern him in the slightest. He flexed his shoulders to limber them after the fight, giving the demons on the benches a challenging glare before he turned around to look at her while Governor Maell helped his defeated brother out of the arena.

Naharan was the first since Eirath to pay her direct attention. This time there was no immediate bid to challenge the demon currently eyeing her like she was a piece of meat, and Selma swallowed nervously as he drew closer to the bars.

Was this it? Would this brutish beast be the one to claim her?

He looked so savage it was hardly a stretch to envision his demonic form. His head was shaved, his eyes possessed of a feral fire that made fear squirm in her stomach. He was terrifying—even more-so than the other contestants who had fought to win her, though she couldn't say why.

"You look so soft." His voice was gravelly, still rough from his battle cries. "I will enjoy mating you."

The demon rested a large palm against the cage, snarling when dark sparks burned his skin at the touch, but he kept it there anyway. "Right here, in front of everyone who wasn't worthy enough to win you. You will be my prize, Breeder."

At least he would touch her ring first until she lost the ability to feel anything but hunger for him. Selma closed her eyes, refusing to see the look of triumph on his face when the Governor declared him the winner. Of her. His prize.

"Three hundred million dollars."

The voice cut through the arena, shattering the muted silence after the last fight.

Now the murmur that rose from the crowd was far from muted, and the prince hissed. She heard the swish of his pants as he spun around to meet the new opponent.

Even Maell seemed mildly astonished for a moment, but then gathered himself again. "The bid is at three hundred million! Your Highness, do you choose to concede, raise the bid, or—"

"Fight!" Naharan snarled. "And win."

Selma opened her eyes again now that he wasn't so close and glanced at the benches to see who'd made the bid. The numbers the challengers slung out had all been outlandish to her, but the leap to three hundred million was outrageous, even if what he sought to buy was her life.

The big male who moved down the stairs with an ease speaking of carefully controlled strength made her breath catch in her throat.

"Kain," she whispered.

He was there. He'd come.

For her.

TWENTY-FOUR
SELMA

Neither demon paid her any attention as she crawled back to the near side of the cage. Their eyes were locked on one another instead.

They were more cautious than previous bidders had been, slowly circling each other rather than jumping straight into the fight. She could see them sizing each other up as they looked for weaknesses, the coils of muscle on each man tensing in anticipation.

Naharan sprang into action first. With a roar deep enough to vibrate every bone in Selma's body, he pulled dark energy from the air and slung it at Kain, who raised his own magic just before impact.

Snarling, he returned it with a flurry of black sparks. The scent of singed flesh and ozone mixed with overwhelming male musk.

"You think you can conquer the Prince of Demons?"

Naharan hissed as they drew apart to reassess each other. "I will tear you apart for your insolence!"

He attacked again, and Selma flinched away from the bars when they half-disappeared in a cloud of magic. It spread through the arena in long, terrifying tendrils. They enveloped her cage, and though nothing penetrated between the bars, it shielded her vision of the fight. She could only see shadows moving in the fog and hear their snarls and roars as they fought.

Her heart was pounding in her chest as she tried to peer through the darkness.

Kain. He was here, fighting for her.

For the first time in weeks, wild hope rose within her. If he won, she'd...

Selma frowned. If he won, she'd still belong to a demon. She would still be his to do with as he pleased, but the thought of Kain keeping her...

It made her womb soften and something pleasant that wasn't connected to the hellish magic in her ring spread through her body. He might have been a demon, but he wasn't like the others. He was here despite his reservations about claiming a mate, which meant he was here for *her* sake, not his own.

A howl of pain cut through the mist and she froze. If something happened to him—

It was a strange thing, suddenly having something left to lose. Not only would her newly sprouted hope be crushed, but she'd also be forced to the ground and fucked against her will while he may be in need of help, wounded and bleeding from the fight.

And she'd never get to see him again.

Her hormones and fear were way too overpowering to let her ponder on why the thought of never seeing him again filled her with even more dread than the idea of belonging to the brutal Prince. Yet as she clung to the cage in a desperate attempt to see the two contestants through the dark magic, she knew without a shred of doubt that she needed to be with him.

When the cloud finally cleared, both males were breathing raggedly from exhaustion, and blood was splattered over both their bare torsos.

Kain had a long, shallow gash running the length of his abs, and Naharan was bleeding heavily from his chest and a split eyebrow.

Growling menacingly, completely lost in primal fighting instincts, they circled each other, ready to leap at the first sign of weakness.

This time, it was Kain who attacked first. The blood from the Prince's split eyebrow dripped down, making him blink—and that was all the advantage Kain needed.

Moving so swiftly Selma's human eyes couldn't follow, he threw himself at his opponent. Naharan failed to evade, and Kain struck hard enough they both toppled to the ground, the Lord Protector on top.

While Naharan fought to throw him off, Kain snarled viciously and brought both fists down hard over the other male's face.

A sickening crunch echoed across the arena, followed by absolute stillness.

For a moment Selma thought he'd killed the Prince, but then she saw him move weakly in the sawdust. Blood covered his entire face.

"Kain wins!" Maell's voice boomed through the silence.

At that, the Lord Protector got up from the ground, leaving his opponent in the sawdust before turning toward the cage—toward her.

His black eyes locked with hers through the bars, and though the wildness in them was clear, her body only responded with throbbing lust. There was no fear, no terror of what he was underneath the facade of strong muscles and angular features—only pure and overwhelming need.

Kain turned his head back to the crowd, cutting their eye contact and leaving her with a pathetic sense of longing. She needed him, needed his closeness, his touch, his hard body against and inside of her own.

"This Breeder is mine!" Kain's deep voice boomed across the circular room. "Any of you step foot in this arena, and I will make sure you regret it!"

Maell, who'd managed to get Naharan up, moved toward the center of the arena again. "You certainly have made your interest in claiming her known, brother, but the auction isn't over yet."

Kain's head whipped around, his profile pulling up in

an animalistic snarl as he growled at the other demon and his shoulders tensing with unbridled fury.

The obvious display of aggression made Maell pause, his eyebrows creeping up ever so slightly. Without taking his eyes off Kain he said, "Does anyone wish to make further bids on the Pure Breeder? I remind you, this is your only opportunity to claim her."

Only silence met his statement—silence, and the unwavering growl from the ebony-eyed demon staking his claim.

"Very well. At the price of three hundred million dollars, the auction has ended! Lord Kain, you may claim your mate."

Kain kept his eyes on the auctioneer for another moment. Then with a slow and deliberate scowl, he let his gaze slide over the spectators—his beaten opposition.

And then he came for her.

Selma scrambled to the cage door just as it swung open—undoubtedly at the behest of Maell's magic—and stumbled out into the arena.

She'd barely taken more than a step before he was in front of her—so big she had to crane her neck back to see his still battle-fierce face, and so amped up on adrenaline and testosterone that he didn't even seem to notice his bruised knuckles or bleeding stomach.

"Selma."

Even his voice was rough and filled with the fire that had been drawn from him during the fight, but it was still not fear that made her shiver in his presence. Just the sound of him, of her name on his lips, made her feel... safe. Even naked and surrounded by demons.

Even knowing what had to happen next.

Arms corded with muscle so thick they were practically the width of her torso wrapped around her waist and pulled her the last bit of the way into his embrace. His body burned against hers, but it only made her melt against his powerful form as tension drained from her.

Safe.

She pressed her nose into his chest and greedily inhaled his intoxicating scent. It was so much stronger than she remembered, so much richer.

"You came for me," she choked out over the appreciative noises her throat seemed to be producing without her consent. "You came."

"I promised to protect you." Strong fingers threaded through her hair, pulling her head back gently, but insistently.

Obediently she tipped her head to look up at him.

"Forgive me." It was a hoarse whisper, so unlike the bellowing roars he'd met the other demons with.

Selma blinked in confusion. Nothing about his behavior had suggested that he was anything but completely and irrevocably grappled by the power of his instincts—and the rock-hard bulge she felt against her stomach now, along with the unmistakable fire in his eyes, made it very clear that he was more than ready to claim his prize.

And yet... he asked for forgiveness? For what?

Before she could ask, his scorching mouth and achingly soft lips closed over hers. She moaned and clutched at his biceps. The kiss was rougher than his words had suggested, but Selma was not even close to being capable of protesting. She simply clung to him and let his hot tongue dance with hers as he tasted and teased her in ways that went straight to her nipples and clit.

When he finally released her lips, she was panting, and her head spun with the onslaught of sensation.

The demon grabbed her by the hair again and pulled firmly enough to crane her neck back.

His teeth grazed her exposed throat, causing her breath to explode from her as more liquid trickled down her thighs.

"Kain!"

He growled at her cry. Then he brushed his fingers against her clit, teasing the already painfully tight ring encircling it.

"Kain..." Even through her need for him and the delightful things he was doing, she felt a sliver of unease. Every time someone had touched that cursed ring, they'd done it to control and abuse her.

"I promise." The whispered words sent more shivers through her. "I will always protect you."

Then he pressed his mouth against her forehead, against the mark blinding her to what he was, and twisted the ring sharply.

Her world went white as agony tore through her pelvis, and she screamed. But heat followed the pain, and the need she'd been battling for so long rose like a tidal wave.

This time, it would be sated. *He* would sate it.

Her next scream wasn't from pain. She tore at his shoulders, his chest, and his pants, throwing herself back against his arms to try and get enough leverage to make any sort of impact on his hulking mass.

Growling deeply at her sudden attack, Kain pushed her to the floor. She landed on her backside in the sawdust, but before she could launch herself at him again to make him fill that horrible, empty void inside of her, he was on top of her.

The heavy feeling of his body was just what she needed, and she keened desperately, spreading her legs wide to try and encompass his hips.

But Kain had other plans.

He grabbed her by the waist and flipped her over onto her hands and knees, and something in her brain clicked into place.

This was it—this was exactly how it was meant to be. Selma arched her back and spread her knees as her lust-addled brain made her prepare to submit her weeping pussy to the dominant male snarling with lust behind her. Her liquids practically gushed down her naked thighs in invitation, and when his large hands grasped her hips to angle her pelvis just right, she sobbed.

"Kain, please! I need you, please! Take me, fill me, *make* me!"

Burning hot flesh pressed against her swollen nether

lips as he slid his hands over her bottom to help spread her pussy open.

The stretch was more than she'd anticipated, but also exactly what she needed. When he'd had her in bed before, she hadn't been cognizant enough to note his size —but she did now.

She groaned with raw lust and curled her fingers against the sawdust when the tip of his engorged meat breached her entrance, stretching her dripping lips as it sank in.

The thick head finally popped into her channel, sending shocks of sensation through her as the ridges along the rim dug in, ensuring she'd stay put during the mating. It hurt—there was no two ways about it—and Selma cried out as she reflexively flinched to escape it.

Kain grasped her harder around the waist to keep her from moving, then he shoved his brutal mass deeper.

"Ngh! Yes!"

Her outburst was involuntary. He forced her pussy wide and it spasmed around his invading force. Then those hellish ridges sank into her swollen G-spot.

Stars exploded behind her eyes as her entire body contracted around him, curling in on itself in delicious convulsions. She wanted to scream, but no sound passed her lips other than high-pitched wheezing, burning pleasure constricting her throat and curving her spine.

He paused, her wonderful tormentor, though his hands tightening painfully on her hips suggested that he was more than ready to finish the job and claim her fully.

Through the rush of blood in her ears she could hear him panting harshly behind her, and the shaking from his attempt to control himself transferred into her from where they were connected.

Even in her state of near-combustion, she understood.

The man behind the beast currently clawing to consume her was desperately trying to hold back, worried he was hurting her with his ridges and size.

"Kain." It was near-impossible to force his name out of her throat, let alone focus on anything but his continued stimulation of her G-spot, but the sheer need she had for him to finish this made her gasp it out. *"More!"*

It wasn't that her body hadn't given him every conceivable hint that she was more than ready for everything he had, but it seemed the sound of her voice—the verbal acknowledgment that she wanted it, even as she shook with the effort to accommodate him—settled the last of his remaining concern.

Roaring like a bloodthirsty beast, he rammed in to the hilt, finally conquering her completely.

"Mine!"

His shout drowned out Selma's wail as his cock forced her pussy wide to its core. Beyond the rough stimulation from his ridges hitting every single sensitive spot along her channel, his girth stretched her so brutally she was suddenly thankful for the days her demon captors had kept her in a state of constant arousal. She could have taken him without the preparation—she was built for him—but as she gasped and panted on his monstrous cock now, she knew it would have hurt. Badly.

Now all she sensed was mind-breaking pleasure.

All the warning she had before he pulled back his shaft of searing flesh was his fingers digging into her hips.

Selma bucked and cried as his ridges rubbed her G-spot again, but the pace was too slow for her to climax. Though she could feel the power the demon put into the movement, he was hindered by the grip of her velvet sheath.

Before his head could pop out of her abused cleft, he reversed the movement, making her take him all the way to her core again. And again.

Over and over the beast bred her from behind, growling with each agonizing thrust. With pleasure or frustration at the pace, she didn't know, though at this point she didn't much care either way.

She didn't know how long the slow mating took, didn't know if it'd been minutes or hours, because all that mattered was how perfectly and completely he took her as his own.

She did, however, notice when he released her hips, grabbed her by the scruff of her neck with one hand, and let the other reach around to press against her pulsing clit.

Selma, who'd been in the process of gritting her teeth as he pushed into her body again, jolted back from the unexpected touch. Kain's thighs slapped against her hamstrings and she yelped at the full penetration, but he locked her aching body in place as he forced her to take the dual stimulation of having both her G-spot and clit roughly rubbed at the same time.

It was too much, too intense. She screamed and thrashed, caught between wanting to escape and needing him to never stop, but although she bucked and wailed, the end was inevitable.

With a final, sobbing moan, her entire body seized. Release so intense it made all sounds fade and her vision turn to pure, blinding white took her.

For once there was only pleasure.

SOUND WAS the first thing to return, albeit distorted, followed by the inescapable sensation of being filled to the brim.

Selma whimpered, fidgeting underneath the heavy press against her back to try and reorient herself.

At her first there were weak movements as the man inside of her rose up off her back. Then, with no further warning, he thrust—fully and with no hesitation.

She mewled in response, but despite her initial desire to escape the continued penetration, the smooth, delicious feel of him as he took stroke after stroke in her swollen pussy soon reignited the fire in her blood.

He was moving easier now. The rhythm of his thighs slapping against hers was no longer slowed by her body's vise-like grip; her orgasm had relaxed her channel enough to finally take him as she was meant to.

Kain grunted every time her velvet heat swallowed him to the root. Along with the obscene way her pussy squelched with each of his thrusts, he filled her ears with the sounds of mating so animalistic and primitive she could barely recognize the man who'd tried to save her.

But it was him. He stoked his thumbs gently over the swell of her hips, even as he picked up the pace so much she had to brace her arms against the sawdust to keep on her hands and knees. And when she cried out from the roughness of the pounding she was taking, that oddly calming tone he'd hummed for her before broke through his snarling.

Kain. Kain was the man claiming her as his own—the one taking her like she'd never been taken before.

Her chest and stomach felt strangely light, even as her throbbing sex was heavy with his presence, and the warmth from everywhere his skin touched hers flooded through her veins.

He was *hers*.

The knowledge settled in her brain with overwhelming clarity even as she panted and whimpered for his big cock. He might have been the one doing the claiming, but even through the haze of forced pleasure she knew that this man was hers, body and soul.

Her moment of revelation shattered when the demon pushed her to the floor with his weight in the ultimate display of domination.

Selma gritted her teeth as the angle of her hips changed, making his ridges ride her G-spot hard and mercilessly. His weight kept her in place, forcing her pussy to milk him with each fluttering spasm despite her high-pitched shrieks.

It took mere moments for her violated core to reach the steep climb toward orgasm again.

She strained against his broad chest, using its surface to steady her body against the convulsions making her jerk beneath him. Kain wrapped his arms tighter around her, supporting her clutching hands for better grip.

Despite the pleasure wracking her mind and body, she realized he was attempting to close her into a protective cocoon of his own flesh, and when he bent his head to rest against hers, she felt encapsulated in muscle and heat, safe to lose herself to the pounding rhythm of the massive girth fucking her to completion.

"Let go, Selma." His harsh gasp in her ear was rough with both pleasure and tension. "I've got you—let go."

It wasn't clear to her if it was his rumbling voice that pushed her over the edge, or just the inevitable result of the mating. Either way, her body obeyed him. Violently.

Once again she seized, clamping hard around his still-thrusting cock as her pussy sent a deep, unbroken shock of release through her flesh and bones. It rocked her in full waves, making her scream and thrash until black and red dots danced before her eyes—until she was nothing but a quivering extension of him, locked to his being by his thick cock grinding against every square inch of her most sacred place.

When she was certain she'd die if it didn't end, he took his own release from her.

Roaring, Kain reared up on his hands to slam his hard length in one last time, and the pulse of his essence bathed her cervix in a flush of warmth, filling her past overflowing with spurt after spurt as finally he seeded her.

Dark energy gathered around them, seemingly penetrating her inside and out, searing into the very essence of her being.

His claim.

Selma collapsed. Not a single muscle in her body felt capable of holding her up a moment longer, and when Kain's warm form came to rest over her, her eyelids fluttered closed. For five full breaths there was nothing apart from soul-deep pleasure, *him*, and hot semen coating her still weakly spasming channel.

Then muted noise finally broke through to her blissed-out mind. Cheering. Loud, rowdy cheering and shouting.

"Shh, relax," Kain murmured when she stirred at the unsettling sounds. "You don't have to deal with this."

This? Her brain slowly woke up from the haze, forced to react to the intrusion into her peaceful sanctuary underneath the male.

They were surrounded by demons. Demons who'd seen her get fucked into oblivion—had seen the sacred moment between her and her protector. Her mate.

Embarrassment filled her, banishing the glorious feeling of peace and completion.

Kain growled low in his throat above her, clearly frustrated with the change in her scent so soon after their mating, and raised up.

She felt the loss of his protective warmth keenly, but it was the tugging between her legs when he gently pulled out that made her whimper—despite his release he was still mostly erect, and though his cock was much softer now, his ridges stimulated her swollen passage with the movement.

"Shh, little one." He placed a soothing hand on her backside when he was finally out, ensuring she stayed put despite her desire to curl up on herself. "Stay still."

Selma obeyed, partly because she could hardly move her sore body, and pressed her face into the sawdust, wishing they were anywhere but there. She needed his touch and comfort, needed his scent—and only his scent—to surround her. Not these strangers staring at her body while she was at her most vulnerable.

A booming roar, even louder than the one he'd issued when he climaxed, ripped through the arena, silencing everyone in its wake.

"The Breeder is *mine! My* mate! I have claimed her for all to see. She is under my protection, now and forevermore!"

"We recognize your claim. Now and forevermore, brother," Maell replied. "Take your mate to the victor's chambers—you have both earned your rest."

Kain bent to pick Selma up, holding her to his chest as gently as if she were a child before he began walking.

She cracked her eyes open and looked up at the man who'd made her his in an effort to save her. His brow was furrowed and his soft lips pressed into a thin line in an expression she couldn't interpret.

"What happens now?" she mumbled.

His black eyes shifted down to her, and his features softened in a way that made her chest feel light. "Now, you rest, my little one."

That sounded like a pretty great idea. Exhaustion tore at her mind now that she was safe in his arms again and no longer in the middle of the group of monsters leering over her naked form.

Content that he would protect her, she closed her eyes again and let his steady gait and the thrumming of his heart against her ear lull her to sleep.

TWENTY-FIVE
SELMA

It was the first time in what felt like a very long time that Selma woke up without need burning in her blood.

Sun bathed her face when she sluggishly cracked her eyelids, but the pleasant warmth penetrating all the way into her bones didn't come from its rays. Instead it came from the big man who'd curled his massive body around hers while she'd slept.

Kain.

She remembered everything from that horrible auction, remembered her fear and the forced lust for every man who'd come close enough for her to smell him. And she remembered Kain winning the rights to mount her after bidding an outrageous amount of money.

A faint blush touched her cheeks at the thought of his claiming.

The last time she'd woken up in his arms they'd done pretty much everything but full intercourse, and at the time he'd been a stranger to her, but now... This time had been about so much more than sating the cruel ring.

She was his—and he was hers. The things he'd done to her to prove that fact made her toes curl.

The warm pulse between her legs at the memory of their wild sex quickly reminded her of the downsides to being fucked by a demon, especially one of Kain's size. Though his semen had evidently ensured that she was not as bruised and battered as she should have been after the pounding he'd given her, her inner muscles were still tired beyond belief. He certainly gave new meaning to the concept of a *demonic cock.*

When she tried to experimentally move the rest of her body, the stiffness in every muscle and joint made it quite clear she'd be spending the day in bed, provided she got her way.

Of course, she had no idea if she would be getting her way or if Kain had plans.

Selma looked at the sleeping male who'd obviously ensured she was safe from any danger by shielding her body with his. His legs were wrapped securely around her lower half, not tight enough to cause her discomfort, but definitely enough that no one could snatch her away from him while they slept.

A smile tugged at her lips. Apparently his instincts had taken the full leap into Crazy Town after he'd given in and claimed her.

Her serious mate.

Gently she reached out a finger to trace his eyebrows,

which for once weren't locked in a frown. He looked peaceful in his sleep. Even beautiful. The lack of a scowl or a frown on his handsome face softened the sharp angles, and with his full lips gently parted, there was nothing to suggest he had any sort of trauma in his past or present.

Her heart clenched when she recalled what had happened to his mother and how that had made him swear to never claim a mate of his own. And yet here he was, lying next to her after taking her as his, because that had been the only way to protect her.

"Kain."

Despite her soft whisper of his name, his eyelids immediately fluttered open and his black eyes found hers.

"Hey." She couldn't hold back a smile at the searching look he gave her—as if he thought she'd awoken him because she was in some sort of distress.

He didn't reply, but he held her gaze. The frown was back.

Selma reached out to smooth the line between his brows with the tip of her finger. "I didn't get to thank you before I fell asleep."

"Thank me for what?" He pulled back a little, looking confused. And unhappy.

"For saving me. I thought you were angry with me—that I wouldn't get to see you again. And I was so scared that I'd... that one of those monsters would take me away forever. But then you came."

A small twinge pulled on his face and he breathed out sharply before lifting off her so he could sit up.

"Kain?"

The big male gathered his legs up underneath him and rested his face in his hands with a groan.

"What's wrong?" Selma frowned and forced her own body to sit up, though her muscles protested wildly at the movement.

"What's wrong?" He didn't lower his hands—didn't even attempt to look at her. "Don't fucking *thank* me, Selma. I raped you. Don't pretend like I'm some great fucking hero sweeping in to save the day. I did exactly what every other monster of my kind does to Breeders. And I *liked* it."

Selma blinked. Repeatedly. "You... You think you *raped* me?"

"That's exactly what I did." He let his hands fall to the duvet covering both of them, giving her a bitter look. "We both know you have no choice in the matter once your ring's been manipulated. I thought I could claim you without... without giving in to the beast inside, but I couldn't. I didn't. I did to you what my father did to my mother over and over and over again, so don't fucking thank me!"

That light feeling in her chest that'd been present since their mating squeezed uncomfortably. Selma gave him a stern look.

"Look, I wanted what you did—all of it. It's not just about the stupid ring. Don't you get it? I was hoping and praying you'd come. And yes, I knew what that would mean. Does it really upset you that much that you liked having sex with me? I liked it too."

Kain gritted his teeth and looked away from her. "That's the ring talking, and you know it. We're both still wrapped up in the post-claiming haze."

Selma barely avoided rolling her eyes. He had severe issues after what happened to his mother, and she would just have to be patient with him.

"So what did you plan would happen after you claimed me? I mean, you must have had a plan, right? Is it to never touch me again? Because I gotta tell you, you paid an awful lot of money just to keep me around to make your morning coffee."

His growl made her jump, then wince thanks to the sore muscles in her abdomen and lower back.

"I did not *purchase* you as a slave. I bid a sufficient amount that none would wish to bid any higher, thus lowering the risk I'd lose you in a fight. And my plan was, and is, to bring you to Colorado." The demon sent her a glare, then pushed off the bed.

Selma watched him as he walked to the other end of the luxurious room and disappeared behind a door. He left it ajar, and she could hear water running.

To Colorado. He was going to bring her to the sanctuary... was going to give her her freedom despite the money he'd spent and the fight he'd won to keep her as his.

Her chest gave an achy spasm. He was going to give her up.

Perhaps he was right—perhaps she was lost in the afterglow of everything that had happened, because a few weeks ago she would have been over the moon with gratitude. Now... she just felt oddly deflated.

The faucets in the bathroom turned off, and Kain reappeared with a bowl in one hand and a cloth in the other. He was still naked as the day he was born, and Selma found herself suddenly distracted from her more morose thoughts. The aching in her chest traveled south of her navel, turning rather more pleasant, albeit still painful.

Kain was a very attractive man. She wondered briefly what he looked like underneath his human disguise, but then lost interest in pursuing that particular train of thought when he bent to place the bowl by her side of the bed and his abs flexed in the process.

"What are you doing?"

"I am tending to my mate. Can you move on your own?"

Tend to her? Intrigued, she glanced at the bowl. "I can move. What do you have in mind?"

He sent her an admonishing glance. "Swing your legs over the edge, little one."

Slowly and awkwardly, Selma obeyed, though it could hardly be classified as "swinging" when she finally pushed her legs out from under the duvet to dangle them over the edge of the bed.

Kain knelt in front of her and proceeded to place his large hands on her knees.

The sweet ache between her legs heated further at the contact, and she winced as her tired muscles attempted to clench in anticipation.

Then he spread her legs with a firm press of his knuckles against her inner thighs, and she couldn't hold back a whimper.

Kain quickly looked up at her with a concerned frown. "Did I hurt you?"

"No." It wasn't a lie—what had hurt her was her body's immediate and overwhelming attempt at welcoming him. Her pussy throbbed, and overworked muscles were forced to tighten as moisture began seeping from her core.

For a moment he looked like he was about to press her further on the matter, but then his nostrils flared and a delicate shiver traveled through his naked body.

"Mm."

It was his only verbal acknowledgment of her predicament, but when she glanced down, she saw his cock strain thick and pulsing between his thighs, eager to heed her body's call. She stared at it, marveling at how something so grotesque could feel so good.

Without further comment he grabbed the backs of her knees and slid her closer to the edge of the bed, ensuring that her exposed mound was easily accessible.

Before Selma managed to as much as squeak, he'd released her and dipped the cloth into the bowl.

She watched him in silence as he smoothed the lukewarm cloth through her curls, rinsing off the dried semen with care that seemed impossible for hands his size. Again and again he rubbed the cloth over her pussy, delving into every fold and even circling her ringed clit a few times.

It felt amazing, and so very different from anything she'd experienced before in the hands of demons. There was no pressure to arouse her, no demand being made of her in any way—just the warm, wet slide of the cloth over her velvet heat as he gently cared for her.

She sighed in contentment, and without really thinking about what she was doing, placed her hands in his mahogany hair.

Kain paused, his large hand coming to rest atop her thigh.

It was an instinctive reaction to stroke her fingers through his glossy strands before grabbing a tighter hold of his head and guiding it to her warm center.

His breath ghosted over her slick folds, sending a delicious shiver through her. Then his tongue flicked out to follow the seam of her pussy from the bottom to the small nub of nerves at its apex.

Selma's breath exploded out in a hoarse gasp. She hadn't been aware she'd been holding it back, but when Kain's mouth opened to suck on her, it left her lungs in soft pants.

He was slow with her, delving his tongue to taste every part of her and only giving her clit a few deep suckles as he explored her soft flesh with the same care he'd shown while cleaning her. Even though her body ached as she clenched and moved for his lips and tongue, his pace was gentle enough that the pain was manageable.

When her gasps turned to needy whimpers, he pushed the cloth aside so he could brush her lips fully open with his thumbs and focus his efforts on her tight clit. Pleasure shot through her, now sharper and much more demanding on her sore body, but it was exactly what she needed.

"Kain!" She called his name as he brought her closer and closer to the edge. A part of her wanted more from him—wanted to be penetrated and claimed all over again —but the demon kneeling between her legs remained excruciatingly careful.

When her muscles finally seized and she cried out in climax, he'd still only stimulated her clit.

Selma slumped over him, resting her shaking arms against his dark hair. Her body was sore from being worked so soon after the rough mating, but endorphins overpowered her discomfort.

"Thank you," she murmured, letting her fingers slide through his soft hair in a gentle caress.

A kiss from his scorching lips skimmed her inner thigh. "My pleasure, little Breeder."

Kain's voice was husky and dark, sending a shiver through her tired body. It prodded at her instincts to awaken and be of service to the male who'd pleased her so, and when she glanced down past his head, she saw the unmistakable sign of his need.

"Let me help you, too."

She smiled when he frowned up at her, then slid her palms over his strong, wide shoulders. He rose obediently when she tugged at his arms, but when she leaned forward and let her tongue swipe at his cockhead, he jerked back as if she'd burned him.

"What?" Selma knotted her brows in confusion. "Doesn't that feel good to demons?"

"Of course it does," he growled. "But I will not take pleasure from you again. I'd rather die than take advantage of you one more time."

Oh, for Heaven's sake! "You're not taking advantage of me! Seriously, can't you employ those damn voodoo senses you guys run around with to know that I'm not scared of you? That I like—"

A roar interrupted her mid-sentence, making her jaw clamp shut from surprise.

"I will not take pleasure from you! You are high from hormones and don't know what you want!"

Kain glared down at her, but seemed to soften at the sight of her startled expression. He sighed deeply and reached out a hand to caress her cheek.

"I will tend to you if you so desire while you're still in my care, but I will not be penetrating your body, nor will I accept a release from you. Once you regain your senses, you will be thankful. Do not press me on the matter, little one."

Selma opened her mouth to argue, but his eyebrow quirked in warning made her change her mind. Nothing would be gained from fighting over it right now.

She wasn't certain what had changed in her to make her actually *want* to be with him like that, but she did know something deep inside needed to feel the brutal stretch of his claim just one more time before they separated.

Ignoring the twinge in her stomach at the thought of saying goodbye, she closed her eyes and let her exhausted body collapse back onto the bed. She'd need rest before she'd be capable of anything, much less spreading her legs for him again.

And she would feel him move within her before he gave her up—no matter how much of a gentleman he was planning on being about it.

TWENTY-SIX
KAIN

It was a pretty surreal experience sitting in his car next to what felt like the small, soft center of the entire goddamn universe—breathing in her intoxicating scent and knowing she belonged to him.

At least for a little while longer.

"Kain?"

He didn't need to turn his attention away from the road to know her gentle brown eyes were resting on him; he could feel her gaze on his face like rays of morning sun.

"Mm?"

"What... What will happen to my parents? After I disappear? Marathin..."

Kain curled his lip at the mention of the demon who'd dared to hurt his mate—who had a *contract* on her. "He will not get to them. I have had them under surveillance since you were taken in, and I will continue to do so until they have lived out their natural lives. You do not need to worry about their safety."

"I'll never get to see them again, will I?"

The sadness in her voice made that uncomfortable, soft thing inside him he'd forgotten even existed before she waltzed into his life throb uncomfortably. It was so much worse now that his claim tied them together, as if the magic had somehow forged an invisible, but physical connection from her to his heart.

"No," he said. "I don't think you will, little one."

The soft touch of her fingers on his leather-clad arm made the permanent erection between his thighs twitch eagerly. It hadn't settled since he'd tasted her sweet pussy three days before, turning every moment of his waking hours into a painful reminder of what he'd done.

Yet even though his insides felt tight with shame and horror from forcing himself on her, his entire body yearned to claim her again. The possessive instincts that'd been released when he mounted her tore at his resolve, demanding that he take her. She was his mate, his Breeder, and when he'd been inside of her, the pain he carried had been blitzed away by the bliss of her wet embrace.

That pain had returned a thousand fold when he regained his senses and realized what he'd done. He'd told himself he was attending her auction to save her—but the possessive roaring in his blood when he'd seared his claim into her had spoken of another truth.

"Will you tell them that I am okay? Somehow make them understand that they don't need to mourn?"

"I will try to find a way."

"Thank you. So much—for everything." She withdrew her hand and blew out a sigh. "Seriously. I won't ever be able to repay you—three hundred *million* dollars? Can you really just pull that out of your budget?"

Some small, primitive part of him wanted to boast about how he could provide for her—and remind her how he'd won a fight against the Prince of Demons to claim her. Apparently she didn't quite understand how much more significant beating demon royalty was compared to the price he'd paid for her.

But he didn't need to nudge her already flaring urge to submit to him any further. It was quite obvious from how she'd been acting that his claim was wrecking as much havoc on her mind as it was his.

"I have to shift some assets around to pay in full, but it will not ruin me. You don't need to think about repaying me anything—it's a small sacrifice compared to what you have to give up because of my kind."

She went quiet next to him, and he smelled a touch of sadness in her otherwise delicious scent.

Kain bit down on his urge to coo at her to make it go away, forcing his focus to stay on the road. She had every right to feel sadness, and the more he indulged his need to treat her like a mate, the tighter he'd get wrapped up in the overpowering instincts that would refuse to let her go.

SELMA WAS quiet beside him until they finally stopped at a small hotel off the highway. It wasn't exactly as high-class as he'd have preferred to offer his Breeder, but at least it was better than the seedy motel they'd stayed at when she was still on the run.

"If we look for something more suitable, we'll have to steer too far off course," he explained as she looked at the Best Western he'd chosen for the night. Mild shame made him slam the car door hard enough to make her jump, which immediately had his protective urges rising. Being mated was seriously hard work.

"You know I'm not exactly a glamour girl, Kain. This is more than suitable." She gave him a sardonic look softened by a small smile. "Come on. I'm tired from the drive."

Frowning, he followed her in to book their room. Despite the lingering sadness in her smell, she still seemed completely at ease around him. Though his claim would continue to have an impact on her for the rest of eternity, he knew of no other newly-claimed woman who acted this calm right after being mated. Even when Breeders had experienced a smooth transition into their new lives, they tended to be skittish and traumatized in the weeks after an auction.

Selma, who'd been so terrified of his kind she'd risked her life to escape them, now seemed to be in complete balance, as if the brutal claiming in front of his peers had mellowed her.

The girl remained a mystery to him.

When they finally made it to the small, plush room, Selma didn't even bother giving it a cursory look before she stripped down right in front of him.

Kain bit the inside of his cheek as he watched her step out of the pile of fabric at her feet and head for the bed —naked.

He'd brought her a few changes of clothes, along with a silken nightgown, but she ignored the luggage he'd carried in as if she had no grasp of how close he was to losing the iron grip he had on his self-control. He'd wanted to throw her down and ravage her all fucking day, and the sight of her bare form didn't exactly help that.

She was still a bit too thin for his liking—Breeders needed plenty of roundness to sustain the rough needs of their mates —but the Governor had obviously ensured she'd been properly fed since coming into his care. And she was a beautiful girl, with that long, dark hair, full lips, and shapely legs.

When she bent over to climb into the bed, he caught a glimpse of the dark thatch of hair between her parted thighs. Flashes of having her on her hands and knees in front of him, the soft cleft hidden there opened wide around his brutal girth, made him groan low with desire and his cock throb painfully.

The inviting sight of her round ass and soft pussy disappeared from view when she slipped underneath the covers, but his need stayed exactly as urgent. It wasn't just the blissful sensation of being buried balls-deep in her tight cunt that had him flexing his hands in a desperate attempt at retaining control—it was everything about being with her and feeling her small body soothe his own in ways he never thought possible. He needed to touch her skin, suckle her breasts, taste her maddening juices—

"Kain?"

He jerked at the sound of her voice, somehow managing to tip his spiraling thoughts back into the present.

"Yes?" Even to his own ears, he sounded unusually gruff.

"Come to bed?"

Maybe she was purposefully trying to torture him.

Moving stiffly, he removed his shoes, socks, coat, and jeans. The erection tenting his boxer shorts was painfully obvious, but she'd be blind if she hadn't spotted it already, and he didn't want the rough material of his pants making her uncomfortable.

When he walked hesitantly toward the bed, Selma lifted the blankets, displaying most of her glorious nakedness with the invitation.

Kain climbed in next to her, careful not to touch any part of her body. He hadn't even settled before the girl rolled over, hiking a thigh over his legs and wrapping her arm across his chest.

"You're so tense," she murmured.

He could feel the soft press of her breasts against his

side and the heat radiating from her core against his thigh.

"You know why." There was no point in pretending he wasn't fighting tooth and nail to rein in the raging monster fighting to take her by the hips, flip her over, and force her to give up that tantalizing little cunt. "You're playing with fire."

Nimble fingers stroked over his skin. "I know you're struggling with the attraction between us. I mean, it's not like it's a secret that you want to make love to me." She raised her leg a little higher, bumping gently against his rock-hard cock for emphasis.

Kain snorted. "What I want to do to you doesn't even come close to being described as *making love*. How have you forgotten what I am behind this disguise? You know what it feels like to be taken by a demon—I want to consume every last ounce of you. Don't test my resolve."

His mate went quiet for a little while, but never stopped caressing his chest. It was oddly soothing, though every touch sent burning heat to his crotch.

"Do you know what Marathin did to make me risk everything and run?"

Kain drew in a deep breath. Just the thought of her helpless and alone like he'd found her, running from the man who'd tried to make her his, sent scalding rage through his veins, dampening the lust in its wake. He'd seen the ancient being's desire for her when he and the Agents cornered them, and he knew what twisted desires coursed through his kind's veins.

"He twisted my ring and made me beg for it. He

enjoyed my humiliation. He threatened me with how much pain I would experience if he sent me to an auction. He manipulated me into pleading to be his so I wouldn't have to endure it.

"He took everything from me. My body, my *soul*... even my mind, because he wanted to possess me in every way possible.

"I don't think you can fully understand what it feels like to be at someone's mercy like that, because you will never have to submit the very core of your being to anyone. *He* wants to consume every ounce of me, until there's nothing left but an empty shell he can fuck and breed."

She looked up at him, catching his gaze with those bottomless chocolate eyes. "Trust me, I know what it's like to be consumed by a demon. That's not what it's like to be with you, even when you make me open for your ridges like he did, fuck me as hard, and say that I'm yours. The difference is that I want you to, because you give me everything you are when you do—because you're going against every instinct you have to give me the freedom I told you I wanted.

"You're not like him. You're not like any of the monsters that showed up at that auction to win the right to force me into slavery for the rest of my miserable existence."

Something felt sore in his chest—the same something he hadn't even been aware existed before he woke up with her in his arms for the first time. He was starting to recognize his claim as an odd and not entirely pleasant mix of fierce, protective urges and something soft and vulnerable that belonged just to her.

"I still have the instincts, even if I fight against them. You don't seem to understand how badly every fiber of my being wants to claim and possess you."

To his surprise, her only reaction to his shameful admission was to put her head back down on his shoulder after kissing his skin.

"I will rip him apart for what he did to you. I don't care if it'll start a war."

"I hope you will."

Her softly spoken admission should have shocked him —she was so gentle and kind, and hearing her say that she wished for someone's painful demise was rather out of character. However, all he felt was warm satisfaction from knowing that she would appreciate the revenge he'd take on her behalf.

They lay in silence for a time before she said, "Tell me about your mother."

Kain turned his head to look at her in the soft light from the bedside lamps. Her eyes were open, but she seemed focused on the hand she kept stroking across his chest and stomach through his T-shirt.

He'd never really talked about her, or about what happened, with anyone besides Thomren. His memory of her was painful and bitter to both him and his brother, and his father could not take the mention of her. His father had once come across an old necklace of hers several years after her death, and had ripped apart several rooms in a fit of rage just from the sight of it.

But not a day went by that Kain didn't think about her.

"She was beautiful. I remember her long black hair and caramel eyes. And she had very soft hands.

"She was in her mid-twenties when my father won her at the auction, and already married to a human man. Her daughter was about a year old. When I was born, she'd been with my father for four years, and not a day went by that she didn't plead with him to let her return to her old life.

"She missed her husband and daughter desperately. My father thought that having me would help her accept a life by his side, but it didn't. She had no interest in me, or my brother when he came along three years later. I remember her referring to us as devil spawn and the product of rape when my father asked her to take care of us.

"Sometimes, when we were very little, she would hold us. She'd cry while she did, but I still remember the feeling of her arms around me. I used to wish I was bigger so I could hold and soothe her instead."

He wasn't entirely sure why he was telling her this, but the words flowed without effort from the place he'd locked away the memories of his mother. The soft sensation of the girl in his arms and her soothing smell seemed to encourage those memories to rush to the surface, eager to be shared with someone who might understand how his mother had felt.

"How old were you when she died?" Selma asked. She moved closer to his body as if she knew how her nearness soothed him.

"I was nine." He stroked her hair gently, pausing for a moment when the bitter pain of the time around his mother's suicide resurfaced. "She'd been growing more and more desolate. Refused to have anything to do with my brother or I, threatened us while my father was in the room. Told us she would kill us in a heartbeat if it meant getting her real child back.

"I don't know if she meant it, or if it was an attempt at making my father set her free, but he couldn't ignore the threat. He had finally had enough of her refusal to accept that she was his mate, not the wife of her human husband, and he did the only thing he could think of to break through her resistance.

"He kept her in the ring's thrall for weeks, only giving her breaks so she could eat and sleep. My brother and I... we heard her scream day and night while he mated her, and cry inconsolably the few hours he didn't. We begged him to stop, because the sound of it... all of it... it was...

"But he said he couldn't, that she was sick and needed help—that he had failed in his duty as her mate to make her content in her life with him, and that he had to rectify his mistakes to save her.

"So he took her until the ring finally broke her. I think something in her mind eventually snapped. She became docile, calm... and he thought she was saved. That she'd just need a little time to recover before she'd become the mate and mother she was supposed to be.

"The first day my father left her side to attend to his business, she slit her wrists and bled out before he returned to find her."

"I'm so sorry," Selma whispered into his shoulder. She pressed her lips against the fabric of his shirt, constricting her arm around his chest and easing the ache there. "For how you lost her, but also for the way you grew up. You should have been cared for by the woman who brought you into this world, despite the circumstances."

He shrugged, fighting the pull of the chasm in his gut at the too-vibrant memory. "She couldn't handle losing her first child, nor her husband. It might have been different, had she not had either when she was caught."

"Did you ever meet her? Her older daughter?"

"My father killed them both the day after she died. He was wild with sorrow and fury and blamed them for taking her away. I never met either of them."

But he'd thought about her—his human half-sister. He'd even wondered if they'd had anything at all in common, despite being of different races.

"Kain."

The pity in her voice cut through his memories, and he looked down at her to see it reflected in her eyes as well.

"Maybe now you see why I can't do to you what my instincts are screaming at me to do." He searched her eyes for the dawning realization of what horrors he was saving her from, but all he saw there were empathy and sorrow.

Selma moved her hand from his chest to his cheek, cupping it gently. "I'm not like her. And you are not like your father."

He opened his mouth to reply, but she pressed her lips over his before he could find the words.

Softly and gently she kissed him, and the tenderness of it made heat rush throughout his body, soothing the old pain in its wake.

"Let me prove it to you," Selma mumbled without lifting her head from the kiss. "Give me this one night to prove to you that you are so much more than your past and your instincts." Another kiss, so soft he could have imagined it. "Let me repay you just a little of everything you've done for me."

TWENTY-SEVEN
KAIN

He should have said no—should have refused her offer, because he knew he'd never get enough if he allowed himself another taste. But it wasn't instinct that made him pull her up so she lay on his chest, nor his body's desperate need that slowly answered her kiss.

It was that soft ache that seemed to be so tightly connected to the little Breeder he'd claimed. It bloomed from where she rested against him, down through his stomach and all the way out into his fingertips, where it transformed into something else—a lightness that soothed his fear.

Her kiss turned just a tad more demanding when he gave in, the pressure of them against his increasing ever-so slightly before her tongue dipped into his mouth.

Kain accepted her without hesitation, his hands traveling down her back until they rested around her full ass before he even realized what he was doing. But Selma just hummed appreciatively at his eagerness, flicking her tongue against his in light, teasing movements that had his head spinning and his cock throbbing.

Just when he was about to lose the will to hold back, she broke the kiss. He caught the mischievous glimmer in her eyes before she dipped her head back down, this time going for his jawline.

With light nips and kisses that went straight to his groin, she traveled down to his throat, continuing the blissful torment. Kain groaned under her ministrations, clutching harder at her backside to keep himself anchored. Her feather-light caresses chipped away at his self-control slowly but inescapably, until his entire body pulsed with the same bone-deep need as his hard cock.

"Selma," he gasped, squeezing his eyes shut in an attempt at keeping himself in check when she pushed his shirt up so she could close her warm mouth over his left nipple. "I can't... *oh!*"

Her deep suction on the little bud sent sharp jolts down his spine, momentarily ruining his ability to form words. No one had ever touched him this way. The human women he'd brought home had enjoyed the look of his body, but he never let them explore much; he had always been too focused on sating the need for a climax between a female's thighs.

"Yes, you can," she said once she lifted her head to focus on his other nipple. "This is how I feel when you touch me."

His eyes rolled back in his head when her pert little tongue swiped out, sending more shocks though his spine.

Kain was so absorbed in the sensations, greedily trying to focus on every lick and every suckle, that he didn't realize where her hand had disappeared to before it grabbed at his cock inside his boxers.

He hissed in surprise, squeezing her ass hard enough to make her mewl.

With some unknown strength of will, he released his grip on her, placing his hands along his sides with his palms down. He wanted nothing more than to grab and stroke her soft body before flipping her over and burying his aching shaft deep inside of her, but the pleasure of her gentle seduction was too intense to ruin with his impatience.

"So eager," she murmured as she stroked her hand up along his pulsing member, freeing it from his boxers. She turned her attention from his torso to the pole of flesh rising proudly between his thighs, biting her lip as she did.

The sight nearly made him come undone.

She was flushed with desire, her breathing coming in small pants, though her need wasn't as unnaturally all-consuming as when she'd had her ring manipulated. His body clearly excited her—not even the pronounced ridges along the edge of his cockhead scared her off—and the heavier scent of her arousal had him clutching at the sheets to stop himself from taking charge.

"I want to bury myself in your slick little pussy," he growled, choosing to voice his desires instead of acting on them. "Every inch, until my balls slap against your gorgeous ass and you cry out from pleasure."

Selma made a squeaky little noise, a mix between a pant and a whimper, and squeezed her hand harder around his cock as she stroked back down with a jerking movement that made his hips lift eagerly.

"Let me touch you, little one," he pleaded. "I want to fuck you, need to feel you tighten around me."

Her lips quirked into a smile, but her eyes stayed on his thick girth. "Soon."

Kain would have argued—was moments away from begging—but before he managed to open his mouth to do so, she wrapped her other hand around his shaft, moving both in tandem to squeeze his hard length.

"This feels amazing," she murmured, not taking her eyes from what she was doing. "You're so hot, so thick... I love how silky-soft, yet relentlessly hard you are against my palms."

He groaned unintelligibly, way too focused on the sensation of her small hands massaging him to take in her praise. He'd known lust since he hit puberty, and had known the pleasures of the flesh for the same amount of time, but never had he felt what she awakened in him with every caress and every squeeze.

The tender thing in his chest throbbed and mingled with the hot burn of lust, leaving him suspended in a near-maddening state of consciousness. When she bent over to lick up along his pulsing head, he growled hoarsely. His fingers dug into the mattress, carving his desire for her deep into the fabric.

"You taste like sex," she breathed, sending shivers through him as the air hit his sensitive skin. Her voice had gone thick and a little shaky with her own lust. Then her tongue darted out again, flicking in between two ridges along the rim, teasing the cartilage meant to keep her in place while he mated her.

The sharp spike of pleasure surprised him—everything about that particular part of his anatomy was about force and pressure, and he'd had no idea how responsive the ridges were to gentle touches.

Selma apparently took his involuntary moans as encouragement, choosing to close her full lips around one of the ridges so she could suck on it.

His vision blurred to black at the pure blast of electric pleasure numbing his entire body. When his breath finally exploded out of his chest and his vision cleared, he was staring down at his mate's flushed face. Her long hair was splayed over the pillow, and a grin spread across her lips despite the low snarl rumbling through his chest and the tight grip he had on her shoulders as he pinned her to the mattress.

Unconcerned with the sudden shift in position, she wrapped her arms around his neck. "Liked that, huh?"

How the hell was she so calm? He could both smell and see the unmistakable signs of her arousal, but even as his heavy cock rested on her stomach, more than ready to penetrate her to the core, she showed no fear of what would happen in a few short moments, nor any desperation to hurry it along.

His confused pause let her pull his head down, and then her lips met his.

Kain released her shoulders as they kissed, letting his fingers smooth down over her breasts and the gentle curve of her stomach until he felt the short hair marking the edge of her sex. When he brushed over her clit, she gasped into his mouth, digging her nails into his nape.

He needed her more than air, ached to feel her velvet heat spread open for his unrelenting girth and make her spasm and clench until she surrendered her very life essence to him in a full, deep climax.

Thankfully, she was willing. Her soft curves molded to his touch, her legs parting wide so he could prepare her, and she didn't tell him to hold back. Finally the sweet torture was over.

When he dipped his fingers lower, they came back soaking wet, and he growled appreciatively. She was ready to join with him. As much as he'd enjoyed pleasuring her the morning after the auction, he didn't have the restraint to repeat it. One taste of her sweet slickness right now and he'd risk losing control again, this time doing much worse than simply flipping his woman over in the process.

Beneath him, Selma pulled her head back from the kiss to look up at him with heavy-lidded eyes. "Take off the rest of your clothes. I want to feel your skin against mine when we make love."

Make love. There was that phrase again.

Kain pulled back from her to do as she asked, ripping the T-shirt over his head and pushing the boxers off his legs without getting out of bed. He didn't know how to make love, only how to fuck, but if it was what she wanted, he would do everything in his power to give it to her.

The small, appreciative hitch in her breath when he knelt naked on the sheets in front of her warmed his skin from the tip of his toes to the top of his scalp. She desired him every bit as much as he desired her.

She belonged to him.

"Come here."

He couldn't hold back a smile at her command. Even the first time they'd been in bed together, she'd ordered him about without hesitation, apparently completely oblivious to the power difference between them.

It was an oddly endearing trait.

Obediently he ranged over her again, holding his weight on his arms so he didn't crush her. He hovered over her for a short time, drinking in the wanton expressions fluttering over her pretty face when he nestled his hips between her thighs.

"Ready?"

He could hardly recognize his own voice, rough as it was with lust, but also with... tenderness. It wasn't exactly a common trait in a demon Lord seconds away from penetrating his willing Breeder.

What is she doing to me?

The thought was fleeting and swept away on a rush of scalding need when Selma nodded, breathily consenting. "Yes."

Resting on one arm, he wrapped his other hand around the base of his heavy cock, aligning it with her dripping slit. Every single drum of his pulse brought the urge to mate his female to a more desperate level, as if the instincts fighting to consummate with her could sense the wet kiss of her swollen labia as keenly as he could.

The pleasurable shock that rocked through him when her soft flesh spread open made him moan. His ridges caught in her eager opening and she hissed in pain.

Without thinking he pulled back, severing the blissful contact to her velvet heat. Even though every instinct in his body and mind roared at him to ignore her complaints and just ram in to the hilt, his fear of harming the Breeder he'd claimed as his own overrode it by a wide margin.

But before he managed to move away from her spread thighs, her hands shot out to grab his hips in a desperate attempt at keeping him in place.

"No, don't stop."

"I'm hurting you," he rumbled. "Without the ring—"

"I don't care!" Fire in her voice made him look up from her inviting slit, catching her hazy gaze.

"Selma—"

"I want to feel you without the ring drugging me. Please... I don't care that it hurts." She dug her fingertips into his hips, attempting to make him apply pressure against her opening again.

He moaned low in his throat at the temptation. Every part of his body ached to be joined with her, and as she lay open and willing in front of him, nothing seemed more enticing than to give in. But...

"I don't want to force you."

At his panted words, taut with the restraint of holding back, the little Breeder rolled her eyes—actually *rolled her eyes*—at him.

"Kain." She looked at him with so much affection it took his breath away. "I need you—and I can take you. Please."

There was not a power on this Earth strong enough to make him deny his mate when she pleaded for him like this.

Groaning, he grabbed at her waist for leverage and thrust forward, spearing her slick cleft wide with his girth. This time she opened fully for his intrusion, and though it was a tight fit, his ridged head pressed into her channel with only a small cry from her.

Bliss. The wet embrace of her pussy was nothing but bliss.

Kain drove in deeper, careful to take her slowly enough that her body could adjust to his presence, until the tight clasp sliding inch after inch up his pulsing cock covered his entire length.

Selma whimpered underneath him, lost in the pleasure. She was right—he never would be able to truly understand what it felt like to surrender the core of his being like she did when they joined.

And she'd offered herself, her very essence, to *him*.

"Selma." He whispered her name, releasing her waist so he could rest on one hand and cup her face with the other.

Her eyes, wild with desire, found his. Even behind the lust he saw the gentleness and compassion that seemed to be a part of her essence, though it was very much overshadowed by her more immediate urges.

Gently, mimicking what he saw in her gaze with the movements of his body, he pulled halfway out, making her gasp as his ridges massaged the sensitive areas inside of her before thrusting back in. The full, tight fit of her had him groaning, but despite the urge to drive into her hard and fast, he kept the penetration slow. Selma deserved more than to be rutted like an animal in heat, deserved to have her offering returned with more than just primitive force.

She gasped at every thrust, biting her lip when he was fully seated within her. Her reaction was evidence of the struggle she still endured to take him, but after a little while of the slow pace, her gasps turned to moans and she wound her arms around his neck, pulling him down over her.

Surprise was quickly overtaken by warmth spreading like wildfire throughout his body. He'd never been embraced like this while having sex, the dirty, rough act not exactly encouraging that sort of intimacy. This... This was something different. Something wonderful.

The deep humming he'd made for her before in an

involuntary attempt to soothe and comfort escaped his throat, flowing in rhythm with his hips' smooth movements.

"Kain."

The way she spoke his name was neither a plea nor a demand. He looked down at her and realized she was watching his face, reading his expressions even though her eyes were still clouded with lust. Before he had a chance to marvel at her, she raised her head and caught his lips in a deep kiss.

And then she canted her hips to meet his, moving in easy waves underneath him, driving his cock deeper into her tight sheath without disrupting the gentle rhythm.

Never had he experienced sex like this.

The bone-deep need to mate and breed her was still there, urging him to go harder and faster. But the new sensations of being one with his Breeder, of feeling her not only surrender to the pleasure, but meeting him for every stroke like an equal—like they were truly trying to become one via the maddening bliss—was even stronger.

When her channel began squeezing him in the tight spasms that signaled the approach of her first climax, he lost any concept of time to the sensation of being so intimately connected with another being. But Selma's nails digging in deep at the back of his shoulders pulled him out of the revelry.

"Harder!"

Apparently, his mate was done making love.

The monster inside of him reared to the surface at her

command, shattering his gentleness. His hips snapped down hard between her thighs, driving his brutal cock in to the hilt before he pulled back to repeat the movement, giving her no time to adjust to the change of pace.

"Yes!" Selma arced underneath him, crying out from the orgasm brought forward by his roughness—but he wasn't done.

When she collapsed back onto the bed, he grabbed her jaw and turned her head so he could bend to claim a kiss not nearly as tender as the one she'd pressed to his lips.

His mate responded sluggishly, winding her arms loosely around his neck again while she hummed as he ravaged her mouth.

"More, then?" she breathed, quirking a small smile at him through her decidedly dazed expression.

"Yes." It was dark growl, and her pussy clenched at the sound.

Kain pulled out of her, and she groaned in protest when his ridges breached her entrance again, undoubtedly tormenting her swollen flesh. She was unable to do anything else before he had her flipped over on her stomach and into the position his instincts would always crave to see her in—submissive and ready to be mounted.

"Oh!" Her small noise of surprise was followed by a grunt when he once more aligned his thick cock to her swollen pussy and pressed in. "Fuck!"

He loved her sounds, even her low cussing when he immediately began pounding her without the gentle warm-up from before, and when she finally gave up on keeping it together and screamed for him, his balls tightened with pleasure.

Yes, this was it. Making love to her was blissful, but this—this was life itself. Protecting her from harm was a powerful instinct, but the raw, unrelenting rhythm of mating his fertile Breeder until she could no longer bear it was every bit as strong.

WHEN HE FINALLY CAME, roaring from primal need to voice his claim yet again, she'd long since lost the ability to scream. The final climax he pushed from her shuddering pussy was only accompanied by her hoarse cry and weakly convulsing body.

Kain collapsed on top of her, only barely remembering to catch most of his weight on his arms before he crushed his small female.

Everything was bliss. Bliss, and calm.

The mating after the auction had been immediately followed by the urge to shield her from his kin, but this time there was nothing to stop the rush of hormones flooding his system. He belonged here, inside of her, protecting her body and bathing in the light of her soul for as long as he remained on this Earth.

"That was beyond amazing."

Selma's sleepy voice pulled him from his thoughts,

and he nuzzled at his mate's hair to let her know he was listening.

"I told you you were worrying over nothing."

Worrying? Kain frowned. Why would he be worrying? He'd never been this unworried in his entire life.

It wasn't until Selma moved a little and gasped in pain when his ridges caught inside of her that he remembered.

The monster within, the one that'd reveled in pounding her ruthlessly as she screamed, had fought its way to the surface despite his promise to never force her like he had at the auction.

"Forgive me." He spoke the words before he could stop himself, biting down hard on his lip after they escaped. He did not deserve forgiveness—not when he couldn't feel truly sorry while his body was still light from having claimed his mate so thoroughly.

"What?" She sounded astounded. "Forgive you for what, exactly? The mind-blowing sex?"

"I was rough with you," he growled as self-hatred nestled heavily in his stomach. He was exactly like his father, and he'd ruin this woman like his father had ruined his mother by his mere presence in her life—because clearly, he was too weak to stay away from her.

As gently as he could, he lifted off her, pulling his softening member from her swollen channel.

She winced at the slow process, fidgeting until he finally popped out of her and his semen dripped out to soothe her red opening.

When he rolled to his back and hid his face in his

hands, Selma scoffed—and then she wrapped her soft body around his, her head resting over his heart.

"Some demon you are," she murmured, "apologizing for being a bit rough. You didn't hurt me—you know that, right? I'm not some fragile little flower."

She clearly had no concept of how goddamn breakable she seemed, compared to his kind.

"You wanted it gentle and sweet, and I ruined it. Like I always will. I'll never be able to hold back with you," he mumbled, too ashamed to even look at her.

To his utter surprise, she chuckled, the breath from her lips brushing against his chest in a teasing caress.

"But you did give me 'gentle and sweet,' you big oaf. You made love to me until I asked for more. And then you fucked me just the way I needed you to. Do you not remember how you let me take charge? I know you have scars that will take time to heal, but this guilt you carry is misplaced. Everything you've ever done to me I've loved. We'll be in Colorado tomorrow, and I..."

She paused, her voice losing steam. "I want the memory of tonight to be about how, even through all the horrors and everything I've lost, there was you—the one good thing in this world of darkness I've been sucked into."

Kain lay still, breathing in her calming scent as her words settled in his mind and body. That sore thing in his chest hummed as if trying to alert him to something, but he was too busy replaying what she'd said to pay it any mind.

He'd never been called *good* before, and he'd most certainly never been the one positive thing anyone held onto in the darkness.

The ironic thing was that she was like a ray of light to him—he could almost see the bright shimmer around her when he looked at her.

And tomorrow he would lose her forever.

She was right—there was no point in wasting this limited time on regrets. He could do that on his way back from Colorado, and—he suspected—every day for the rest of his existence.

Pulling her in closer to where his chest ached, he bent his head to kiss the crown of hers. For tonight, he would forget everything apart from how perfectly the woman he could call his for one more day fit in his embrace.

TWENTY-EIGHT
SELMA

The closer they drew to the place circled on their map over Colorado, the gloomier Selma's mood became.

Waking up that morning wrapped in Kain's warm embrace had been bittersweet because she knew it was for the last time. He'd given her the one night she'd asked for —a night without worries or regret—and now it was time to face reality again.

A reality in which she had been given the gift of freedom.

Selma pressed her forehead against the car's passenger-side window. Even acknowledging the small murmur of reluctance at accepting her freedom was an insult to the man who'd claimed her. She knew every instinct in his body would be screaming at him to keep her by his side so he could breed her the way his kind always had with women like her, and yet here he was, bringing her to the Sanctuary himself.

If he could fight against his instincts for her, then she could do the same for him.

The slowing of the car made her turn to look at the demon. "Why are we stopping?"

"It's here. I can feel it." His nostrils flared and he clenched the steering wheel in obvious agitation. "There's a pretty strong repellent along the border—it's making me itch to turn around and leave."

Selma frowned. "Are you sure? I can't feel anything, and we're in the middle of nowhere."

"Oh, I'm sure." He gave her a short glance before unbuckling his seatbelt and opening the driver side door. "It's got demon-specific wards mixed in with it. I'm guessing regular humans will also avoid the place without ever thinking about why, but there's a little extra in there to ensure we stay out."

She followed him out of the car, looking in the direction he was staring at with narrowed eyes. "So... somewhere in there is a sanctuary for women like me? It just looks like a normal road and woodland."

"Yes, in there you can be safe, little one." His voice turned soft despite the discomfort making him fidget. He raised a hand, letting dark tendrils of magic flow from his palm. "Watch."

She did, and gasped in surprise when the dark mist hit an invisible wall. Sparks flew at the contact and the tendrils shifted, outlining the border as it sought a way through.

"I've never asked how your magic works," she said,

suddenly realizing how little she actually knew about Kain and his race. It felt... wrong, somehow—like she was leaving behind an unfinished puzzle she should have completed.

Everything in her life had always revolved around the monsters she saw, and now she was leaving it all behind without ever fully understanding the purpose of it.

Without ever fully understanding *him*.

"It doesn't matter." He turned around, cupping her face in his hands. "You are free from it all now."

Her heart clenched as she let her eyes find his black gaze. "Kain, I..."

"Go." Stopping her words before she even knew what she wanted to say, he bent down and kissed her lips so softly she only felt his heat as a gentle brush before he pulled back. "Please go before I stop you. Be free."

Selma swallowed thickly, the sinking sensation of loss in her gut making it almost impossible to take a step back. But she did because he was giving her the gift of freedom, the only thing she'd ever wanted.

"Goodbye, Kain," she whispered, turning from him before she could change her mind.

He didn't respond, but she felt his dark eyes on her back as she walked toward the once-again invisible barrier. Though she couldn't see it, the moment she stepped through it the magic washed over her skin like a light mist.

Her senses lit up as if someone'd dropped an extra dose of caffeine in her coffee, her brain hyper aware of every rustle of wind in the trees lining the narrow road and the smell of woodland filling her nostrils. Everything seemed... *more,* somehow, but softer at the same time. It was like the dome of magic was made of cotton, filtering every sensation with a gentle touch. Protecting whatever lay inside.

She couldn't feel Kain's gaze on her any longer, but when she looked over her shoulder, he was still there, staring at her with those haunting eyes.

Her abdomen clenched hard, and she gasped at the twisting agony low in her belly.

Loss. She'd known him so briefly, yet everything in her screamed to run back to him, to safety—

But *this* was safety, a literal sanctuary, and one he'd brought her to. There was no turning back, even if her chest tightened as she returned his gaze.

With a force of will, she turned back around to focus on the road ahead.

She made it twenty more steps before the pain in her abdomen returned, only this time it was hot knives shredding her from the inside out.

Agony blasted through her and she fell to the ground with a cry, clutching her stomach as her body violently spasmed.

A deep ringing like someone striking a massive church bell echoed through the sanctuary, making her bones vibrate, but she didn't have the focus to care about its source.

Through the blinding waves of pain, only one clear

thought thundered in her brain: *It's killing me.* Whatever magic permeated this sanctuary, it was trying to force its way into her every cell, tearing at her like a vicious dog.

Kain.

Selma twitched on the ground, trying to force her limbs to drag her back to him, but she didn't have the strength. She only managed to turn halfway over, but the effort let her see back where she'd come from.

Kain was there, his features marred with fury as his black magic struck the barrier separating them.

Another deep ringing echoed around her as he did, his lips forming one single word around a roar. Her name, she dimly realized—he was screaming her name.

Another torturous wave blurred her vision into red-dotted black, erasing the demon trying so desperately to save her once again. She floated into unconsciousness knowing he'd be too late this time.

TWENTY-NINE
KAIN

When she stepped through the barrier, every cell in Kain's body felt the loss of his claimed mate like a sickening emptiness spreading from where the ache in his chest pulsed.

He would never, ever be whole again without her, just like his father had never truly recovered after the loss of his mate, but it didn't matter. This burden he would gladly carry if it meant the light within the woman who'd unwittingly claimed his soul would never be dimmed by the darkness inside him.

But the sight of her walking farther and farther away would haunt him for eternity.

As if she felt his pain, her steps faltered maybe ten yards in, and then she turned around to look at him, her brows drawn.

Something was wrong.

"Selma?"

The urge to protect her was stronger than the repellent nature of the barrier, and he stepped closer to the invisible wall in a futile attempt at reaching her.

She turned her back on him again, taking a few more steps, and everything in him clenched with terror. *Something was wrong!*

Before he could call to her, her entire body seized as if stricken. Then she keeled over, both hands pressing against her abdomen.

"Selma!"

Without his bidding, Kain's dark magic welled up from his core. He slung it at the wall with as much force as he could muster, wild with fear. She needed his help, and she needed it now!

"Selma!" Kain roared again, but she didn't respond. She twitched on the ground, writhing in pain and clutching at her abdomen.

She was trying to push herself toward him, and their eyes connected for a second. Then hers rolled back into her skull and she collapsed, lying so still he could no longer tell if she was breathing.

Dark, thick panic clenched his sternum, stealing his breath. His powers poured through his body and out of his hands, hammering against the barrier again and again. It was made from old, strong magic, but even if he had to drain every drop of his essence to bring it down, he would do so to get to her, because if she died...

If she died, he would cease to exist.

Nothing could have prepared him for that overwhelming certainty. Not his father's miserable existence, not the keen sense of loss when Selma had been taken into custody, nor when she'd walked through that blasted barrier.

Yet as he stared at her crumpled form, he knew he wouldn't be able to break through in time.

Still, he would never stop trying.

"Selma!"

Kain threw yet another violent wave of energy at the wall separating him from his mate. He knew she couldn't hear his call, but the sound of her name helped him focus his efforts.

He should never have let her go—should have kept her by his side where she would have been safe forevermore. But he had felt *guilty* for tying her to a life she didn't want, and because of that, she was going to die.

"Selma!"

With the next surge of power, he felt as well as heard the faintest hint of a crack in the barrier. It wasn't enough to break through, but it was something. He would get to her, even if he had to drain his own life essence to do so.

Just as he was about to let another discharge free, movement farther down the road behind the wall caught his attention. There were people coming down it—three women on foot.

Kain snarled. Though he knew they couldn't hear him, they could most definitely see his rage, judging by their terrified faces.

Slowly, deliberately, he gathered his dark power in a

mist around his body before pointing to Selma's unmoving figure.

The gesture was clear—either they help her, or he would pull the fucking barrier down around their ears—and it seemed to register with the women. Two of them noticed Selma and rushed to her side while the third kept a wary eye on him.

They were talking to each other, but he couldn't read their lips. Couldn't see what they said about his little mate's condition.

The anxious wait made him pace as the women took her pulse and pressed at her body. After a moment, the female not at Selma's side disappeared back down the road.

It felt like an eternity until finally the two remaining women lifted her up between them. But instead of carrying her straight to him, they paused on the other side of the wall, sending him nervous glances.

As if he gave two shits about them!

Angrily he gestured at them to bring her out, but they still hesitated. Then one of them pointed down the road behind him.

They wanted him to back away.

It was physically painful to put more distance between himself and his mate, but he understood that it was the only way they would dare leave the safety of the barrier. So he did.

Only when he was about fifty yards away did they finally move forward, breaching the wall as if it was nothing but air. They carried her limp body out with them, and despite his near-painful concern over her unconscious state, something dark and hollow deep within eased.

"What's wrong with her?" he called the second they were through, worry making his voice hitch.

They looked up, startled, but didn't reply. As soon as they'd lowered Selma to the ground, they retreated back to the safety of their Sanctuary.

Cowards. But it didn't matter—they had brought her out to him, and that was all he cared about.

Kain was by her side in seconds. He knelt on the ground so he could examine her himself.

She was still breathing, and when he checked her pulse, it seemed to be getting steadier. They'd gotten to her in time.

"What happened, little one?" he whispered, gently stroking her hair away from her face. Now that he could touch her and see she wasn't in overt danger anymore, the terror bubbling in his stomach was settling. Still, until she opened her eyes and spoke to him, he would not let his relief distract him from his need to keep her safe.

As gently as he could, he lifted his human mate so she was resting against him. Underneath the worry, there was relief at having her with him again. Every part of his being had felt the loss of her when she crossed through the barrier, and now every part of him felt her return. It was intoxicating.

The low hum he made just for her rumbled from his

chest before he even realized what he was doing, but he made no attempt at quelling it. It was the sound a male made to soothe his mate, and at this moment, it didn't matter that she'd told him goodbye. She was still his to protect.

"Selma, wake up for me, my precious."

The soft cooing he couldn't hold back, however, and the sound of it made him cringe. He'd overheard Thomren do that for Meredith on the few occasions he'd been allowed into their home after Thomren claimed her, and the ridiculousness of speaking to a grown woman like that had made him roll his eyes at his second-in-command.

As it turned out, it wasn't all that easy to control.

"I take it she's your mate?"

The clear, feminine voice rang across the silent road and made Kain's head snap up. His muscles tensed and his lip curled in a snarl. Without taking his eyes off the faintly shimmering blonde woman who'd just stepped through the barrier, he got to his feet in front of Selma, hunched over and ready to repel an attack.

She wasn't the first goddess he'd seen, but she was the first one who'd snuck up on him when he had been too preoccupied to notice.

"Why are you here?" she demanded. Though she didn't take a defensive stance, she was watching him closely. "Did you follow the girl?"

"I brought her here for protection, but your barrier harmed her. I swear by the stars themselves, if you have injured my mate, I will rip your heart out through your throat!"

The goddess' eyebrows crept up a millimeter. "*You* brought her here? Why?"

Kain's nostrils flared at her disbelieving tone. "That is none of your concern. What did you do to her? Why? She's an innocent!"

Golden eyes leveled a haughty stare at him, but then they shifted behind him, fixating on Selma.

"Yes, she is. Move aside, demon. I will tend to her."

"I am going nowhere," he told her flatly. "Answer my question or I will tear you limb from limb, you gilded cunt."

The goddess huffed. "You don't have the strength, not after how much power you poured into my barrier. And you can't heal her, either. The fact that you've yet to try proves you know she needs me—what my barrier did to her can't be healed by your twisted magic. Now *step aside*, or risk your mate dying in your arms."

Kain dared a glance back at Selma's quiet form. She seemed stable, but the goddess wasn't wrong. His magic could heal many human conditions, even if he'd never particularly bothered to, but this? It wasn't simple biology that ailed his mate. It was divine magic.

"If you harm her, I will not only kill you—I will butcher every woman hiding in your sanctuary, desecrate their remains, and trap their souls in eternal damnation. Do you understand?"

His voice was low, but the threat came across loud and

clear. Despite the goddess' attempt to remain stoic, a touch of green marred her flawless skin.

When she bowed her head in a single nod, Kain slowly took two steps away, allowing her to move past him to the woman curled up on the road behind him.

She knelt by Selma's side and let her hands slide over her face and down her torso. Kain had to dig his nails into his palms to stop himself from tackling the goddess to get her away from his mate. Everything in him screamed *danger* at her presence, and allowing her to *touch* his Selma...

"Wake up, child."

Kain blinked at the gentleness with which the goddess spoke. It was so very different from the tone she'd used on him, and it made his anger level just a little.

Golden light shimmered around her hands and flowed into Selma's abdomen. When his mate groaned softly and shifted underneath the goddess' touch, he could barely contain his relief. It would be okay, she was okay—

"Kalam!"

The Word of Power slammed him backwards so hard he hit the uneven tarmac of the small side road. When he fought his way back up, a cocoon of golden light arose around his awakening mate and the goddess who'd just attacked him.

THIRTY
SELMA

"You silly girl."

The motherly scolding tone that broke through the sensation of bathing in light made Selma frown before cracking her eyes open. More than a little confused, she stared up into the most beautiful face she'd ever seen—high cheekbones, full lips, and dazzling golden eyes surrounded by golden-blonde hair. Behind the incredible woman was a starry sky beyond a shimmering veil of light.

"Who are you?"

"I am Bealith, Goddess of Seers. What is your name, my child?"

Goddess? She must be the one in charge of the Sanctum. "I'm Selma. What... happened?"

"You tried to cross the boundary while carrying one of them in your womb. The barrier expels all demons, including the unborn." Bealith's hand skimmed over her belly in a gentle caress.

If Selma hadn't been so dazed by the shining light and waking up staring at a Goddess, she might have felt a bit more than mild surprise at that revelation.

"Oh. I thought it was supposed to be difficult to conceive with a demon."

The goddess' perfect lips quirked into a smile. "I take it the father is the demon who single handedly tried to tear down my defenses?"

Selma frowned. "Is he all right?"

The smile turned decidedly mischievous. "A bit upset, but perfectly fine. He claims he brought you here for protection. Is that true?"

"Yeah. Why is he upset?" She struggled to sit up, annoyed at the dizziness making her head buzz. It felt a bit like being drunk, only without the fun parts.

A shining wall came into focus when she was finally upright, and behind it was her mate, his face almost unrecognizable with rage as he slung wave after wave of pure black energy against the shield. A faint echo hummed through the air with every hit.

"What did you do?" Shock cleared her head and she whipped around to stare at the goddess again, anger filling her. "Drop that shield! He thinks I'm in danger—I need to calm him down. Now!"

Bealith cocked her head as she looked at her. "I will, but first you and I need to talk. However, if you could convince him to stop attacking my shield, it would be much appreciated—he's very strong for someone who just poured enough magic into my Sanctuary's barrier to crack a few of the wards, and I need time to explain."

Selma narrowed her eyes at the beautiful woman. "If you trick me, he will kill you." There was an odd feeling of calm in saying those words, in knowing that someone as powerful as the demon Lord raging just a few feet from them would stop at nothing to protect her.

"I know, but you have no need for his violence to shield you from me, little Seer. I will never harm my daughters. Please, tell him to stop and I will explain everything."

Seer? Daughters? Selma gave her a hesitant look, but then nodded. Whatever a goddess had to say would be worth listening to.

She wobbled a little as she got to her feet and had to place both hands against the wall of light to balance herself. Her palms buzzed pleasantly at the contact.

Kain's black gaze locked with hers through the wall, fear plain on his face. He put his hand against the barrier opposite hers, but pulled it back with a growl when sparks flew at his touch. Dark energy burst from his injured hand against the wall above her head, making the entire thing vibrate, and anger once again marred his features.

How did one go about calming down a demon Lord seemingly hell-bent on wreaking havoc?

Selma waved a hand to get his attention, and when he paused his assault, she shook her head determinedly.

His dark brows drew into a frown and he gestured agitatedly at the goddess, who remained seated on the ground with her back halfway turned in an obvious attempt at seeming nonthreatening.

Selma nodded at him, hoping he'd understand. He seemed to, because despite the less-than-amused expression on his face, he nodded once and stood back, arms folded over his chest. Waiting.

She smiled in thanks and then turned back around to the goddess.

"I don't know how long he will hold back for, so you should hurry with that explanation. Please."

She tacked on the last word at Bealith's quirked eyebrow—it was undoubtedly bad form to make demands of a goddess, and Selma blushed at her poor manners. Apparently, being around demons for too long wasn't good for her social skills. Carefully, she sat back down.

"Why are your here, child?"

Selma blinked in surprise. That wasn't exactly what she'd expected to hear. "You mean at the Sanctuary? I was told it—you—take in Breeders who escape their Masters."

Bealith wrinkled her nose delicately. "You are not a 'Breeder,' Selma. You are so much more than what those meatheads can imagine. You are a Seer, one of my beloved daughters.

"Yes, I take in those of my daughters who cannot accept a life by a demon's side, if they are lucky enough to make it here. But you seem to care for the one who has chosen you, so I ask again: Why are you here?"

"I..." That question should have been a lot easier to answer. Selma glanced at the man who called her "mate" and felt her heart clench. "He gave me my freedom. If I don't take it, I will forever be a slave to them."

"Do you know how many demons have willingly given up their mates before?"

Selma shook her head. "Few?"

"None." The goddess stared unblinkingly at her, those odd, golden eyes piercing right through her. "Not a single one. Yet here that big brute is, bringing you to my doorstep for protection. He is the first demon I have ever heard of to go against all those primal instincts they're filled with in order to do what is right. Do you think if you chose to stay with him, he would enslave you?"

A shameful heat rose in her cheeks. No, Kain would never do anything to her she didn't want him to do, and she'd done him a great injustice by implying he would.

"No. Never."

"The Seers who find their way here are damaged. They have suffered at the hands of these beasts, and I suspect you have too. But his seed has taken root in you, and I cannot offer you sanctuary. I never wanted this for you—for any of you—but I wasn't given a choice."

She bit her lip in a very human gesture, glanced at Kain's impatient form, and then looked back at Selma. "What I want to tell you was never meant to be shared with anyone who isn't a god, but I need you to hear it nonetheless.

"The war between gods and demons has waged for millennia, and before the fertility goddess Mattla intervened, we were losing. They were too many compared to us, and had we not done something, the balance would have shifted in their favor—and trust me when I say that neither we nor the humans would have fared well had that happened.

"But then Mattla put forward her plan. She suggested a way we could make the demons fight amongst each other whilst also lessening their number of offspring. The gods—all of us—agreed to the plan, and the female demons who'd been forced into subservience by the demon king accepted.

"It seemed perfect, and for many years, it was. The female demons birthed only more females, and with their increasing numbers, they had the strength to fight against the Lords. The upheaval among the demon race meant they lost their focus in their war with us. But after decades of dwindling numbers and lost battles, they opened negotiations. And we had to act."

Bealith reached out to grasp Selma's hand between her palms. The buzz of her touch was oddly exhilarating —like drinking too much Irish coffee.

"That's when I lost my children, the Seers. I was always so proud of you—the gentle souls who carry the light within you. You spread joy and hope among the people you lived with, and were revered as wise women and shamans.

"Unfortunately, the demons have always favored you —they cannot resist the light you hold, even though they shun goodness in most other forms. They tricked or captured many o you into servings lifetimes by their sides, and that is how Mattla got the idea to grant the male demons sons birthed by humans—but only Seers. It would greatly reduce their rate of procreation, seeing how rare you are, but it would break the negotiations between the males and females, ensuring that the demons would not unite and overrun us.

"I tried everything to plead for my children, but the other gods had already decided. Because the demons favored you, you were selected, and the only way I am allowed to interfere is by ensuring that there is a sanctuary on each continent where those who cannot endure their fate can seek refuge."

Selma stared at her. "I'm sorry... I'm some sort of a... shaman? I don't mean to be disrespectful, but I've never been accused of being particularly wise. And I haven't given a whole lot to charity, either. No beacon of light within me, no superpowers of any sort. I can just see demons."

Bealith smiled. When she spoke, her voice pitched with sorrow.

"It was the trade-off for ensuring you could reproduce with demons. Naught but an echo remains of what you were—the light in you had to be dimmed to make room for a demon's claim. But your sacrifice has meant the world isn't overrun with their darkness."

Sacrifice? Something about that phrasing made it sound awfully willing, and Selma didn't remember being asked to swap magical powers for the ability to be impregnated by demons.

"Why are you telling me all this? If you can't protect me, then... then I will need to go back to them." To Kain. There was a distinct lack of despair at that thought. Then she remembered what—or who—else she would be bringing, and anxiety finally nestled in the pit of her gut.

She was *pregnant*. With a demon's offspring. Kain's offspring. He was going to lose whatever control he still had over his temper once he found out. Noble intentions or not, he'd made it clear he never wanted a mate, and even though he'd sacrificed his beliefs to save her, she didn't think he would be particularly happy with adding a baby to the mix.

Not to mention how she'd cope once she allowed the knowledge to take root, which wasn't something she could do just yet—not when she had to focus on getting enough information out of the goddess in front of her to ensure her survival.

Swiftly she pushed away the hazy image of a white picket fence and sunny afternoons on a porch swing, even as her hand found and rested against her lower belly of its own accord.

Bealith smiled softly. "I am telling you this because I believe you have a chance at breaking this cycle of abuse and despair. Most demons who claim a mate will walk through fire to keep her, but the one who brought you here? He sacrificed his own needs for your benefit—no one's ever thought these beasts were capable of selfless love, but this might be proof that the seed is in there. If you can nurture it and spread it to your children... my daughter, you could be the catalyst who finally defeats evil."

Selma's mouth dropped open. "Whoa there! Kain was capable of love from when he was a child. I have nothing to do with that—and I think love is a fairly strong word for what's between us! We're doped up on each other's pheromones, and he's a good guy. That's why he's helping me.

"As for this catalyst nonsense? If what you've told me is true, then I've had quite enough of being a tool for gods to play with. All I want is to live in peace!"

To her frustration, all her minor rant got her was a chuckle from the glowing woman in front of her.

"My dear, you're the only woman in history to call a demon a 'good guy' while knowing his true nature. Even Breeders who grow content with their fate would never claim he is good. That *guy* on the other side of this shield has crushed many humans' lives—it's in his very nature. Yet you see kindness where others see evil.

"Deny your heart if you wish, my daughter. When you have given birth to the demon in your womb, you will be able to live behind my walls—assuming you wish to turn your back on your mate and his son.

"But if you don't—if you can find it in your heart to nurture the love and gentleness within them both—then no one's to say that you cannot have the peaceful life you desire, along with helping light spread throughout a race that's been ruled by darkness since the very beginning. The choice is yours."

With a final glance in Selma's direction, Bealith got up and turned to the wall, looking at the demon glaring at them.

"I can tell you that love is the way to connect to the power you were meant to have. You are so much more than a Breeder, so much more than a damaged woman defined by the monsters who want to use you. It's up to you if you want to take that power."

She turned her head to look at Selma over her shoulder, a small smile playing on her lips. "I am needed elsewhere tonight, my child. Please do make sure your demon doesn't wreak any more havoc on my sanctuary's wards—he has already done damage that will take weeks to repair, and terrified your sisters residing here."

Selma frowned, the weight of the goddess' words making her fold her arms protectively over her midriff. Just the thought of leaving a child behind, even a demon child she couldn't even face the reality of just yet, sent cold shivers down her back.

"Choose wisely, daughter."

A flourish of golden light and shining fabric made Selma squint to protect her eyes, and when she looked back up, the goddess was gone. So was the golden shield that had separated her from Kain.

"Selma." He wrapped his arms around her before she fully realized she was alone with him again, and she gasped at the strength that crushed her against his hard chest. "I swear, I'm going to kill that fucking bitch! Are you all right? What happened? Ew, you reek of her!"

Selma laughed at his disgusted expression as he pulled his nose away from where he'd buried it in her hair. "I thought she smelled pretty nice. Like flowers and sunshine."

The dark-eyed demon sent her a look which suggested that he was considering dunking her in the nearest river to lose the scent. "What happened to you? And what did that deceitful hag tell you? Whatever it was, you need to know that none of them are to be trusted. They are as dangerous and tricky as demons—they just go about it differently."

She was pretty sure he was unable to be objective about the trustworthiness of gods, but ironically, if she did take the goddess' words for truth, then he had a point.

"Tell me what happened to you." Concern was still evident in his voice, but his words bore the unmistakable air of a command. This demon had had enough of waiting.

"Er..." She'd hoped to have a little more time to digest everything before deciding on how and what to tell him, but when she looked up into his eyes, she knew he wasn't going to accept anything but the immediate and full truth.

"Don't freak out, all right?"

Both his eyebrows arched. "You do realize that is anything but a calming statement, right?"

"Sorry, it's just, ah... So you know how that barrier keeps demons out?"

"Yes?"

Selma bit the inside of her cheek. They hardly knew

each other. Despite the incredible intensity of their time together, they had only been around one another for a handful of days. Yet when his arms were around her, it felt like they'd known each other for a lifetime.

"Seriously, I need you to promise me you won't freak out, because I can't deal with that right now. I think I'm pretty terrified, and I don't need you to—"

"Tell. Me. Now!"

Kain accentuated his growl by grabbing her arms and shaking her—gently, but it stopped her rambling.

"Right, sorry. So the barrier... it, uh, keeps demons out. All demons."

His expression didn't change to a look of understanding.

"Also baby demons," she clarified. "So that's why I got knocked out."

For the longest time, he just stared at her. Selma stared back at his frozen face, not entirely sure if he'd grasped what she was trying to say.

"I'm pregnant."

Actually saying it out loud did nothing to soothe her nerves, nor did his continued blank stare.

"...so I can't stay at the Sanctuary. And I... I really need you to speak now, because I don't know what to do and you're freaking me out."

When air wheezed out of his lungs, she realized he'd stopped breathing while she spoke.

"Selma..."

Her name on his lips sounded pained, and when he

carefully released his grip on her arms, she felt the loss of contact way too keenly. Fear of rejection pierced her heart, making her wrap her arms around herself and the child she was apparently carrying to stem the ache.

"I know this isn't what you want, but I need your help, okay? Please don't leave."

Shock finally cracked his frozen mask. "Leave? You think I'd—" He interrupted himself with a foul curse and stroked a hand through his hair in an obvious attempt at soothing the agitation that seemed to flow out through the broken facade. "You're carrying my... my child?"

She nodded, more than a little confused at his reaction. "Bealith told me so, and it makes sense given what happened with the barrier."

Kain went quiet again, his body stilling.

"Kain?" Gently she placed a hand on his chest, searching his eyes for a clue of what was going on. Her panic mixed with her confusion, resulting in an unpleasant roll in her gut.

That was when she saw the single tear drawing a path down his cheek.

"Why are you crying?" She could hardly press the words out as complete terror closed around her lungs. He was so strong, so stoic... and a freaking demon! Tears were not something she'd even thought him capable of.

He gasped in the night air, and when his nostrils flared, his eyes went dark, the moisture leaving them. The scent of her fear had finally cut through.

"I can't let you leave." It was a hoarse murmur. "If I

touch you right now, I will never let go again. I can't. Not now, not when he's been born. Never."

Oh. The motionless state of his body suddenly made sense—he was doing his very best to rein in instincts that were undoubtedly clamoring to grab her and lock her up somewhere.

Yet he was still trying.

Something in her chest loosened at the sudden realization that even now, even when his instincts were strengthened immeasurably by his upbringing with a mother who tried to leave him, he was still fighting tooth and nail against himself. For her.

Wordlessly she pressed herself against his powerful body. When he shivered, she wrapped her arms around his waist.

"Do you want this?" she asked, afraid of the answer, but nevertheless needing to know. "You planned on freeing me when you went to the auction, but instead... Do you even want a mate and a child? I know your instincts are probably making you feel certain things, but do *you* want it?"

Carefully, as if he thought she were made of spun glass, Kain raised one large hand and let it stroke through her hair.

"I want you with every fiber of my being. Both of you. I have never been... I am..." Kain bit his lip, raw emotion cutting across his angular features. "I am scared." He said the word as if it was a foreign concept to him.

He wanted them. Wanted her and the life she was

carrying. Relief made her shudder and bury her nose in his chest. As long as that held true, as long as he was there to lean on, she could do this.

Love.

The goddess' words rang in her mind, and she frowned at the sweet pull they caused in her chest.

It was too soon—too much to deal with right now on top of everything else.

With sheer force of will, she pushed the swirling tangle of emotions aside and focused on the here and now —on Kain and the life growing inside her.

"I'm not going to leave. I don't care that it's a demon child. It's mine, and I will love it always. I would never do to *him* what your mother did to you and your brother. I just need a bit of time to... well, to adjust."

Kain's strong arms encircled her again, pulling her tighter against him. A calm settled over her mind as his heat encompassed her.

Home. This was home.

"You will care for this child?"

Despite the coarse note, she heard the fear in his voice clearly.

"Yes." Selma pulled her head back so she could look at him. "Always."

Finally, relief seemed to wash over him, filling his eyes with a joy so strong it made her heart flutter. When he buried his face in her hair, the tune he hummed just for her rumbled out of his chest and into her body.

"I am going to take such good care of you." His voice

dropped, turning husky in her ear. "You will want for nothing, I promise."

Selma laughed and let go of his waist to press against his chest when his hands began sliding down her body in a rather familiar way.

"Really? *This* makes you horny? I practically had to rape you when we were at the hotel, but now—in the middle of nowhere, after I tell you I'm pregnant, you suddenly want it? I thought I smelled bad."

"You stink. I don't care."

It was pretty impossible to hold back the smile pulling at her lips at his sudden change. She hadn't seen him like this before—unrestrained, yet still in control. It made her chest feel light.

"I'm not having sex with you right now. There's too much to discuss. Like what do we do now? This wasn't exactly in the plan."

He rubbed at her hips with his thumbs, the gesture still suggestive, though he kept his palms still. "Now you come back with me."

"And then what?" She frowned, trying to wrap her head around the crazy turn this evening had taken. A few hours ago she'd thought she would be saying goodbye to him forever, and now here they were, on a road in the middle of nowhere discussing their futures. "No offense, but I'm not about to raise a kid in a penthouse on top of a casino."

His soft lips quirked in a smile. "No? And where would you prefer to build a nest, my little mate?"

"Nest? I was more thinking a house. You know, in the country. With fresh air and..." She blushed when the damned picket fence popped into the forefront of her mind again.

"And?" he asked, eyebrows lifted in amusement. "If you want it, it's yours."

"We can talk about that later. I... I also want you to meet my parents, and preferably make such a good impression that they don't think you're in the modern slave trade and have brainwashed and/or abused me while I've been missing for the past two months. They've got to be worried sick."

"Hmm," he said, the amusement withering on his face.

"What?"

"Breeders usually don't keep in contact with their human relations. It's... too complicated."

Selma arched her brows until they met her hairline. "Too complicated? You mean because the poor woman has to explain to her family why she's suddenly not allowed to be farther than three feet from her new boyfriend?"

Kain looked distinctly uncomfortable. "That and the lack of aging, along with a few other... issues."

"Kain, I'm going to see my parents. They've been through enough because of my condition. I'm not just going to disappear."

Though his expression remained grim, he nodded. "We will find a way. I suppose I will have to officially introduce you to my family too, once we've settled in a bit."

The prospect did not seem to please him, but given his upbringing, she didn't really expect an uncomplicated relationship between him and his father and brother.

Selma leaned forward to rest her cheek against his chest, her eyes fluttering closed at the contact with his strong, warm form. If she could help him heal, she would, not because of Bealith's plan to break the darkness within the demon world, but because he deserved the care and tenderness his mother had denied him.

Kain stroked her hair in a gentle caress. "Come, little one. Let's get you home."

THIRTY-ONE
SELMA

This time, the silence emphasized by the soft hum of the car's engine was pleasant.

On the way here, Selma had been weighed down by the prospect of never seeing Kain again, of never getting the chance to explore what it was about him that called to her on more than just the most primal of levels.

She glanced to her left something fluttered low in her belly. His dark eyes trained on the road ahead of them were illuminated by the dashboard, his strong hands resting on the steering wheel. Eyes that could make her blood burn with just one look and hands that could melt her with a simple caress.

Okay, so maybe she was eager to explore the primal levels with him, too.

His low growl made her sex clench and her panties suddenly dampen. How did a growl do this to her?

"I can smell you," he said without taking his eyes off

the road, but when she glanced at his hands, his knuckles were white around the wheel. "Your need."

"Handy." She couldn't keep the breathy note from her voice. "When we get to a motel, will I have to forcibly seduce you again? Or are you over the belief that you're molesting me?"

"My morals are irrelevant. You carry my son and will need my seed to survive the pregnancy."

Her eyebrows arched. "Uh... what?"

He let out a low sigh. "My semen will strengthen your body when we mate so that you may endure the full nine months with a demon growing inside of you. Without it, you would soon weaken and die."

She blinked. Repeatedly. Some of the warm, fuzzy feelings that had been spreading inside her since she'd accepted her pregnancy faded.

"My child will *kill* me?"

"No, I would never let that happen. But he needs a lot of power, and he will drain your life essence to grow if not supplied with another source. He may look human to you once you hold him in your arms, but he will not be a human baby. Which brings me to something else you should know."

His eyes darted to her for a brief moment, a certain measure of worry evident in them despite the lack of light in the car. "We normally know our Breeders are pregnant when they, ah, see through our disguise."

"See through...?" Selma paused to stare at the male by

her side. "You mean I will see your demon form? When? Why?"

Another sigh. "It usually happens within a few weeks of impregnation. Our son's magic will protect you against the brand blinding you to our true nature. It is... upsetting to many Breeders, and I want you to be prepared. I will need to mate you regardless, to ensure your survival. Even if you find it... disagreeable."

It took her a moment to process his words. If she refused him, he would force her in order to keep her alive.

Memories of the demons she'd seen before she'd been branded made her shudder. While some had been like her Procurer—mainly human with horns or odd eyes—others had been terrifying. Submitting to him if he looked like that...

"What does your demon form look like?" This time her whisper was more hoarse than breathy.

He grimaced. "Different. Bigger. Less human."

Well, that wasn't overly helpful. She glanced at him again. Maybe it was better if she didn't think too much about it until she absolutely had to.

"You demons sure seem to forget to mention a lot of the small print beforehand."

Kain's mouth twisted into a small grin. "It's sort of in the job description."

One of his large hands left the steering wheel to rest on her knee, and calm spread through her body at his warm touch. "We still have a little time before it happens," he continued. "Hopefully, it will be manageable by then."

She somehow doubted it, but right then, it didn't matter. He was there, looking like his human self, and they were going to work everything out. Together.

Her heart fluttered pleasantly.

Perhaps the goddess was right—perhaps what she felt was love.

Kain made a soft noise next to her, squeezing her knee gently as if her scent somehow conveyed her emotions. He didn't look away from the road again, but the soothing hum she was starting to recognize as their personal thing soon emanated from him.

Content, Selma leaned back in her seat and closed her eyes.

Demon or not, he was hers. She had recognized it when he claimed her for the world to see, and in her heart she knew it now.

He was her savior.

THE SCREECHING of tires and jolt of brakes being slammed ripped her from sleep.

Selma gasped against the seat belt's strangulating hold, her eyes popping open wide just as the car came to an abrupt halt.

"Kain, what the fuck?" she gasped as she reached up

to rub at her throat. Apparently she'd been sitting in a less than ideal position for emergency braking.

He didn't turn to look at her, his gaze locked on the road ahead. "I will get out. The second I am, you take the wheel, turn around, and drive as fast as the car will go. Head east on the first exit road you come across, but do not come back this way.

"My phone is on the dashboard. When you are at least half an hour away you find 'Kesh' in my contacts. Tell him who and where you are and follow his instructions."

She blinked in confusion at his command, but then she spotted what was blocking the road ahead.

Dark, sparkling mist lit up the sporty-looking car parked across both lanes before swirling up along the body of the man standing in front of it with a grim smile.

Prince Naharan.

He lifted an arm and beckoned them.

"Kain..." The icy panic making its way through her body was more than evident in her voice too.

"There's no time," he hissed as he undid his seatbelt without taking his eyes off his enemy. "I spent too much power on the barriers—I can't beat him, and if he captures you, he will kill our child. Do as I say."

"But—!"

He looked at her for the briefest of moments, and the urgency in his black eyes quelled her protests.

There was nothing she could do. And if she didn't obey, his sacrifice would be for nothing.

"Kain..."

"Drive, my love."

And then he was out of the car, walking toward the Prince with his broad back to her, shielding her from the other's sight.

Selma fumbled with her own seatbelt, struggling to loosen it with fingers that were stiff with fear and adrenaline. She couldn't think about the despair in his voice, nor the words themselves—she had to do as he'd asked, and if she paused to think, she'd never be able to leave him behind.

As the leftovers of Kain's magic whirled up around him, she finally managed to get free from the seatbelt and throw herself into the driver's side.

The engine was still running, but she had to scoot the seat forward to reach the pedals. After what felt like an eternity, her hands finally closed around the steering wheel.

She threw the car into reverse, ignoring the angry shout up ahead. Kain would hold Naharan off until she'd escaped, of that she was certain.

Only when she'd managed to turn the car around did she allow herself one final look in the rearview mirror at the man who'd claimed her as his, but what she saw made her wish she hadn't.

He was on the ground, the last of his power constricting around Naharan's body as the Prince knelt on top of him, rage evident on his face. And behind them stood six women, looking dispassionately at the two males as if waiting for Kain to be subdued.

What the fuck? Were they female demons? Why were they with the Prince?

Selma desperately flicked through scenarios even after she rounded a bend, leaving them behind as she sped along the winding road at much higher speeds than was wise. Distance was the only thing that could save her, the only thing that would make Kain's sacrifice mean something.

My love. He'd called her *my love.*

Her heart clenched and she gasped as tears threatened to blind her.

He'd saved her yet again, this time giving his own life. She prayed to any power, divine or otherwise who might have been listening, that he would live through this—that the man he'd told her to call would be able to help save him.

None of it made any sense. Why had Naharan ambushed them? The laws were meant to protect a mated couple—their union was meant to be sacred, as far as she had understood.

And the females? If they were demons, then why were they just standing there, looking on? They were the males' sworn enemies.

Nothing about the scene made sense. The only thing that was clear was the aching hollow in her heart that seemed to grow with every mile she put between herself and Kain.

When she finally pulled over forty-five minutes later, she'd given up on holding her tears at bay.

With shaking hands, she grabbed the phone off the dashboard and opened the car door to get out. She needed to calm down if she were to have any hope of making this "Kesh" understand a word she was saying.

Selma wiped at her eyes to stem the steady trickle of tears before leaning against the car and breathing deeply. The quicker she got a hold of herself, the sooner she could get Kain help.

That thought dried her tears. He needed her to be strong now. The father of the life growing inside of her needed her.

Her hands were still shaking when she pulled out the phone and scrolled through his contacts, but she managed to find the entry with Kesh's number and press "call."

The silence of the dark roadside seemed to press in around her as she listened to the phone ring. Over and over the sharp tone buzzed into her ear, each time making her panic bubble closer to the surface.

What if he didn't answer? What on Earth was she going to do? She could try to call Thomren if his number was listed in Kain's phone, but if he was home with his pregnant mate it would take him way too long to get to Colorado.

"Yes?"

The gruff voice broke through her spiraling thoughts, and Selma exhaled as relief and adrenaline made the muscles in her legs soften.

"Kesh?"

A moment's silence. *"Yes. Who's this?"*

"Selma, Kain's Mate. He told me to call you—"

"What happened?" he interrupted. *"Where are you?"*

"In Western Colorado, off Route 40. Prince Naharan and some women—I think demons—attacked us. They've got Kain. Please, we need your help."

A growl burst through the phone at her explanation, but the sound of it soothed her. His anger was directed at their attackers.

"I'm on my way. Do you have access to transportation?"

"Yes," she said, glancing at the fancy car Kain had driven her straight from the Governor's mansion to Colorado in.

"Good. I'm going to text you directions to a cafe in the nearest town. Drive straight there. I will be there in less than an hour. Do not stop for anything, understood?"

"Okay." Knowing that someone who sounded as competent and in control as this Kesh was would be taking charge of the situation was a huge relief. Selma slumped against the side of the car when her muscles threatened to give in to the delayed shock. "Thank you."

He grunted, then disconnected the call, leaving her alone on the side of the road.

Now that the reassurance of Kesh's voice was gone, the darkness seemed to press in on her again, making her every hair stand on end. Somewhere out there, demons were hunting her.

The phone in her hand lit up with a text message—directions from Kesh.

But before she managed to read the text, a scraping sound from the other side of the car cut through the darkness, chilling her blood.

What the hell was that?

"Hello?" she called stupidly before biting down hard on her tongue. If whatever made that sound was capable of responding, she didn't exactly want it to.

Moving faster than she'd thought possible Selma lunged at the driver side door. The sooner she got out of here, the better.

Her heart drummed hard in her throat as her adrenaline spiked for the second time that evening, but when her fingers pulled frantically at the handle, it didn't budge.

How was it locked? She'd made sure to leave it unlocked when she got out, leaving the keys in the ignition. Frantically she pulled on the door again, but it still wouldn't budge.

"Even when you reek of fear, you are the most delicious thing I've ever seen," a deep, familiar voice purred.

Cold shock froze her to the spot, her fingers still curled around the handle. *No.*

Movement in her peripheral vision made her snap her head around just in time to see a large shadow move around the back of the car. It was too dark to see his features in the faint light of the stars, but she didn't need a visual to know who it was.

"Hello, sweetheart."

"Marathin." She whispered the name of the man who'd first captured her, hoping against all hope that she was mistaken—that the demon who'd promised to bend her to his will wasn't here, about to take her away and break her. "No."

"Now, now, don't say it like that, my sweet. You'll hurt my feelings." There was a distinct smirk in his voice—the sound of a man who knew he'd won. "After everything I've done to ensure we could meet without the interference of that brute who thought he could claim you after you'd given yourself to me."

Oh, god. Sick realization nestled in the pit of her stomach. "*You* are behind this? *You* captured Kain?"

"Oh, no—only another Lord could do such a thing. But I may have been the one to suggest to the Prince that he should take care of your unworthy mate. No royal can ignore a direct threat to their power, and His Highness was more than willing to listen to my suggestion of how to get rid of the Lord who challenged and beat him.

"You see, once *Kain*—" He spat the name as if the very taste of it tongue disgusted him. "—got out of his mating high for long enough, he may have decided to lay claim to Naharan's position. It's his right, after all, since he defeated a royal in an equal fight. So as you can imagine, Naharan didn't need much persuasion. I mainly provided the contacts."

Contacts? Those females...

"What's going to happen to him?" Despite her fear of

the dark creature slithering around the car, she needed to know her mate's fate. Somehow, she would make it through this nightmare and she would find him again. As long as he was alive, this monster couldn't break her.

"Oh, the queen was most receptive when I approached her. You see, while Naharan worried he couldn't take your mate on by himself, he couldn't very well involve other Lords in this. Killing one of their own without provocation? It is treason, even for a Prince of Demons.

"So I came up with a simple solution: The females are struggling because our Lords are so much stronger than them—the males they can kidnap and breed with do not produce sufficiently powerful daughters. But if we were to offer them a Lord and a Stone of Power? Let's just say that it's very beneficial to me that the Queen of Demons owes me big."

The chill in her blood reached her heart. "You're going to... *breed* him? He'll never stand for that!"

Marathin chuckled and finally stepped close enough that she could make out his face in the darkness.

"I care nothing for the Lord's fate—what happens to him will be in the hands of the queen. I only care about *you.* The Prince thinks he's procured my services on the promise that I get to mount you for a night, along with a sum of money, before he hides you away as his secret mate so no one will discover what he did. You and I know better."

"You're betraying him, too." At this point, the fact that

he would double-cross even the Prince of Demons didn't shock her—it was merely a statement as she watched him slide a gloved hand over the side of the car. "You're going to give up everything just so you can claim me."

He smiled, faint starlight reflected in his teeth. "That is how much I love you, yes."

Love. The word seemed to mock her as the face of the man who had truly given her his scarred heart flashed in her mind.

"You're sick," she snapped, anger suddenly welling up to mix with her fear. "You know nothing of love—you only want to possess me like some trinket! And you ripped my mate from me, thinking you could ever replace him. I will never be yours, you sick bastard!"

His smile turned into a sneer. "You signed my contract—I own you, every ounce and every breath. Did you truly think I was going to stand by and let someone take what's mine? *I* found you—I was the one who first mounted your little cunt, the first to teach you how to take a demon's ridges. You *begged* me to keep you, remember?"

Before she managed to react, he took the final few steps to reach her and his hands came down on each side of her, clamping onto her shoulders. This close, she could see his face clearly, and the rage marring his handsome features was terrifying.

"I've given up so much for you. All I demand is that you obey the contract you signed. Once you've learned who your true master is, I will be good to you again."

Selma squirmed to get away. Though she knew it was

pointless, instincts for self-preservation took over, and she fought and kicked at him in her desperation. Once, he'd been able to sway her with his handsome features and kind mannerisms, but whatever attraction she'd had for him was gone.

Even if she hadn't seen him brutally murder the people who'd tried to save her from him, Kain's claim to her had erased other demons' ability to influence her, and she felt nothing but disgust as Marathin's hot breath puffed against the side of her neck.

"Let go of me!" she screamed as he lifted her up, only to press her against the side of the car a moment later. "I'm his, and nothing you do will change that!"

Marathin's eyes glowed dangerously as he bent over her, blocking her view of the night sky.

"We'll just have to see about that. Once I remind you of how perfectly we fit together you will change your tune, Breeder. But at least he should have given you enough cock that I don't have to twist your ring—you will be fully conscious through every moment while I reclaim your sweet little cunt. You'll have eternity to regret running from me—and I suspect you'll start when you're howling for mercy on my ridges!"

Oh, god. No.

Cold realization set in just as he started ripping at her clothes. He'd raped her before, but this time, the dark magic welded around her clit wouldn't ease the violation.

There'd been pleasure the first time he'd forced her. Her body, while at first struggling with his demonic anatomy, had been open and eager from his manipulations. Now every muscle in her body tensed with repulsion at his closeness, nausea churning in her gut as she struggled against him.

The pain of being forced to take his ridged mass while her body was unwilling terrified her, but what made her heart clench was the realization that someone other than her mate would demand access to the very core of her being, would take what only belonged to Kain.

She couldn't live through that.

"No! Let me go! Stop!" Selma clawed at his face and kicked frantically at anything she could make contact with, but Marathin was much too strong.

Snarling, he ripped open her shirt to let her breasts spill into the cold air, then yanked her pants down so hard the zipper broke.

"*Yield!*" he growled. "Yield, or I'll make it hurt even worse!"

He'd once claimed he'd never harm her, promises made by a demon cajoling his victim. Kain had made her promises too, promises he'd given his freedom to keep. The juxtaposition thundered in her head as she struggled against him, the twisted mockery that was Marathin's claims of love finally making it crystal clear what'd been between her and her mate who'd sacrificed everything for her.

Love.

Bealith was right. But she'd never get to tell him.

In the end, it didn't matter how much she resisted.

Marathin was much too strong, and despite fighting and screaming as best she could, nothing she did made him stop.

When his hand brushed between her legs, separating her nether lips, there was nothing she could do to resist it.

Marathin grunted at her low sob, squeezing her wrists painfully tight. She tried to clamp her thighs together, but he simply lifted her to rest against the hood of her car and stepped in between her legs, separating them with his hips.

But where despair and violation had sprouted, something new rose from the very core of her being: a white-hot fire burning through her veins in a flash faster than she could fully comprehend, eradicating her fear until only deep, seething anger remained.

He dared! He'd ruined her life, had hunted for her across the entire country, and now he'd taken her mate from her just so he could violate her once more.

She'd cowered before him for the last time.

"I said no!" This time her voice was not a pleading whimper. She screamed in fury as the fire in her blood rushed up her arms and into her hands.

Marathin released her wrists with a startled shriek, stumbling back, and she didn't pause to think. The second she was free, she grasped his face in her hands and squeezed.

His skin lit up with bright white light drawing fissures from where her fingers bore into him. He screamed then, his eyes wide with fear as he stared at her, but his body seemed limp, only held aloft by her grip.

There was nothing but grim satisfaction as she stared at his panicked eyes lit up from within with the raw, pulsing power rushing from her core.

With a crack like thunder, his head exploded between her palms in a burst of light. Selma tumbled to the ground, thrown by the shockwave. Belatedly she shrieked and cussed as her exposed skin grated against the rough road. But once she finally lay still, nothing but silence met her.

Slowly she sat up, panting from pain and a kind of soul-deep exhaustion that was wholly new.

On the ground a few yards over, Marathin's headless body lay sprawled on the tarmac. Bits of bloody skull and brain matter were scattered around them both.

The nausea came before she could fully process the horrific scene, and she only just managed to lean over to avoid vomiting all over herself.

Once her stomach settled enough that she could fight against the dry heaves, she somehow found the strength to hoist herself up by grabbing onto the car.

She'd killed him. She'd killed her rapist. Her kidnapper. And she felt no remorse.

She didn't know what that white light was or where it came from, but she knew without a doubt that it belonged to her.

Slowly she turned to look at what remained of the demon who'd ruined her life. This time, numbness quelled her nausea.

"I should have made you suffer for longer," she whispered to his mangled corpse.

It was several moments before the faint hum of a motor finally tore her attention back to the present.

She may have escaped one enemy, but she was still being hunted. Mysterious white light or not, she needed to get to safety before the Prince found her, or both she and Kain were doomed.

THIRTY-TWO
SELMA

The café Kesh had directed her to turned out to be more of a pit stop for truckers, with only a few patrons at the tables, thanks to the late hour.

Selma paused at the entrance to let her gaze sweep the shop in hopes of spotting the man she was here to meet.

At the farthest table facing the door, an obscenely handsome man looked up, his eyes widening in outrage at the state of her.

Selma tugged self-consciously at her ruined coat. Underneath it her clothes were even more ripped from Marathin's attack, but she hadn't exactly had time to do anything about it.

The stranger got up from his chair, his movements carefully measured in a way that more than hinted at inhuman strength as he made his way toward her.

She swallowed automatically, fighting an instinct to

flee. He was most definitely a demon Lord, given the way invisible power radiated from his huge form.

"Kesh?" Her voice cracked when he stopped in front of her. She had to tip her head back to look at his face.

He nodded as his black eyes narrowed to slits. "Naharan did this to you?"

Oh, great. As much as she appreciated his anger on her behalf, now was not the time to deal with primitive demon instincts, and Kesh looked an awful lot like Kain had when he'd sworn to kill Marathin.

"No, but can we please get out of here? I don't know if they're still after me." Even though she felt distinctly uneasy about being this close to a demon Lord she didn't know, Kain had trusted him with her safety. No matter his overwhelming presence, she much preferred to be in his company than out in public where the Prince could get to her.

Kesh growled low, but nevertheless placed an oversized hand on her shoulder so he could steer her out the door.

"How many were there?" he asked when they made it to the parking lot.

"Seven. Prince Naharan and six females." Selma turned to look up at the demon accompanying her. "They made a deal—the females helped the Prince secure Kain, and in return he'll be used for... for breeding. We need to save him."

Kesh's eyebrows rose at her words, but instead of commenting, he simply guided her to a black motorcycle.

Selma squirmed away from his grip on her shoulder. "Are you even listening to me? Kain's in trouble. You need to help him!"

The demon let out a small sigh, his dark eyes gleaming with impatience. "Trust me, he didn't have you call me for his sake. You said it yourself a moment ago—they might still be hunting for you, so right now we need to get you to safety. We can talk about my brother once you've been secured."

Brother? Selma stared at him as he took off his leather jacket, zipped it around her, and then shoved a helmet over her head. Finally he mounted the bike and twisted to lift her behind him.

So this was the other son of the woman who'd killed herself to escape an eternity as a Breeder.

"Hold on tight. It's a long drive," he grunted, and she wrapped her arms around his T-shirt-clad midriff.

He seemed about as approachable as Kain had the morning after their first meeting, but despite her instinctive wariness of a demon his size and less-than-talkative nature, she felt substantially safer on the back of his bike than she had on the car ride here.

If he was Kain's brother, he would most definitely help get her mate back—and make Naharan pay.

THEY RODE FOR HOURS.

When Kesh finally pulled up to a large estate, Selma's

entire body was stiff from the ride, and despite her worry for Kain and the trauma she'd endured from Marathin, she found it hard to stay awake.

Yet she peeked up from behind Kesh's wide back when he stopped in front of the iron gates flanked by armed men. They were somewhere in the countryside, in which state she didn't know, but the security seemed as vigorous as it had been at Kain's casino. Apparently all demon Lords were anal about surveillance.

"Alert Kirigan of my arrival," Kesh said to the guard.

"Yes, sir," the guard replied as the gate swung open to allow them entry. He glanced curiously in her direction before Kesh kicked the bike back into gear and they roared up the long driveway to the manor house.

"Who's Kirigan?" she asked once they'd stopped again. "Your second-in-command?"

"My father," Kesh grunted before unceremoniously lifting her off the back of his bike.

Selma froze, staring up at the imposing house. Despite her fatigue and aching joints, she suddenly felt rather hesitant at the prospect of walking inside.

Kain's father... What little she had heard of him had been enough to scare her, and meeting him like this, without the protection of her mate? It was more than a little daunting.

"So Kain told you about him?"

She looked up at her companion. The slight flare of his nostrils gave away what he'd picked up on—the smell of her fear.

"A little," she croaked.

Kesh grimaced and placed a hand on her shoulder, gripping her gently through the much-too-large leather jacket. "He won't harm you, Breeder. And we need his help. Come—after you provide what details you can, you will be cared for."

There wasn't really anything else to do. Kain needed help, and this seemed the only way to get it.

With the constant presence of Kesh's large hand on her shoulder, as if he thought she needed the support, Selma climbed the stairs to the grand doorway where yet another man stood guard.

"Does your dad expect an attack?" she asked when the armed male sent her a curious look.

"Who knows?" the demon Lord behind her grumbled. "Most Lords keep their private domain well-protected."

The guard opened the door for them without comment, even though he looked like he was bursting to ask about the Breeder being hauled into the estate.

Selma saw his nostrils twitch in her direction when they passed over the threshold and managed to smother an eyeroll. Smelling like catnip for demons was starting to lose its novelty.

Inside, the house was every bit as manor-like as the exterior. Selma looked around the grand hall they'd stepped into with raised eyebrows. "Did you and Kain grow up here?"

"Yeah." Kesh gave the exquisite paintings on the far wall a disgusted look. "Grossly pompous, isn't it?"

There wasn't a lot she could say to that. She'd grown up in a lower middle-class household, and the only things they'd had on the walls were her drawings and various art projects as she was growing up. This level of wealth was far beyond anything she could relate to.

Of course, the fact that Kain could pay what he had for her just by "shifting some assets around" should really have warned her of the kind of home he'd grown up in.

Kesh led her down a marble-floored hallway and into what looked like an old-fashioned library or drawing room. Floor-to-ceiling bookcases in dark wood lined the walls, and a chesterfield sofa with matching armchairs sat by one of the two large windows that probably offered a lovely view of the grounds in the daytime.

By a large fireplace stood a tall, broad-shouldered man with a crystal tumbler full of amber liquid. He was wearing a loose shirt and black pants, and his naked feet suggested he'd gotten out of bed to meet them.

"Father," Kesh greeted him, "I'm afraid we have a problem."

"Of course we have a problem," Kirigan said. His voice was dark and rich, and it reminded her painfully of Kain's. His hair was black as Kesh's, but she could see the resemblance to both of them in his angular features and soft lips.

He also looked to be exactly the same age as his two sons, but before Selma had a chance to reflect on that startling realization, the demon's black eyes landed on her, and all her contemplation halted as she tried to suppress a shudder. Something was off in his deep gaze—like she was staring into an abyss, not a person's soul.

Thankfully he shifted his disturbing eyes back to Kesh after perusing her for only a few seconds.

"Why else would you come? I take it the woman is the Breeder your brother claimed a few days ago. Is he dead?"

His calm tone made Selma frown. He was talking about his child's potential death with no more emotion than if they'd been discussing the weather.

"No, but the prince attacked him and gave him away to the queen so she can breed him. He needs our help."

Selma hadn't meant to draw the disturbing demon's attention back to her, but his apparent lack of care made her push past Kesh's protective shoulder to glare at the man who'd raised her mate.

"*Our* help, little Breeder?" Kirigan's eyebrows crept up a few millimeters. "You care what happens to the beast who raped you?"

Unexpected anger flared in her chest at hearing the gentle giant who'd protected and cared for her spoken about as if he were anything like the monster who had *actually* raped her.

"He's no rapist. He was going to set me free. Yes, I care for him—he's my mate and the father of my child, and I don't care what fucked up relationship you obviously have with him! I am going to save him—and if you're not going to help me, I'm wasting my time."

Something shifted in the dark, dangerous depths of Kirigan's gaze, and realization of what she'd just said set in like a cold shock. Reflexively she stepped back, plastering her back against Kesh's strong torso in instinctive search of protection.

"Well, well, aren't you a little firecracker?" Kirigan mused before taking another sip of alcohol. "And pregnant? I suppose that explains why Kain would send her to you for help." He raised an eyebrow at Kesh.

The demon behind her let out a low rumble, almost imperceptibly putting his shoulder back between her and his father.

"Apparently. Nevertheless, if he's still alive as she says, I'm going to go get him. I assumed you would care what happened to your oldest son too, or I would not have brought his mate here."

Kirigan's upper lip curled in a snarl—the first expression of emotion she'd seen on him. "Of course I care. You and he are the only reason I still suffer through the torture of walking this Earth, despite what hatred for me still festers in your hearts.

"However, one does not simply charge into battle against the Queen of Demons, nor sling accusations of betrayal against our king's heir. We need to plan, and you need to take care of the female—she's dead on her feet, her sharp tongue notwithstanding."

"As you wish. We will speak further in the morning."

Kesh's large hand found her shoulder again, and when he practically herded her out of the room, she got the distinct impression he was happy to put distance between them and his father.

"And Kesh?" Kirigan's deep baritone called after them just before the door shut in their wake.

Kesh paused, and she could have sworn she heard a muted profanity slip past his lips. "Father?"

"Make sure the Breeder does not roam around unescorted. It would be a pity if she came to any harm."

Selma's heart jumped into her throat at the casual threat, and she gladly followed Kesh when he steered her down several long hallways and up a winding flight of stairs.

"What the hell did he mean by that? Did he just threaten me?" she finally asked when she was absolutely certain they were out of earshot.

The demon by her side sighed. "He is... not entirely stable, and he will occasionally lash out. It was not a threat—he likely doesn't want to accidentally hurt you if he comes across you while he's in one of his moods, and that was just a reminder for me not to let you out of my sight."

She glanced up at Kain's brother, frowning. "Is it because I might remind him of your mother? My scent, I mean."

An odd expression crossed Kesh's features and he gave her a long look out of the corner of his eye. "He told you?"

"About how she died? Yeah. I'm... I'm sorry. You were even younger than Kain—it must have been so hard for you, too."

Despite the horrors of the night and the near-debilitating exhaustion starting to creep up along her limbs, she felt sadness for the tragedy that had ripped this family apart—and a stab of guilt for springing the subject on him.

Kesh's dark eyes narrowed. "He knew you before that auction, didn't he?"

Selma bit the inside of her cheek as she remembered the first time she'd seen Kain. "Yes. He saved me. It's a long story. I didn't think he was going to come to my auction, but he did—to save me again."

"So that's why he went. When I heard my brother was going to attend a Breeder's auction, I didn't believe it —until I saw him march down the stairs and challenge the Prince of Demons himself. Never thought he'd bid on a mate."

Kesh opened a wooden door, revealing a rather large bedroom with a plush carpet and antique-looking furniture.

"Wait..." Selma paused as she realized what that sentence meant. "You... You were *there?*"

Her mate's brother had seen her naked—had seen them have wild and obscene sex in front of a bunch of strangers. Heat flushed her face and she had to fight herself not to hide it in her hands. Fucking demons and their fucking barbaric customs!

"Yes." He walked into the bedroom, pulling her with him before shutting the door. "I heard Kain would be attending and I was... curious. Of course he was going to save you—I should have realized there was some noble motive behind it. He always did have a soft spot for vulnerable women, after..."

He fell silent for a moment, but then seemed to gather himself with a deep intake of breath. "But he got you pregnant, you say? I bet that came as a nasty surprise to him."

Hurt and some oddly protective instincts made her press a hand against her stomach to shield the small life growing there.

"He was happy," she said, more than a note of frost in her voice. "Scared, but happy. Don't you insult him, or me, by insinuating anything else."

A wry smile pulled on Kesh's devious lips, offsetting his look of mild surprise. "You really are a little firecracker, huh? Back-talking a demon Lord mere days after your claiming. Is that why he chose you?"

In truth she had no idea why Kain had fallen for her, but she didn't feel like telling this stranger anymore of their private business. He may have been Kain's brother, but she was done talking about Kain when he wasn't here. If Kesh hadn't heard about his brother's decision to attend the auction directly from him, they obviously didn't have a close relationship.

Selma set her jaw. "Instead of worrying about that, maybe you could tell me when we'll go get Kain?"

"As soon as we're able. My father isn't wrong—it's a rather delicate situation, and we, at the very least, need to know where he's being kept before we can act. But this is not something you need to worry about, Breeder. I will take care of it—you just need to rest."

Great, another overbearing male who'd decided she was too delicate to do anything but nap.

She *was* pretty exhausted, though, and that four-poster bed *did* look pretty inviting—and despite how annoying Kesh's assurance that she didn't need to worry because he was in charge now was, some embarrassing part of her responded to his self-assurance by letting go of her anxiety and fear. Somewhere along the line, her hormones had evidently gotten the upper hand, and she now instinctively trusted big brutes who said they'd take care of everything so she didn't have to.

It was infuriating.

Annoyed with herself as much as with him, Selma turned toward the bed. However much she wanted to throw a fit, she needed to sleep more than she needed to assert herself right now. Tomorrow, however, was another matter entirely.

Determined to climb in and disappear from the world under what looked to be extraordinarily thick and fluffy blankets, she kicked off her shoes and unzipped and removed Kesh's leather jacket—and was halted by a sharp intake of breath from the demon behind her.

"I want the name of the one who did this."

Selma blinked at his angry tone, then remembered what state Marathin had left her clothes in.

"Oh. It's... a bit of a long story. One of Naharan's accomplices chased me down when I fled."

She pulled uncomfortably on her ruined shirt, ensuring that she wasn't flashing him anything inappropriate, then finally climbed into the bed. It was soft and heavenly, and she felt her muscles relax into the mattress on contact. She didn't want to think about Marathin and what he'd done to her, or even what she'd done to him.

"Who is he?"

The low growl from the end of the bed had the small hairs on her arms standing on end. Selma cracked her eyes open halfway to look at the demon Lord.

"He's dead. I don't want to talk about it right now, okay? I'm so tired."

Kesh grunted an assent, though he still looked rather scary and angry as he hovered by the end of the bed. When she let her eyelids slide closed again, she heard him move quietly around the room, undoubtedly to turn off the light and ensure that everything was safe for her.

She sighed. As infuriating as it was to be treated like a china doll, there was still something rather endearing about these big brutes' obsessive need to care for the women whose scent drove them loopy.

Besides, the somewhat familiar pattern reminded her of Kain, and she dozed off with a feeling of being safe in the hands of people who would help her save her mate.

THIRTY-THREE
SELMA

The pleasant scent of male musk slowly penetrated her consciousness as sleep released its hold on her. She was warm and comfortable, and the feeling of hard, sculpted flesh by her side made her feel safe. Home.

Selma nuzzled in closer against her mate and was rewarded with a sleepy rumble that sounded just like it should, but also... not.

Before she'd managed to push away the haze of drowsiness, the big male by her side rolled over, letting a large hand stroke down over her hip and in between her thighs, then up against her clothed sex in an unmistakable suggestion.

A myriad of images and sensations coagulated in her mind in the span of a split-second—Marathin touching her, spreading her apart, trying to force his way inside of her.

"*No!*" She fought wildly against the questing hand, punching and kicking until the man in her bed rolled away with a startled grunt.

Relief mixed with flashes of a broken skull and brain matter splattered across the tarmac, and she only just managed to scramble to the edge of the bed before she vomited.

The rest of last night's memories finally set in while she dry heaved. She was in Kain's father's home—not among enemies.

"Are you certain he's dead?" Kesh's voice was so gravelly with restrained fury it set the hairs at the back of her neck on edge.

Forcing a deep breath, she rubbed both hands against her eyes, slowly regaining control of herself. What Marathin had tried to do to her last night hadn't been much different from the first time he'd taken her against her will—except it had. But what she'd done to him was so much worse, and so very satisfying.

Selma drew in another deep breath and lowered her hands, her frantic heartbeat calming as she replayed the grim satisfaction of murdering her molester until the horror released its grip on her body.

"Yeah. I'm certain."

Kesh let out a breath behind her, and she got the fleeting impression that he was disappointed with that answer. He had likely been hoping to murder the offender himself.

She looked over her shoulder, and sure enough Kain's

handsome brother was frowning, an air of agitation rolling off him.

He seemed to pull it together when her gaze caught his, rolling his shoulders with a grimace. "All right. Well, if you're done puking, we best get this over with. Do you have a preferred position?"

Selma blinked. "Position for what?"

Kesh arched an eyebrow at her, his expression suggesting he was starting to suspect she was clinically slow. "To be mounted."

She stared at him, his words not quite making sense until she remembered his hand between her legs.

"Are you… Are you actually serious right now? You're my mate's brother, for fuck's sake! I'm not sleeping with you, and if you try and force me, so help me I'll *end* you!"

Perhaps it should have been fear that gripped her when she realized his intentions. He was so much bigger than Marathin and so much stronger. But the feeling of power still tickled in her palms, as if her body was reminding her that she would never have to submit against her will again.

Not that she knew *how* to access that bright energy, but the buzz in her hands seemed a promise that she would, should she ever need to.

The black-haired demon just stared at her. "You think I *want* to mate with you? It's my duty, Breeder. This is why Kain sent you to me—so I can ensure yours and his child's survival."

Kain's explanation when he'd driven them back from

the sanctuary came back to her—about how her baby would drain her life essence if she wasn't supplied with... an *alternative.* She grimaced.

"Look, I appreciate it, but I'm fine. *We're* fine. Focus your efforts on bringing my mate back to me so *he* can take care of us."

Kesh sighed, running his fingers through his dark hair. "Fine. But if you grow weak while we look for him, we're doing this. Understood?"

Selma nodded once, having absolutely no intention of complying. But it was obvious her overprotective brother-in-law wasn't dropping the issue without some concession. The sooner she got him off the idea she needed his magic semen, the sooner he'd refocus on getting Kain back.

"Why are you in my bed, anyway?" Selma glanced at his shirtless body. At least he seemed to be wearing his jeans from last night, and she was still in the torn clothing she'd worn when she collapsed in bed.

"It's technically my bed. This is my old room. You were having nightmares and whimpering in your sleep, and you wouldn't shut up until I climbed in and held you."

Oh. The morning just kept getting better and better.

"Um, sorry."

Kesh grunted dismissively. "It's fine. Are you done sleeping? I'll bring you down for breakfast after you've had a shower."

SELMA SPENT the better part of the morning pacing the ground floor of the house while trying to keep hold of her patience.

Kesh had cleaned her vomit off the floor while she was showering and presented her with some overly elegant—and absurdly expensive—silk garments with the price tags still attached. Then he'd proceeded to hover over her while she ate, insisting she pile on the cream cheese and sliced meats "for the baby."

He was even worse than Kain, who at least hadn't threatened to force feed her, and she was beginning to find his special brand of protectiveness more than a little aggravating.

Her mood wasn't helped any further by the lack of apparent urgency in freeing Kain.

"You should sit down. You need to conserve your energy."

Selma leveled a glare at the big man leaning against the door frame to the study, watching her with slightly narrowed eyes as if she was to blame for his need to keep her under constant watch.

"You do realize that this fetus was conceived like, five days ago at most, right?

"You do realize it's a demon's offspring who will suck you dry of energy if he needs to survive? You're not carrying a human child. The more energy you expend, the sooner you'll need semen."

Well, wasn't he just great at making her feel all at ease with being an expectant mother?

Just as she opened her mouth to hiss at him to back off, a large, dark form appeared behind him, and her jaw clamped shut at the sight of Kirigan. She may have given him attitude the night before, but he still made her insides tight with fear. There was just something utterly disturbing about him, from his dark gaze down to his unsettling aura.

"Don't argue with the Breeder, Kesh." Kirigan moved easily past his son and walked toward her, fixing his terrifying eyes on hers. It was all she could do not to shrink back when he stopped right in front of her and placed a single finger under her chin to tilt her head up. "There is spark left in this one still. Do not seek to quell it."

Kesh seemed to materialize by her side out of thin air, looming over her shoulder as if to press his father back a little with his presence.

"Kain left her for me to protect. I will care for her as I see fit. Father." The last word was tacked on in a somewhat more demure tone when Kirigan lifted his unsettling gaze from her to his son.

"Indeed you will." The hot finger finally moved from her chin, and despite how annoyed she was with Kesh, she was pretty thankful for his protection at that moment.

When he placed a hand on her shoulder and gently pulled her back a step and out of his father's dark aura, she breathed a shaky, and embarrassingly audible, sigh of relief.

"Any news of Kain?" she asked.

Kirigan pursed his lips and finally stepped away. He headed toward a small wooden table hosting several bottles of expensive-looking liquor.

"Yes. My connections have managed to locate him. He is being held in a secure location up in Manitoba—far into their territory. Extracting him will be... challenging."

Selma stared from him to Kesh. Hope surged in her chest, but Kirigan's pause made her guess there was more to it than what he let on. "Challenging?"

"Nothing for you to concern yourself with, my dear. We will find a way." He poured a measure of whiskey and sipped it calmly before turning back around. "However, there is one thing I would discuss with you.

"It's a curious thing, really. My connections also said that one of the Prince's lackeys was killed the night they took my son. Only he wasn't killed by Kain. He was found several miles away, by the side of the road with scratch marks on his arms as if someone had tried to defend themselves against him. Someone small and weak.

"And, as if this wasn't puzzling enough, his head was scattered across the road. As if it'd exploded. I believe you know him—Marathin. Marathin Hershey, your Procurer, according to the records."

Oh.

Fuck.

Selma gave him a nervous glance before she steeled herself. Somehow she doubted that even the demons trying to protect her would take kindly to knowing what kind of power had awoken in her after her run-in with Bealith. Nor the demon world in general, judging by how they treated the women they called Breeders.

"Is that something you would happen to know anything about, little one?"

Kain's preferred term of endearment for her spoken by this frightening creature startled her for a moment, but she still managed to stick out her chin in defiance.

"I have no idea what happened."

Kirigan's lips curled in the smallest hint of a smile. "Do not try to lie to a demon, Selma. You will rarely deceive them."

Selma did her best to keep her gaze firm, though she pressed back into Kesh's strong chest for support. "I'm not lying. I'm scared and worried about Kain."

The older demon's smile turned a little sharper at the corners. "You mistakenly believe your scent is the only indicator of your deceitfulness. You are young and inexperienced, and there is little you can do to hide a lie from a demon my age. It's painted in the tensing of your jaw, the slight dilation of your pupils. My sons may be stricken by your pheromones, and easily manipulated by the call from your sweet little cunt, but you will not find me so easily distracted."

Her mouth fell open at his sudden vulgarity, but that wasn't the cause of the fear curdling in her stomach. No, that came down to his eyes—those dark, soulless eyes that seemed to swallow all light that touched them bored straight into hers, demanding her surrender. It was as if she was staring into the depths of madness, realizing that just below the surface there were true horrors to be found.

"Father," Kesh interjected. He squeezed Selma's shoulder comfortingly, trying to draw her into his own protective aura, but there was no escaping those terrifying eyes as long as Kirigan chose to keep them locked on hers.

"Did he force himself on you, Breeder? Is that how it happened?"

The feeling of Marathin's hands on her body, ripping at her clothes and touching her as if he had every right to, made its way to the forefront of her mind, and she couldn't repress the shudder it caused, nor the sense of dread.

She stared up at the demon in front of her, shaking her head in denial, but his gaze was alight with whatever it was that normally lurked just beneath the surface. The twisting emotion in her gut was no longer fear—it was pure terror, too strong to rationalize away with the fact that Kesh was here to protect her, or that as mad as Kain's father was, he wouldn't want to intentionally harm her. Instead her instincts screamed of danger, and she grasped at the protective body behind her, desperate to escape.

"That's enough!" Kesh grabbed her by both shoulders and easily lifted her behind him, squaring up in front of his father. "Get a hold of yourself—you're terrifying her!"

Selma had a moment's worth of relief that she was no longer in the enraged demon's direct line of sight. She wrapped her arms protectively around her midriff to try to gather her composure and quell her racing heart, but it shattered to pieces when Kirigan's face contorted in a snarl.

In the next second, his hand cracked against Kesh's jaw, sending her protector flying into the nearest bookshelf. Dark magic shot up around his limbs, pinning him in place.

The small whimper that escaped her lips sounded like it had come from a scared little animal—and it apparently didn't do anything to dampen Kirigan's rampage. His face lit up with feral ferociousness when she cowered back against the wall behind her, and he followed her retreat with slow, measured steps.

"Lying little Breeder. So small and soft. You reek of fear—which is why my foolish son is trying to break himself apart to get free and save you. Do you enjoy the power you hold? Is that what happened with Marathin? You made him mad with need, only to kill him when his desire got out of control? Show me what you did to him!"

"I did nothing!" she shrieked.

He snarled again and grabbed her shoulder. "Show me! Now!"

Kirigan dug his fingers into her flesh, not quite firmly enough to cause her pain, but it triggered her panic nonetheless. With a cry she brought both fists up to punch at him, hammering them against his unyielding flesh.

"Let go! Let go of me!"

"Fight me all you want, girl. Unless you do to me what you did to Marathin, I will make you scream. And if you still don't show me what I want to see, perhaps I will take the baby in your womb."

Maybe she should have questioned his claim to want to hurt his own grandchild, but in that moment, all she saw was his terrifying, distorted face. His features morphed before her eyes, adding a layer of red and black scales and long, black, coiled horns.

And his eyes... his eyes no longer had any white to them, their emptiness swallowing the last remotely human thing on his face.

Selma screamed.

It had been so long since she was faced with the visual aspect of her lifelong nightmares, and all the years of living in terror crashed back into the present at the sight of the monster who had her in his claws.

She didn't think—she only reacted. Something warm and powerful rose within her, and she grasped for it in desperation, using its strength to strike at the demon.

Bright, white light rushed from her hand like a current, blasting into Kirigan.

Black and white sparks flew around them as he lifted dark magic around himself at the very last moment, causing the air to vibrate with a high-pitched screech like the sound of a braking train. It didn't stop the shockwave of the impact from throwing him to the ground.

Selma stood frozen, staring at the man the power

within her had tried to destroy—that *she* had tried to destroy in her terror for her child's life. His features were once again human, and the zealous fire in his eyes no longer reflected danger so much as absolute awe.

THIRTY-FOUR
SELMA

"I knew it!" Kirigan's voice was raw with emotion. "The light! So pure. I knew it was inside of them! Kesh, did you see? That is their call—that is what drives us mad!"

By the bookshelf, Kesh slowly got to his feet, his bindings gone. He was eyeing her carefully, as if he didn't know if she would attack.

"I'm sorry," she whispered, not certain her voice would hold. "I didn't mean to."

Kirigan got off the floor, his disturbing gaze focused on her. "Marathin was the first time?"

She nodded, confused at his apparent excitement. She'd expected anger. Retribution.

"You are not a weak little girl. You have strength to rival ours." He was still staring intently at her as if he was trying to see the white light through her eyes. "I always knew it was buried within you, but I could never... And then *you* come waltzing into my son's life, bringing us new life, and *this*."

Now he turned away from her, murmuring to himself in a language she didn't know.

Kesh stepped forward as his father went to one of the bookshelves farthest from them. He glanced from the mad demon to her, wariness still evident on his features. A faint trail of blood trickled from the corner of his mouth.

"You all right?"

"Yeah." As all right as she could be after having been subjected to an insane demon, at least. Her pulse was still drumming rapidly in her throat.

"I'm... sorry I let him do that. I was unprepared, and I failed you."

Kesh looked distinctly uncomfortable, and it suddenly dawned on her that despite how mistrustful he might be of her, she likely still reeked of fear. Undoubtedly, that scent was wreaking havoc on his instincts. But like his brother, he was fighting to control himself.

"Why doesn't it affect him?" Selma lowered her voice a tad and glanced at Kirigan. "My scent?"

Kesh growled as he gave his father's back a dirty look. "Who the fuck knows?"

"It does, in a way." Kirigan turned back to them without looking up from the leather-bound book he was leafing through. "But your pheromones work by upsetting our ability to calm our nervous systems, and I have lost the ability to feel much of anything. Therefore, the added aggravation of a frightened Breeder isn't too difficult to ignore."

Selma kept quiet, though she had a hard time believing he was telling the full truth. The way he clung to his liquor-filled glass suggested he was more likely trying to desperately numb feelings too painful for him to cope with—and she'd seen a glimpse of what lay beneath his dead gaze.

Agony. Madness. Despair. It was more likely he could ignore her scent's effect because he was drowning in a nightmare much worse than what her scent could compete with.

Despite her fear of him, and despite what Kain had told her he'd done to his mate and her human family, she pitied him.

"I first came across a reference to what you just showed us many years ago," he continued as if he hadn't just threatened her with killing her unborn child to make the light inside of her burst out against her will. "This text mentions 'the powerful light within the Seers.' I am old enough to remember when your kind was something other than our mates and mothers. Did you know we weren't always able to mate with the women who see us for what we truly are?"

Selma nodded, errantly wondering exactly how old the being in front of her was. As far as she understood, her kind had been known as Breeders for centuries.

He smiled, though it looked more like a grimace. "Then you also know we have the gods to thank for that—

and the traitor queen, of course, may she burn in the fiery pits of the Earth. What I don't understand is how you can access it when there have been no other incidents as far as we know."

Love. Bealtih had claimed the key to unlocking the lost power was love. Though Selma highly doubted no woman had ever loved her demon captor, at least after some time. Stockholm Syndrome was a thing, after all.

Maybe it was because of Kain. If no other demon had ever loved his mate so unconditionally that they were willing to give them up, perhaps he was the reason for her newfound strength.

Not that she wanted to test Kirigan's mental stability by talking about love and gods.

Thankfully he didn't seem to be expecting an answer, and his gaze remained thoughtful and distant rather than burning into hers as it had when he was determined to force her to speak.

"Yes, well, whatever it is, musing about it won't help us get Kain. Let's just focus on bringing him back—he chose to claim a mate, so he can also deal with her unstable power," Kesh interrupted. He'd folded both arms over his chest, looking like he was more than ready to pawn her and her unexpected issue off on his brother at the first opportunity. Apparently this demon Lord had had enough of babysitting a wayward Breeder.

"But on the contrary, my son." Kirigan's mouth quirked lightly at one corner, lending his expression a wicked slant. "This is exactly what we need to focus on to get Kain back. A Breeder capable of killing our kind? The females will never see it coming, and it will lend us the element of surprise we need in order to overpower them."

"Absolutely not!" Kesh's scowl dropped in favor of pure outrage, and in the next moment, he shoved her behind his back. "I am not taking her into the middle of the queen's territory! Kain left her for me to protect, not you, and there is no way I'm risking her life on such a folly!"

"In case you haven't noticed, she's not exactly a helpless little darling. Do you have a better plan?"

"She is untrained. We have no guarantee she'll be able to call on her power at will, not to mention what will happen to whatever men we bring with us. The second something scares her, they'll likely abandon their positions to protect her, risking the entire fucking operation. It's not going to happen, and I don't care how bloody you beat me—I'd rather risk your wrath than have to live with the knowledge that I caused a Breeder's death!"

The last sentence hung in the air between them like a solid entity in the room. Selma winced, desperately praying that the harsh words didn't cause Kirigan to go over the deep end.

But when he spoke, his voice was quiet and controlled.

"If you learned anything from your mother's death, it should have been that no one can force these creatures to bend to our urge to possess them. Not in the long run.

Now do yourself a favor and ask the little one what she wants to do."

"It doesn't matter what she wants," he hissed, though his voice had lost some of its power. "She's my responsibility."

Selma sighed from her protected vantage point and placed a palm against his back. From what little she'd managed to learn about them, a demon as agitated as Kesh needed a gentle hand.

"I'm going, Kesh."

Slowly the big man turned, staring down at her with both dark eyebrows pulled into a frown. "Do you understand how ludicrous this idea is? You and your baby would be in mortal danger—the exact thing Kain sacrificed himself to prevent. No."

It was just his instincts—he couldn't help the urge to treat her like she was made of porcelain. Selma did her best not to show her brewing annoyance.

"If I can help in any way, I'm going. As you said, Kain sacrificed himself for me. I'm not going to abandon him."

He narrowed his eyes. "He did not send you to me so I could drag you back into their claws. You are not going, and that's final. Have I made myself clear?"

IT WASN'T that she had complete faith in her ability to control the light inside of her—far from it—but despite Kirigan's less-than-stable sanity, she knew from their discussion that he was right: she was their best shot at getting Kain out, because no one would think her capable of doing any harm. If they were spotted while trying to sneak in, Kain and Kirigan would distract the females so she could finish them off.

It was curious, really. She'd never imagined herself capable of killing, but the thought of ending the life of one of the monsters responsible for imprisoning Kain didn't disturb her as much as she'd thought it would. Marathin's death had proved that through her power, she finally had agency over her own life. She wasn't weak like they'd tried to tell her she was, and she didn't have to sit back and let others decide what was going to happen to her.

The monsters who'd taken her mate were going to regret what they'd done.

When she looked at the men in the helicopter transporting them as close to the queen's residence as they could get, she caught Kesh's angry glare and failed to suppress a mildly teasing smile.

The demon Lord had gone so far as to threaten to lock her up to keep her safe in his father's house while they attempted to rescue Kain. Neither of them had been prepared for the sudden outburst of tears his last shouted "no" had caused, but while Selma was fairly sure it was just due to pregnancy hormones, Kesh had looked like he'd just accidentally killed a litter of puppies.

He'd cradled her and cooed and soothed with a clear undertone of panic, and that was when she'd realized how she was going to get her way.

He'd still not forgiven her for the borderline cruel manipulation of his instincts that followed.

"We're at the meeting point in two minutes," the demon Lord said, his voice clipped and cool. "You will stay behind me at all times or I will abandon the mission and drag you home, no matter how much you cry. Is that clear?"

Selma sighed, but nodded to placate him. None of them would benefit from distractions, and she knew he needed to believe her safe so he could focus. As long as they got to Kain, she didn't care what she had to do to make that happen.

THIRTY-FIVE
KAIN

The shackles around his wrists cut into his already bleeding flesh, but the pain was easy to ignore.

Snarling, he crouched by the wall he was chained to, ready to lunge the second the female came within reach. He would snap her neck as he had the last of his captors who'd made that mistake.

"Now, now, big boy. I just want to chat," she purred from behind the bars of his cell. She cocked a hip and looked him over with hunger in her cold eyes. "You're such a handsome one. And strong. I just want to make you feel good. Don't you want to feel good?"

"I want to rip the head from your shoulders. That would make me feel good."

Her laughter echoed off the stone walls, its pitch modulated for seduction. The only impact it had on Kain was to further fuel his rage.

"I bet your offspring will be as fierce as their daddy.

Would that be so bad? To make strong children who will bring honor to your name?"

Children. His chest gave an achy spasm, and he gritted his teeth against the onslaught of emotion that word brought.

He had a child—or at least he'd *had* a child. He didn't know if Selma managed to escape, and he would likely never find out. All he could do was hope that she'd made it to Kesh and that his brother would treat her and their child well.

If a mated demon died, it was customary that the Breeder went to a sexually mature family member if she still had young children. It was the only way to ensure her new mate didn't kill the offspring not related to him in a fit of jealousy.

To Selma and his family, he was dead. No one knew where he'd been taken or that he was even alive, and Kesh was smart enough to know not to draw attention to Naharan's betrayal. An all-out war with the royal family would risk destroying them all—including his mate and unborn child.

"I have sent you willing female after willing female, and you have denied them all. And of course you killed poor Freidha. She was in heat, which is why she was silly enough to get too close, but I really did expect you to at least sniff her a bit before breaking her neck.

"Yet nothing has tempted that lovely cock of yours—which, let's be honest, is pretty out of character for your kind. I've been told you Lords enjoy raping those of us you capture, so why not take it when it's freely given?"

Kain spat at the ground and showed his teeth in disgust. He knew what they wanted from him—his seed to strengthen their offspring. Maybe before he'd mated his little one his body would have given in to the alluring scent of a female in heat, but now all he felt was repulsion. Nothing and no one would ever make him yearn like Selma did, and mounting another would only sully her memory.

He was fully aware that the image of her pretty face and the way she made him feel things he hadn't even known were possible were the only pleasantness he would ever know again.

"You know," the female said, the purr in her voice changing ever-so slightly to a more threatening sound, "you will give me what I want eventually. I am your queen, and sooner or later, you will yield to me. You produce stronger sperm when at full health and vitality, but I will starve and torture you to get what I need."

Kain's only response was a growl. Let her try to break him—he would rather die than give her what belonged to his mate.

Selma.

If she had made it to safety, nothing they did to him would matter.

The queen sighed and uncoiled the whip hanging by her hip. "I see you've made your choice. Very well."

HIS BODY still trembled long after the queen had left the dungeon. He wasn't exactly unfamiliar with pain, but even his exceedingly high level of endurance had started to crack after hours of being whipped and beaten.

Kain breathed in deeply to calm himself, and the scent of his own blood filled his nostrils. He leaned his head back against the cool stone wall he was slouched against. Closing his eyes, he groaned at the ache in his marred shoulders when they pressed more firmly against the surface. He'd heal quickly enough, but he had no delusions that the bitch queen wasn't going to draw more blood the next time she came.

And the time after that, and the time after that.

Hopefully, one day soon, she would let her guard down for just a second. When she did, he would strike, and maybe—just maybe—he would escape and find his mate again.

He smiled wryly. Succumbing to romantic fantasies... what a little torture and emotional turmoil could do to a man—even a demon.

During the beating, he'd indulged himself and let his mind escape to those moments in the car when he'd been driving Selma back. While looking at her sleeping form all curled up on the passenger seat next to him, he had finally realized what that sore thing constricting in his chest every time he thought of her was.

Love.

How ridiculous that such a folly had his insides twisting and his very being yearning. Yet he'd felt nothing but warmth flood his body as he'd watched her sleep, knowing that what he felt was love.

She'd chosen him. She'd chosen him and his child, had assured him that she would never leave their son—and in her scent and beautiful eyes, he'd seen the truth to her words.

For nearly an hour of his life, while the sound of Selma's deep breaths and her beautiful scent filled the car he was bringing her home in, he'd known true happiness. It was enough—it was more than he'd ever hoped for. More than he'd known to hope for.

No matter whether he escaped, they could never take that away from him.

Rattling at the dungeon door made his jaw clench and his thoughts slam back into the present. He'd hoped to get some sleep and to gather a bit of strength before the next session, but the queen was undoubtedly determined to make him break sooner rather than later. He still had the marks to prove as much.

The sharp fluorescent lights flickered on, and he could now make out two sets of individual footsteps. With a low growl he got to his feet, though he remained crouched and prepared to attack.

"Kain?"

The soft voice made his breath catch in his throat, choking off the growl.

No...

He hadn't finished the denial before the owner of the voice came into view. She paused for a second, her soft mouth dropping open in shock. Then she ran to the bars.

"Kain!"

Panic, desperation, and overwhelming joy blended into a knot of emotion in his stomach as Selma pulled uselessly at the door to his cell, rattling it in her attempt at getting to him.

"You can't be here," he gasped, panic taking over as he envisioned his beloved mate in the hands of the ruthless queen. "You have to get out!"

"We're not planning on hanging around, if that's what you mean." Another figure came into view, gently prying Selma's fingers off the bars so he could get to the lock.

Kesh.

Dark light flickered around his hand as he pressed his black energy into the lock, melting it off.

The moment the door was open, Selma rushed through it as if she was going to jump at him. But she stopped short, looking his bruised and bleeding body up and down with horror in her eyes.

"Oh, Kain."

The scent of her anguish pulled the rumbling hum from his chest before he closed his arms around her, shackles and all, and pulled her soft body against his. His lashes hurt when she pressed against them, but the soothing comfort of her already familiar weight far overshadowed any discomfort. Lost in the sensation of her, he buried his face in her long hair to inhale her intoxicating aroma, never pausing his deep rumble.

His mate. His beloved.

"Could you guys maybe wait with the reunion shit until we're out of here? I don't know if you've noticed, but we're in a fucking dungeon underneath one of the queen's residences. If we want any chance at getting out, it needs to happen before they manage to call for reinforcements."

Selma pulled away at his brother's snide comment, her brown eyes filling with worry instead of joy.

"He's right," she said, her voice tight. "Kirigan is trying to contain the guards upstairs. We have to hurry."

His father was there? Kesh had taken her to their father?

Through sheer force of will, Kain pushed away the worry clenching in his stomach. He could have words with his brother about putting his entrusted mate into danger—which damn well included bringing her here —later.

He glared at Kesh over the top of Selma's head, but the other demon was too preoccupied with examining his chains to care.

"Resistant to our magic," he muttered as he gave the lock an experimental prod with the tip of his knife. "It'll take forever to pick this. They sure didn't want you getting loose, eh? Selma, give it a try."

Kain frowned as his mate grabbed the shackles around his wrists and stared intently at them. His unasked question was soon answered when pure white light burst from her palms and into the metal, cracking the lock open as efficiently as a rock to a walnut.

"What the fuck was that?"

Kesh quirked a sardonic eyebrow at him. "Oh, that? Yeah, turns out your Breeder is capable of killing even the strongest among us. And may I take this opportunity to congratulate you on your choice of mate? Well-picked. She sure is worth the shit-ton of trouble your claiming has caused."

A defensive growl rumbled from his chest even as he eyed Selma with some hesitation. Had she always been capable of this? Had she somehow manipulated him into believing she was defenseless?

Her face contorted under his scrutiny, giving way to lines of anxiety and exhaustion.

"I didn't know, Kain," she whispered as if the questions were plain is his eyes.

No, she wasn't pretending to be weak—he'd smelled her terror when she was cornered and abused the first time he saw her, and now... she looked so frail, tired. Whatever was going on with her unexpected power, she obviously wasn't in control.

His protective instincts drowned any lingering doubt, and without a care for his many welts and cuts, he lifted her into his arms. They could talk later—right now, he needed to get his mate to safety.

Instead of objecting to being carried, she sank further into his grip and buried her head in his shoulder.

"I was so afraid I'd lost you," she mumbled, her voice

soft and intimate. His heart throbbed oddly in response, but just as he went to nuzzle against the crown of her head, he caught Kesh's exasperated eyeroll out of the corner of his eye.

Right. Reinforcement of their bond had to wait until they were in safer, and more private, quarters.

Kain followed his younger brother out through the dungeon, silently promising himself to also have a chat with Kesh about the exact reasons he'd thought it wise to bring his mate into enemy territory.

On the other side of the dungeon door, the body of a female demon lay crumpled against the wall, her skull bearing the undeniable marks of having been crushed with a great amount of power. A similar sight met them at the top of the stairs, and in the adjoining hallway they found three more bodies. Clearly the operation hadn't gone seamlessly.

Kesh paused at the end of the long, marble-tiled hallway, his hand hovering over the doorknob.

"I can't hear anything."

His hoarse whisper made Kain freeze, his senses straining to push past the limits of his fatigued body. Complete silence met him.

There should have been noise—the sounds of fighting.

"We have to go," Kesh hissed. "We can't attempt to save him without endangering her."

"Him" being their father.

Kain shook his head, determined not to let any lingering loyalties to the man who'd brought him up risk his mate. There was no choice to make—she was his only priority.

They shared a short look before Kesh kicked open the door, ready to cover their escape.

Yet they didn't manage more than two steps before dark magic wrapped around Kesh's throat and brought him to his knees with a gurgle.

Kain cursed and let Selma slide to the floor so his hands were free and his body between her and their attackers. His powers enveloped them both just in time to block a crushing blow of magic.

He growled at the cowardice behind the invisible attacks. These were filthy traps placed by weak enemies!

"I see I didn't tire you nearly enough."

The queen stepped out of thin air. She yanked on the chain in her hand, pulling his father out in the open too.

Kirigan stared straight ahead. Not a single hint of emotion flickered in his gaze despite the blood trickling from the barbs on the thick metal collar around his neck.

Kain pushed the odd pang in his gut away and bared his teeth at the queen.

"You will not stop us from leaving," he snarled in return. "Without your little tricks, even a queen has no hope against a Lord."

The queen's painted lips quirked. "Perhaps not under normal circumstances. But as you might be able to spot, I've already incapacitated two Lords without breaking a sweat, and despite all your bravado, you are not even at your full strength. Are you, my Lord?"

She had a point. How had she managed to trap both Kesh and Kirigan this easily?

He narrowed his eyes in concentration as he focused his powers. She was right—he was not at his best, and it was more challenging than it should have been to keep the protective barrier raised around himself and his mate while pushing his magic outward.

A faint shimmer filled the room, outlining the forms of several dozen crouched figures—hidden females ready to attack, no doubt. Yet that didn't explain how the magic constricting around Kesh's neck kept him kneeling and immobile, nor how his father, one of the most powerful demons he knew of, had been captured.

"A parting gift from His Highness," the queen purred. "For a son of one of those empty-headed cunts you all fawn over, he is quite crafty."

She held out the wrist on the hand not around Kirigan's chain, letting the jewel mounted on her silver bracelet sparkle.

Kain gasped, almost losing his grasp on his magic. A Stone of Power!

"Now, don't look so surprised. You didn't think I'd offer to help my sworn enemy just for a stud—even one as handsome as you? Lucky for me, your Prince thought you a great enough threat that he was willing to bargain this stone for our help in taking you out of the equation.

"Not that I doubt the little bitch hiding behind you had something to do with his compliance. I do wish I understood what you saw in the pathetic little cretins, but

I suppose I will have the chance to test her myself before Naharan picks her up."

Blinding rage surged through his veins, partly at the threat to Selma and partly at the depth of the Prince's betrayal. The three Stones of Power were as ancient as their race and had been safeguarded by their rulers for millennia to ensure the gods never got within breathing distance of them. Giving one to a sworn enemy who had already proved she would cooperate with the gods was treason.

If he had to give his own life to stop her, he would.

Kain grabbed at the very root of his essence, forcing his magic to burst out through his marred hands in a sudden blast that covered his leap toward the queen.

The room exploded in movement and shrieks as the hidden females sprang to aid their ruler, but they were too late to stop him.

He grabbed her shoulder, her bones snapping with a satisfying crunch when he closed his fist. The chain holding his father captive fell from her grasp.

The queen shrieked and twisted, throwing him over her hip and to the ground faster than he could anticipate.

He rolled to get back on his feet, but it was too late. Black power closed around his windpipe, and when he looked up, he saw the Queen bent over him, her features pulled into a fierce snarl. The Stone of Power shone at him, keeping him down.

"For that I will kill you," she hissed. "I have two other Lords I can breed now."

Kain tensed, trying his best to free even an ounce of his power, but the magic from the stone kept him completely pacified. He had failed.

"Kain! No!"

Selma's scream, shrill with anguish and fear, cut through to his very soul.

His mate. He would leave her behind to endure unspeakable horrors and a future as a breeding slave for a demon who would never treat her with the respect she deserved—and there was nothing he could do to change it.

Nothing he could do but die.

"Now, child!"

Faster than his eyes could follow, a dark chain wrapped around the Queen's throat and pulled her back. Kirigan's head appeared above her shoulder, grimacing at the strain of holding her back with his own chain.

With a grunt he spun her around before she could activate the Stone of Power, as if using her body as a shield for both himself and Kain.

Bright white light exploded through the room.

Kain gasped and tried to roll over to escape its destructive power, but there was no need. Before he could move, it was gone, leaving stunned silence in its wake. Silence, and ashes.

It took him a moment to realize that the fine, white powder drizzling over him like snowflakes on a quiet December night was what was left of the queen.

"Such beauty."

The reverent mumble came from his father. Kirigan

smiled with uncharacteristic softness in the direction the light had come from before turning his attention to Kain.

"Get up, son. Your Breeder is about to pass out, and I'm not entirely sure the females will honor her claim to the title once they come out of their shock."

Selma!

Kain's head snapped in her direction. She was swaying on her feet and her face was ashen.

He was up and by her side in a second, lifting her into his arms just as her knees buckled and consciousness left her still eerily glowing chocolate eyes.

The light had come from her.

THIRTY-SIX
SELMA

The burning need from someone twisting the ring clasped around her clitoris pushed through the black nothingness with muted force.

Selma groaned sluggishly, but her body refused to obey her attempts to spread her thighs wide or lift her hips for easier penetration.

"Is she responding?" The deep voice sounded like it came from somewhere far away.

"Yes. Be quiet so I can concentrate."

Though her fuzzy brain distorted the growl which followed, something at the very core of her being recognized it.

"Kain?"

"Yes, I'm here."

Relief nestled in her heart, even as her pussy contracted pathetically. Kain was here. He would make everything better.

"Do you really need to concentrate to fuck?" The faraway voice took on a clear note of sarcasm.

"Kesh, if you don't shut the fuck up, I'll beat you until you do!"

Despite the deep need pulsing between her thighs and Kain's dark snarl sending pleasurable shivers through her, enough reality filtered through the darkness surrounding her to make her understand that Kesh was about to see them have sex. Again.

Selma whimpered, wishing he would go away.

"Shh, little one." Kain's voice turned soft again. Intimate.

Warmth brushed over her abdomen and down her legs, spreading them, and then the heavy pressure of his hips settled in between her thighs. All thoughts of anything other than Kain evaporated.

Yes, yes!

Burning expectation swept through her lethargic body, priming her for what she knew would follow at any moment—what she needed more than air, even in her half-conscious state.

Thick, hard flesh pushed in between her legs, spreading her lower lips obscenely wide. If she'd had the strength, she would have cried out the moment he thrust in, filling her to bursting. Instead she could only groan into the darkness as Kain's heat claimed her in one long, slow push.

He was so deliciously big that even in her weak state,

her pussy clutched desperately at his girth, and every nerve ending sang with the violent pressure.

"Fuck!" His growl was low and rich, marking the moment he bottomed out in her tight sheath. "Selma..."

No sound followed her hoarsely whispered name—only the spine-breakingly intense sensation of his hips drawing back and his thick cock and primed ridges rubbing deeply at every sweet spot inside her. She may not be able to feel most of her body, but she certainly felt him and the places his scorching flesh made her come alive with his touch.

It was almost too much, despite her ring making her pussy weep and open for his punishing girth. When they'd mated before, she'd been fully in her body and capable of squirming and screaming as he pummeled her into oblivion. This time all she could do was lie there and take it, her focus solely on the sensation of his grueling length pushing into her over and over.

"Feel me, my love," her mate gasped from the empty space above her. "I got you. Just feel me."

Just feel him? She could do little else!

But behind the violent stretch and her pussy's desperate grip on him was something else—something more. It almost felt as if every thrust into her core brought life with it, as if the pleasure of his presence inside of her anchored her fleeting consciousness to her slowly waking body. Where his skin brushed against hers, her presence of mind slowly returned, and every thrust produced shockwaves of pure pleasure.

Selma floated in the suspended state of semi-consciousness, unable to grasp any sense of time in the darkness. There was only the full, slick thrusts of Kain's body as he brought her back from the brink of something she wasn't sure she could have found her way back from on her own.

Soon her pelvis was straining against the intrusion in an increasingly urgent search for just a little more, just that final thrust—

"Yes!"

She screamed the word in her mind at the same time her lover roared it, following through with a hot flood of liquid deep between her legs. It filled her with the heat of the sun, spreading warmth through every cell in her body as if spring had suddenly set in after a long, cold winter.

"You risked your life to get me. You little fool."

Selma hummed quietly at Kain's tender, yet scolding whisper, enjoying the sensation of her mate's hot breath against her ear. Her arms were still heavy and lethargic, but at least she could feel them again.

With some effort she lifted them and wrapped them around his torso, knowing her caress would soothe him as much as the heavy press of his body soothed her.

"Can you move yet, my beautiful? We need to get to safer quarters."

She frowned at his question. Safer quarters? She felt safe and warm in the protective cocoon of his heat. Why would they need—

The memory of the Queen's residence snapped back with unpleasant force.

They still weren't safe.

The surge of adrenaline that followed made her eyes open wide and dig her fingers into Kain's strong sides.

Faint daylight filtered in to replace the darkness she'd floated in for uncounted hours, suggesting it was just on the cusp of dawn. She didn't have time to reflect more on what that meant for how long she'd been out, because in the next moment, her eyes managed to focus on the man resting between her thighs.

Black and red scales covered his naked body and long, ebony horns sprang from his skull. Though his angular features were eerily familiar, they were also those of a monster.

Selma screamed, reflexively striking out at the beast on top of her in a panic.

The unwavering knowledge and trust of who she had just made love to was replaced by her worst nightmare come to life, his brutal girth still lodged deep inside of her.

"Get off, get off! *Get the fuck off me!*"

With a grunt of surprise the demon obeyed, moving swiftly and easily off her still-flailing body. He only paused to pull out of her swollen pussy, gently dislodging himself from her flesh despite her attempts to kick him.

"Selma..." Her name was a deep rumble from the back of his throat. His eyebrows were knit in either concern or frustration.

The second he was out of her body she scurried backwards, only stopping when metal hit her back and shoulders. It was the side of the helicopter they'd flown in to save Kain; it was still on the ground, and the demon had pulled back far enough that he was now crouched outside the opposite door, giving her space.

"Calm her down, Kain. It's just the mark's effect wearing off. Your baby must have needed that infusion of power to be strong enough to protect her from it."

The calm voice came from somewhere behind the demon hovering by the open door.

Someone else snorted in amusement, and movement outside the helicopter made her curl into a tighter ball.

"Well, that is some seriously awkward timing. Could you hurry this up? We need to get moving, and her scent is driving me crazy."

"Shut up, Kesh," the demon who'd mounted her snapped before turning back to her, his features smoothing from the scowl he'd leveled at the other.

"Selma, listen to my voice. It's just me—it's Kain. You know me, little one. Close your eyes and just listen."

His suggestion made her stare at him in shock. Close her eyes? He must be insane.

Yet the moment's pause gave logic time to rear its head. Despite what he looked like, this was Kain. *Kain.*

Reluctantly, she let her eyelids flutter closed.

A soft, rich humming made her heart rate drop almost instantly.

"It's just me, little one," Kain's deep voice called softly through the unwavering sound of his hum. "It's Kain, your mate. I told you this would happen, remember? There's nothing to be afraid of, I promise you. Our son is just fighting the mark for you. You know I would never hurt you."

Selma breathed deeply as her fear subsided. While she couldn't see him, there was little doubt in her mind that this was the man she'd been longing for ever since she'd met him. His voice rumbled richly from his chest, cooing to her as if she were a wild animal. Trying to make her as comfortable as possible.

"Let me smell you," she croaked. His smell was her favorite thing about him, and if she could focus on that along with his voice, then maybe she could accept this.

The helicopter swayed when his heavy weight entered, and then heat radiated against her face and body. He was close, but not reaching for her.

Slowly, she leaned forward and breathed in.

Warm, heady musk caressed her senses and allowed calm to filter through her system, settling her frazzled nerves.

Yes, this was Kain. This was the man who'd risked everything for her.

Selma's palms found his bare chest of their own accord, stroking over his scaled flesh. It didn't feel much different than when she'd seen his human illusion—maybe a bit tougher, but still warm and smooth.

Her hands continued upwards, exploring his face. It also seemed pretty much the same, if more chiseled.

Only when she let her fingertips slide up to his coiled

horns did things start to feel out of place. They were ridged and sharply pointed at the ends.

It doesn't matter—it's still Kain, she silently insisted, even as her hands trembled at the feel of something so unreal on the crown of her lover's head.

She opened her eyes again.

Kain looked up at her, worry marring his demonic features.

"Are you okay?"

"Okay" was probably a strong word, but Selma nodded nonetheless. At least she no longer felt like her heart was about to burst from her chest.

"That's good. Will you let me wrap this blanket around you and pick you up? We really do need to get out of here—the Queen's subjects may very well decide to give chase. I'd rather not have another confrontation out here."

He was still talking to her as if she were a scared little bird, but her frazzled nerves appreciated the effort. His soothing noises went a long way toward helping her keep calm enough to let him cover her naked body in a thick blanket.

When he lifted her out of the helicopter like a child and carried her around to the front, she saw two other vaguely familiar demons standing by the vehicle. It looked like at least the members of Kain's family had made it out relatively unscathed, though she had little recollection of events after the light had burst from her body.

Both males turned their gaze away when Kain growled low and threateningly, staking his claim.

As if that was necessary after screwing her while they were apparently just hanging around, waiting for them to be done. Fucking demons and their lack of propriety.

She knew Kain had initiated sex because she'd needed his seed, but while there were plenty of other things to feel uncomfortable about—such as everyone suddenly looking like the monsters she'd spent her entire life fearing—Selma was not exactly pleased with yet another couple of demons having seen and heard her in such an intimate moment.

AS SHE SAT on Kain's lap watching the land disappear beneath them, her mate's hand rubbing slow circles on her belly, Selma gave up on trying to make sense of the creatures who had filled her world from the moment she was born. They were not human, and even when she gave birth and her mark would once again blind her to their otherness, they would never be human.

Yet that didn't stop her from knowing, despite the unease in her stomach at her lover's current look, that she belonged here with him.

Perhaps Bealith was right. Perhaps it was her fate to bring love to the demon who held her in his arms, as well as to the one growing in her womb.

THIRTY-SEVEN
KAIN

"You know what will happen the moment this gets out!" Kain threaded a hand through his hair in agitation as he stared at his father. "A Breeder with power? Someone will try to kill her. I won't allow it! I'd rather let Naharan get away with treason than put Selma in more danger."

Kirigan lightly tapped at the glass of bourbon in his hand. "Nothing you do will stop this from getting out. We left way too many of the Queen's subjects alive for this not to spread like wildfire. We're better off nipping it in the bud and facing the royal family head-on."

"You mean confront them? Publicly?" Kesh cocked an eyebrow in surprise. "That will lead to—"

"A coup." Kirigan smiled wryly, though it didn't touch his black eyes. Nothing did anymore. "We have one of the Stones of Power and your mate killed the reigning queen. She does have a legitimate claim to the throne, despite being a Breeder rather than a demon."

"You're mad. I'm not bringing her to Europe, and I have no desire to challenge the royal family in their own territory. We may have one Stone, and I am sure we will have supporters once we divulge Naharan's treason, but they have the other two Stones *and* it's their home," Kain said. As much as he wanted to tear the prince limb from limb, it wasn't worth risking his mate's life. "All I want is to find somewhere safe to bring up my family."

"That's the point; nowhere is safe until we have dealt with the threat of the traitorous royal family." Despite the nature of the topic, Kirigan's tone remained calm. "You will never find a safe place for that girl unless you seize power over those who would harm her."

"Fuck!" Kain slapped his palm against the nearest wall hard enough for the structure to shake. He was right—his insane monster of a father was right. Unless he established himself at the very top of the food chain, they would always be looking over their shoulders.

If they seized control of the demon world, not only would they annihilate the threat of Naharan, but they would also curb the fear of a Breeder with power by making her Queen, thus establishing her in a position of authority—even if that would initially cause an uproar, especially among the demon females.

"We don't have to go to Europe," Kesh said, his brow wrinkled in thought. "We make our claim here. We find Naharan and make his crimes public, then execute him and claim dominion over the Northern Americas in the process. If the rest of the royal family objects, they will come to our territory and we will have the advantage. Or they give up control of the New World and we still accomplish what we set out to do."

"It is a good plan," Kirigan agreed. "If you truly care for the Breeder's safety, you will do this, Kain."

Kain grimaced. "I will think on it. When I return, I will let you know what I've decided."

Without waiting for further input, he turned and walked out of the library.

As a Lord, he'd always had a natural inclination toward leadership and domination, but he'd never had any desire to rule more than his assigned city. After Selma... Well, shit, he'd hardly had time to adjust to having not only a mate, but also a child on the way. Yet every fiber of his being longed to be with her—to create a future with her.

Ruling a continent was not on his list of priorities.

Still, he could see no other way to ensure her safety. Even without her disturbing powers, he would need to kill Naharan to ensure the snake never tried to touch her again, and killing royalty... that meant war.

He hadn't had time to talk to her yet, to try and figure out where the fuck the destructive light within her came from. Though he would have preferred to keep her in his arms, he'd needed to discuss their next move with his brother and father first, and Selma was clearly still more than a little unsettled at their demonic forms.

So instead of keeping her by his side where she belonged, he'd locked her in his old room to give her a little peace—a peace he now had to break. She deserved to know what was happening, and he would need to mate her again.

As much as his cock appreciated that prospect, his heart twisted unpleasantly. The pure horror in her eyes when she'd woken up and seen his true face would haunt him for an eternity, and knowing he would have to mount her while she was still able to see him like this caused dread to nestle in his gut.

Yet he would do it to save her life, even if it would cause irreparable damage to their fledgling relationship. Even if she would never be able to return his love after being made to mate with a monster.

Kain paused in front of his bedroom door and raised a hand to rap against the wooden surface with a knuckle.

"Kain?"

His name on her sweet voice made him smile, even if she did sound wary.

"Yeah. Can I come in?"

"Of course."

When he opened the door, she was sitting on the wide four-poster bed with her legs folded beneath her, looking as lovely as ever.

She drew in a deep breath at the sight of him, her brown eyes widening, but at least she didn't cower, scream, or even look away.

"How are you feeling?"

"I'm okay." Selma gave him a weak smile, and he could see the tired lines already marking her pretty face again. Not being seeded while he'd been captured had taken its toll on her newly pregnant body.

"You should have let Kesh mount you. He told me you refused him."

He frowned at the thought of another man on top of her, but he'd sent her to his brother with the expectation that she would belong to Kesh forevermore. He hadn't expected to make it out alive, and despite his rage at the prospect, she would have been in much better condition if his brother had fulfilled his duties between her thighs.

She flushed. "Yeah, well, I wasn't about to have sex with anyone else, especially not your brother."

His possessive nature purred at her statement, but he knew he had to make her see sense, should the need for her to accept another demon ever occur.

"Should something happen to me again, you need to allow it. Your life is more valuable to me than anything else. And if I die, I would want Kesh to provide for you."

Selma frowned. "Nothing more will happen to you. Promise me."

The sore thing in his chest—the place that connected him to her beyond anything he could ever have imagined—spasmed at her demand. Perhaps her need to see him safe was born from a place of realizing he would always provide her and their child with safety, but it nevertheless warmed his very core to know that she wished for him to stay alive—and with her.

"I can promise you that I will do anything and everything in my power to remain with you for the rest of eternity. But we still have dangerous times ahead, little one. This business with Naharan..."

"You will have to kill him."

The way she said it, so completely calm, made pride swell in his chest. She was tougher than he had ever thought a Breeder could be.

"Yes."

"I killed Marathin." She caught his gaze and held it. "He was scheming with the Prince, but planned on double-crossing him to steal me away. He tried to rape me, and that power inside of me you saw at the queen's palace awoke. What does that mean for the contract he had on my soul?"

"My father told me as much. It means you're free. The only thing that can break contract magic is the death of the demon who created it."

Despite his pride in her, Kain's lip pulled up in a snarl at the mention of the scum who'd tried to lay a hand on his mate. For her sake, he was happy she was the one to kill him—the quiet strength that radiated from her now wouldn't have been there if she hadn't put an end to the monster herself. Still, every cell in his body ached to maim the man who'd hurt his mate.

"I hope it was slow and painful," he added.

A smile ghosted across her lips. "You're very demon-y when you say stuff like that—while looking like this." She made a vague gesture toward his horns.

Kain snorted and eased himself down on the bed next

to her. She didn't flinch at his proximity, but he noticed she kept a hesitant eye on him.

"I know this is hard for you. It would have been easier if we'd been together longer and you had known me better before you saw my true form."

She rubbed a hand over her belly and sighed. "Apparently Maell wasn't kidding when he said I'm extremely fertile. What happens now, Kain? With Naharan and... and my powers? I'm not an idiot—I understand we're in pretty deep shit."

We. Even when he was in his demon form, she accepted that they were a unit with a shared future. It occurred to him that while neither of them had wanted a mate, they were both remarkably quick to accept their new bond. Surely it couldn't all be hormones? It didn't feel like hormones.

"We go to war," he said softly. "There's no other way."

His mate nodded, her lips narrowed in determination. Yes, she'd grown infinitely tougher since he'd found her alone and scared in that warehouse.

"If you are Queen, no one will question your powers —even if you are a Breeder."

She looked at him then, something he couldn't quite identify shifting in her eyes. "And you? Will you question them?"

"There is nothing to question," he said.

In reality there was much to question, but he didn't want to rattle her any further. As brave a front as she was putting up, it likely wouldn't take much more before she'd break.

And he still needed to mate her. Whatever that powerful light within her was, they would have to talk about it later.

She looked like she wanted to interject, but when he paused to let her speak, she didn't. Instead her shoulders slumped, the dark circles underneath her eyes seeming more bruised than ever. She needed him.

"Selma... We need to make you better, little one."

She shrugged and attempted to straighten, but he could still see the strain on her face. Their previous seeding had not been nearly enough to make up for her depletion of energy, and he suspected that her usage of the powerful light hadn't helped things.

"I'm okay," she said, though her gaze slipped from his to where her hands lay in her lap.

"You're not okay. I need to take you again. And I will need to do that every day until he is born."

She paled noticeably, and Kain's heart sank into his stomach. If he had to force her, he would never be able to look at himself in the mirror again, but he would do anything to save her life. Even this.

THIRTY-EIGHT
SELMA

She knew he was right. No matter how much she tried to ignore it, bone-deep exhaustion was lurking right underneath the surface, threatening to break through and render her helpless.

She hadn't thought much about it when they were preparing to rescue Kain—had written it off as a natural reaction to the stress and trauma she'd endured since the attack in Colorado. But after she'd collapsed at the queen's residence, she'd come to realize that it was so much more than that.

In her bones, she knew that if Kain hadn't done what he did—as mortifying as it was to be fucked on the side of the road with his father and brother watching—she would have died, along with the life she was carrying.

Selma glanced at the large demon perched on the bed next to her. He was frankly terrifying; there was just no way around that. Though she'd been able to accept that he was her mate, the thought of willingly submitting to his monstrous cock while he looked like this made her heart pound.

The grim determination displayed by the set of his mouth made her remember what he'd said in the car after she told him she was pregnant—that he would take her, regardless of her protests, as long as she carried his child. She knew it was to ensure both she and his son survived, but it had been a lot easier to accept when he still looked like the incredibly handsome and more human man who'd saved her time and time again.

This... She shuddered as memories of being chased and tormented flooded in. The attack she'd endured before coming to Ravenswood House was all too vivid in her mind—big, scaly monsters with horns and fire in their eyes pushing her to the ground to force their way into her body.

And then Marathin, who had more than once shown her what it was like to be forced into submission.

A tremor traveled up her spine. This time, there would be no escape.

"Please don't fear me."

It was a hoarse plea, so completely contradictory to his brutal appearance, that for the briefest moment, her heart ached for him.

He was still Kain.

Selma closed her eyes and bit her trembling lip hard enough to taste blood. She had to submit without a fight. She owed him that much.

"Just do it." It wasn't the most heated of permissions, but it was all she could manage right now.

Judging by his relieved exhale, it was enough.

The bed dipped underneath his weight as he moved closer, a waft of his heat brushing against her skin before his large hand came up to cup her cheek.

"I will never hurt you," he murmured, and then that soothing hum that resonated within her core vibrated from his wide chest.

What was it about that sound? Selma breathed deeply as every muscle in her body slowly relaxed, inadvertently filling her lungs with his heady scent. Though she was still very much aware of the hulking demon whose touch warmed her skin, it was as if his hum numbed her anxiety. Her fear was still there, of course, but as long as he made that sound deep in his chest, she could deal with it.

Kain pressed his scorching lips gently against hers.

He tasted like heat and male and something wild she couldn't name as anything but *Kain*. The soft pressure of his lips teased her mouth open with its gentle insistence.

Selma sat frozen in place as he slowly devoured her mouth, her eyes firmly clenched. Her body recognized the taste and feel of the demon's kiss, and a thread of desire wound its way through her apprehension. It wasn't enough to alleviate her tension, but it was something.

Kain's low growl told her that he'd sensed her wakening response to his ministrations. The sound sent another shiver down her spine—this time not purely from fear. While the animalistic growl was a disturbing reminder of what sort of creature had her trapped on the bed, it also spoke to something warm and needy in her core.

She had more or less expected him to twist her ring and immediately take her to get it over with, but as the demon moved in closer, wrapping his strong arms possessively around her waist, she knew that had been a foolish expectation. Even when in the throes of the mating thrall after the auction, he'd taken the time to explore her body and set her skin aflame with more than just forced lust.

This time she knew he would be trying to awaken her body to pleasure, to ease the guilt of forcing the coupling.

Guilt. His terrifying appearance aside, he was capable of feeling guilt. Of feeling love...

Drive, my love. His desperate plea when he'd sacrificed himself to the Prince rang in her mind as he eased her onto her back, large hands skillfully ridding her of one of the silken dresses his brother had supplied for her upon her arrival.

This creature—this man—loved her, even as his form filled her with horror.

"Oh." Her lips parted in a soft moan when he closed his mouth around her nipple. Gentle pulls that went straight to her unprepared clit followed, and she grasped at the sheets to keep from clinging to him.

This was what she needed—to forget that the beast on top of her was more than just her lover and mate. She needed his gentle seduction, but if she let herself get too lost in the sensation and allowed herself to touch him, the spell he was so methodically weaving around her mind would shatter.

So Selma clung to the bedding as Kain sucked first one and then the other little bud, followed by his tongue and teeth gently nibbling and flicking at them until she was writhing and a warm ache settled between her legs. Unwittingly she spread her thighs for him, inviting his touch where she needed it most.

Kain growled again, the beast in him voicing its appreciation of her surrender, but before she could clasp her legs tight at the unpleasant reminder of what sort of creature she was begging to claim her unprotected core, he snaked his hand down to cover her panty-clad mound.

He didn't hesitate, possibly sensing her returning unease, and instead pushed two nimble fingers in behind the flimsy fabric and against her clit.

Selma couldn't hold back her gasp, nor could she keep her hips from bucking at his touch. The demon didn't give her time to rein in her body, instead deciding to push his advantage. Without lifting his mouth from her breasts, he let his finger rub circles over her bundle of nerves and across the metal entrapping it, not stopping even when she began to moan and spread her legs wider.

Despite her mind's weak attempts to resist, his touch blazed through her hesitation as it coaxed her body into submission. His hum was unwavering, never allowing her a moment to panic, and as her pleasure built between her thighs, she gave in.

"Yes!"

Just a little more... She arched up against the pressure as her arousal mounted into a tight knot, desperately close to finding her release. *So close, so close!*

"Kain...!"

At the sound of his name, the demon twisted his fingers around her ring, making it bite savagely into her swollen nub and activating the magic within.

White-hot fire shot through her pelvis and up into her torso, setting her every cell aflame.

"Kain!" Unthinkingly she grasped at his shoulders to press herself closer to the source of the need crashing through her. Her eyes popped open wide as she gasped for air in the heat of her desperation.

The horrifying features of his demonic form met her wild stare. Even through the call of the ring forcing her to arch in a plea for his monstrous cock, fear coursed through her at the sight of him poised over her naked body.

Oh god...

Kain's face contorted around a snarl above her, making her pussy clench and weep with the primal sound, even as her fear made her stomach tense.

"No," he growled. Then he lifted off her, leaving her burning body to writhe on the bed.

"Please," she gasped. He couldn't leave her, not now. As much as he frightened her, she needed his heavy cock to soothe the burn wracking her body and making her spread her thighs wide for the monster. "Please, I need...!"

He grabbed her hips and her body instantly paused its

writhing, instincts forcing her to submit to the dominant male.

When he flipped her onto her stomach she groaned with need, even as her mind reeled behind the lustful haze the ring inflicted on her. She wanted this—needed this with every ounce of her being, despite her terror at his demonic form. She would have to endure being mounted from behind, needed to let go of the final shred of her will desperately fighting against the torrent of lust pulsing through her from that needy place between her legs so she could submit willingly. If she didn't, they would never be able to get past this, and—

Selma's thoughts came to an abrupt halt when Kain pulled her into position, but instead of the expected pressure from his massive girth pressing at her dripping opening, he lifted her so he could twist his head and shoulders in underneath her.

Before she managed more than a gasp of surprise, he had her knees spread wide on each side of his thick neck and his hands were securely around her ass, pressing her down toward his face. His intentions became obvious shortly after when the tip of his scorching tongue teased over her wet slit.

The white spike of pleasure as his devious mouth found her clit had her eyes rolling back in her head. A long, drawn-out groan escaped her lips.

"Your pleasure tastes like life." His hoarse whisper vibrated through her slick folds and up through her spine.

Her pleasure. Selma arched into his mouth, pressing

her aching nub closer to the heat of his skilled tongue and lips. She knew from the burn in her body that he was fighting his instincts roaring to mount her rough and deep, yet the sight of her fear when she'd seen him hovering over her, more than ready to penetrate her defenseless pussy, had stopped him.

Once again he was going against everything he was so she wouldn't suffer.

Kain pulled his hot mouth back from her dripping flesh, only to let his tongue lash at her throbbing clit until she writhed on the edge of orgasm. He pushed two of his thick digits into her rhythmically clenching channel, and she moaned loudly at the sudden pressure.

"Yes, like that," she gasped into the sheets she'd buried her head and fists in. "Please, yes, don't—*oh*—don't stop!"

As if on cue, he hooked his fingers behind her pelvic bone, pressing them into the spongy area there. Sharp, uncontrollable pleasure so intense it passed the border to pain rocked through her, driven forth by his tongue and that unrelenting pressure against her G-spot.

Her vision sharpened to pinpoints before everything turned white within the hurricane of sensations roaring through her blood, and the flood of her climax peaked.

"Ah! Fuck! Kain, yes!"

Her scream echoed through the room as her pussy convulsed around his invading digits. She ground her clit against his mouth, too far gone to care if he could breathe.

Thankfully, he didn't seem to care either, his tongue moving rapidly over her pulsing clit again and again until she collapsed on top of his face with a whine, pleasantly spent.

Endorphins clouded her mind, momentarily quelling the still-burning need deep in her pussy. The ring had yet to be satisfied, but the orgasm her lover had provided allowed for a short reprieve.

Along with the endorphins came an overwhelming sense of gratitude toward him—the man who'd brought her nothing but protection and pleasure since the day she met him.

And through the hormonal rush came something else —the clear and unwavering courage to finally put into words exactly what he meant to her.

"I love you."

Kain stilled underneath her. Only the waft of air over her nether lips as his breath left his lungs let her know that he'd heard her.

"What?" he croaked, sending more pleasurable tingles through her spent flesh. "What did you say?"

His tone suggested his refusal to believe what he'd heard.

Where such a statement should have made her stomach contract with nervous energy, all she felt was peace brought on by the wake of the orgasm, and the stirring of the ring's magic breaking through her moment of calm. Selma rocked her hips uneasily, trying to stave off the onslaught so she could rest in that perfect cocoon of contentedness for a little while longer.

"I said I love you." She sighed in frustration as she

fidgeted above him. Her need for sex was increasingly difficult to ignore, every second bringing the urge to mate back to progressively insistent levels. As always, the ring craved his ruthless penetration.

Her pussy was starting to throb again, and the teasing brush of his hot breath over her softened cleft didn't help matters. With a small whine, she arched her back and pressed down a little, searching for the stimulation she knew would appease her needy body for another moment.

"Kain, more! I need more."

He growled underneath her again, a sound caught somewhere between frustration and desire. His fingers bit into her hips, making her mewl. Before she realized he'd moved, she was balancing on her hands and knees on the soft bed and the demon was now behind her, snarling.

"More," he spat, spreading her dripping pussy wide with his fingers to prepare the way for his assault. "Do you forget what I am the second you can no longer see my true face? I can taste your fear on my tongue every time you lay eyes on me, yet a little pleasure with your back turned and you declare your love as if it's something to give away for a fuck."

The thick crown of his pulsing cock pushed against her opening, making her breath hitch in her throat and her fingers clench in the already crumpled sheets. He was so thick, and this time she was awake to feel the full force of him.

"How could you ever love someone like me?" Kain's voice was still a dangerous snarl, but behind the fury, there was unmistakable despair. It resonated deep in her core despite her focus on the pressure slowly increasing between her legs.

"Or is this really all it takes to break you, my love? The promise of a climax on my cock, and you're ready to give me everything?"

The rasp of his question was punctuated by her loud wail as he shoved in, burying his head and the brutal ridges inside her soft channel.

"I'll give you what you need, Breeder—and when I'm done, you can tell me if you still have the capability to feel anything but fear for me."

Every thought in Selma's whirling mind snapped to a halt, her consciousness turning solely to the invasion of her most sacred place. Kain's wide cock filled her spasming channel, and though her body was more prepared to take him this time than when he'd rutted her at the auction, it still took all she had to remain on her hands and knees as he slowly pressed himself all the way in.

His ridges ground mercilessly against every sensitive nerve ending inside of her, and when he finally bottomed out, he possessed her so completely the beat of his pulse resonated within her as if it were her own.

"Kain...!" She cried out for him, lost in the sensation of being one with the demon who'd chosen her—of the knowledge flooding her mind that he belonged to her. *This* was where she needed to be, suspended on his massive cock and wrapped up in his inhuman strength, even if her body was being forced to its limits to submit to him.

Kain dug his fingers into her hips once more. Then he began the rough, agonizing movements in and out of her stuffed pussy. His ridges tormented her as they slid over her G-spot, forcing screams and cries from her throat as he fucked her.

It was impossible for her to think about anything but the delicious agony of being spread and taken, so she gave herself over to it—to him—the hazy knowledge of his disbelief in her love disappearing into the hormonal fog of pained pleasure and submission.

Soon her cries took on the note of an impending climax and the demon responded. He released her hips to let one hand get at her clit, rubbing it roughly while he grabbed her by the hair with his other hand.

The sharp tug on her scalp as he pulled her head back, combined with the dark pleasure from her spasming pussy, made her body surrender. Her orgasm blasted through her, and she cried out as she tried to lunge forward in an instinctive attempt to escape the violent sensation.

His grip on her hair kept her in place, helpless to endure his unrelenting pounding into her quaking channel while she came so hard the world blurred and blackened.

Kain didn't stop. Even when she sagged in front of him, spent from pleasure so intense she could hardly keep upright, he kept up the punishing pace, letting his hips slap against her bottom and not giving her a moment's reprieve from his full and grueling penetration.

It was when her vision finally returned that she saw him. His hand was still fisted in her long hair, keeping her head up, while the other forced more pleasure into her weakened body with its insistent ministrations underneath her.

She was still on her hands and knees, held up by his hold on her body more than by her own strength, but when her eyes locked on their mirrored reflection, her mind snapped back into place.

In front of the four-poster bed was a large wooden dresser, and mounted on the door of that dresser was a mirror reflecting her naked body and the monster violently shoving his cock into her.

Even the ruthless fucking wrecking her pussy couldn't draw her startled attention away from the display.

Since Selma had hit puberty, her fear of the monsters haunting her had taken on a slightly different flavor. In her darkest moments, she'd feared what would happen if one day they no longer just stalked and stared at her. Her worst nightmare had always been this—being forced to spread her pussy for something that didn't even look human.

Yet as she stared at Kain's huge body moving behind her, it wasn't fear that tightened her aching muscles.

He looked even larger than normal, the way his blackish-red body hovered over hers, and along with his color, his horns and demonic features made him look exactly like every monster she'd feared all her life. Yet watching him fuck her pale body like she didn't have a choice was the most erotic thing she'd ever seen.

There was no comparison to the monster who'd truly forced her. Somehow the knowledge that the demon brutally ravaging her like an animal was Kain banished the last vestiges of her terror and replaced them with depraved excitement.

Not even when his grip changed back to her hips so he could increase the speed of his thrusts even more did she look away, too fascinated with the way his abdominal muscles flexed with every thrust, making her breasts sway with the motion.

Her face contorted with pain-laced pleasure every time he drove in to the hilt, her swollen lips shaping themselves after her yelps and moans. Everything about their reflection was as raw and perverted as the feeling of his massive cock forcing her soaking pussy wide, and his ridges gave her pleasure no human was built to withstand.

When Kain slid his massive hands up her stomach to squeeze her breasts, she gave in.

The tight coil low in her stomach snapped in a burst of ecstasy, and her pussy spasmed around the thick intrusion as her vision turned to pure light, obstructing her view of their fucking. Her body convulsed around the unending torrents of sensation rocking through her from where they were connected.

Through her own screams, she heard Kain growl out his climax, and then—while she slowly came down from the peaks of rapture—his hot spurts of semen against her flexing cervix marked the completion of their mating.

Selma slumped into the bedding, utterly spent.

Kain's large body nestled on top of hers, his panting breaths huffing against her ear as he curled his warm shape around her, protecting every inch of her quivering skin.

They lay like that for a long while as they both came down from the intense mating high. Only instead of just the usual lethargic endorphins swarming her system, Selma felt her energy slowly return. Her limbs were not nearly as heavy as they'd been before he mounted her, and though her mind hummed with sated satisfaction, she didn't have to struggle just to stay awake.

The wonders of demonic semen.

She smiled wryly at that thought, because while it was clearly giving her the energy she needed, it was also making a hell of a mess between her thighs. She felt sticky and full, but it was far from uncomfortable. He was hers, body and soul, and he belonged inside of her, around her —even when he looked like a monster. It didn't matter. He was her Kain.

"I still love you," she murmured, coughing to clear her throat when it ground out hoarsely from all her screaming. "You said to wait and see until after you'd fucked me. Well... I still love you."

The demon stiffened on top of her, and she heard his breath catch for a moment before...

"You're high on hormones."

Selma rolled her eyes at his dismissive grunt. "Fucking hell, Kain. Is it that hard to believe?"

He snorted, then lifted off her, slowly pulling his cock from her leaking pussy. She gritted her teeth when his ridges caught on her entrance before finally popping out, leaving her feeling unpleasantly empty.

"Don't worry about this, Selma. I'm not some lost little kid in need of love."

She turned—somewhat carefully as her abused abdomen protested the movement—and glared up at him. He'd gotten off the bed and was in the process of straightening out his shirt and zipping up his pants, all while carefully avoiding her gaze.

Both anger and pity burned in her stomach. He was so goddamn infuriating. She knew why he was doing this—why he was so adamant that she couldn't love him. But if she could get over her childhood trauma of being haunted by monsters because of him, if she could mate with him despite everything that had been done to her, he would have to get over his abandonment issues. Right fucking now.

"Get down here."

Her sharp tone made him glance at her, surprise evident on his harsh features. The demon Lord was undoubtedly not used to getting ordered around like this.

"Get down here, now." She sat up on the bed and pointed to the crumpled up sheets in front of her.

Slowly he obeyed, likely more from sheer surprise at

her change in mood than any feelings of actual intimidation.

When he was perched in front of her, eyebrows raised in silent question, Selma reached out and grabbed his strong jaw in one hand. Her fingers closed around his warm, soft skin covered in the reddish-black scales, and the difference to her own pale color momentarily paused the slew of words from spilling from her lips. He was beautiful, even like this.

Selma let her eyes roam over his face, taking in the pain in his fully black eyes, the strength in his brow, the sharpness of his features, and the coiled elegance of his black horns. Further down, his body stretched and dipped over hard muscle in just the right way. He was all male, and so incredibly beautiful.

"Selma—"

His exasperated tone and the dismissive look on his face made her anger return full-force.

"No, you listen to me—I'm done with being told I don't know my own thoughts and feelings. *Done.* Yeah, we had sex, but that doesn't mean that I don't know the difference between a hormone high and what my heart is telling me.

"I love you. Through all the horrors and all the confusion, you're the only one who's been truly there for me since this all started. Stop trying to take that away from me because you have issues.

"And this strange new power that's popped up to make everything even more complicated? It's because you loved me enough to let me go—you showed me what true love really means, and I...

"Don't ask me to pretend like that doesn't matter. I have been afraid to be taken and forced and used all my life. With you, I am finally free. You see me for who I truly am, *what* I truly am. How could I not love you?"

Her chest heaved and her cheeks burned with the remnants of her frustration, and she felt more like she'd been in a battle than declared her love.

Kain looked as if she'd struck him, his lips slightly parted. He didn't say anything—just stared at her with something that looked a whole lot like fear painted over his strong features.

Fear. He was afraid of her.

She understood. His mother, the woman who was supposed to love him more than anything else in this world, had shunned him, and in the black depths of his eyes she saw his soul-deep terror to let himself believe in her words—because if he did and she left him like his mother had, it would destroy him.

Selma moved even before she felt her heart clench with agonizing sympathy. She wrapped her arms around Kain's brutish body and buried her face in his neck, pressing her naked form against his in an attempt to give the comfort every ounce of her was aching to provide him.

"I love you," she said again. Though her voice was muffled against his skin, the soft groan he let out in response made it clear he'd heard her. "And I'm never going to leave. You're mine as much as I am yours.

Please don't let your fear shut me out. I need you, Kain, more than I ever thought I could need anyone or anything."

Slowly he closed his strong arms around her, as if he was hesitant, yet powerless to accept her comfort. He buried his face in her hair, breathing in her scent with a shaky gasp.

They sat in silence for a long while, the only sounds Kain's soft panting against her hair along with the gentle brush of her lips against his skin as she placed kisses along his shoulder and neck.

When he finally seemed to calm, she lifted her head from the crook of his neck, though her arms remained locked around his powerful body.

"You know, this is where you're meant to say something back," she noted.

Kain let out a shaky laugh and finally lifted his head to look at her. "You sure are a bossy little thing."

"I was thinking something slightly more romantic, maybe." It was impossible not to return the wry smile playing across his decadent mouth, and warm tingles danced across her skin and up her spine at the unwavering affection in his dark gaze.

Kain lifted a hand from her waist and gently cradled her cheek, letting the thumb ghost across her lips. "There are no words I could say to you that would ever..."

He bit his lip and looked away for a moment. When he looked back up, the unadulterated love and worship in his eyes took her breath away.

"There is nothing I wouldn't do for you, my love. My mate."

She gasped into his mouth when he pressed his lips to hers, only to melt against him when he gently coaxed her lips apart. As his tongue slowly delved into the cavern of her mouth to stroke alongside hers, she groaned in defeat and clutched at his body to avoid collapsing from the overwhelming burst of sensation.

Kissing Kain was quickly becoming her second-favorite thing to do, eclipsed only by the raw pleasure of sex with him.

He pulled back some time later, separating with gentle pecks to her now swollen lips, and smiled at her undoubtedly drugged expression as she sagged in his strong embrace.

"You okay?"

"Mmhm," she sighed, then wiggled a bit to get more comfortable on his lap. The intimidating length between his legs had grown decidedly hard during their kiss. "More than okay. You?"

"Always, my love."

That particular pet name would be pretty easy to get used to.

"I do have a few questions, though," he said, and to her annoyance, some of the softness left his face, a more serious expression highlighting the sharpness of his features. So much for spending the day in bed, basking in the glow of having finally put words to her feelings.

"You said your new power is caused by my love for you. What exactly did you mean?"

"Oh." Selma frowned, thinking back to everything Bealtih had told her that night in Colorado. It seemed like an eternity ago. "The goddess talked to me about what I am—I mean, what my kind were before we became Breeders."

He narrowed his eyes. "You cannot trust the words of a goddess, Selma. They lie and deceive as easily as you and I breathe."

A wry smile pulled on the corner of her mouth. "Yeah? Says the demon who's some sort of crime lord back home. I'm not just taking her word for it, Kain. I can feel it inside of me. She didn't lie, not about that at least."

Keeping her tone calm, she told him what the goddess had said, but despite her best efforts, the demon holding her didn't exactly take the revelation of the depth of the gods' deceit well.

"They used you?" he hissed. "*They* are the reason for every Breeder who has ever been forced to bear a demon child! And this Bealith has the audacity to claim that we are the ones who need to be controlled. By the fucking stars—"

Selma placed a hand over his mouth, interrupting what was undoubtedly about to end with some form of violence. "It doesn't matter. I don't care about the gods' plans—I care about you and our child. Does anything else really matter? Let them scheme and plan. I am taking no part in it, whether they want me to or not."

His enraged expression softened minimally at the reminder of the life in her womb, but dark determination was still etched into every line of his face. “I am going to make you Queen, and when I do, you and your kind will no longer be mere pawns in their twisted game.”

THIRTY-NINE
SELMA

"Exactly how did you get Kain to agree to this ridiculous idea?"

Selma sighed and glanced out the dark window. Nothing but the faint light of the street lamps on the other side of the metal gates cast any illumination over the deserted warehouse's grounds. If someone was hiding in the shadows, she would never be able to tell.

"We talked about it like adults. He agrees that it's the best way to lure out the Prince."

Kesh scoffed by her side and readjusted his grip on what looked like some form of a rocket launcher. "You cried until he caved, didn't you?"

A faint blush rose to Selma's cheeks at the casual accusation. She had indeed had to resort to tears to ensure Kain was pliable enough to listen to her reasoning for putting herself and his baby in harm's way, but she wasn't about to admit to that. It wasn't exactly a dignified tactic.

"It's the best shot we have at capturing the prince. He thinks I belong to him, so when our double agents let him know I'm being kept here and guarded by you while Kain is out looking for him, he's likely to try to steal me away. Without me, you would have a hard time luring him out."

"And without you here, this wouldn't be so fucking dangerous," he shot back, giving her a less-than-approving glance. "You do know what will happen if you're hurt, right? I mean, you've seen the husk that is my father—you must realize that Kain will end up exactly like that if you're lost to him. And yet here you are, willingly playing bait."

Selma cocked an eyebrow. She wasn't entirely sure if Kesh's reluctance was toward her personally, or if he just resented her pheromones and their effect on him.

"Well, I'm certain you'll keep me safe." There was just a touch too much sweetness in her voice.

He grunted and leaned back against the wall. "Or you could just blast the bastard with that pretty light of yours. Oh, wait—that's right. You still have little to no control over it."

"Is there something you'd like to say?" she snapped, finally fed up with his attitude. Ignoring his demonic appearance, she rested her hands on her hips and rounded on him so she could give him her best glare.

Kesh ignored her combative stance, not even bothering to afford her more than a short glance. "Only that my brother is way too lenient with you. You'd be far less likely to get anyone killed by knitting a blanket or painting a sunset, or whatever Breeders normally do."

Selma's mouth fell open in outrage at his casual sexism, but before she managed to form a ripping retort, the window exploded inward.

SHE COULD ONLY HAVE BEEN out for a moment, because when the darkness retreated she was still on the floor and sporting several stinging cuts from where the glass had sliced her skin.

Someone said something above her, but it sounded like it came through water. She shook her head to clear the foggy sensation, only to be hoisted up by her waist the next second and shoved behind a wide, leather-clad back.

Kesh's back.

Her hearing returned with a sharp pain in both ears about the same time as she saw the ten demons standing in the shards she'd lain in only moments ago. Most of them looked somewhat female, apart from the huge creature standing in the middle, pointing at Kesh with a clawed hand the size of a dinner plate.

"...over the girl and I won't rip your throat out."

Selma just caught the tail end of the biggest of the demons' sentence, but it was enough to make her shudder. That rough voice laced with cruelty could only belong to Naharan.

"She doesn't belong to you—she belongs to my

brother, as you well know. Remember how you tried to steal her from him, and in the process betrayed everything that is sacred to our kind?"

Kesh nonchalantly tipped the rocket launcher so it rested against his hip, but despite his seemingly relaxed pose, he was obviously ensuring he kept his body between Selma and the danger before them.

The Prince snarled at the mention of Kain and spat on the floor. "The presumptuous filth is not worthy of her. She belongs with me—with royalty. Besides, where is he now? Not here, guarding the Breeder. He left his imbecile of a baby brother to do that. It seems to me he doesn't deserve the honor of a mate. This is your last chance—give me the girl or die."

Kesh's response was to fire his weapon.

Everything exploded into movement and noise. The demons managed to throw themselves out of the way in time, causing the rocket to connect with the far wall with a fiery boom.

The concrete shattered into pieces. Selma threw herself to the floor behind Kesh as the demons attacked, shrouded in a black cloud of sizzling magic and protecting her head with her arms.

Shouts and growls tore through the air, and through the mayhem she heard Kain's voice. Their trap had snapped shut. Now all that was left to do was hope they were stronger than the prince and his followers.

"Let's get you out of the way, hmm?" a dark voice

grunted above her, followed by a set of strong arms lifting her from her the floor.

Selma shrieked at the unexpected touch, but she caught a glimpse of the demon who pulled her from the center of the battle's face and relaxed some. It was Kirigan.

He took her to the edge of the warehouse, his fingers skimming over the cuts on her face in a brief check of her wellbeing. Then he put her down behind a couple of crates.

"Stay here. You cannot get hurt."

She stared up at the demon who looked so much like his eldest son, apart from the dark hair and soulless eyes. He'd been the first to side with her when she'd suggested that they use her as bait, seemingly not too concerned with any risk the plan might pose to her.

Yet as he stared down at her now, she could have sworn that there was genuine worry somewhere beyond the pained despair in his deadened gaze.

Then he was gone, returning to join the fight, and Selma was left to cower alone behind her shelter.

It was never the intention that she should join in; Kain had been very, very firm on that point, reminding her how completely her attack on the queen had drained her.

Yet as she saw the man she loved fight against the creature who had tried to force them apart—saw his broken family rally around him to protect the two of them from being torn apart again—she knew she couldn't just hide in the corner like some damsel in distress; not when she had finally been given the power she needed to defend herself after years of being a victim.

The two groups—Naharan and the nine females on one side and Kain, Kesh, and their father on the other—seemed evenly matched. After the attack on the roadside in Colorado, they hadn't expected Naharan would bring along many, if any, supporters, opting instead for speed and stealth.

They had obviously miscalculated, and Selma didn't like the sudden chance they might not win. That Kain....

The real risk that he might die suddenly became clear when the Prince leapt across the room, twisted his body out of the way of Kain's dark magic, and landed a blow to her mate's head. The claws on his other hand ripped a long, red gash across Kain's back, making him roar. He swung around just in time to shove Naharan off him, narrowly avoiding decapitation.

Selma's heart stopped dead as the man she loved staggered. It only took him a few seconds to regain his momentum and turn on Naharan with a fierce snarl, but it was enough for her to realize exactly what she could lose this night.

Everything.

The white light burst out of her before she'd even made a conscious effort to summon it.

FORTY
KAIN

He'd only seen her light twice before, but Kain instantly recognized the bright shine of power out of the corner of his eye when he faced off against the Prince.

Selma.

Worry made him look toward her to see if she was in some sort of trouble, despite his need to focus on his attacker. The absolutely murderous intent in her eyes, fixed on Naharan, had him diving for the floor just as a wave of white energy crashed through the room.

Glass and wood shattered where it connected, catching two of the Prince's accomplices in its wake, though Naharan himself managed to duck at the last moment.

That girl was going to be the death of him—literally, if she didn't work on her aim.

Pushing aside his urge to rush to her and ensure she didn't use any more of her life essence, he dove for the gobsmacked prince. At least his little mate had bought him a moment's advantage, and a moment was all he needed.

Roaring with triumph, he clasped both hands around Naharan's throat. When he saw his enemy's eyes widen with terror and felt his spine finally snap, Kain pulled his lips back in a snarl.

Deep satisfaction throbbed through his veins and pounded in his temples as he tore the Prince's throat from his body. Blood sprayed from the ghastly wound, and he opened his mouth to taste its metallic pulse, letting his senses fill with the sweet rush of victory.

No one would ever try to take his beloved from him again.

Kesh and Kirigan had gotten the upper hand on the remaining demons, and the dusty air filled with the scent of blood and guts as they systematically slaughtered their enemies.

Kain stared down at his fallen opponent—the male who'd thought he could claim his mate—and felt nothing but grim satisfaction at his ruined throat and glazed eyes. There was no turning back now; he'd killed the Prince of Demons, and from his demise he would grasp the political power needed to keep his family safe.

Selma. The need to hold her in his arms overwhelmed him now that the threat had been eliminated. He rose and looked for her.

She was still standing by the crates where she'd been when she let her power wash over the room, but instead of the deadly determination she'd exhibited before, her expression was now wary and a little frightened as she looked out over the destruction.

His little mate. He was so fiercely proud of how she rose to the occasion when she needed to be strong, but at her core, she was still a gentle soul.

She startled a bit when he rushed to her side, but her hesitant look seemed to be reserved for the blood spatter covering his face and body rather than his demonic form.

"You shouldn't have done that." He placed a hand upon her cheek and frowned at the lines around her eyes. He had mated her a few hours before they separated, but drawing on the white energy seemed to drain her fast. "You promised me you wouldn't try to interfere."

"Excuse me for saving the day," she bristled, full lips drawing into a pout.

Their softness tempted him, and he swallowed a groan as his instincts demanded he mount his prize after defeating the challenger to her warm little cunt.

"He almost killed you—did you really expect me to just do nothing?" she continued, her tone more than a little indignant.

Kain found it hard to focus on her words, his eyes roaming her soft form hungrily. His battle rage had been momentarily displaced by his concern for her well-being, but now that he had ensured she was safe, the testosterone in his blood was roaring for a different kind of outlet.

With a low growl, he pulled her body flush with his and lifted her, reveling in the way her curves molded against his hard muscles. Everything about his little Breeder was inviting and soft, and he loved the way her flesh dipped under his strong fingers.

"Oof! Kain!" Selma protested as he crushed her against him. He quelled her objections by claiming her lips and demanding access to her mouth.

For a moment she relented, turning pliable as he kissed her deeply, and he'd already decided to have her then and there, sparing no thought to his father and brother or the mangled bodies.

But then she stiffened in his grasp. Before he had even tasted her, she pulled her head away and whacked his chest with her palm.

"Ew!" Her outburst was followed by wild spitting at the floor, and she squirmed violently in a clear effort to be put down. He didn't oblige.

"You taste like blood! That's so fucking gross! Don't even think about doing that again before you're clean!" The last bit she snapped at him when he leaned in to silence her protests once more.

Kain hesitated, the need in him to mount and claim her for just the briefest of moments making him consider shoving a hand down her pants to twist her ring so she'd be more agreeable. But her angry glare brought him back from the edge of his instinctual madness.

With a sigh he let her slide to the floor, though he kept both arms around her. Forcing his mate to couple in the middle of torn-off limbs and pools of blood was unlikely to earn him any favors, though he personally found the thought quite appealing.

Selma rubbed at her mouth with the back of her hand and shot him another dirty look, but at least she didn't try to break away from his hold. "And that one? What do we do with her?"

He looked in the direction she nodded and saw Kesh holding the last surviving member of Naharan's group by the neck with casual ease.

Kain's lip curled with renewed anger—his instincts were snarling at him to kill every last one of the bastards who'd thought they could take his mate from him, but he knew he couldn't give into the urge to rip out her guts. Not yet at least.

"We need a witness who can attest to our claims when we take over control of the continent. We need as many of the Lords on our side as possible, and the more proof we have, the better. You will tell everyone exactly what happened, won't you?" Kain raised his voice slightly toward the end, giving their captive a pointed stare.

Whatever conviction had made the female join forces with the Prince, it had withered after seeing her comrades slaughtered like animals. She made a raspy sound until Kesh eased his hold on her neck.

"Y-Yes, my Lord," she croaked. "Whatever you want, my Lord."

"Your *Majesty*." Kirigan strolled over to the captive and put a finger under her chin, forcing her to look up.

"My son is your king now, wretch. Get used to addressing him as such."

The smaller demon looked stunned, but when Kesh dug his claws into her neck, she came around quickly enough.

"O-Of course, Your Majesty. I'm sorry, Your Majesty! Whatever you say, Your Majesty!"

Kain smothered a sigh. He didn't give two flying shits about his title, but his family's insistence on drilling it into their surviving witness was undoubtedly a wise decision.

All that mattered was keeping Selma and his unborn son safe, and for that to happen, he needed every Lord on the continent to bend their knee to him.

Reluctantly, he let go of his mate and stepped over to the fallen Prince. He grabbed him by the horns, and with a twist, tore his head clean off his body before turning to his father and brother.

When he'd left his father's house on the same day he'd matured into an adult, he'd turned his back on them, never once wishing to lay eyes upon them again. Yet in his most desperate hour, they'd both rallied behind him, all for the sake of the woman who'd brought love into his life at last.

Perhaps in time, there would be more than the loyalty of blood between them.

"Let's go," he said. "We have a continent to conquer."

FORTY-ONE
SELMA

"I do not appreciate being strong-armed into hosting a meeting for the continent's Lords without first being given a reason. I hope you understand that if this turns out to be a waste of my time, and that of everyone else who travelled here, there will be consequences."

Selma fidgeted by Kain's side at the less-than-amused look the large demon across the desk was giving her mate. Being back at the Governor's mansion did not bring back entirely pleasant memories, even if she couldn't recognize her auctioneer in his current form.

"Naturally, Your Excellency." Kain gave her shoulder a small squeeze and then stepped forward, leaving her flanked by Kesh and Kirigan, the latter of whom had the female demon they'd captured on a chain.

Behind them stood five silent demons from Kain's personal forces. One of them had greeted Selma with a familiar smile, but she hadn't recognized Thomren before

Kain called him by name. They were all here for her protection in case things went bad.

"So? What is it?" The Governor looked irritably to her mate, drumming a clawed hand against the desk's mahogany surface. "I am not letting you into the arena before I know exactly what's going to happen."

With a shrug, Kain turned the bag he was carrying in his right hand upside-down and shook it. Naharan's decapitated head landed on the thick carpet with a *thunk*.

The Governor stared at the head as if fascinated by the fluids slowly seeping into the fibers. When he finally lifted his fiery eyes to Kain again, there was apprehension behind his gaze.

"So... you're planning a coup?"

"Yes."

"May I ask why?"

Kain glanced down at the head by his feet. "He ambushed me and gave me to the queen to breed, all so he could steal my mate. I saw no other option."

The Governor's eyebrows rose incrementally. "That sounds... unlikely. Your mate is lovely, to be sure—" He nodded at Selma as if paying her a compliment before continuing. "—but no sane man would commit the highest form of treason, even for a Pure Breeder. Do you have any proof to support these allegations?"

"Selma."

Her name on Kain's lips sounded less like a lover's caress than she was accustomed to and more like the command of someone who was used to being obeyed. She stepped forward nonetheless, glancing up at her mate before looking at the Governor.

"Would you please show His Excellency the object you claimed when you defeated the queen?" Kain said.

He was stretching the truth a bit here—she hadn't taken anything after more or less accidentally killing the queen. She had promptly passed out, leaving Kain and his family to get them out of there, but she'd been told that claiming ownership of the Stone of Power would more firmly secure her position—even if she had no idea how to use it, or even what its significance was.

Fumbling a little, she pulled the smooth rock out of her pocket and held it out. It fit perfectly in her palm and shone with a dark light that pulsed warmly against her skin.

The Governor gasped and jumped to his feet, his chair clattering to the floor behind him. "How…? How did you get that?"

"The queen was using it to control my mate and his family. She said it was a gift from the Prince in exchange for helping him capture Kain and myself. I killed her and was told it now rightfully belongs to me." She closed her hand around it and pushed it back into her pocket.

The Governor licked his lips as if they'd suddenly gone dry. "You killed the queen?"

Kain's large hand came up to rest on her shoulder, his protective aura wrapping more firmly around her at the other male's shift in tone.

"Before she shows you, I must insist that you acknowledge the lack of deceit in her scent when she told you of Naharan's betrayal."

The other demon's eyes didn't stray from her face as he nodded. "I acknowledge your words as truth, Breeder."

"Good. Selma?" Kain gave her shoulder another comforting squeeze and took a step away from her, undoubtedly ensuring she didn't accidentally singe him with her less-than-reliable powers.

Selma bit her lip and concentrated, drawing her focus inward to that place the white light seemed to come from. As cautiously as she could, she pulled it out of her core and pressed it into her right hand. When she felt her arm hum with the vibrations of the unstable energy, she opened her palm, letting the power gather in a fizzing ball of light.

"By the stars!"

At the Governor's outburst Selma closed her hand again, letting the energy evaporate harmlessly into the air. Exhaustion swept over her, and she sagged gratefully against Kain when he reached out and wrapped an arm around her. These powers would be a whole lot more convenient if they didn't completely drain her.

"I told you, Maell. I told you there was something dangerous inside of them." Kirigan's voice resonated through the room from behind them, the same note of zealotry in it as when he had first seen her light. "The ancient texts more than hint at this."

The Governor looked like he would have been pale as a sheet, had she been able to see his human disguise.

Without a word, he slumped back down in his chair, his eyes still lingering on Selma, though he seemed to be looking straight through her.

"And the prisoner?" he finally asked after several minutes of silence.

"Our witness. She helped the prince along with several other females. She will testify to our claim when we speak to the Lords. Will you speak on our behalf as well, Governor?" Kain asked.

Maell nodded slowly, his eyes finally leaving Selma to settle on Kain. "I will attest to the truth of the Breeder's story, and I will support your claim to the throne based on the treason and defeat of the Prince, *Your Majesty*."

Kain straightened by her side, the subtle hint of power in his aura growing stronger. "Good. Then call the meeting—we have a war to prepare for."

AS SELMA FOLLOWED the demons through the wide hallways and listened to their deep voices discussing the politics of the coup, the magnitude of the entire affair finally set in.

It wasn't that she hadn't understood how much trouble the prince's kidnapping and the awakening of her powers had caused—and every event since then, too. But the understanding that the demon who'd saved her from his own kind time and time again was about to overthrow the entire structure of demonic society in an effort to keep her safe hadn't fully dawned on her until now, and a fresh wave of terror made her gut clench.

Kain stopped next to her, his grip on her hand making her follow suit.

"We will be with you in a minute," he called to the others who had paused when he did.

Obediently they continued, disappearing around a corner soon after.

Kain turned to her, letting his free hand cup her cheek. "My love, there is nothing to fear. I promise."

The softness in his eyes contrasted with the firm conviction in his voice, and she leaned in toward him like a flower reaching for the sun. She needed him with every part of her body and soul.

"I just want to live in peace—you, me, and our baby. And I want a white picket fence and a porch swing, and Sundays spent in the garden. But instead we're preparing for war. How can you say that there's nothing to fear? If I lose you..." Just the thought made her throat close up.

Kain's mouth pulled into a wry smile. "So that's what you wanted instead of my casino apartment? A white picket fence and little demon kids running around, setting fire to the begonias?"

Selma blushed and smacked his chest with her free hand. "Now is not the time to mock my dreams!"

Kain grinned at her reaction, but instead of continuing his teasing, he bent his head and pecked her lips. When he straightened again she was breathing shallowly, and something lower down murmured about forgetting war plans and worries and focusing on more interesting things instead—such as the thick cock she knew rested between his powerful thighs.

Her mate chuckled when her gaze drifted downward, propping her chin up with a finger. "I can promise you that there is nothing to fear because as turbulent as the next few months will be, I will not allow anything to happen to you or our little one.

"Furthermore, no power in this world will stop me from being by your side—not now, not ever. And once we take over control of North America, there won't be a male demon on this continent that wouldn't lay their life down for you.

"That is my pledge to you, Selma. I will love you for an eternity, and you and every child you bear will be safe and happy."

There was nothing more to say—nothing more he *could* say. In his eyes she saw the truth of his promise, and in his face, the strength he needed to keep his word.

Selma raised up on her toes so she could wrap her arms around his thick neck. Without a word, she kissed the man who'd finally set her free from a lifetime of fear. All that mattered was his love, because in that she had found her own power, along with the knowledge that even in the darkest of nights she would never again be alone.

PRINCE OF DEMONS

READ THE NEXT BOOK IN THE DEMON'S MARK SERIES

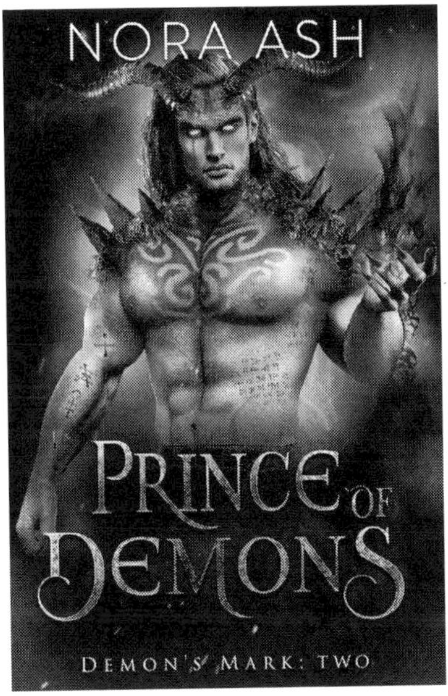

I bargained my soul. Not my heart.

Kesh knows better than most how much hassle a Breeder

can be, thanks to his brother's willful woman. With a war on his hands and enemies at his door, the last thing he needs is a mate of his own...
Read his story in Prince of Demons – Demon's Mark: Two.

---

* SNIPPET *

Kesh

"There's a demon at the gates who insists on seeing you. Says it's urgent."

Kesh sighed deeply, pulling his attention from the war map he'd been trying to update with the latest news of their enemies' movements.

"More urgent than stopping the Europeans from taking Maine?" Kesh asked, his voice deceptively gentle.

Mallorn, more than accustomed with his Lord's ways, took a slight step back, bringing him out of arm's reach. "I said you were busy. I more than hinted at what happened to the last underling who claimed an emergency and found you disagreed. He still insists."

Kesh growled, scrunching the map in his fist as irritation flared hotly. "Do these fools not realize the importance of what we're doing? How fucking close we are to annihilation? Why must they pester me with their petty squabbles? Who do I have to disembowel to get some peace?"

"Weight of the crown, I'm afraid," Mallon said, infuriatingly uncowed by his Lord's anger. "He's waiting outside the throne room."

Kesh shot him a glare and straightened up. "Fine. Send five troops to Maine. Tell our warriors I'm sorry I can't help them take down the invaders—I have a fucking contract dispute to settle, or whatever the hell it is this time."

THE THRONE ROOM still looked like the casino it'd been up until recently. His men had done a decent job at taking out the gambling tables and slot machines, but the bar still remained along the eastern wall, and the stains of alcohol and stench of desperation weren't coming out of the carpet no matter how many times Mallorn had had it dry cleaned.

Kesh strode to the throne—and imposing chair bolted to the hastily constructed dais—and slung himself down, propping a foot on one armrest as he drummed his irritation into the other.

This was the part of the job he hated the most. If he'd known how much time he'd have to play referee for minor demons bitching about someone screwing them over in contract negotiations, or listen to some Lord or another wax poetic about how he thought the Kingdom should be run—or, stars forbid, try to curry favor with the prince—there was no way Kesh would have helped his brother claim the Americas.

"Right. Send him in," he growled, motioning for the man guarding the door to open it.

The guard obeyed, pulling the painted-over glass door open with more pomp and circumstance than the situation required. Kesh swallowed his annoyance—the guy was doing his job. Ceremony was part of the illusion needed to claim a kingdom.

The man who entered looked like your standard low demon, more muscle than true power. Not exactly known for their interest in contracts. And one hundred percent not capable of having the sort of problems that'd be worthy of Kesh's attention.

"What do you want?" Kesh growled, staring holes through the demon's skull as he imagined hanging him from the rafters by his tongue.

"I... I bring you a gift, your Highness." The slight quake in his voice betrayed his unease at standing before the prince.

"A *gift?*" an outraged voice squawked. "What the hell do you mean, *a gift?*"

Kesh blinked, focusing on the human girl he'd barely noticed when the demon first entered. She was plump with unkempt dark hair, dark circles under her eyes and something between terror and fury plastered across her pale features.

"A gift?" he parroted, turning his attention back to the

demon. "You demand an audience with the Prince of Demons to give me a *human*? Have you lost your mind?"

"She's a Breeder, Highness," the demon said. "I wouldn't have disturbed you from your important work if she wasn't in desperate need of your protection."

Kesh blinked again, his gaze turning back to the female. "A Breeder?"

"Yes, my Lord." The demon pushed the girl forward, despite her obvious reluctance. "I... found her. She sees us for what we are."

"And you didn't keep her?" Kesh arched an eyebrow, but kept his gaze on the girl, who was staring back at him, chin thrust out in defiance despite her wide eyes betraying her terror.

"N-no, my Lord. That would be treason. I would never—"

Kesh silenced him with a raised hand. He knew the fucking laws—his brother had written them.

A Breeder.

He sent his sister-in-law a less than grateful thought. She might be the new Queen, but she was also a gigantic pain in the ass. *And* the reason for the whole bloody war.

But of course, Selma was a Pure Breeder. This sorry little thing might be exactly what he didn't need to deal with right now, but at least she'd be out of his hands soon enough.

If she even was a Breeder.

Kesh sighed deeply and scrubbed a hand over his face, wishing his idiot brother hadn't rewritten the laws concerning Breeders, and motioned for her to step forward with a flick of two fingers. “Come on. Let’s have a look, then.”

The girl didn’t move—only kept her blue eyes locked on him, the stubborn set of her chin wobbling.

Kesh narrowed his eyes at her disobedience. He leaned forward on the throne and ground though gritted teeth, “Come. Here. *Now.*”

She stumbled a step forward, as if jerked along by a chain, and Kesh leaned back, his smoldering temper calming ever so slightly.

The girl paused for a second, but the command in his gaze made her continue forward and up the dais, one hesitant step at a time until she stood in front of him. Her body shook ever so slightly as she stared at him, and her fear wafted against his nostrils, stirring a delicate sensation of unrest in his gut.

Ugh. Not a promising start.

Kesh pushed his foot off the armrest and reached for the girl. She was taller than most human females, but still only came to around eye-height with him when he was seated.

Her eyes went impossibly wider at the approach of his hand and she tried to jerk away with a startled squeak, but she wasn’t nearly fast enough. Kesh wrapped his fingers around her throat and brought her closer, ignoring her clawing to get out of his grip.

He pushed his index finger up, forcing the girl’s head

up and to the side, and buried his nose in her exposed neck.

Instantly, his senses were alight with a wash of scents, smells of other demons, hospitals, human decay and chemicals clawing at his throat. But behind that...

Kesh closed his eyes and drew in another deep breath, his skin prickling with the sensation of her hair brushing against his face. Her fear was the strongest of the scents that belonged to her and not other pollutants she'd come across. It was thick and acrid and made him growl before he could stop himself.

She whimpered at the sound, and he huffed with irritation and breathed in again.

There was warmth underneath that fear. Something sultry and rich, tangled with something he couldn't quite put his finger on. Mindlessly, he sniffed her again, pulling her closer to his body to find the source of that enthralling scent.

She whimpered and pushed against him, babbled some unimportant words of protest, and he smothered the annoyance of her resistance by wrapping her closer to his body, quelling her squirming with the strength of his arm around her back.

She was soft and warm agains his chest, the press of her breasts and the small gasps of her breath sending fissures of excitement through his skin. He breathed her in in greedy gulps, wishing he could wash away her terror so its scent wouldn't disrupt those beautiful notes underneath. It was disturbing, her fear—making unease spread from his gut to his blood, until all he could comprehend was how he needed her to be content.

"You're safe," he rumbled, his lips brushing over her skin and raising goosebumps along the slender column in his grip. Mindlessly, he loosened his grip on her throat, brushing his hand along her back to calm her.

The girl spluttered, outrage tinging the sounds—and then, without warning, sharp pain bloomed through his arm.

Kesh jerked back, more from surprise than anything else, and blinked down at the little creature in his grasp. Her blunt teeth were still firmly lodged in his forearm from where she'd bitten him.

What...?

It was only then he realized what he'd done. He stared down at the woman in his arms in horror, sick dread clenching in his gut. He'd wrapped himself around her body like a fucking meat shield, the urge to protect and soothe still thundering in his blood, making his temples throb and his cock ache.

"*Shit,*" he muttered, pushing her off his lap so she stumbled a few steps backward, nearly tripping down the two steps of the dais.

Yeah. She was a Breeder, all right. One of the few human women capable of bearing a demon's offspring. And so fucking valuable, even the war would have to wait while he prepared her for a mate.

There'd been a time, before his brother took control of the Americas, when specialized Procurers would seek out and train these women, then auctioning them off to the highest bidder. But since Kain had met Selma, that was no longer how things were, because stars forbid anything be simple. His brother had literally gone to war with the previously reigning family to protect his mate—and by extension, the sweet-scented little cunts she was part of.

These days, any potential Breeder was to be brought to the nearest Lord, and he'd then be responsible for gentling the woman into her new life, and finding a suitable mate for her.

And Prince or not—Kesh was the only Lord within a fifty mile radius.

He scrubbed his face with both hands, trying to steady himself from the onslaught of her scent as he gathered his thoughts. He'd have to ring- and mark her, find some unlucky sod who wouldn't mind spending the rest of eternity getting mind-fucked by her pheromones, somehow persuade her to allow a mating... and at the same time not lose the entire fucking Eastern coast to the European king while he was preoccupied with playing matchmaker.

He should have left his brother to rot in the old Queen's prison.

Of course, then he'd have been responsible for Selma.

Kesh suppressed a shudder at the thought of claiming his brother's mate as his own and refocused on the current cluster-fuck at hand.

The girl was huddled at the edge of the dais, seemingly too scared of him to try and run away yet clearly not in any hurry to get closer either, and when he tore his gaze from her to address the sorry demon who'd brought him this nightmare, he found the rest of the throne room empty, save the guard.

"Where the fuck did he go?" he snarled at his guard, getting to his feet to take up pursuit. The Breeder stumbled another step back at the sudden movement, lost her balance—and fell down with a hard thump.

Without thought, Kesh took the stairs in one leap, kneeling by her side to cradle her head in his hand as he ensured she wasn't hurt.

"Get away from me!" she hissed, cringing away from his touch. She pushed herself along the rug, scrambling to put distance between them.

"He left, your Highness," the guard said.

"I can fucking see that," Kesh growled, irritation flaring in his veins both at the renewed smell of the Breeder's fear and his own inability to hunt down the demon who dropped her off. He had *questions*—but the girl was obviously not in a good state. And his first priority was to calm her down.

"Curse it all," he muttered, finally straightening up and taking a couple of steps back, putting enough space between himself and the girl to hopefully calm her down. If she was an unmarked Breeder, she'd be able to see his true form. Even if she'd been among demons before—which her scent suggested—he knew he would be frightening, his features much less human than most lowly demons'.

"Is she truly a Breeder, my Lord?" the guard asked,

the note of longing in his voice unmistakable. Kesh rolled his eyes—at least it'd be easy enough to find a man willing to mate her.

"Yes," he bit out. "And you will tell *no one.* Understand? We don't need the entire territory to be distracted."

"I would never," the man said, sounding more than a little aghast at the suggestion he might betray his Prince.

Kesh sighed, shooting him a glance over his shoulder. He'd hand-picked every single man in his service. He knew they would never betray their loyalty to him.

"My Lord..." the guard began.

"Once she is settled, I will put you on the list of potential suitors, Sefron," Kesh said, returning his focus to the girl still huddled on the floor. "Now, go. Have the servants send food to my chambers." He wrinkled his nose as he looked the Breeder over, for the first time noticing how grimy she was. "And have a bath drawn. Then make sure I am not disturbed."

"Yes, my Lord."

The sound of the doors closing behind Sefron echoed through the throne room, leaving Kesh alone with the Breeder.

ALSO BY NORA ASH

DEMON'S MARK

Demon's Mark

Prince of Demons*

Demon Hunter*

ALPHA TIES

Alpha

Feral

Protector*

THE OMEGA PROPHECY

Ragnarök Rising

Weaving Fate

Betraying Destiny

ANCIENT BLOOD

Origin

Wicked Soul

Debt of Bones*

DARKNESS

Into the Darkness

Hidden in Darkness

Shades of Darkness

Fires in the Darkness

MADE & BROKEN

Dangerous

Monster

Trouble

Made in the USA
Columbia, SC
23 September 2023

23227452R10295